THE NIGHT WILL FIND US

THE NIGHT WILL FIND US

a novel

MATTHEW LYONS

Turner Publishing Company
Nashville, Tennessee

www.turnerpublishing.com

The Night Will Find Us

Cover design: Erin Shappell
Book design: Erin Seaward-Hiatt

Library of Congress Cataloging-in-Publication Data Upon Request

9781684425501 Paperback
9781684425518 Hardcover
9781684425518 eBook

Printed in the United States of America
17 18 19 20 10 9 8 7 6 5 4 3 2 1

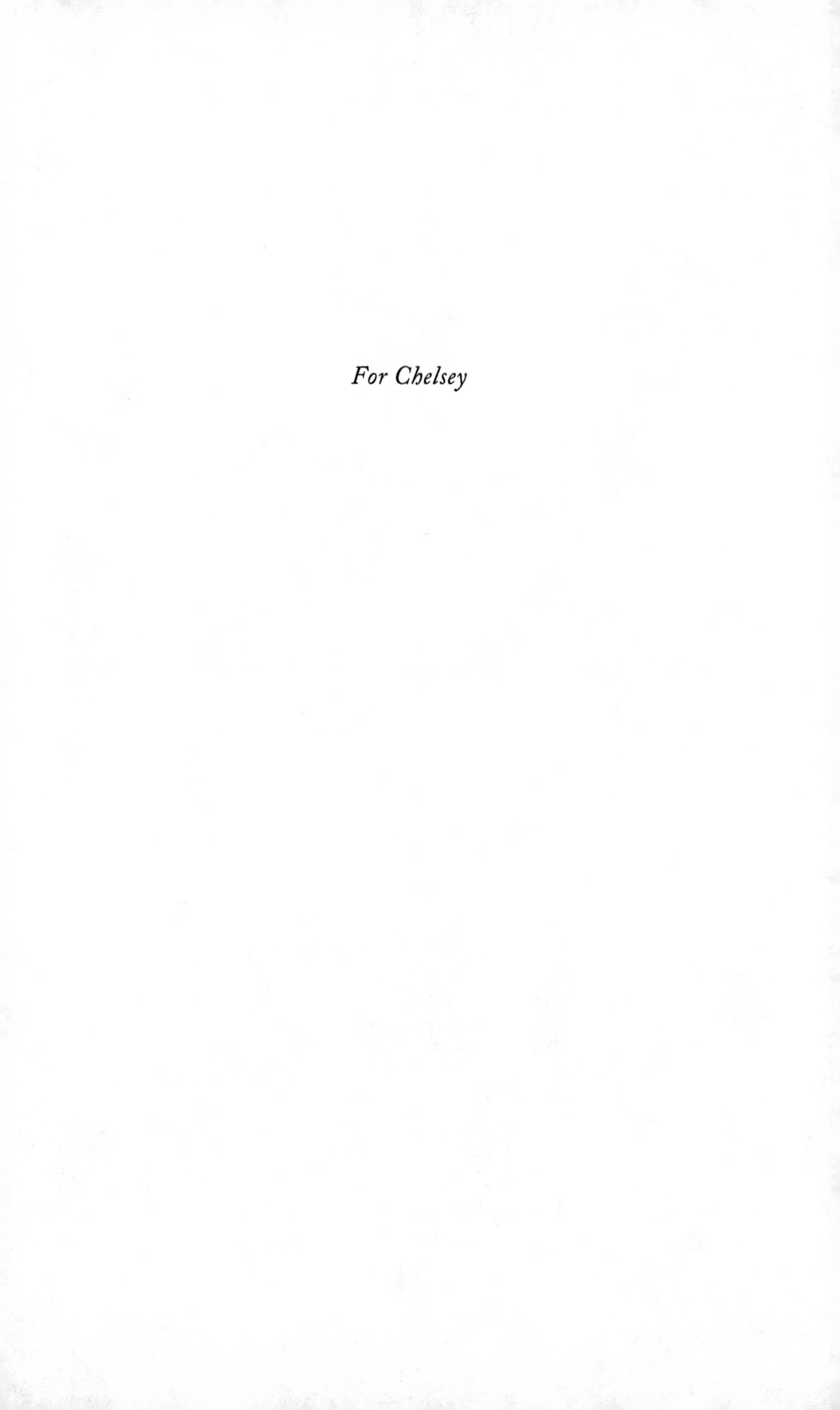

For Chelsey

I tried to warn you when you were a child
I told you not to get lost in the wild
I sent you omens and all kinds of signs
I taught you melodies, poems, and rhymes

—Lord Huron

1692

She used to watch Simon start fires with the hatchet. He'd had it made special so he could do just that, designed it himself with the blacksmith up in Mount Holly. It was a long, spindly thing with a thread of hard, ash-white flint embedded along the blade's edge, the wood and metal stained dark with ink or coal 'til the hatchet was so black, it nearly devoured the light. Mary had seen him use it a dozen times or more, catching a flame by striking stone or brick in just the right way, sending a spray of thick white sparks flying out like a fan. Simon had always liked fire, looked at it like he would an old friend. Maybe that should have been her first hint that there was something wrong with him.

Mary ran through the trees, ducking through the shadows and moving as quietly as she could. She tried to keep her breathing under control, tried to keep it from spiraling out into another panicked sobbing fit, but that proved nearly impossible; Simon was burning the trees as he followed her. Overhead, smoke stained the blue sky a muddy gray, filling the air with a sweet, charred smell that slashed at her nose and throat, making it difficult to draw a full breath without shuddering.

She could hear him in the distance, crashing through the branches and singing his hymns at the top of his lungs: "A Mighty

Fortress Is Our God," "All People That on Earth Do Dwell," "Now Thank We All Our God." She could hear the sick smile in his voice, the way his thin lips curled and parted like an open scar with every word. He wasn't far behind her, closer now than he'd been since she first fled the estate house.

Inside her head, Mary could still hear the sounds of the Ganders family dying—their desperate, gurgling wails and the horrible silences that followed soon after. They were sleeping when he came for them, a grinning scarecrow carrying that goddamned black hatchet, his dark cloak snapping in the wind like torn sackcloth.

She should have known he would follow her. She should have known he'd never stop. He never was any good at knowing when to quit.

Mary ran until her lungs burned, until her legs turned to warm jelly and her vision blurred from the exertion. But even as she flirted with collapse, she kept going. She couldn't stop now. Not when he was so close behind her.

Dashing through another clearing, she closed her eyes and listened.

These woods made so much noise on their own: the chirping of birds, the rustle of leaves in the wind, the scruff and snarl of nearby animals. But behind all that, Mary could hear . . . something else. It'd been there since she crossed into the forest, a gentle murmuring sound underneath the chatter of the woods and Simon's cruel songs, so quiet and subtle that she couldn't be certain she was hearing it at all. It was like a whispering in the trees, or perhaps beyond the trees—small and sharp, like a silver fishhook pulled through her soul, dragging her ever forward despite the pain and exhaustion, growing louder with every step. It sounded just like her beloved grandmother, gone to the Lord some fifteen years ago.

Mary broke free of the tree line, finding herself at the edge of a great blue lake, the surface of the water still and undisturbed, like glass. In its mirrored face, she could see the sky and trees and thin drifts of smoke, the world reflected. For a moment, she couldn't help but stare. The lake was beautiful; it was almost perfectly round, as if it were crafted personally by the hand of the Almighty. Some childish part of her desperately wanted to kick at the water, disturb it somehow, make sure it wasn't as solid as it seemed, but something inside her cautioned against that. No good ever came from disturbing God's plans.

On the far shore, the trees were thicker, denser, older. More shadow there than light.

Go, the silver voice whispered to her. *You can hide there. You'll be safe.*

Behind her, the sound of Simon's voice swelled, the notes growing richer and rounder. He was gaining on her.

Mary broke into a sprint. Circling around the lake, she picked up speed, less running and more throwing herself along the shore as she made for the shadows. She could make it. She was going to make it.

At the edge of that great darkness, she ducked behind one of the thicker oaks and waited, her heart hammering against her ribs as she struggled to pull more air into her lungs. She peeked out, gazing across the lake to where she'd stood only a few minutes ago, willing him away, praying to God that Simon had taken a different path through the woods. She held her breath and counted, as if getting all the way to ten would be proof enough that she'd finally shaken him free from her trail.

She'd made it all the way to nine when he stepped out of the trees, his heavy black boots sinking into the damp soil at the water's edge. Except for all the blood, he looked exactly as she remembered him: tall and post-thin with socked-out, dark-ringed eyes and a permanent rictus grin pulling his papery, haggard cheeks in opposite directions.

Mary watched from the shadows as Simon owled his head around, scanning the shore of the lake, his eyes eventually coming to rest on her own. It took everything Mary had inside her to not scream. Damn the shadows, damn the trees—he looked at her as if they weren't there at all, as if there were nothing in this world except him and her, trapped together in a perfect void.

Grinning so wide it threatened to split his head in half, Simon raised a hand and waved. Standing there, behind the oak, she could almost hear his reedy voice, calling out to her: *Miss Kane . . . Miss Kane, I see you . . .* Then he started to move, strolling purposefully along the lakeshore, lazily striking sparks off the rocks with his hatchet.

Mary watched him for longer than she should have, transfixed by the jerky way he walked, like a marionette guided by an inexpert hand. Then, remembering herself, she turned and ran into the thick of the old forest, following the whispers to wherever they led her.

Eventually she'd find a place to hide.

Eventually she'd reach where she was going.

FRIDAY

1

Chloe hadn't really known how bad things had gotten until three weeks before the end of the school year, when Parker went and beat the shit out of Kyle Terletsky in the White Castle parking lot.

All their friends were there with them: Adam; Nicky and her new boyfriend, Josh; shit, even Nate was there, though he was too busy looking at porn on his phone to pay attention. They were all sitting together at one of those crappy molded-steel tables when Terletsky and his buddies walked by. As he passed, Kyle leaned in and said something to Parker, though Chloe didn't hear what. None of them did.

What happened next was so sudden that, for a moment, Chloe didn't even notice anything had gone wrong. One second, Parker was sitting next to her, eating his way through a small pyramid of sliders; the next, he was dragging Terletsky across the blacktop and putting him in the hospital. None of them could stop him from doing it. Parker had always been a big kid, but he'd seriously taken off over the past year, growing taller and broader until he was roughly the size of a small house.

He didn't even say anything while he did it; he just tossed Kyle to the ground like a rag doll, then went to work on his skull with his big, milk-jug fists, pounding the kid's face into chunky tomato soup. Adam, ever the peacemaker, tried to pull Parker off the kid, but football star or not, Adam could only do so much. Parker was so much bigger than him, and by the time Adam closed the distance, it was too late. The damage was done.

When Parker finally let up, Terletsky looked like he'd been hit by a truck, backed over, then hit again.

Before anyone could call the cops, the five of them ushered Parker into Chloe's mom's Chevy Astro and got the hell out of there. They rode in silence back to Nicky's house. Once they were safely there, Chloe asked everyone to give her and Parker—still sitting in the way, way back, nearly vibrating with rage—a minute alone to talk.

When they climbed out to join their friends a few minutes later, Chloe's face was dark and knotted with worry from the things her cousin had told her through his tears. It wasn't until Parker had gone home for the night that Nicky and Adam were able to coax the story out of Chloe.

Terletsky had called him *orphan*.

The story got around school real fast; it even filtered all the way up to the administration. But since *the incident in question* had occurred off school grounds and nobody—not even the Terletsky kid with his shattered, fucked-up face—was about to snitch, the school officials couldn't actually do anything about it. Parker was in the clear.

Thing was, Chloe had told her friends only some of what her cousin had confessed to her, sitting in the back of the van. There was so much she'd left out, things she couldn't wrap her head around, things she wouldn't have believed Parker could have said had she not been there to hear them. Like how good it felt to beat on Terletsky until he spat blood and went limp. Or the horrible way Park had smiled when he'd told her how Kyle had begged for mercy through broken teeth.

And she didn't tell them that since Christmas, he'd been carrying his dad's gun around with him wherever he went.

* * *

By the time the final bell had rung and Chloe reached the parking lot, almost everybody else was already there, impatient to get going. Adam, tall and casually handsome, leaned against the grill of the van, hands in the pockets of his letterman jacket, backpack slung *just so* over one shoulder—so picture-perfect, Chloe would have thought it was a put-on if she didn't know him as well as she did. Adam saw Chloe first and raised a hand to wave as she crossed through the parking lot, weaving between cars and crowds of relieved-looking kids, finally free for the summer. Chloe waved back as she got closer, fishing in her backpack for her keys. She clicked the remote once, and the van chirped, the doors unlocking with a satisfying *ka-thunk.*

Nicky sat in front of Adam on the concrete wheel stop, her shock of bright-red hair tied back into a ponytail that exploded from the back of her head, smoking her menthol cigarettes and holding hands with Josh, who sat faithfully by her side, eyes narrowed under the bill of his ball cap, Instagram feed wheeling by on his phone. Chloe and Parker had known Nicky almost as long as they'd known Adam, the four of them going through school together all the way back from Mrs. Johnson's second-grade class.

Nicoletta Rosetti—everybody just called her Nicky—was the new kid in school back then, but after being seated together that first day in second grade, the four of them had become inseparable. They just . . . clicked, in that special way little kids can when they find out they have more in common than they have differences. The things that set them apart from each other just didn't really matter. They were always different, but they liked that about each other. Chloe had her academics, Adam and Nicky did school sports (football and track, respectively), and Parker was a sensitive kid who liked to just sit and read more than anything else.

It was the four of them from then on, their own little tribe against the rest of the world—or at least the rest of New Jersey. They were together when Adam's brother went to jail the first time, when Chloe's parents separated for half of freshman year, when Parker's dad went missing last October. Even when Nicky and Josh got together, all of them had gone on the first date, a group thing to see some stupid movie.

Nicky and Josh had been dating since just before Valentine's Day, but even now, at the end of the school year, none of them had stopped calling him her *new* boyfriend, as if there were any other boyfriends in the past to speak of. Chloe liked Josh, generally speaking. He was nice, a little boring, but he seemed to love Nicky as much as she loved him, which Chloe supposed was really the important part of it.

Over on the sidewalk, Nate was busily upending his backpack into the trash can, shaking papers loose, gleefully muttering "Fuck you, fuck you, fuck you" as a whole year's worth of work spilled messily into the waiting mouth of the green drum. Being built like an oversized potato, he had to stand up on his tiptoes to do it, but he was making it work. They'd all met Nate in eighth grade, when he was assigned to their group in Earth Science. Adam was the first one to suggest they invite him along to hang out that first time, but he fit in with them right away, almost as if he'd been there all along. Nate was a funny kid, and he meant well, even if he didn't know when to shut up sometimes.

"What took you so long?" Nate asked Chloe without looking up, whipping his backpack from one end like a dusty blanket, making sure it was totally empty. "We've been waiting for like an hour."

"It hasn't really been an hour," Josh said offhandedly, eyes still trained firmly to his phone. "It's been five minutes. Maybe a little bit more."

"Traitor," Nate said. Looking satisfied that he'd erased all traces of his junior year of high school, he turned away from the trash can and crossed over to stand by his friends, smiling and wetly smacking his lips against his teeth in the same disgusting way he always did.

"It's been five minutes," Adam echoed. "If that. Don't listen to Nate."

Chloe cracked a grin. "Why, Mr. Jarvis," she said. "Have I ever?"

"You can both eat my shit," Nate said with a chuckle, then nodded at the cigarette Nicky held pinched between her knuckles. "Can I get one of those?"

Nicky shook her head. "No."

"Why not?"

"Because it's never just one with you," she said, rolling her eyes. "You'll smoke half the pack if I'm not careful. You know how long it took me to get these? Scam one off someone else, or find a senior to buy you your own."

"We are seniors. I mean, we are *now*."

"Not senior enough to buy our own smokes."

"Come on, give one over," Nate wheedled.

"Sorry, bud. Nothing doing."

Nate gave her the finger and looked around at the rest of them. "So are we going to get this show on the road, or what?"

Nicky blew smoke. "Soon as Parker gets here, yeah."

"Well, shit, where is everybody's favorite angry boy? Haven't seen him since free period this morning," Nate said, looking around. "Chloe? Seen your cousin around today?"

Chloe shook her head and then plucked her phone out of her pocket and thumbed off a quick text to Parker:

Hey, you around? We're ready to get out of here.
12:15PM, 5/25

"I don't think he was here today," Josh said, sounding disinterested. "He's in Algebra Two with me, and he didn't show up at all this morning."

Chloe looked around at her friends. "Anyone else?"

Nicky held her hands up, Newport pursed tightly between red lips. "Not I."

Adam nodded toward Millbrook Avenue and the Shop-N-Go situated across the street from the school parking lot.

"There he is."

As if on cue, a giant, hulking shadow stepped through the Shop-N-Go doors, decked out in a red-on-black Slayer T-shirt and a pair of busted jeans, cable-thick arms heavy with a pair of fully loaded plastic bags. A shopworn camping pack was strapped tightly over his shoulders, and his black-rimmed glasses were fixed high on the bridge of his nose. Parker.

Looking at him from here, Chloe couldn't help but think that of course Terletsky never stood a chance—it was like a field mouse trying to fistfight a freight train. None of them said anything as they watched him cross the street, brow furrowed under his shock of black hair, capping the scowl that never seemed to leave his face anymore.

Parker walked up to them and set the bags down in the middle of the group, then looked around at his friends.

"What are you all staring at?"

"Nothing," Chloe said, pulling her cousin into a brief hug. "Not a thing. How was your last day of class?"

Parker looked away. "Fine, I guess. I don't know. Why?"

"No reason."

"Josh said he missed seeing you in Algebra Two today," Nate said, grinning.

Josh reddened. "I . . . no, it wasn't . . . I don't know. I just noticed you weren't there, is all. I wasn't . . . like, making a judgment about it. Or anything."

"It's fine. Got busy, is all," said Parker, waving Josh off. He nodded toward Nicky and the cigarette in her lips. "Can I get one of those?"

"They're menthols."

"Menthols are fine."

"Sure then, knock yourself out," said Nicky. She tossed him the crumpled white-and-wintergreen hard pack.

Nate stitched his face up into a play-scowl. "Hey, seriously, what the hell?"

Nicky waved him off, keeping her eyes on Parker. "Need a light?"

"No, I got it." Parker shook a smoke free and lobbed the box back to Nicky. He produced a battered silver Zippo from his jeans pocket and snapped it to life, touching the flame to the tip of the menthol. Beside him, Chloe could just make out the engraving on the side: *DAC*. David Allan Cunningham. Parker's dad.

"That's one big-ass backpack, man," Nate said.

Parker nodded, but from where she stood, Chloe could see something in his eyes she didn't like.

"We're going camping," he said measuredly.

"Yeah," Nate said, "*we're* going camping. It looks like *you're* prepping for doomsday or something. That shit is oversized as fuck, dude."

Chloe shot Nate a hard look. "Why does it matter?"

"Because the rest of us just have our bags and shit while Parker's busy showing up like the Boy Scouts of America or something. 'Be prepared,' right?"

"I never was one," Parker muttered.

Nate's face twisted into a mean little smile. "Shocker."

"I was," said Josh. Everyone looked at him, and his face flushed red. "For like three years," he added sheepishly.

"I rest my case," Nate said with a sneer.

Chloe watched Parker's shoulders knot up as he turned to stand square with Nate, easily looming a foot over the fat kid. Parker rolled his head back and forth, eliciting a meaty *crack-crack-crack* from his neck.

These two. They'd been at each other's throats the whole year, needling and posturing, typical guy bullshit; it had only gotten worse since Parker's dad—Chloe's uncle Dave—went missing last fall. No one knew what had happened to him. One day he was there, the next, he was gone. It was as if he'd just . . . disappeared.

For a moment, Chloe was sure Parker was actually going to smash Nate to pieces, like he did the Terletsky kid, but then Adam shoved his way in between them, meeting Parker's gaze and holding it, keeping the big kid's attention off Nate.

"Hey, hey. Ignore him." Adam kept his sky-blue eyes locked on Chloe's cousin, leaning in and dropping his voice so only the three of them could hear.

"Look, I get it, okay? I do. You've done this camping shit before, we haven't. You know best here. No big deal. Nate's just, y'know . . . being Nate. The more he sees he's getting on your nerves, the more he's going to do it. You know how this works."

He wasn't wrong. They'd all seen the animosity growing between the two of them for the whole school year; barbed comments, mean jokes, and other microaggressions were the norm for Nate and Parker these days. When it was one or the other and everyone else, it was like nothing had really changed. They were still *them*. Nate was a wiseass, but he meant well; Parker was as intense as he'd ever been, though he never stopped being a sweetheart underneath. But when they were in the same room together, it felt like things were just waiting to boil over, and both guys kept turning up the burner.

From where she stood, Chloe watched Parker's eyes flare, then cool.

"All right," he said after a moment. "Fine."

"Okay, good," said Adam, raising his voice to a normal volume. "So, what'd you get from the gas station?"

Parker shrugged his churchdoor shoulders and looked down at the bags by his feet.

"Candy bars, soda, beef jerky. Chex Mix. Stuff like that."

Adam's face softened. "Sweet. Let's get everything in the van and get out of here, okay? We've got a long drive ahead of us—probably a couple hours, right?"

"Probably," said Chloe.

"Well, let's get going then. We want to be there and set up before it starts getting dark." Adam nodded to the bulging plastic *Thank You For Shopping With Us* bags on the blacktop. "Help me get all this into the back with the rest of our shit."

They piled into the Astro and hit the road, everybody but Parker and Chloe leaning out their windows to give the scrolled city limit sign the finger as it whipped past and quickly disappeared into the distance.

Randolph, New Jersey: Where Life Is Worth Living! Fuck you twice. Just another nothing bullshit suburb in New Jersey, the nothing bullshit capital of the world. Anytime they managed to get out of their hometown alive wasn't just a mercy, it was a miracle.

They'd been planning this trip for months, an end-of-the-school-year expedition down to the Pine Barrens to camp and drink and burn shit and kick summer break off right. Parker had picked the place, a campground he said he'd gone to a bunch when he was a kid—not too far out of the way, but remote enough that nobody would bother them. Nicky had spent months gradually swiping Bud Lights from her dad's garage fridge, one at a time so he wouldn't notice, stashing them in an old cooler in a far, spider-filled corner of the basement. Adam snaked an eighth of half-decent weed and a bottle of Everclear from his big brother's room. Nate started stockpiling fireworks, and Parker spent a lot of time in his basement, getting together all the camp gear he thought they'd probably need. They each bought their own food to add to the pile: granola bars, cans of SPAM and sardines, precooked bacon, oatmeal, and Pop-Tarts. Add to that Parker's two bags of gas station junk food, and they were stocked up for a midyear Thanksgiving Dinner if they wanted to have one.

Chloe was the one who spun the lie they each fed to their parents. None of that *I'm sleeping over at her house and she's sleeping over at his house and blah-blah-blah* crisscrossing bullshit; that was amateur hour and almost guaranteed to get you busted. No, this required a little actual creativity—a few well-aimed lies braided together with the truth, so if anybody slipped, it would get written off as forgetfulness or whatever instead of outright forgery. They were going camping, sure, but so were a lot of kids. Just an overnight, nothing serious. Yes, there were going to be adults there, a couple of the newer teachers were chaperoning, they'd said. No, it wasn't an official thing, it was more casual than that. Just some kids from their class, the new seniors. No, they weren't going to drink or do any drugs. Yes, they were going to be as safe as possible. Promise.

Chloe angled the van down Route 10, then took a hard right onto 287 a few miles later, eventually heading south on the turnpike toward the Barrens. When they turned off the highway almost two hours later, the forest rose up from the horizon in a green-and-brown wave that crashed over them and dragged them under, leaving the sky and sunlight behind, obscured by densely packed trees. The Pine Barrens were massive, a sprawling wood that blanketed most of the lower half of the state, stretching out to cover something like a million acres of land, all told. It wasn't just a forest; it was a green ocean that stretched on and on forever, punctuated by the occasional column of sunlight that managed to break through the treetops to spear into the earth below.

Scanning the road ahead, Chloe reached over and turned the radio down, reducing the music to a soft background buzz as she followed the arrowed signs labeled CAMPGROUND.

"Cell service just shit the bed," Nate announced from the middle of the van, clicking his iPhone off and tossing it onto the seat cushion next to him.

"You can get by without porn for seventeen hours," said Nicky.

"*You* can get by without porn. I'm a growing boy, and a growing boy needs tits."

"You've already got tits," said Nicky, nodding at the moth-eaten T-shirt drawn tightly across his chest.

Nate winked at her and made a show of looking her up and down. "You're just jealous," he said, licking his lips.

In the rearview, Chloe saw Nicky blush and look down at her knees, self-conscious. "Fuck you, Nate."

"Only if Josh is cool with it."

"What? Ew. *God.*"

Nicky made a grossed-out face and chuckled despite herself while Nate grinned. Beside Nicky, Josh's face turned a bright, pinched red, and he turned to look out the window like he hadn't heard anything at all.

"Hey, Parker?" Chloe called back. "Can you come up here? I need to know where we're going after this."

Surprisingly nimble for a kid his size, Parker moved up the length of the van with ease, kneeling down as best he could in the narrow space between Chloe and Adam to look out the windshield at the road ahead.

"The turnoff should be right along here," he said, squinting through the little light still squeezing through the trees. A moment later, he darted a hand out, pointing a finger at a rough dirt turnoff ahead.

"There. That's it. Turn there."

Chloe cocked her head to one side, not taking her eyes off the road.

"Uh. Is it?"

Beside them, Adam turned to regard Parker. "Are you sure? I mean, it doesn't look like anything."

"I'm telling you, that's the turnoff. What, you don't believe me?"

Adam's hands went up in supplication. "Look, I'm not being an asshole here, I'm really not, it's just . . . When was the last time you were up here, man?"

"A couple of years."

"How many is a couple?"

"I dunno, a couple is a couple. Why does it matter?"

"I guess it doesn't," said Adam.

Parker turned his head to look intently at Chloe, his big brown eyes full and pleading.

"I remember, Chloe. Trust me. This is it."

Chloe hesitated for a moment, then swallowed her doubts and said, "As long as you're sure."

"I'm sure." Her cousin's voice was nearly a whisper, so soft and fragile, Chloe was sure she was the only one who heard him say it.

She eased her foot off the gas and slid it over to the brake, spinning the wheel to turn off the two-lane blacktop. The second they hit the dirt road, the tires started to judder and rumble, sending loose rocks pinging off the underside of the van, but Chloe could already see that Parker was right on the money—the road wound back and forth through the thick trees in a relatively clear path that went on and on into the distance.

"Just take this all the way to where it ends, okay? Another twenty minutes, maybe. We can park there, and then we'll hike the rest of the way up," said Parker.

"Hike? Nobody said dick to me about having to go on a hike," Nate called out. "I don't want to go on some fucking death march, guys. I'm wearing flip-flops over here, not like boots or whatever."

"We did say," said Adam. "Like a week ago, and then again yesterday. It's not our fault you didn't listen."

"It's not far," Parker said, keeping his eyes on the road. "Just a couple of miles, and then we're there." Chloe didn't have to look over at him to know he was smiling a little bit.

"A couple of *miles*? Are you kidding?"

In the rearview mirror, Chloe saw outrage flicker across Nate's face and then ease back into scowling, brooding silence. Fine by her. At this point, she was willing to settle for whatever kept the two of them from going shithouse on each other any more than they already had.

She followed the dirt road carefully, keeping the speedometer pinned at a safe twenty miles an hour, navigating the twists and turns and switchbacks that led them deeper and deeper into the Pine Barrens. The trees were closer to the path than she was used to, keeping them in shadow, but every so often, she'd catch a glimpse of sunlight poking through the trees, a yellow blade jabbing into the ground.

The parking area Parker had told them about was a little gravel cul-de-sac at the end of the dirt road, really only big enough to accommodate two or three cars—four if they really squeezed in—but luckily, there wasn't anyone else around. Chloe nosed the van in along the far side and killed the engine, throwing on the e-brake before announcing, "Okay, we're here. Everybody out."

They unloaded their packs together, splitting the supplies evenly so everyone carried their fair share. Nicky and Josh took most of the cookware and water while Adam and Parker carried the beer cooler, heavy with cans and gas station ice. Nate grabbed the tents, which left Chloe stuck with the extra bags of food Parker had gotten from the Shop-N-Go.

Parker assured them again that the hike wasn't going to be too bad—maybe a little hilly, but it wasn't like they were traipsing up the side of a mountain or anything. Everybody seemed to be fine with it except for Nate, who grumbled under his breath and kept glancing furtively down at the sandals he'd strapped to his lumpy hobbit feet.

Christ, but it was humid. Everybody had said that the coming summer was going to suck, boiling hot from June to late September, but May hadn't exactly been comfortable, either. It was already pushing the high eighties a couple weeks ago, but out among the trees and the plants, the heat and humidity were almost unbearable. The air was thick with condensation that laid on them like a blanket, plastering their shirts to their skin, drawing beads of sweat down their spines to pool in their jeans.

Hiking her pack higher on her shoulders, Chloe fixed the nylon chest strap in place and clicked the remote at the Astro. The van honked its horn in response, just once, a sound that echoed through the trees and vanished just as quickly.

"Here," said Adam, making a grabby-hand in her direction. "Let me hang on to those. I've got more pockets than you."

Chloe shrugged and tossed him the keys. Beside her, Parker lifted the beat-up old Coleman on his own and nodded toward one of the rough trails branching off and away from the gravel.

"Okay, this way," he said. "Not far now."

Everybody followed him into the woods.

2

From out on the highway, the Pine Barrens was enormous; from inside, it was never-ending. Branches hung low in heavy canopies, and dead old leaves from seasons long past covered the forest floor in a carpet of soft rot. On their uphill path, the fronds and leaves obscured the distance in a lattice so dense and complete that Chloe could see only about fifteen feet to either side. She could almost feel the woods closing around their little bubble with every step they took—as if the forest was slowly eating them alive.

The sound was another matter altogether; it was so weirdly loud out here, teeming with life. Insects buzzed against the wind as it whistled through the trees, and the caws of birds bounced brightly overhead, paired against the rustling of nearby hooves and paws. It spoke to her, it *whispered* to her, as if the voice of this place were a radio signal she was gradually tuning into. The sounds of the forest all swirled together inside her head, a natural symphony without beginning or end. This was the voice of the earth that she was hearing, what it was like without human beings around to screw it all up, as they so often did.

The forest was ancient and absolute, humbling in its vastness and startlingly beautiful both from afar and up close.

It didn't take Nate long to start complaining about it.

"I hate you all for making me do this. Especially you, Parker—this was your idea," he called from the back of the group. "I can't believe I let you talk me into this lame camping shit."

Parker didn't say anything.

"Did you hear me, Parker? I'm serious. You're gonna pay for this. You owe me big time now."

Parker still didn't say anything.

"Nobody's making you do this," Nicky snapped back at Nate. "You can walk back to the highway and hitchhike home or whatever. We don't need you here if you don't want to be here. Especially if you're going to keep bitching like this."

"Sure, I could do that. Or Chloe could just give me the keys so I can go sleep in the van tonight." Nate slapped at his neck. "There's air-conditioning, and not as many fucking bugs, probably."

"Chloe isn't going to do that," Chloe said, deadpan.

"Because Chloe can't, or because Chloe won't?" The feigned sweetness in Nate's voice was like burned aspartame.

Chloe looked back at Nate and allowed him a patient smile that didn't reach her eyes.

"Pick one."

Nate threw his hands up in the air.

"Jesus. Is nobody on my side about this? Josh?"

Beside Nicky, Josh spiked his eyebrows and looked back over his shoulder at Nate.

"We're all out here to have fun, Nathan," he said mildly. "We all agreed on the trip. You don't have to be here if you don't want to, but the rest of us are staying the night when we get to the campsite."

"If I die of exposure out here, it's all your faults, understand? I'll haunt each and every one of you," Nate grumbled.

"You're not going to die out here," said Adam, sounding impatient. "You're going to get drunk and stoned and throw shit into a campfire and eat hot dogs until you puke, same as all of us. Then tomorrow morning we'll drive back home and it'll be summer break and you won't have shit to do for the next three months."

"When you put it that way, I guess it kind of sounds like fun," Nate said. "But officially, this is still all bullshit."

"Duly noted," said Adam.

Eventually, they came to a natural clearing with a blackened, circular stone firepit in the middle. The whole area wasn't much bigger than the living room at Nicky's parents' house. Overhead, the trees seemed to bow in over them, forming a natural baldachin between the clearing and the sky. Orange afternoon light danced through the wind-rustled leaves, casting a warm glimmer across the ground that seemed to make the soil glow.

Chloe watched as Parker set down the beer cooler and crossed over to the far side of the clearing, drawing close to one of the trees, inspecting its trunk closely. He glanced back at the rest of the group from the tree line, and for a second, he looked like his same old self, as if the moody, angry kid that had replaced him over the past year was just a bad dream that had finally, thankfully evaporated.

"This is it," said Parker, truly smiling for the first time that day. "This is the place."

Everybody got to work setting their own tents up around the clearing. Since they were sharing a tent, Nicky and Josh finished theirs first, then climbed inside and zipped the front flap shut after them. After a moment, they started giggling and rustling around inside, eliciting raised eyebrows and shared, embarrassed smiles from all their friends.

"You know those things aren't soundproof, right?" Nate called out, pitching a pine cone at the side of the tent. Josh and Nicky quieted down some, but they didn't come out or unzip the flap for a while afterward. Nobody much minded. The two of them had been waiting a while for some alone time—free of the watchful eyes of their parents—and nobody, not even Nate, seemed interested in taking that away from them.

Chloe had brought one of her grandpa's old tents. It wasn't huge, but neither was she. Standing at only a little over five feet tall, she didn't need a lot of space—just enough to curl up in, like a cat. She'd pulled her chestnut-brown hair off her slender shoulders into a messy ponytail, her big green eyes bright against the sunny afternoon. Across the dead firepit, she could see that Adam's tent (all his gear, really) looked fresh off the shelves from REI, while Parker's was shabby but well-cared for, no doubt formerly his dad's.

In the far corner, Nate dropped his stuff on the ground and sat down on one of the fallen trees, then cracked open a water bottle and poured its contents over his dusty, battered bare feet.

"Fuckin' flip-flops," Nate grumbled. "Fuckin' hiking. This is bullshit."

From her side of the clearing, Chloe watched him wipe his soles dry with the bottom of his shirt before pulling his duffel bag into his lap.

"Okay, so, check it out," he said, unzipping the bag and holding the top wide for them all to see. "Fully loaded, as requested."

The duffel was filled to the brim with fireworks: Black Cats, Saturn Missiles, sparklers, bottle rockets, Roman candles, a couple of fountains, even a big box of M-150 Salutes—those little half M-80s that you could still buy at roadside stands if you asked the guy behind the counter just right.

"Oh, I brought something special too," said Nate, digging in the bag down to his elbow. "Know I put it in here somewhere . . . maybe near the bottom . . . Ah, there we go."

From his duffel, Nate pulled a heavy gallon ziplock bag filled nearly to bursting with coarse black dust, holding it high for everyone to see.

"Check it out," he said. "Black powder. Thought we could really fuck some shit up with this."

Adam looked at him and cocked an eyebrow.

"Uh, Nate, my dad uses that stuff to make bullets when he goes hunting. That's like, real-ass gunpowder."

"Shit yeah, it is." Nate beamed. "Like four pounds of it. Swiped a couple bags from my dad's gun safe this morning. Old man still doesn't know I know the combination. Like, *holy shit*, it's Mom's birthday. Real clever, Doug. Dickhead."

Nate glanced over at Parker, who was busy pounding stakes into the dirt through metal eyelets, securing his tent in place, keeping his head down.

"Wait, should I not talk about dads right now, Parker? Is that still a touchy subject? I'm sorry. I didn't mean to make you feel left out."

Parker didn't look up, but Chloe saw his hand tighten around the little camping hammer, squeezing until his fist was white and bloodless.

Beside Nate, Adam's face was grave. "No, listen. Black powder's what those guys on the news make car bombs out of, the ones who live in shacks in the woods and write manifestos or whatever. That's a serious explosive, man."

"So what? You said bring fireworks."

"Yeah, *fireworks*, not bomb-making supplies. What the hell are we even going to use that for?"

Nate spat and grinned. "Hell if I know. Something really cool, though, right? *Pow*. Up in smoke."

"Come on, be smart about this," Adam said. "Black powder's not the kind of shit you play with, okay? It's not a toy. Somebody could get hurt. You could start a fire with it or something."

"Yeah," Nate said, his voice dripping with sarcasm. "That's kind of the point, *Dad*. You're welcome, by the way."

Adam's shoulders fell. "Nobody asked you to bring that. We just wanted some fireworks. Sparklers or whatever."

"I've got sparklers," Nate cried. "Sparklers and Black Cats and all that other stupid baby bullshit. You can have it, it's yours. But I was trying to do something nice for you guys. For *us*. So if you grow your balls back and decide that you want to come play with the big kids, you let me know. I'll be out in the woods, blowing shit up with my dick. Everybody else can fucking fuck themselves—you most of all," he said, jabbing a finger at Parker.

"Nate, I'm asking you nicely here. That shit is not to be played with. Just go pour it out in the fucking creek or something, please," Adam implored.

A smile crept along Nate's thin lips.

"Nah, I think I'm good."

"Seriously?"

Nate just kept smiling at him. Chloe watched Adam swallow back his irritation and turn to walk away. A second later, Nate did the same, carting his bomb-bag into the trees. Soon they could all hear the machine-gun popping of firecrackers, accompanied by Nate's loud whooping.

Chloe let out a sigh and went to join her cousin, who seemed to be trying to make himself as small and invisible as possible as he drove stake after stake into the earth. She couldn't blame him for that; Nate's shit had gone from cute to cancerous real fast.

"Hey, are you okay?"

"I guess," said Parker. "I don't know. Yeah."

Chloe jerked her head in the direction Nate had stormed off. There was another rolling crackle of fireworks, farther away now.

"I just want you to know, we all know that it's not you," she told Parker. "He's the one who's starting shit. None of this is your fault."

Parker nodded curtly. "Sure."

"And it's not okay, what he said to you before," she told him. "When we were hiking, and just now, about your . . . yeah."

"I know."

There was a nervous quaver in his voice, the sound of too much emotion welling up in the pit of his throat. She knew that sound well; it always came just before he started to cry. She'd heard it a lot in the last year.

"Hey, I've got a present for you," said Chloe.

Parker looked at her. "What . . . ?"

"Hold on," she said, forcing a smile. "Let me get it."

She crossed over to her own tent and went inside to get her backpack, returning to kneel down next to her cousin. From inside, she pulled out a black package with two walkie-talkies sealed inside, COBRA 32-MILE RADIO written across the top. She handed it to Parker with a grin.

"*Ta-daaa*! Just like when we were kids, camping out in Grandpa's backyard," she said. For a moment, the ghost of a smile crept into the corners of Parker's lips.

They'd done it a lot back then, when they were littler and the whole family would get together on Friday or Saturday nights for family dinners. They used to beg their parents to let them sleep over at Grandpa's so they could camp out. They'd set up the tents in opposite corners of the old man's big backyard and spend the night looking up at the stars and telling scary stories and going inside for microwaved s'mores.

Parker was the one who had found the old walkie-talkies in Grandpa's basement, buried in a steamer trunk full of old toys from when their parents were kids. They needed a fresh set of batteries, but they still worked fine. Chloe had beamed when he brought them out to the backyard.

"Now we can talk even after we go to bed," he'd said, eager in the way that only nine-year-olds could be.

After that first time, the radios became a crucial element of any backyard camping trip, as important as the tents or cans of Coke or comic books. They'd talk to each other all night, sometimes even going to their tents early to chat wirelessly until one or both of them fell asleep in the glow of their dollar-store flashlights. It was nice, having him there with her the whole night through. She used to get scared of the dark. That was why she'd learned about the stars and the constellations in the first place; knowing about them made the darkness seem less scary. The stories made her feel less alone.

Parker made her feel less alone.

Chloe tapped a finger against the plastic packaging, smiling at her cousin.

"This way I won't lose track of you," said Chloe.

Parker smiled again, and for a second, he looked just like the little kid she remembered from way back then—the one who helped her set up her tent and then would lay in the grass next to her, listening raptly while she told him all about the different constellations and the ancient stories behind them.

"Well, what are you waiting for?" Chloe asked. "Open 'em up. Let's see what we're working with here."

He unfolded his pocket knife and used it to split the hard plastic at the top, then pulled both radios free from the package and passed one over to Chloe. Parker turned his radio over a few times in his hands, then switched it on, checking the battery before clipping it to his belt.

Chloe held her radio to her lips and pressed the talk button, her voice erupting staticky and speaker-loud from Parker's hip: "You think these'll really work from thirty-two miles away?"

"I don't know. Maybe," said Parker. "But even if they can do only half that, it'll still be pretty cool. Thank you for this, Chloe. Really."

She gave him a side hug. "You're welcome, really. Keep it on, just in case I have something brilliant to say and you're not like, right next to me, okay? Channel six."

Parker reached down and switched his walkie-talkie over to the sixth band. It squawked and then settled back into silence. A second later, Chloe did the same.

"Okay. All set."

"Awesome."

Eventually Nate came back, barefoot and sweaty from blowing off steam out among the trees. He didn't say anything to Adam or anyone else when he returned, instead going over to his spot to haphazardly putting his tent together, muttering curse words to himself. He got this way sometimes, all moody and shitty. They'd learned that it was just best to let him sulk it out; he'd get over himself eventually.

"Ignore him," Chloe advised Parker. "Okay?"

"He's hard to ignore."

"Then just try your best, okay? Eventually he'll calm down. He always does," Chloe said, trying to believe it.

Parker merely nodded in response, almost to himself. As if she wasn't even there.

Everything was fine. Everything was going to be fine.

Chloe didn't see what started the whole thing off, but later, if anybody had asked her, she'd have guessed *probably nothing* and would have been basically right on the money. Nate had been spoiling for a fight all day, after all, so it wasn't much of a surprise when she heard him start snarling at Parker again.

"Okay, seriously, what's your problem? Huh?"

Normally, it wouldn't have been a big deal, but there was something in Nate's voice—a hard, mean edge—that made her sit up and pay attention. Parker was sitting on the ground next to his tent, whittling a stick with his pocket knife while Nate glared at him from across the clearing, his eyes wide with rage.

"I said, what the fuck are you looking at?"

"Nothing," said Parker.

"Really? Because it sure seemed like you were staring at me," Nate accused. "Were you not just staring at me? Yes or no?"

"No."

"*Bullshit.*"

"Whatever." Parker went back to his whittling, angling the knife down and swiping another thin scroll of wood from the stick.

"*Whatever,*" Nate mocked.

"Nate, just once can't you just fucking back off?" Adam called to him from across the firepit. "You're just starting shit to start shit. You know he wasn't—"

"You back off, Jarvis," Nate snapped, eyes still locked on Parker. "Hey. Hey. Look at me, you big freak. Look right here, in my eyes. I asked you a question. Were you or were you not staring at me? Tell the truth."

"I guess I was," Parker said, keeping his eyes on the stick.

"What the hell for?"

"For nothing," Parker said. "I was just looking."

"Fuck you, just looking," Nate snarled, whipping a handful of dirt Parker's way. "What exactly were you *just looking* at?"

"You."

"Why?"

Parker raised his head to look over at Nate. Chloe could see a messy mix of exhaustion, sorrow, and barely restrained rage on his face.

"Because you're doing it wrong."

"Doing *what* wrong?"

"The tent," Parker said with a sigh. "You're putting the tent together wrong."

"Who gives a shit? You're not sleeping in it, are you?"

Parker held his eyes firmly on Nate. "No."

"Then what do you care?"

"I guess I don't."

"Fuckin' right," Nate said, sneering. "You know, I gotta tell you, man, you've been a real drag all this year, and I'm so sick of it, I really am."

"I'm . . . sorry?"

"Sorry doesn't count for shit if you're not changing shit. You know, I think I speak for everyone when I say that if you're going to act this way all night, maybe you should do it somewhere else. Away from us."

"Nate, seriously, lay off already," Nicky said from beside the firepit. Next to her, Josh was blushing and averting his eyes. Nate shot her a sour look.

"Don't act like it's not true, *Nicoletta*. All of you know what I'm talking about, don't pretend like you don't. He's been acting like a champion asshole all year. And what he did to Kyle Terletsky?" Nate shook his head in disgust. "Guy had his jaw wired shut. You remember what he looked like. He's going to be in a fucking neck brace until the middle of senior year, and what for? So Parker could express some anger? *Fuck. That.* I don't want to live my life around that kind of psycho shit, do any of you?"

None of them said anything. Not a single one spoke out against him or contradicted what he was saying. Nate was an asshole, but he wasn't all the way wrong, either. Still, it didn't take a super-genius to see he was taking it too far. Nate always took shit too far.

Chloe saw real hurt in her cousin's eyes—hurt mixed with fury and hate and fear and loneliness.

"I didn't mean to hurt him," Parker mumbled.

"You got a real funny way of showing that. But the thing is, even after you did it, all of these guys stuck by you, for some stupid reason."

"I didn't ask them to."

"No shit."

Parker looked around at his friends, his face gray and fractured. Only Chloe met his eyes, but even she could barely hold his horrible, sodden gaze for a second before looking away. It was too much. Her lips and cheeks felt hot and puffy, and tears blurred the outside corners of her eyes, smudging out the edges of the world.

"Nate, don't," she sputtered. "You know Terletsky was the one who started it, and . . . it's not like that, it's, it's not."

"It's exactly like that," said Nate.

Adam took a step closer to them. "Nate—"

"What'd I say to you?" Nate snarled. "Stay. The *fuck*. Out of this, Adam."

"It's fine," Parker said, rising to his feet. "I get it. I'll go."

"Good. We don't want you here anymore," Nate said, his voice cold and hard. "Just go. Get out of here."

Parker's shoulders fell. He dropped to one knee and started gathering up his sleeping bag and the rest of his stuff, packing it by handfuls into his backpack.

He was really going to go. "Parker, don't. Please. It's him. It's not you. It's him." Chloe reached a hand out to her cousin, but he shook his head at her, pulling his bag onto his shoulders as he stood again, keeping his eyes on the ground.

"It's fine. I get it," Parker said, that wretched tension climbing in his voice again. "I can go. I'll go. It's okay."

"That's the most reasonable thing you've said all day," Nate jeered. "See you later, you piece of shit no-dad asshole."

Parker looked up and zeroed in on Nate, and for the second time in her life, Chloe saw something in her cousin's eyes that scared her. The sadness and the pain were still there, but they had been frozen over by an icy hate that she'd seen in his eyes only once before, in the back of the van after what he'd done at White Castle. But even that didn't hold a candle to what she was seeing now. Chloe had never seen this kind of hate in *anyone* before. It was like Parker had completely unplugged from himself.

"Wha-what . . . what . . ." Parker stammered. "What did I do to you, Nate?"

"You were born," snarled Nate.

"Okay, let's all fucking *quit it*," Chloe barked, but she could see it was too late to stop Nate now. He'd gone full tilt, his eyes wide and mean, his lips drawn back to show off every crooked, yellow tooth in his head. It was easy to see that even though he was keeping his face serious, he was enjoying this. He was having fun jamming knife after knife into Parker's hide. And up until this point, Parker had just stood there and taken it. But for that awful freeze in his eyes, Chloe would have thought he was doing it still.

Nate prowled across the clearing to stand close to Parker, gesturing broadly toward the rest of their friends.

"None of them give a shit about you or your problems, dick. Up until now, they've just been pretending, to keep you quiet. But now that you're leaving, I suppose we don't have to worry about that much longer, do we?"

"That's not true," Nicky protested. "That's a lie."

Nate ignored her, remaining focused on Parker. "You've been acting like a big baby this whole year, man. You used to be cool. At least you weren't such a moody pussy all the time. But you know, I just can't do it anymore, okay? I'm sick to death of walking on eggshells around you all the time, like you're going to fly off the deep end and take all of us with you, just because your dad blew town or finally did himself in or whatever the fuck. I'm done with your moody orphan bullshit. Go kill yourself."

None of them saw Parker pull the gun. One second it wasn't there, and the next second it just was, as if Parker had plucked it out of thin air to point at Nate's head like a black metal curse, all lethal curves and angles. The muzzle was so close to Nate's lips that he could have kissed it if he wanted to. Wouldn't have even needed to lean forward. That mean grin, though—it hung on Nate's face like it was stapled into his flesh. Like there was nothing in the known universe that could wipe it off, not even when he was looking down the barrel of his own annihilation. Behind the gun, Parker's eyes had gone blank and still.

Adam gasped. "Parker, what the fuck!"

But Nate laughed—he actually *laughed* when Adam said it.

"Jesus Christ, chill out, Jarvis. We both know he's not going to shoot me."

"Shut up, Nathan. Just shut. Your. Mouth." Nicky's voice was drawn tight as a drum, nearly exploding with nerves.

"Oh, whatever," Nate snarled back. "None of you want to call him on his shit, that's fine by me. I'll say it—I don't give a fuck anymore. Enough is enough. Ooh, scary, you're a big man with your gun, right? What a joke." He took another half-step forward and jabbed a finger into Parker's chest. "You're not gonna do shit, because you're a fuckin' loser, just like your fuckin' loser dad—"

The gun made a sound that slapped them all in the lungs and startled a wave of birds from the trees above as a red curtain blew out from the back of Nate's head. Everything around them froze in place.

For one long, horrible second, Nate stayed standing, trapped in time, his face twisted into something Chloe could nearly call a smile. You could almost look at him and think everything was okay, like there wasn't a black, finger-thick hole poked in the middle of his forehead. The gun bucked in Parker's hand, but he kept it outstretched, the muzzle still even with Nate's face.

The silence of it was terrible. It was as if Parker had cut the valve and cinched off every sound in the woods—the birds, the wind, everything—leaving only a great sucking emptiness behind. Chloe watched as Nate's thick throat bobbed and worked against itself, wrenching a panicked, meaty noise from his lips.

"*Gkkk . . . guk . . . gggggkkk . . .*"

Nobody said anything. None of them even breathed, stuck in that moment just half a second too late to take it back or make it better. *Better* was little more than a myth now. A legend. A ghost story. Nothing was ever going to be better ever again.

Nate tilted backward and toppled to the ground like a felled tree. Nicky screamed and buried her face in Josh's chest. Chloe was frozen in place, unable to move, finding it impossible to process the horrible thing she'd just witnessed. Beside her, Adam stepped forward, hands out, moving slowly toward the big kid and the revolver in his hand.

"Park, don't—"

Parker turned and ran into the trees.

3

Chloe had never seen a dead body before, not really. She'd seen them on TV, in documentaries and articles on the internet, sure. But never up close, never like this. She'd never even been to a real funeral. The grown-ups in their family had kept her and Parker away from their grandpa's service three years ago, telling them that it would be *too much* for them, no matter how many times the two of them had insisted otherwise. After a while, she'd figured out that when her mom said that, what she really meant was that it would be too much for the grown-ups, not for Chloe and Parker, and Chloe had spent years hating her for it. They—she and Parker both—felt like they'd been robbed of something, somehow. An essential part of growing up, of becoming a whole person.

It all seemed so goddamn unfair at the time. But now that she was here, staring at a bright, bloody mess spilling out of a body that wasn't even cold yet, all she wanted was to go back to a time before she knew what this felt like.

In the middle of the clearing, Nate bled into the earth from both sides of his skull, leaking red into the soil and dead leaves, his eyes rolled so far back into their sockets that all Chloe could see were the wet, gummy whites.

She screamed. And then she kept on screaming. Standing there, watching her friend die, she couldn't stop the sound from pouring out of her.

It was Josh who moved first.

Jumping to his feet, he broke away from Nicky and crossed over to Nate in four long, quick strides, dropping to his knees in a cloud of dirt and dust. Chloe watched as Josh felt at Nate's soft, bloody neck with two fingers, searching for a pulse. Searching for anything that could take it back.

"Nate? Hey, Nate, can you hear me? Listen, I need you to blink if you can hear me, man. Just give me something here. Anything." His voice was strong and sure, nothing like the Josh they'd come to know up until now.

Over by the tent, Nicky started to cry, collapsing to the ground as the sobs ripped their way out of her in giant, wracking heaves. Chloe had never heard Nicky cry like that before; if anybody had asked her an hour ago, she would have told them that it simply wasn't possible. On numb legs, she went to Nicky and wrapped her arms around her, holding her as tight as her thin arms could manage until the worst of Nicky's sobbing had abated.

When she was sure Nicky wasn't going to start crying again, Chloe stood and went over to Josh, helping him off the ground. He gave a little shake of his head, then went over to hold his girlfriend. Chloe's eyes drifted back to Nate's body and the horror show above his shoulders, feeling a sort of cold obligation take her over from the inside. Nate was an asshole, but he deserved better than this. They didn't have to leave him sprawled out like that, all bent, twisted angles.

"Adam, can you help me straighten him out at least?"

Adam didn't respond. Chloe looked around, but Adam wasn't there anymore.

Inside her head, the pieces clicked together.

Of course he had. Probably didn't even think twice about it.

Adam had followed Parker into the forest.

"Parker, wait up, man!"

Adam's voice rang out from behind him, but Parker ignored it, barreling through the scrubby underbrush, away from the blood and the looks on his friends' faces and all the noise inside his head. The gun was still in his hand, his dad's Smith & Wesson 586, the one he had taught Parker to shoot with once he was old enough to learn on pistols. Black with a worn-smooth walnut grip, it seemed so much smaller now that he was older. Back when he was a kid, he remembered thinking it was the same kind of gun old ships used to sink other ships. It sure made a noise like it was.

"Parker, stop, please!"

Louder now. Adam was getting closer. The panic and the rage and the hateful emptiness still raked at Parker's ribs, white-hot claws bleeding him from the inside. He wanted to scream, to drop to the ground and cry, to put the gun in his mouth and pull the trigger.

He did none of it. He kept running.

Up ahead, he could see a grove. Charging toward it, Parker wiped at his burning eyes with the backs of his hands. He wasn't going to stop, not when he was so close. He was going to stick to the plan.

Just behind him, there was a crashing of branches, and Parker knew that Adam was nearly on top of him. Fucking Adam. He couldn't ever just leave shit alone, could he? He always had to be Captain America.

"Parker, please—"

Parker whirled around, gun out, finger on the trigger, muzzle trained on Adam's face. His friend looked panicked, and angry, and scared. Out of control was a bad look on Adam.

"Leave. Me. Alone," Park said, punctuating each syllable with a small thrust of the gun.

Adam shook his head. "You know I can't do that."

"You have to."

"Why?"

"Because I have a gun," Parker snarled, "and you don't."

Adam's face was gray and drawn. "Nate's dead, man."

A lump of bile formed in Parker's throat, and he swallowed it back. "I figured."

"What, then? You wanted him dead? You wanted to kill him?"

"I wanted him to shut up," said Parker.

"You don't get to shoot someone just because they're being an asshole."

In his heart, Parker knew that Adam was right. But Adam being right hadn't been enough to stop Nate from scraping at him. Being right couldn't put Nate's brains back inside his skull, the breath back in his lungs. Adam could be right all he wanted. It was still too little, too late.

"Come back with me," Adam said. "We can still set this right."

"You know that's bullshit," said Parker.

Underneath his gray tee, Adam flexed his muscular shoulders. At his sides, his hands knotted themselves into tight, bone-white fists.

"Don't make me make you," he said.

"You can't *make* me do anything, Adam. You never could."

But Adam wasn't listening. He was already moving, barreling toward him at what seemed to Parker like Mach 5 speed. Adam crashed into him, hard, and Parker went off balance, twisting against the impact as both of them spilled to the ground.

Together, they scrabbled for the pistol—Parker trying to keep it away from Adam, Adam trying to wrench it free from Parker's big hand as he peppered his ribs with sharp little rabbit punches. It felt like someone was setting off little flares in his belly every time Adam landed a blow, but Parker held on to the gun.

Using little more than brute strength, Parker forced his best friend off the top of him, throwing Adam back so he could struggle to his feet. But Adam was already rushing him again. God, he was so *fast.* Adam hit him like a speeding car, leaping into the air to spear his shoulder into Parker's chest. They both went tumbling back to the ground once more, a tangle of limbs and muscle. Adam locked both hands around one of Parker's knees to try and drag himself up on top again, but the angle was bad, and Parker saw him coming. Sitting up quickly, he swept the pistol down into the side of Adam's mouth, sending the smaller boy tumbling away with a yelp, clutching at his mouth, rivulets of red already leaking between his fingers.

Unsteadily, Parker got to his feet once more, stepping back, creating distance between the two of them. He wiped the blood off the side of the revolver and raised it to point square at Adam's heart.

"Cheap shot," Adam groaned as he stood, swaying unsteadily.

"I told you." Parker thumbed the safety off the pistol. "I told you to go away."

"Come on, you know I can't do that."

Behind the black gaze of the gun, Parker rose to his full height, towering half a foot over the crown of Adam's head, rolling his own broad shoulders, spreading them out like vulture's wings.

"No?"

Adam wiped a trickle of blood from his lips. "You can't just walk away from this. That's not something you get to skate on. I can't let you. I won't."

"Yes, you can," Parker said, hating himself for begging. "All you have to do is turn around and go home. Please."

"I'm not going to do that. I'm not ever going to do that. I'm your friend."

"So it wasn't true, what Nate said? All that mean shit about you guys being sick of dealing with me, that was just Nate being Nate?"

Adam's mouth dropped open an inch, like he was searching for the right words. "I mean, what do you want me to say, man?"

"Say that he was wrong. Say that he was just being an asshole because he liked to hurt people."

Adam's eyes darted away for a moment, and Parker could see the shame burning there. In that second, hiding behind the revolver, he knew.

"Parker . . ."

A bitter sting drove itself deep into Parker's heart. "Never mind. Sorry I asked. I'm going."

As he turned, he saw something change inside his friend. It was like all the kindness left in Adam's body fell away from him in a single, awful rush, leaving only a hard, unfeeling mannequin in its wake. Parker barely recognized him.

"Just put the gun down already!"

Adam's words came out sounding cruel and childish—so unlike the boy that Parker had known since elementary school. He'd always been the kindest of all of them, but it was clear that kindness didn't apply to Parker anymore.

Before Parker could react, Adam was racing toward him again.

On a good day—hell, on any normal day—Adam was fast. Faster than Parker ever had a chance of being, even if he'd spent years training, which he hadn't. Parker could never move the way that Adam could move. Parker was big, and he was tough, but speed, *true* speed, the kind that Adam held like a gift from the gods ever since they were little kids—that was something that had always eluded him.

Adam could sprint a whole mile. He could tackle an obstacle course like he was standing still. He could run a marathon without breaking a sweat. Adam could move like nobody Parker had ever seen.

Except right now, this wasn't about fast. This had nothing to do with fast.

Parker dropped the gun's barrel by a hair and pulled the trigger. In a burst of bright red, Adam's knee exploded.

A scream split the air between them, an unbroken wail of agony almost as loud as the gunshot had been. It filled the forest, that scream. It sliced through Parker's body and echoed inside his skull. He hadn't ever heard anyone make a sound like that before; that it came from Adam Jarvis just didn't compute.

Adam collapsed to the ground in an instant, hands jumping to his leg, blood spilling out from between his knitted fingers in a messy rush. Parker watched him go down and let the gun hang by his side, momentarily forgotten. Standing still, he watched his friend, curled up in the dirt and yowling like a wounded animal.

It felt good to watch him twist and writhe like that. It felt good to see someone else hurt.

Inside Parker's belly, the rage slowly cooled to a dim glow, while Adam screamed through his teeth and clutched at his mangled knee. His eyes had gone wide and white and full of fury, but it was obvious that Adam wasn't going to do anything but lie there and bleed. Park could feel tears prickling the backs of his eyeballs again, and when he spoke, the words came out shaky and uneven.

"I'm sorry. I'm . . . I'm so sorry. I didn't want to," Parker said. "I swear I didn't. But I told you to leave me alone."

Adam twisted his head to look up at him, and for the first time in his whole life, Parker knew what real hate looked like. Not even Nate had looked at him like that. Nate had been a mean shit, but he hadn't *hated* Parker—he'd just wanted to hurt him. But Adam? Yeah, he definitely hated Parker now. How could he not? It burned there in his movie-star blue eyes, a pair of red-hot coals fresh from the fire. There was no coming back from this.

"I'm sorry," Parker said again, as if it would help anything.

Then he turned and walked away, leaving Adam to seethe and bleed while he headed deeper into the woods. He had other things to worry about now.

* * *

They all spun around to look when they heard the second gunshot roll through the trees in a single sharp *POP*. It sounded so far away; how had Adam and Park gotten so far already? The first shot had been so huge, like a car crash or something. The sound of it had hung in the air for what had seemed like forever.

As one, Chloe, Nicky, and Josh all twisted in place and ran in what they thought was the direction of the gunshot, dashing away from the clearing and their tents and their gear and their dead friend, heading straight into the depths of the Pine Barrens.

"Adam? ADAM!" Nicky screamed into the empty distance, pumping her legs as Chloe and Josh struggled to keep up. *"ADAM, WE'RE COMING!"*

It was Chloe who realized, after a moment, just how stupid they were being.

"Guys, we need to stop," she chuffed. "Guys, stop!"

Skidding along the ground, Chloe whipped her hands out to try and stop her friends from going any farther. Nicky was well out of arm's reach, but Josh was closer than she'd thought. Pivoting to try and intercept him, Chloe crashed into Josh with a bone-shaking *smack*. The two of them went tumbling to the forest floor. As she fell, she belted the back of her head against something cold and hard buried in the dirt. A second later, she heard someone approaching.

At first, she saw double. Nicky loomed over her, hands on her knees, eyes wild. But there was another girl there too—older, dressed in all black, her face slashed with tears as she lurked behind Nicky's shoulder.

Who . . . ?

Chloe blinked hard enough to see stars, did it over and over until the vision evaporated and it was just the three of them again.

"Chloe, what the shit?" Nicky panted, her eyes big and wet with tears. "Why would you do that?"

"We need to stay put," Chloe said, prying herself off the ground, rubbing at the back of her head with dirt-smeared hands.

"What!"

"We have to go back."

"No, the hell with that," Nicky snarled. "Adam is still out there. He could be *hurt*."

"Chloe has a point," Josh said, rising to his feet. "Parker is out there with a *gun*, Nicky. He knows how to do this wilderness shit better than we do, and he's already killed one of us, maybe two. What makes you think any of us stand a chance against those odds?"

"Don't say that," Nicky said. "Don't you fucking even—"

"Nicky, listen." Chloe shook off a fresh surge of panic, forcing a kind of calm into her voice that she truly didn't feel. "Whatever made Park pull that trigger, are you so sure it won't make him stick that gun in your face next? Or Josh's? Or mine? He's dangerous, and none of us knows where the fuck we're going. We need to call the cops, and we need to stay put. Anything else puts us in harm's way."

"No, no, no!" Nicky cried. "Adam's our friend! We need to *do* something!"

"Nicky, we *are* doing something," Josh interjected, pulling his phone from his pocket and thumbing at the screen. "I'm calling the cops, okay? They'll be here soon. An ambulance. Our parents. Anyone. Everyone. But until then, I think we just need to hold tight."

"The hell with that, and with both of you," Nicky dropped down to the dirt, stretching one long leg out in front of her.

Chloe stepped in close to her. "Nicky, please, don't do this."

But down in the ratty earth, Nicky was already retying her sneakers with a singular focus, all traces of the crying fit gone from her face, save for her puffy red eyes and the clean tear tracks cutting through the grime on her cheeks.

"I'm not going to wait around to get killed," she said. "If you want to stay here and wait for him to come back, that's on you, but

I'm not going to hang around like a sitting duck. We're *witnesses*. You know what happens to witnesses, right?"

She double-knotted her laces and punched the sides of her trainers with rigidly balled fists, apparently satisfied. Walking between the trees, Josh circled around and around, his cell phone held aloft, eyes squinting to focus on the screen.

"I can't get a signal," he said. "We should be able to get some kind of signal out here—we're not that far out of service reach. A bar or two maybe. Especially for 911. They have contingencies built in for 911 calls. This doesn't—"

"Cell service died back when we pulled off the highway," Nicky snapped. "Remember in the car, Nate was . . ."

Chloe watched as the sentence died on her lips at the mention of their dead friend's name. Nicky stood and looked at her boyfriend, then at Chloe, face set in a stony scowl.

"You guys coming?"

Chloe shook her head. "Nicky, don't."

The tall redhead's eyes narrowed. "He needs my help. That was a *gunshot*, Chloe. You heard it as well as I did."

Chloe held her hands out to Nicky in what she hoped was a placating gesture.

"That's exactly the point. Even if he's hurt, Adam's smart, and he's strong. He might still be okay. But Parker's been going camping out here since he was a little kid. He knows what he's doing in the woods."

The words were out of her mouth before she even really knew what she'd said. Instantly, Nicky's eyes flashed with fury.

"Are you *kidding* me right now?"

"Nicky, *stop it*," snapped Chloe. "You know what I mean. What Parker did was fucked up and horrible, but you can't deny he knows how to look after himself out here better than any of us do. The three of us need to stay together. We can't just freak out and go running in some random direction. We don't even know which way they went."

"But what if he comes back for us?" Nicky's voice was coiled like a spring, all of her nerves slashing through to the surface. Chloe couldn't blame her; she felt like she was barely hanging on herself.

"Then we'll deal with it," Chloe told her. "Whatever happens, we'll deal with it. Together. I promise."

"And Adam?"

"Adam'll find his way back," Chloe said, sounding way more certain than she actually felt. "And if he doesn't, or can't, we'll hike back to the van at sunset and drive until we get a signal and we'll call the cops. We'll call the FBI, the National Guard, whatever you want. The army or something. But right now, we have to wait. Just for a little while, and then we'll go. I promise. But we have to give Adam a chance to find his way back to us first."

She watched Nicky's eyes twitch back and forth, from her to Josh and back again, then farther. Toward the clearing. Toward the tents, the firepit, and the body. A silence passed between the three of them. Nobody wanted to say the words again. Doing that, repeating those words, would make it completely real, and it couldn't have been real—not *really* real. The truth was too big, too gruesome, too awful for any of them to look at head on. The truth would leave them all in shreds if they let it.

Finally, something in Nicky's face softened, the tiniest bit of give.

"A couple of hours," she said at last, her voice small and fragile. "Just until it starts getting dark."

"A couple of hours, then we'll go," Chloe agreed.

Nicky swallowed. "Okay."

She turned and stalked back to the clearing, Chloe and Josh trailing behind her. When they reached the campsite, Nicky went straight to the tent she shared with Josh, getting down on her hands and knees to climb in.

Josh gave Chloe a resigned look, then followed his girlfriend inside.

"Guys, can you not zip that thing up? If you don't mind?" Chloe said. "I really don't want to be alone right now."

She counted eight whole breaths before Nicky answered.

"Fine."

Back by the firepit, Chloe pulled a ratty old blanket out from the shambles of Nate's tent and went to lay it over his body. He already looked so much worse than he had a little while ago. His face had gone loose and slack in death, hanging half off his head like a wet rag as the hole above his eyes seemed to grow and spread. Standing there looking at it made her stomach turn, so Chloe spread the blanket over the top of him and beat a quick retreat, sitting down on the farthest stump, and ran her fingers through her hair, pushing loose locks away from her face and tucking them behind her ears.

Eyes shut for a moment, she tried to do the breathing thing that the school counselor had taught her after Uncle Dave had gone missing—four in, six out; inhale the good, exhale the bad. Visualize it like white light and black smoke, cycling in and out of her lungs, purging all the stress and fear from her system, one breath at a time. She stood and crossed the clearing to the far side, to the tree that Parker had been examining when they first got here. There were carvings in the wood, six letters ringed with deep tally marks, counting the years.

DAC/PDC

Chloe understood at once. She knew those initials well.

Parker had led them to his and his dad's old camping spot.

Some faraway part of her brain knew he'd told them that before, but for some reason it hadn't really clicked into place until this moment. She didn't want to worry about Parker, but she couldn't help it. He was alone too—even if he did it to himself. He was still her cousin, after all. That cold thing she'd seen in his eyes when he pulled the trigger—that wasn't really him, was it? She had to believe that it wasn't all that was left of him. The Parker she knew better than maybe anybody in the world had to be in there somewhere. Parker was so much more than the bundle of fear and nerves and rage and hate and sorrow that lived inside him.

And now he was out there on his own. But then again, he'd been alone for a long time. Ever since his dad went MIA.

The details, such as they were, were few and far between. One day last October, for no reason at all, Chloe's uncle Dave had told Parker and Aunt Lori that he was going camping so he could get some time alone. He hadn't told them where he was going or when he'd be back; he'd just packed up some gear and left. At the time, it hadn't seemed like a big deal. Dave went camping all the time, with and without his family. He was an outdoorsy guy. This was just what he did sometimes. So, thinking nothing of it, Parker and his mom had told him that they loved him and to be careful.

Then he never came home.

Chloe pulled her cell phone from her pocket and clicked the screen to life: 4:16 p.m. Up in the corner, the battery indicator read 40 percent, and beside that, just like Josh had said, zero bars.

That was okay. They could last. It wasn't long until they would hike back to the van and get the hell out of here. Come nightfall, this whole place would be swarming with cops and state troopers. Their parents would come and get them. Everything was going to be okay. All they had to do was make it to the highway, and then it would be over.

And yet, Chloe couldn't shake the feeling there was something wrong with their plan. It was like a burr caught in her brain, biting deeper into her whenever she turned her attention toward it. She was forgetting something. What the hell was it?

Wait. Shit.

Oh, shit.

The realization hit her like a cartoon safe falling from the sky.

She'd given Adam the keys.

4

Adam crawled.

Despite the agony, despite the nausea, despite it all, he crawled. He had to get back to his friends, to the camp. It would be dark soon, and Adam had been camping in the woods before—he knew what it was like when it got dark in the forest. Night in the city, in the suburbs . . . it was nothing compared to how it was in the woods. The darkness out here was absolute, a living thing that flooded in around you to eat you alive.

Unless he was totally mistaken, he still had an hour or two until the sun dropped past the horizon. Plenty of time to crawl back. They could start a fire, wrap his leg, keep him warm while somebody went for help.

He was going to be okay.

He kept telling himself that as he dragged himself along the forest floor, digging his bare hands into the dirt and rocks, heading inch by bloody inch in the direction he thought he'd come from.

He was going to be okay.

Over and over, he told himself the lie, *knowing* it was a lie, but bereft of anything else to cling to. The truth was ugly, and it was brutal, and it only made things worse. Better to cling to the lie and press on for as long as he could. That's what people did in these situations. They kept going, even when there was nothing left to keep going for.

Stopping to rest his head against a rock, Adam closed his eyes and drew a deep breath to scream out again.

"*Chloe! Nicky! Anyone!*"

He lay there and waited, hearing his own voice bounce off the distance in diminishing returns, then fade out entirely. Where the hell were they? How far had he followed Park off the trail? He counted to ten and then started to crawl again, grinding his teeth against the astonishing pain radiating out from his injured leg. Up until this point in his life, Adam hadn't known that he could feel this much of anything. His whole world had been reduced to this hot, sick glow burning out from his ruined knee to fill his whole body, like firing a flare gun in the middle of a small, dark room.

Adam slowed and then stopped and rolled to sit up, leaning forward to get a better look at his bloody knee. He had to see. Holding his breath, he peeled back the torn denim, then immediately wished he hadn't.

Underneath his shredded jeans, the skin hung off his leg in rags, blood pulsing steadily from its messy edges, staining the bottom of his pant leg dark and shiny. In the middle of the mess, Adam could see something cracked and white, like the shards of a broken plate sticking out of the pulpy meat, clustered around a little black hole in the middle that looked like it went on until forever.

Adam felt sick, staring at it like that, and another warm, slurry wave of nausea rolled up from his stomach to the back of his throat, impossible to swallow back. The wave turned into a flood, and a second later, he twisted to the side and puked, a cord of bile jetting from behind his lips, splashing across the leaves in a thin spray.

Hopelessness danced through his body again, stronger now than it had ever been. He wasn't used to being empty. He didn't know how to hurt and keep going, no matter how many times he told himself otherwise. Looking back, he could see an uneven trail of red in the dirt behind him, leading off into the distance, tracing his path all the way from where Parker had shot him.

Where was he, even? He thought he'd been heading back toward the camp, but now he wasn't sure. None of this looked familiar. He should have paid more attention when he was trailing Park. He should have been on the ball. Now he was lost out here with a blown-apart knee, all because of Parker fucking Cunningham.

Adam closed his eyes and felt his whole future crumble, all the puzzle pieces blown off the board in a single, awful blast. His football scholarship was gone now, that much was obvious. Nobody was going to give a full ride to a running back who couldn't run. And it wasn't like he had the grades for an academic scholarship. He was fucked. Even if he got out of this forest alive, he was totally and utterly fucked.

In a single second, with a single bullet, Parker had destroyed Adam's whole life. Parker had ruined everything.

Alone and bleeding in the woods, Adam pressed his face to the earth and started to cry, feeling the heaving gasps twist and bow his body. When they finally subsided, he took another deep, rib-cracking breath and howled out again,

"*CHLOE! NICKY! ANYBODY! HELP!*"

There was nothing but silence to greet his cries. Fine. That was fine. Adam didn't need their help. He could do this on his own. He was strong, he was capable. He was Adam Jarvis, and Adam Jarvis could do anything he set his mind to, trashed leg or not.

Rising to crawl again, he pounded a fist against the ground, splitting his knuckles open on the rocks, summoning up all his rage to wash the fear and sorrow away. It was what they'd spent years drumming into him during practice: anger was useful. Anger could be harnessed.

After another second, he started crawling again. He was going to find them. He was going to be okay. He just had to get back before dark, and that was still a long way off.

But he was going to be okay.

* * *

Parker ran for as long as he could, feeling his lungs burning and his head starting to pound. He ran until Adam's screams faded off into nothing, until the only thing he could hear was the thrush and hum of the woods behind his own wheezy breathing. Slowing to a lumbering trot, he slung his pack around one shoulder and opened it up, trading the still-warm pistol for the busted old canteen he'd taken from the kitchen at home. The water inside was already a little stale, but it tasted good.

Parker knew this place. He'd been out here plenty of times with his dad, fishing and hiking and starting campfires, grilling hot dogs on sticks and telling ghost stories. They'd come out here as far back as Parker could remember. His dad loved it out here, which made Parker love it too. There was something serene and perfect about a forest like this being square in the middle of New Jersey, like it had been dropped there, in between the highways and townships, right out of the clear blue sky.

There was another campsite up ahead. Parker pushed through the brush to have a closer look. This site was far older and smaller than the one he and his friends had stopped at, but the layout was similar: a rough clearing surrounded by trees, with a blackened firepit in the middle, filled with ashes.

Step by step, he paced around the outer edges of the clearing, taking it all in. It was peaceful here, like this. He couldn't hear anything but the soft buzz of the woods, the blood thumping in his ears, the crunch of his boots on the soil. This could work, at least for the night. Everything else could wait until tomorrow. He'd left his tent back with his friends—could he even still call them his friends, after what he'd done?—so he'd have to make a shelter from whatever he could find. But that wasn't a problem; he'd done it before. His dad had shown him how.

He'd need a fire, though.

Park knelt beside the firepit for a closer look: the stones had been burned as black as the thick mounds of ash inside. He'd have to clear it out before building a fresh fire. He jabbed at the dead cinders with a stick, then thrust his hand into the firepit and felt around. The ashes were warm. Someone had been here just a couple of hours ago. Inside his ribs, Parker's heart jumped despite his common sense. *It's not him*, he told himself. *It's not him, it wasn't him.*

But what if it was?

Parker dug through the pit, scooping out handfuls of ash until his fingers brushed against something smooth, solid, and cold. What the hell was that?

He gently closed his hand around the object and drew it from the ashes.

It was a hatchet, heavy and stained black as shadow. Parker shook the loose ash from its length and turned it over in his hands, inspecting it from handle to blade. It was old, ancient even. The blade was long and curved the wrong way at the top, the handle thin and almost delicate. It seemed like it would be fragile, but it wasn't; the wood was worn smooth and stained pitch-black to match the head, but it felt sturdy. Parker had never seen a hatchet like this before.

At the base of the handle, someone had carved a cross like two nails stacked together.

Who had left this here? Who'd tried to burn it, and why hadn't it taken?

Dropping his pack on the ground, Parker took the hatchet over to one of the trees at the edge of the clearing, set his feet, and sunk the blade into the wood with a satisfying *thunk*. Yanking it free, he did it again, and again, leaving thick gashes behind in the trunk. He didn't know how old this thing was, but it was still strong, still sharp, and he was definitely going to need something like this out here. He'd left his knife and his camp hammer in the dirt at the main camp, and it wasn't like he could go back and get them now.

With his thumb, Parker brushed the last few dovewings of ash from the head and went to work. The sun was going down fast. He had to make some shelter while he still had the light.

Chloe went through all of it again.

"Okay, we've got a box of cinnamon Pop-Tarts, a couple tins of Vienna sausages, six beef jerkys, some Mountain Dew, a handful of candy bars, the water, the beer, the Everclear, the hot dogs, and the granola bars. We've also got like two cans of SPAM, three of sardines, plus Adam's precooked bacon and that oatmeal you brought, Nicky. Also I think there's some gum and breath mints in there, but I'm not a hundred-percent sure on that. You guys sure you don't have anything else to add to the food pile? Guys?"

Neither of them were listening. Josh was kneeling by the firepit, sweat pouring off his face as he tried to build them a campfire from a pile of dead branches baked dry by punishing New Jersey summers past. Meanwhile, Nicky was circling the tree line around the clearing again and again, her eyes increasingly frantic in the sharp glow of her cell phone light.

"I'm telling you, the path is gone, Chloe."

"It's not gone. Paths don't just vanish."

"Then you try and find it."

Chloe gestured vaguely to the far side of the campsite. "It's somewhere over there. That's where we came in, right?"

"You're not sure?" Nicky asked, incredulous.

"Are you?"

"No, I'm not, and I've been looking for it for an hour."

"Nicky, it's just dark, okay? It's going to be okay."

Dark was an understatement. Night had closed in over the forest like an executioner's hood, blotting out everything but the shadows of the trees that stabbed up at the stars shining in the sky. Nicky turned her light toward Chloe, the little LED blinding in the drowning blackness.

"I'm not crazy, Chloe."

"I never said you were."

"You thought it."

"No, Nicky, I didn't. All I said was that paths don't vanish."

"But it's *not here.*" There was an edge razoring into her voice, the first signs of panic starting to bubble up to the surface. Chloe stood and went over to her, trying to keep her expression kind, despite how annoyed she was beginning to feel.

"I don't think you're crazy, Nicky. But I don't think the path vanished, either. It's just dark. Things get lost in the dark all the time. That doesn't mean they're gone. I know you're scared, okay? I'm scared too."

Nicky's lower lip twitched, and her eyes widened, just a little bit.

"Why are you going through the food again?"

Chloe shrugged. *To distract ourselves so we don't freak out. So we have an anchor. To pass the time. All or none of the above.*

"Just . . . to have something to do," she said.

"What if we're out here all night?" Nicky whispered.

"Then we're out here all night. We have food, we have our tents and our gear, and Josh is going to get that fire going any second now. We'll be okay until morning. When that happens, we'll find the path again and walk on out of here. I promise."

Nicky made a face and nodded, then went back to walking the tree line. As if she just wasn't looking hard enough. Chloe hadn't told her about the missing keys yet—what would be the point? Without a path back to where they'd parked, what good would the keys do? The plan had already gone to shit, and the three of them were already wound up nearly to the breaking point; anything else might just shatter them completely. Shamefully, she was actually a little thankful that the dark had swept over them so fast. It bought her time. Maybe by morning she'd have a chance to get her bearings, find a different way out of here. Maybe she'd wake up and magically know how to hot-wire a minivan.

"Guys, I think I've got it," called Josh. He stood back from the firepit, arms raised in triumph, a stupid grin cut across his face. By his knees, the little pyramid of gathered wood he'd assembled there had finally caught, a flash gathered in shadows blooming into something more substantial. The wood crackled and burned, a real campfire.

They all huddled around it for safety as much as for warmth. There was something comforting about a fire in the dark. Nicky folded herself under Josh's arm, while Chloe got in close and hunkered down, holding her palms out to absorb as much heat as she possibly could.

"Thank you for this, Josh. Really," said Chloe.

"It's no problem. Nothing I couldn't do again given another thirty or forty tries. I've basically gone full mountain man at this point."

Chloe closed her eyes and kept them shut. She appreciated the attempt at humor, but kneeling only a few feet away from their friend's body, jokes seemed destined to fall flat.

"What do we do now?" Josh asked.

"Stay put 'til morning," said Chloe. "We've got food and our tents and a fire. It's not going to do us any good charging ass into the trees if we don't know where we're going and can't see shit."

"So what? We just go to sleep, try again in the morning?"

"Honestly? Kind of, yeah," said Chloe. "You guys okay with that?"

"No," Josh said. All the humor had gone from his eyes. "Very, very no. But it's not like we have any other choice." He sighed. "I'm going to go try and close my eyes. My head hurts, my back hurts, my everything hurts. Sleep will probably do us all some good, and maybe if we're lucky, tomorrow will be less screwed up than today."

"Hope you're right," Chloe said.

"If you two need anything, let me know? And be sure to feed the fire, otherwise it'll go out."

"Will do," Chloe said. "Sleep well."

Josh nodded to Chloe, hugged Nicky and kissed her on the cheek, and then went to their tent and climbed inside, burying himself underneath one of the sleeping bags until all they could see was the general shape of him beneath the green polyester.

Chloe raised her eyebrows in Nicky's direction.

"You heading that way too?"

Nicky looked around, giving a final, half-hearted search for the trail out of the woods. "Yeah, I guess. You going to stay up?"

"For a little while, yeah. Just have to make a pit stop, and then I'm getting in my tent and not coming out until it's daylight again. Hopefully there will be sleep somewhere in there too."

"Do you think that's a good idea? Just going to sleep like that?"

"Given the lack of options, I'd say it's probably fine, yeah," said Chloe. "Why?"

"Shouldn't one of us stay up, and . . . you know, keep watch?"

"Watch for what?"

The fear in Nicky's face was unmistakable; it seemed to have taken up permanent residence there over the course of the last few hours. Still, Chloe understood what she was really asking.

"Nick, I don't think he's going to come back."

Nicky gave her a distrustful look.

"How can you be sure?" Her voice was a blade-sharp whisper.

More than anything, Chloe wanted to reassure her. She really did. Except she didn't know any more than Nicky, and given the circumstances, she could hardly blame anyone for freaking out. But someone had to be the grown-up right now.

"Because if he was going to, he probably would have already."

Nicky made a strangled noise in her throat, probably trying to hold back another round of sobs, but she didn't say anything. She just wiped her eyes and nodded. Chloe reached an arm out and gave her shoulder a squeeze, hoping the gesture was comforting.

"You go on ahead and get into bed," Chloe told her. "I've got to go pee, and then I'll stay up for a while longer, keep watch, feed the fire."

Nicky nodded. "Don't go far, okay? I don't think we should go much past the tree line if we can help it. Feels weird out here."

Chloe squeezed her shoulder again. "I'll be fine. You get in there and spend some time with your boyfriend. I'll be right back."

Tears twinkled at the corner of Nicky's eyes.

"Where are you going, exactly?"

Chloe pointed. "Just right over there, a little ways into the trees so I can pee in private." She tried to give Nicky a confident smile. "Not far at all. And I've got the fire to lead me back, don't I?"

Nicky scrunched her face and neck up, then shook it off. "Fine. Just be back soon."

"I will. I'll shout if I need anything. Anything at all."

"Promise me you'll come back."

Chloe held back a sigh. "Of course I'll come back."

"Promise me." Nicky's eyes were like saucers in the flickering light.

"Alright, I promise."

"Okay."

She watched Nicky turn and climb back into her tent to lie down beside Josh, zipping the tent flap up behind her. A second later, she thought she could hear a faint, muffled sob, but it faded out as soon as it had come. From the pile Josh had gathered, Chloe tucked a few extra branches into the blue heart of the campfire, watching them catch and burn. For a second, she could almost forget all the myriad ways this trip had gotten so completely fucked up. For one fleeting moment, it just felt like she was camping. Then the feeling passed, a cloud drifting across the thumbnail moon, and all she was left with was the horrible, shitty reality. No escaping it now.

Chloe headed out into the shadows and trees.

Adam saw the tree before he saw the cave.

It rose like a broken bone from underneath the earth, bare and jagged and so white it nearly glowed in the dark. At first, he thought he was hallucinating it, so different was it from the black, imposing pines that surrounded him on all sides. It didn't have any branches to speak of, just a bent trunk that split in two imperfect halves near the top, like a pair of broken fingers.

He'd been on the ground for what felt like forever, feeling worse with every six inches he dragged himself forward. First it had been the space between his shoulders knotting up, then his stomach had started to churn, followed by chills and a fist of pain throbbing behind his forehead, opening and closing over and over, rough fingertips scraping the meat and bone inside his skull. Having to endure all of it together was almost worse than his knee, which had gradually ebbed back to a constant, swollen agony instead of the screaming death grip it had been before. Looking down, he saw that he was still bleeding, though it had slowed from a constant surge to a heavy trickle. That was something. Still, he hadn't stopped feeling like he was going to puke again at any moment, or shit himself, or maybe both.

He crawled toward the white tree, gawking. He'd never seen anything like it. It stood at the mouth of a low cave cut into a rocky hillside, like it was guarding whatever was inside. He'd initially thought it was some sort of aspen, but aspens had branches, features, those textured stripes that came from scores in the bark. This tree didn't have any of that; it was totally smooth, except for the tiny knots and grain grooves that Adam only saw once he got in close.

The thought that it might be some ancient elephant bone sticking out of the dirt came back to Adam twice as hard, but as he drew closer, he could see clearly that it was certainly a tree, definitely dead, maybe even petrified, though he didn't know how that would be possible. He ran a hand along the trunk, feeling the ashy dryness of the wood with bloody fingers, leaving red smudges behind as his hand came away dusted white and gritty with some sort of spore or something.

He wiped it away on his shirt. So weird. So totally alien.

Adam turned his attention to the cave. It was dark, wet, and rough, but it might do for the night. Not like he had any other options at this point. He stopped and dug in his pocket for his phone. The screen was cracked and falling away in chunks from his fight with Parker, but it looked like the flashlight was still working. The white light exploded in his face, and he turned it toward the stone interior. The cave wasn't very deep, but there was a bend down near the back that he didn't like the look of. There could be anything—or anyone—hiding back there behind the rocks, just waiting to do him in.

"Hello? Hello!" he shouted, pained, into the cave, trying and failing to keep the words from cracking where his mouth met his throat, like a creaky seesaw. His voice bounced off the damp, mossy stone, reflecting back at him in a fun house mirror version of itself: *hEllOooO . . . HeLLoOoOo . . .*

Adam waited there for a while, laid out on the rocky earth, trying to fight back the hurt and summon up the energy to crawl inside.

When he started to drag himself forward again, every little movement was agony. Hot coals in his knee, rotten teeth in his guts, a dripping fist of fever in his skull, knives up and down his back. He only had a few feet to go, but he already knew he wasn't going to make it all the way. It was too much, too hard. He'd done all he could do, gone as far as he could go. He'd burned everything he had in him, getting here. He wasn't smart like Chloe or Josh, or resourceful like Parker. Everything he had that was worthwhile had been taken away from him, and now he was going to die right here, right now.

No one would find him. He was lying in a grave carved just for him.

Halfway inside, Adam twisted and tried to get a better look around, but his phone slipped free from his numb fingers and went skittering across the cave floor, making bizarre, warped shadows dance and coil all around him. Pulling hard against the pain, he reached for the phone but it was too far, all the way across the rough stone floor, the light pointed straight up, illuminating the cave like a cold white campfire. At least he wouldn't die blind.

Something rustled behind him.

Contorting to look over his shoulder, he tried to get a better view, but there was nothing there that he could see past the tree. Everything beyond had been blotted out, as if reality had been stained over with ink or paint. Feeling uneasy, Adam shifted in place, trying to get comfortable. He laid his face down against a cold, smooth spot on the stone floor, and the relief that followed was incredible, maybe the best thing he'd ever felt in his life. Sleep, or something like it, was already grasping at him from the depths with thick, banded tendrils that he knew wouldn't let go once they took hold.

He heard the rustling again, louder now, closer. He rubbed at his eyes with grimy, bloody fingers, but he couldn't see anything. Holding his breath, he tried to stay as still as the night around him. He didn't want to be killed by some awful unseen thing. He didn't want to die at all.

The last thing he glimpsed before he passed out was the bone tree starting to shimmer and bow in the wind.

* * *

Using the hatchet, Parker sheared branches from trees and wove them into a sort of curtain that he braced between the dirt and a cluster of trees on the edge of the clearing where the trunks had grown closest together. The little lean-to wasn't perfect—it wouldn't keep out anything but the lightest rain, if it came to that—but he figured it would do for the night. At the very least, it might stem some of the wind and the cold. It was a hell of a lot better than whatever he'd left Adam with.

Jesus, *Adam*. A swirling chemical mix of shame and anger pulsed through Parker's system as he stopped and thought about what he'd done to his best friend just hours before. Adam hadn't deserved a bullet to the knee, no matter how he'd acted, no matter what he'd said. He was just trying to help, and when it didn't work, he'd got angry, he'd got desperate. Anyone could understand that. Parker, on the other hand—well, Parker had shot two of his friends today; killed one and left the other for dead. Parker was the bad guy. Parker was the fuckup. No matter what happened now, no matter how he felt about it, there was no coming back from that. Ever.

He leaned his broad back against one of the trees and sank down, scraping a curtain of bark dust free to fall across his broad shoulders. His ass hit the dirt with a quiet *whump*, and he let his head tilt back, his eyes looking up at a small window punched through the distant treetops, the darkness beyond filled with stars. He focused on them until they were all he could see, and imagined himself drifting among them, lost in an empty sea speckled with spots of distant white light. He felt cold and adrift, alone in an escape capsule ejected from some larger vessel, the control panel off and the engines long gone dead. Nothing to do but float here, through the absolute dark, and wait for time to pass. Nowhere to go but forward now—wherever *forward* led him.

Right now, he supposed that meant sleep. For a little while, at least. After that, he'd figure out his next move.

Down on his hands and knees, he crawled into the little shelter, angling his giant's frame to fit in the small space he'd afforded himself. For any normal person, it would probably be pretty comfortable, but it fit Parker like a coffin. Parker positioned his backpack on the ground to use as a pillow; it was lumpy and wet and cold, but it was better than a rock or nothing at all. Beside his head, he laid the black hatchet down on a bed of dried pine needles, right where he could grab it if he needed it.

Tomorrow he'd start looking for his dad. He was out here somewhere, and Parker was going to find him. He had all the time he could ask for now.

On his hip, Parker's walkie-talkie crackled to life.

"Parker, are you there?"

He snapped the radio off his belt and held it up in front of his face, eyes slitted and suspicious. He'd forgotten he was wearing it, or that he'd left it on. A second later, the red light on top of the handset fluttered with signal, and the speaker crackled again, that same familiar voice coming through as clear as a church bell.

"Park, it's me. If you're there, please pick up."

Once she was far enough away from the clearing, Chloe sat down on a log and hung her head, trying to breathe. In the distance, she could still see Josh's campfire dancing inside the circle of stones, casting jagged shadows through the trees as much as it did flickering orange light. She knew for a fact that the moment she got into her little secondhand tent she'd have no problem falling asleep. At this point, she could probably sleep through a forest fire. Exhaustion was in her muscles, in her spine, in her eyes and the back of her head. If she were to lie down right here, right now, she'd be out before she took her next breath. But she couldn't do that. Not yet.

Sitting alone in the dark, Chloe counted to 120, then unhooked her walkie-talkie from the waistband of her pants and held it to her lips, pressing the *talk* button down with her thumb.

"Parker, are you there?"

Nothing.

"Park, it's me. If you're there, please pick up."

More static silence, then:

"I'm here."

Chloe sighed, relieved despite herself.

"Are you okay?"

There was a long pause on the open channel.

"Not really."

"Yeah, there seems to be a lot of that going around right now," she said.

"How are you guys?"

"Not good, Parker. Really not good at all."

There was another pause. "Yeah."

"Where are you?"

"Woods," Parker said. "I'm not sure where, exactly. I found another place to camp, so . . . Are you guys still, you know, there?"

"Most of us, yeah." The words came out of her mouth soaked in poison.

"Are you mad at me?"

The air caught in Chloe's throat, coming out in an incredulous splutter. She didn't even have to think about what she was going to say next. It was all just right there, waiting.

"Mad? Yeah, Parker, I'm pretty fucking mad. How could you even ask me that? Of course I'm mad. I'm mad, and I'm scared, and I'm so goddamn tired I could scream. And you know, there's nothing that anyone can do about it, least of all you. I don't have any idea what to do with all of this shit. I don't know if I should hate you or if I should feel sorry for you, or both, or something else. What you did was so awful that I'm not actually sure how I should react. Honestly, I feel guilty even talking to you like this right now."

The rage pulsed in electric arcs along her skin, up and down her arms, raising the tiny little hairs there to stand straight up. Saying it felt good, and saying it felt awful. The radio felt so small and flimsy in her hand then, like Chloe could crush it to powder if she just squeezed.

"You don't have to talk to me if you don't want to," he said after another moment.

A fresh surge of white-hot anger tore through Chloe's brain. "But I do, though. I do have to talk to you, because thanks to you, everything is now so profoundly fucked up that I think the only way we're all getting out of this and going home is if we do it together."

"I'm not going home, Chloe."

"Of course you are."

"No. I'm not."

"Why?"

"It's complicated."

"So explain it," she snapped. "If you're worried about the cops, or your mom, or Nate's parents—"

"It's not that."

"Then tell me what it is."

The radio fell silent for a moment. "Did you find Adam?"

"No . . . wait, what do you mean *find* him? We heard another gunshot, but that was all. Is he dead too?" An image flashed across the surface of her brain of Parker and Adam standing across from each other between the trees, knee-deep in vines and brush—Parker with that gun held out in front of him, just like before, Adam with a jet of blood and brains streaming out the back of his head. She could almost hear the gunshot again, the horrible way it seemed to pinball off the trees and the sky and back again.

"I don't think so," Parker said.

His deep, calm voice brushed away the nightmare image. The relief that blossomed in Chloe's gut at anything he had to say right now made her feel like such a traitor.

"But you did shoot him?"

Chloe heard him sigh. "Just in the leg. The knee. He was still alive last time I saw him. Probably still is."

"How merciful of you," she jeered.

"You don't understand. He tried to rush me."

"I don't care! You don't get to shoot people just because you're carrying a fucking gun! That's not how this works!"

"I didn't want to."

"That doesn't mean shit," Chloe said. "You still did it."

Another long pause. "Yeah."

"We're going to go to the cops once we get out of here, Parker. You have to know that by now, right? As soon as we can call 911, we're going to."

"That's a good idea. You should."

There was no inflection in his voice; all the feeling had bled out, leaving him sounding flat and blank. She couldn't tell if it was exhaustion or if he had finally just totally disconnected from reality. There was a hot surge in Chloe's chest, like she was going to start crying again. She gulped it back and stood up from the log, pacing back and forth in the dark, quickstepping from one tree to another, hoping to distract her body from the sobs that were threatening her from her deepest core.

You don't get to cry. Not now. Not in front of him. Not like this.

"You know you don't get to walk away from this, Parker. You shot Nate dead, maybe Adam too. The police are going to find you, and they're going to make you pay for it."

"Yeah, probably. Eventually."

"You know you deserve whatever it is they do to you for all of this."

"I know."

"Can I ask you something, honestly?" For a second, her voice shook, but it held steady.

There was a long pause on the line, an extended feedback hiss; then Parker said, "Sure."

"Do you even feel bad for shooting him?"

"Which one are you talking about?"

Jesus. The sobs rose up in her one more time, and she had to take a few deep breaths before she was steady again.

"That's not funny, Parker."

"I'm not trying to be funny."

"Then what are you doing?"

A silence settled across the radio, more complete than it had been before. Chloe punched the *talk* button again, even though she already knew what had happened.

"Parker? . . . Parker?"

Parker had turned off his radio. He was gone.

5

Nicky lay awake in her tent, listening to the woods and the night while Josh slept next to her, snoring softly. She couldn't hear what Chloe was saying, but she knew that she was talking, and since she had never been the praying type, there was only one person she could be talking to right now. Nicky had seen the two of them pop open those radios, smiling in that secret way they didn't think anyone else noticed. The two of them bulwarked together against the rising tide of reality, same as they'd been since elementary school. Like it was the world that was wrong for not running at their speed, rather than the opposite way around.

She thought for a second about going and having a smoke. She'd been half-heartedly trying to cut back, but whatever Chloe and Parker were talking about out there, it didn't sound like it was going to be over anytime soon. She could get one or two in before Chloe came back, if she puffed fast.

She got as far as rolling over to reach across Josh for her pack and her lighter but at the last second decided against it. She didn't want to be away from him, and she didn't want to leave him alone. Asleep, he was already farther away from her than she would have liked. And the smokes would just keep her awake, anyway.

Screw it. She'd just lay here until her eyelids got too heavy to hold up.

Eventually, she heard Chloe's voice strain and rise before settling back into a more restrained whisper, then silence, punctuated by a soft weeping that seemed to float along through the air like birdsong. It was a few minutes before Nicky heard Chloe's footsteps getting louder as she returned to the camp. Nicky pulled Josh tight against her and closed her eyes, wishing she'd never agreed to go on this stupid trip.

Chloe tiptoed around the campfire and fed a couple of thicker branches to the flames to keep it going as long as she could. It would surely go cold by morning, but in the meantime, more warmth and light weren't bad ideas. She watched the branches burn, the bark curling back and blackening in the flames while the heartwood took its time, swipes of dark brown trembling along their lengths before joining the fire proper.

She wanted to hate her cousin for everything that he'd done, but she couldn't quite bring herself to it. She was furious and heartbroken, but she couldn't crest that final hill that stood between rage and hate.

She really hoped Adam wasn't dead. The next morning, after they found the path again, she'd take Nicky and Josh out and try to find him before anything got any worse. Parker said he'd only shot him in the leg, but saying you'd *only* shot someone was like saying you only committed a *tiny bit* of arson. Doing it at all was bad enough.

A chill wind snaked its way through the trees and across their campsite, making the fire pop and dance as Chloe's clothes twisted and pulled against her thin body. She waited for it to pass, then tossed another three branches on the flames. The fire contracted for a moment, then latched onto the new fuel and grew larger, the flames half as tall as Chloe. The heat felt good. Turned out, even in summer in New Jersey, the woods got cold at night, so she was thankful for the warmth.

She didn't look at the trees. She didn't look at the tents or the sky or the covered-over dead body only a few feet away from her. She kept her eyes on the campfire, fixated on the way it curled up and chewed on itself, perfectly content to burn. For a second, she wondered what it would feel like to throw herself on top of it, to just surrender and let the flames eat her up. Chloe wondered how long it would take her to die from something like that. Would her clothes and her skin melt together, or would they turn separately to ash? What would the embers do to her hair? How long would it take for her eyes to boil and burst into jelly?

Christ, but she needed sleep.

Banishing the fantasies of burning from her head, she went to her little tent and climbed in. Inside, she zipped up the flap behind her and lay down on her belly, burying her face in crossed arms. She was out almost immediately.

Adam came to drenched in sweat, curled up in an awkward ball against the far wall of the cave. The pain was still there, his knee was still a mess, and aches like broken bones still wracked the whole of his body, but his head had stopped feeling like it was going to burst like an infected zit. He was cold, though. Really cold. A chill, sharp and merciless, had sliced through the night air while he'd been out.

He pulled himself to a sitting position against the cave wall and tucked his hands into opposite armpits, trying to return some feeling into his numb digits. Hunger clawed at him, a panicked animal set loose to scrabble around in his belly. The fever had burned away his appetite, but it had come back twice as hard now, alive and awake and undeniable inside him. He wished he'd brought something along with him from the camp, but he hadn't been thinking that far ahead. He'd just wanted to keep Parker from getting away, so he'd charged off after him like an asshole—and he'd paid the price for it.

Nobody likes a hero, Adam. His mom had told him that a million times, whenever he got too full of himself during football or baseball, or tried to get between his brother and his dad when they were having another knock-down-drag-out. *It's not like you see in comic books or movies. Whether they mean to or not, heroes have a way of complicating everything for everyone else.*

Heroes only get people hurt.

Adam shucked off his overshirt and held it up against the guttering light from his phone to find the cleanest sections, then tore into it with his teeth, biting and gnawing at the tough fabric until he could rip the cloth away in thick, frayed stripes, one after another. When he had enough of them, Adam tied the biggest one into a knot and fit that between his teeth.

This was going to hurt.

He went to work, bandaging his destroyed knee up tight with the flannel strips. Touching the wound shot butcher knives into his brain, but he kept going, gnawing a scream into the knot. Each time he got one strip wrapped around, he tied it off, then moved on to the next one until he was out of strips. The makeshift bandage wasn't hospital quality by any means, but it would do for now.

Adam spat the knot out into his hand and tossed it toward the mouth of the cave. That's when he noticed it. The dead white tree had grown branches—branches heavy with fruit—while he was asleep.

It was one of those brief, nonsense thoughts, there and gone in a flash. It must have been that way all along. He'd just missed it when he first dragged himself in here. The fever had played hell across all his senses, and then it had knocked him out flat. But he was past all that now. He was on the mend, or at least stable for the time being. Seeing clearly for the first time in what must have been hours.

The lumpy fruit glistened in the dark, oddly shaped bulbs so red they were nearly purple, like a blister or a bruise. Dew had started to collect where they hung, rolling down to drip off and splash onto the cave floor. Looking at them, Adam's stomach churned and gurgled. Jesus, he was hungry.

Peeling himself away from the damp rock wall, Adam slowly crept over and picked one of the misshapen fruits off the tree, holding it up to inspect in the scant moonlight. Up close, it was fist-sized, with a stem jutting out the top of it like an apple, with soft, supple skin. There were thin blue-black streaks running through it, too, branching off of each other to crisscross the whole thing in web-like veins.

The logical side of his brain was aware that eating this could be a really bad idea. For all he knew, it would be poisonous and kill him, or maybe just wreck his insides and leave him screaming in curled-up agony while he filled his pants with heaves of hot, bloody shit. He wasn't stupid. But the animal in his belly slashed at him, immune to his logic. It wasn't going to take no for an answer. He had to put something in his stomach, or his stomach was going to eat itself.

He looked around the cave for anything else to eat. Maybe moss, or some kind of plant—hell, he thought he remembered hearing that people could eat lichen in a pinch—but there was none of that in here. It was just the rocks, and the lumpy fruit, and him.

He brought it to his lips and breathed in its scent. There was a perfume to it, a sweetness that wasn't quite cloying, a tartness that wasn't quite rotten, with a tang of something simmering just underneath the surface. Iron? Copper? What fruit smelled like that? It wasn't unappealing, more just that the fruit smelled exceptionally *whole*.

His stomach groaned, its protests growing louder. Looking at the fruit in his hand, Adam imagined how delicious it would taste, could almost hear it humming to him—*Eat me, eat me, eat me all up*—in some familiar tune that he couldn't quite place. The growl in his guts turned into a snarl, and a second later, the snarl grew teeth and bit into him, deep. The pain was impossible to ignore.

Adam didn't need another invitation. He didn't even hesitate. He sunk his teeth into the meaty skin and chomped down. The fruit burst between his lips in a torrent of flavor that flooded his mouth, better than he'd ever imagined, like sweet steak. Adam chewed hastily, like a starving animal, before swallowing the mouthful in one throat-wrenching gulp. Juice spilled down his hands as he inhaled the fruit, making short work of it in four enormous bites, each a bit larger than the last. When he'd swallowed the last of it, stem, core, and all, he stopped for a moment and breathed, fully expecting it to hit like a brick in his belly.

Except he didn't feel poisoned. In fact, he felt better already. His stomach shuddered with pleasure at the sensation, then growled for more.

Adam plucked another swollen, lumpy fruit off the tree and tore into it like a bone-thin street dog. He'd never tasted anything this good in his entire life. When he finished with his second, he reached up for a third, and a fourth. He'd eat every fruit on the tree if he could.

SATURDAY

6

Parker woke with the sunrise. It shot blades of yellow light through the trees, setting the forest aglow. Laying there, without his glasses on, he thought the blur made it look like the Barrens had caught fire while he was sleeping. He rolled over in his evergreen lean-to, then rose to a sitting position, arching his back until his spine popped like a string of Nate's firecrackers. He'd slept well, a lot better than he'd expected, actually, especially after how things had gone with Chloe. He'd half thought he'd be up all night, but it had gone the other way; his eyes had fallen shut like a pair of portcullises as soon as his head hit the backpack again.

Parker pushed the wall of braided branches away, tipping the majority of his shelter over onto the ground, where it landed with a soft *thrush*. Fresh air rushed in around his body, prickling the spots of skin he'd left uncovered with a hard chill that had no doubt waited for him all night. He'd been smart enough to sleep in his clothes and his boots, but even so, the cold was enough to make his neck and cheeks and the backs of his hands tingle something stubborn.

The radio was still where he'd dropped it the night before, next to the black hatchet. Parker felt a pang of regret for ending the conversation the way he had, but he couldn't keep talking to her like that.

Of course he felt bad for what had happened. He didn't want any of this, but he couldn't take it back now. The best—shit, the *only*—thing any of them could do was keep moving forward. Looking back was only going to screw everything up worse.

He rubbed at gummy eyes with clumsy fingers and ran his hands through his short black hair before fitting his glasses over his face, shuttering the world into focus. That's when he saw that he wasn't alone.

A figure crouched in the middle of the campsite, its back to Parker, broad shoulders hunched up to bend its silhouette into a nearly perfect square. Park had to blink a few times before the shape lost its shimmering blurriness, its edges sharpening as the seconds crept on around them.

It was a guy, Parker could tell that much, and he—whoever *he* was—had knelt down next to the blackened firepit to poke at the ashes with one bare hand, humming tunelessly to himself. The man's bulk was impressive, his broadness enough to rival Parker's, but even squatting down, Parker could tell that the guy was clearly a lot shorter than him, maybe by a foot or more. Moving quietly, Parker reached over and lifted the black hatchet, getting a good grip around the black wood before rising to his feet.

"C-can I help you?"

Nate turned to regard Parker with a wide grin.

"Hey, prick. You sleep okay?"

Parker didn't even think—he just screamed and tried to put the hatchet through his dead friend's face.

It didn't work. The blade whizzed through Nate's head like it wasn't there at all. Set off balance, Parker stumbled back, while Nate only smiled wider. He ran a hand across the length of his face, as if checking for damage, then held it up for Parker to see.

"Yeah, nice try and everything, but I'm pretty sure shit doesn't work like that anymore," he said.

Parker looked at the hatchet in his hand, then back to the dead boy in front of him. This wasn't possible. There was no way. Parker took a few more backward steps, slower this time, keeping the hatchet blade between them like a talisman. "You're dead. You're supposed to be dead."

"No, I'm supposed to be *alive*," said Nate, jabbing a finger in Parker's direction. "You're the reason I'm not." He held his hands out in a lazy Christ-pose. "*Ta-da*!"

"So you're what? A ghost now?" There was an embarrassing shake in Parker's voice.

Nate shrugged. "Man, hell if I know. Last thing I remember was telling you that you weren't going to do it, and then . . . you did it."

Parker remembered things differently. His skin still stung from all the mean, ugly shit Nate had sprayed at him the day before. He could still feel where Nate had jammed a finger into his chest.

"It didn't hurt or anything, dying. In case you were wondering. It just felt like somebody'd poked me in the forehead, and then everything sort of got cold and blinked away, and then there was just nothing. Like, *noth-ing*. Like yanking the sheet clean off the bed, but instead of a mattress and box springs underneath, it was just . . . void. Empty black space where real life should have been."

"That sounds terrible."

"Yeah, it was pretty goddamn horrible, Parker. Then, like a second later, I opened my eyes, and I was in the woods again. And I gotta tell you, I have never been happier to be anywhere. Like, at least I was *somewhere* instead of *nowhere*. I fucking cried, no shit. I sat down and cried for like an hour, and when that wore off, I realized I could hear this . . . ringing in my ears. At first I thought it was nothing, just leftover noise from you blowing my brains out, but I figured out that wasn't actually the case pretty quick. You know the sound I'm talking about, like one of those headaches you can kind of hear? Yeah, that. Fully drumming inside my brain too. Faint to begin with, but it got quieter or louder depending on which way I was walking. First I tried walking away from that shit, but the thing was, the headache got worse the farther away I got from the sound. So I figured, hell with it. I'm already dead, might as well try going the other way, see what happens, you know? Not like it was gonna kill me, right?

"Anyway, I walked all afternoon and all night. Followed the sound through the trees until it was the only thing I could hear. Followed it all night. Then, the second I walked up and saw you sleeping, the noise just—" He snapped his fingers on both his hands. "Gone. Like it was never there at all. You gotta figure that means something, right?"

"I don't know. You tell me."

Nate rolled his eyes. "Fuck makes you think I know? I woke up like this. You're the one who paid attention in school and shit. You learn anything there that could help us out here? This kind of shit usually means something, right?"

"Everything means something, or nothing."

"Helpful, Parker."

"But now that I think of it," Parker mused, "there is one thing that I learned. Might be helpful."

"Yeah? What's that?"

"Ghosts aren't real," said Parker. "So you're not fucking real."

Nate cracked a smile and prodded at his own body with sausage fingers. "I don't know, I feel pretty real to me. Not exactly a hundred-percent *solid*"—he reached down and tried to pick up a rock from the ground, but his fingers passed right through it—"but, you know, I'm here. Real quick, though, you ever have a deer run *through* you? It's real weird, I'll tell you that much for free. I don't think it was a lot of fun for the deer, either, honestly."

Nate took a step closer, and Parker took a step back, jabbing the head of the black hatchet out at the dead boy.

"No, no, no, don't, okay? Just don't," Parker said. "I'm having a bad dream, or a nervous breakdown, or I don't know what, but there's no way that you're really Nate, incorporeal or not. You're some broken part of my brain fucking with me for whatever reason. Nate's dead. You're. Not. Him."

"'An undigested bit of beef, a blot of mustard, a crumb of cheese, a fragment of an underdone potato!'" Nate crowed, doing a little dance where he stood. "Now you say it. C'mon, Park. You know the next part—'There's more of gravy than of grave about you.' Say it."

Parker didn't say anything. Nate gave him the finger.

"Fine. You make for a shitty Scrooge, anyway, and I'm not too hot on playing Marley, either."

Something inside Parker softened, then broke. "When did you read that?"

"What?"

"*A Christmas Carol.* When did you read it? You hate reading. You always said that it was gay, which doesn't mean anything. I didn't know you'd read any Dickens."

Nate gave him a sour smile. "I didn't. I liked the version with the Muppets and the old English guy from those Batman movies when I was a kid, though. My dad always made us watch that one before we opened presents." A shadow passed over his eyes. "But I guess that's over and done with, huh?"

Something cold and weird climbed up Parker's back, from belt-line to shoulders, and stayed there, weighing him down.

"You shouldn't have made me do it," he said, his voice a hoarse whisper.

"I didn't *make* you do anything, Parker. You brought the gun, you stuck it in my face, and you pulled the trigger. Everything that happened is one-hundred-percent your fault. All because you couldn't keep from losing your stupid temper. You don't get to ignore the truth because it sucks."

That same old anger flared behind Parker's ribs, bright blue and burning hot, but he didn't scream at the ghost, he didn't curse, he didn't do anything. He just watched Nate for three long breaths, and then he knelt and collected his things, hefted his pack onto his shoulders, and walked away into the woods.

Parker didn't have any interest in putting up with Nate's shit dead any more than he did when he was alive.

He shoved through the trees at a death-march pace, using his long stride to put as much distance between him and the old campsite as he could, driving his boots into the earth like they were punishments from God, splitting the branches in his path with bone-breaking cracks. It felt good to break things, all of a sudden.

Up ahead of him, Nate stepped out from between the trees, wagging a finger like a disappointed babysitter.

"Oops. *Sowwy.* You can't get rid of me that easily," Nate said. "Not twice, friendo. This time, I'm sticking around. We're going to be best buds."

Parker wove around him and kept walking, kicking sprays of pebbles and dirt from his path.

"Seriously, man. I'm not going anywhere, so you might as well start getting used to it," Nate called after him. After another second, Parker stopped in place and looked at him, his shoulders falling in a two-slope avalanche.

"What do you even want from me?"

Nate made a face like he'd tasted something disgusting. "From *you*? Nothing. Do you honestly think I want to be stuck with you for the rest of my afterlife, or whatever the hell we're going to call this? Honestly, I'd rather cut my own tongue out with a pair of my mom's sewing scissors than spend eternity with you. But I've got this, remember?" He tapped two fingers against his temple. "The farther I get from you, the more it feels like somebody's pounding nails through my skull. So until we figure out how to unfuck this glitch, curse, whatever it is, I'm sticking next to your big ass like stink on shit."

Parker shook his head and sighed.

"Fine. Whatever. I don't care. Could you at least do it quietly?"

Nate showed him that same sick grin he always made when he was being too clever by half. "That doesn't sound like me to me."

Parker walked around him, studying the angle of the sun, trying to get his bearings. A moment later, Nate stepped out from behind another tree and fell into lockstep with him.

"Stop doing that," said Parker.

"What?"

"The teleporting thing. Stop it. If you have to be here with me, just be here with me. Stop messing with me and just be a decent person for once in your life."

"Says the murderer."

"Nate, *please*."

The ghost-kid threw his hands up. "Fine, Jesus. Have it your way. See if I care. You were never any fun anyway."

They came to a sunken clearing and wove around the bog-like wet patch in the middle that boiled with mosquitoes to crest the slope on the other side. Parker swept low branches and brush away with the hatchet, getting a better feel for it with each swing. The trees were thicker here, so far off the paths, much older and denser. He hacked through another dry tangle and caught Nate watching him with squinted, riverstone-black eyes.

"What?" Parker asked.

"You know, I didn't see it yesterday, but I think I get it now," said Nate. "Why you came out here."

Parker didn't even turn his head to look. "Enlighten me then," he said, still carving a path through the trees.

"You came looking for him."

Parker stopped in place, just for a moment, feeling his guts spool out the front of him like a broken measuring tape, trying to keep his face from betraying him. *Don't say it. Please don't say it.*

"I don't know what you're talking about."

"Sure you do. You didn't really want us to come out here and camp together, because who gives a shit about camping? No, you came out here to find your dad. Didn't you?"

The words hit Parker like a truck, and for the second time in two days, he wanted more than anything to shoot Nate in the face.

Chloe heard the sound before she even opened her eyes: a coo and warble, followed by the airy, fluttering snap of wings. Slowly, she sat up and unzipped the flap of her tent, careful to make as little noise as possible, then peeked her head out to see.

The blanket had blown off of Nate in the night and now hung awkwardly in the branches of a tree on the far side of the campsite. Something black and thick had settled over the top of his body, like a sort of horrible, writhing moss. It took her eyes a second to adjust to the light before she understood what she was seeing.

Crows. Nate was covered in crows.

Crouched in her tent, Chloe watched with mounting revulsion as the horde of birds clustered and shifted on top of her dead friend, flapping and lashing their dirty black wings at each other, jockeying for position as they stitched their sharp beaks into their cold perch. Chloe scrambled to her feet with a revolted wail. They were eating him.

They tore at his body with short beaks like scissor blades, snipping at his bulk through the holes they'd torn in his clothes, coming away dipped in red and dangling bloody strips of his insides. Horrified, Chloe threw a rock at the churning black mass. It sailed in a high curve, flying wide and hitting the ground in the distance with a *thud*.

"Go!" Chloe barked at the birds. "Get out of here! *Get out of here*!"

She sent another stone flying at the murder of crows, harder this time. This one flew lower, bouncing off the ground to glance across Nate's slack face, opening up a stripe of sour purple-red along his cheekbone. The gash didn't bleed; it just hung there in his skin, like a punched-in smile. She heard the other tent unzipping, and out of the corner of her eye, she saw Nicky and Josh emerge, blankets and arms wrapped around each other.

Nicky saw it first.

"Chloe, what the hell is . . . Oh, god. Oh, *Jesus*."

She bent at the hip and retched onto the ground while Josh stared. Chloe didn't wait. She'd had enough of this shit. She hefted one last rock and sent it flying true, landing dead center in the mass of birds, smashing one open against Nate's body as the rest took flight in a frightened black wave that disappeared into the trees like smoke.

Chloe toed the rock off of Nate's chest and watched as it rolled down and away, coming to a rest by the dead campfire. On top of the body, the dead crow was half-flattened against Nate's bulk, its skull split open and leaking, body bent and warped, broken wings glued with fresh blood to the corpse below it. Underneath the bird, Nate was a mess. His face and chest looked like someone had gone after them with a flathead screwdriver, pitting out little red divots of skin that didn't bleed. Some of the birds had been at his eyes too; his lids hung in rags over hollow-looking sockets that wept a kind of clear jelly that Chloe didn't want to look too closely at. His lips were torn to shreds, same with the outside edges of his nose. He didn't even look like Nate anymore. Now he was just this big, bloody dead thing on display before them.

"We can't leave him like this," Chloe said in a strangled voice. "We can't."

Josh absently turned to look at the blanket still splayed in the branches. "I don't think I can reach that without climbing."

"No, we need to bury him or something. We should do it together."

Nicky made a sick, sad sound in her throat and turned away from them.

"I'm sorry, I can't take this shit," she said. "I won't. Just, goddammit. *God fucking dammit.*"

Nicky stepped back and then launched herself back into the tent. A second later, Chloe heard the muffled sound of her sobbing, a noise she'd already gotten too used to. Josh didn't even seem to have noticed that Nicky was gone. His face had gone pale and queasy.

"Alright, that means it's you and me," said Chloe. "Come on, help me drag him. Josh?"

But he didn't say anything, staring at the picked-apart mess that used to be their friend. Chloe leaned in to break his sight line, waving her hand at his face.

"Hey. Hey, Josh. Right here."

A second later, his eyes cleared, and he saw her again.

"Sorry, what?"

"We have to cover him up, or they'll come back. Let's go."

He nodded to himself. "Right. Yeah. Okay."

They dragged Nate by his arms to just beyond the edges of the campsite, out where the trees got a little thicker, looking for a place where he'd fit, laid out like he was. The feel of his cold skin against hers was awful and unnerving; it made her want to scrub her palms until they bled. It wasn't natural, dealing with the dead like this.

When they found a spot that would work, they left him there and went rock hunting, gathering up as many as they could carry. After twenty or so minutes, they were pretty sure they had enough to do the job, so they began to cover him over. First they laid an outer ring, tracing Nate's silhouette in stone, then piled whatever they could on top, building their friend a loose, formfitting coffin piece by piece.

"This isn't really how I thought I'd spend the first day of summer break," Josh said, stacking stone after stone across the summit of Nate's big belly.

"Me neither."

"I'd at least thought I'd be a little hungover by now. Or a lot hungover."

"Same."

"I was looking forward to that hangover," said Josh. "I was really going to earn that hangover. Nicky was too."

Chloe kept her head down and stacked stones. "I think we all were."

"She's not as tough as you guys think she is, you know," Josh said. "She likes to play the hard-ass, but she's so not that. She's sensitive. All that toughness—it's just a front."

Faint annoyance crackled along Chloe's neck hearing him say it, doubly so because he was right.

"I know, Josh," she said, biting back her irritation. "We've known her since elementary school."

"I'm not saying you haven't. I'm just saying, I think I might see parts of her that you guys don't."

"You're saying you know her better than we do? Better than I do?"

"No, no, that's not it at all. I'm just saying that, you know, this is a screwed-up situation—"

"For all of us."

"What?"

"It's a screwed-up situation for all of us, Josh. Not just you, and not just her. Everybody."

"Well, sure, I was just—"

"I know what you were *just*," Chloe said wearily. "But do me a favor and save it. We don't need more shit to deal with right now."

Josh closed his mouth so quickly, Chloe heard his teeth click behind his lips. They went back to piling stones on top of Nate in silence.

"I'm sorry," Josh eventually said. "I wasn't trying to be an asshole. I just . . . I worry about her, you know? I really like her a lot, Chloe. I love her. I want to make sure she's going to be okay."

Chloe placed another rock, then another. "She likes you, too, man. She likes you a lot. And, honestly, if you can help her be less scared sometimes, then god bless."

Josh blushed, just the tiniest bit.

"I know."

Chloe shot him a sideways glance. "But you gotta back off when it comes to telling people shit about their friends. You've been around for a few months now, and I like you and all, but that doesn't mean you've got the right. This isn't your place, and it's not your circle. Maybe someday, but not now, and definitely not for a while. I'm glad you're looking out for her, but right now is a profoundly shitty time to try and make people pick sides. We're all on the same side, at least until we get out of the Barrens. Okay?"

"Sure, yeah," Josh said. "Of course."

"Good answer."

It didn't take them long to finish building the cairn, and when it was done, the stones were piled half as high as Chloe stood. It would do for now; at least it would keep more crows from getting to Nate's body. She wasn't sure about anything bigger, but she didn't know what else lived out here. Were there coyotes in the Pine Barrens? Wolves? Bears?

When they got back to the campsite, Nicky was already dressed and sitting by the firepit, hanging her head between her knees. Chloe exchanged a look with Josh, who nodded over toward his shared tent.

Go, Chloe mouthed to him. *I've got this.*

Josh peeled off and went to the tent to change, while Chloe crossed the distance to Nicky and stood next to her, looking at the back of her head, gazing at the wildfire hair tumbling down around her shoulders.

"Hey, Nicky."

"Hey yourself," Nicky said, her voice flat and empty.

"How are you doing? You okay?"

Nicky twisted around and fixed Chloe with red, dark eyes. "No, I'm not. Are you?"

Chloe shook her head.

"No, I don't think so."

"Great. Glad we got that cleared up." Nicky pushed her hair back and gestured to the place the body had lain. "What did you do with the . . . with him?"

"We took him out into the trees and buried him."

"You don't have a shovel," said Nicky.

"We piled rocks over him," Chloe said. "Started with an outer ring and moved inward. It's called a cairn. Learned about it in Euro History last year. I think it'll keep things from getting at him, and that way the cops won't have any problems finding him when they come."

"They won't," Nicky said with a sneer.

"Won't what?" Chloe asked, startled.

"The cops aren't coming, Chloe. Nobody's coming. Our phones aren't working. It's just us now, and we're all going to die out here. I know it, and you know it too."

Chloe sat down next to her. "I don't know that, because it's not true."

"Yes, it is. We're not getting out of here, because the forest doesn't want us to leave."

"Come on, that's crazy."

Nicky's eyes flashed with anger.

"I looked for the path again," she said. "While you guys were out burying him. It's not there. It's just gone. Like the forest just ate it all up."

A cold thread of trepidation crept up Chloe's spine. "It has to be there."

"It isn't."

"That's not possible."

"Apparently it is."

Frustration roiled in Chloe's belly. "Look, you're just not looking for it right, okay? It's there. I know it's there," she insisted.

Nicky's eyes filled up with fresh tears, and she turned away from Chloe, back to the dead campfire. "Why don't you look for yourself then, if you're so sure. See what you find."

"Fine." Chloe stood and went to the nearest edge of the campsite and started to walk a careful circuit around its perimeter. She knew she was going to stumble on it after a minute. She had to. Nicky was just upset. She wasn't thinking straight.

Chloe took small steps, tracing the entire outside edge of the campsite, waiting for the dirt path to open up before her . . . but it didn't. After a minute, she'd walked a full circle to stand right back where she'd started.

Nicky was right. The path was gone.

Chloe clenched her guts against the horrible vertigo drop that opened up inside her, clinging to rationality like a life preserver. This was not the time to be freaking out. She couldn't do that. She wouldn't.

Solutions. They needed solutions right now, not more panic.

"Nicky, I promise you, there is a way out of here," Chloe told her. "We just have to find it. If it's not the path we came in on, then there'll be another, or we pick a direction and just start walking until we hit asphalt. This is New Jersey—there are highways everywhere."

Nicky got really quiet for a second. "I heard you talking to him."

Chloe's stomach dropped. She'd overheard. Of course she'd overheard. The Barrens got so quiet at night it was probably impossible for her to not. But Chloe was pretty sure that she could still defuse this.

"Sorry, what?"

"Last night. On your radio, when you said you had to pee. You were out there talking to Parker. I heard you."

Chloe's face flushed. "Nicky, I—"

"Don't lie to me, okay? Just do me the courtesy of not standing there and lying to my face. I know what I heard, so don't try and tell me I didn't."

Chloe lowered herself to the ground next to Nicky, but it felt more like a collapse than anything—like the little bit of strength left in her body had just rushed out of her, leaving her to fall like a dropped puppet.

"I had to see if he was okay, Nicky," she said quietly. "He's my cousin. I love him."

"You should have told me you were doing it, instead of sneaking around. You always tell me everything. You always have."

"I know I should have told you. I know. I'm sorry. I just . . . I know how pissed you are at him," said Chloe. "I'm pissed too."

"But you still talked to him."

Chloe sighed. "Because he's still my family. The fact that he did what he did doesn't change that."

Nicky's face was a bitter tangle. "What did he have to say for himself?"

"Not much. You know him. He wasn't doing okay—"

"Oh, yeah, poor him."

Chloe ignored her. "But he didn't sound like he was hurt or anything. I asked him about Adam."

"And?"

Chloe hesitated for a moment, unsure if she should tell Nicky the truth. "It's probably a good idea for us to go and try to find him while we still can."

"Why? So you and my boyfriend can drag him into the woods and bury him under a pile of rocks too?" She was playing hard-ass again, armor all the way up to mask her real feelings. Chloe couldn't really blame her. Vulnerability had never really been Nicky's strong suit.

"That shot we heard yesterday . . . that was Parker putting one in Adam's leg. He might not be dead, but he's definitely hurt."

"Oh my *god*," Nicky groaned.

"He was alive when Parker left him, Nicky. People don't die from being shot in the knee, at least not right away. I think that if we can find Adam—soon—maybe we can help."

"What about Parker?"

"Parker's a nonissue."

Nicky gave her a hard look from under a furrowed brow.

"I meant what I said last night, Nicky. I don't think we have to worry about him right now. Whatever he's doing out there, it doesn't have anything to do with us. If he wants to be alone, we'll leave him alone. We've got other problems to deal with right now."

Nicky craned her neck to look up past the trees, toward the bright blue sky that seemed so much farther away this morning than it had the day before.

"Okay. Fine," Nicky said. "We'll go find Adam. All of us. Together."

"That sounds good to me."

"Maybe we can help him. I hope we can, at least."

Chloe rose to her feet. "Great. I'll let Josh know, and we can start packing up camp."

"Sure. But, Chloe?"

"What?"

Nicky fixed her with a cold, empty glare. "If I see Parker out there, I'm going to kill him. Family or not, I swear to god I'll do it, and if you try and get in my way, I'll kill you too. Got it?"

Chloe nodded, swallowing the jagged lump of fear in her throat. "Got it."

"So were you ever going to tell any of us what you were really doing out here? Or was it supposed to be a surprise?"

Parker kept moving, drawing his pack higher on his shoulders, evening the distribution of its weight across his back. They'd been going for an hour or more, tromping through the trees, following the path of the sun. Parker watched the woods around them, keeping his eyes narrowed for movement, for something out of the ordinary, for anything. He didn't know exactly what he was looking for out here, only that he'd know it when he saw it.

"You weren't supposed to notice I was gone until it was too late for any of you to catch up."

"Wait, seriously?"

Parker nodded. "That was the plan, yeah."

"So what, you were going to get us all partied out and then disappear into the woods in the middle of the night?"

"Basically, yes," said Parker.

"That's cold, man. Really cold."

"I didn't say that I was going to feel good about it. But it was easier than explaining. I don't know. I figured you'd all go home without me. I was going to leave a note."

"Wow, a *note*? How goddamned magnanimous of you. You do understand how screwed up doing that would have been, right?"

"More or less screwed up than killing someone you've been friends with since middle school?"

Nate bugged his eyes out at that. "Oh-ho! Was that a joke? Did the great and serious Parker Cunningham just crack a joke? That might be a first, folks. I'd say it's too soon, but it's not like we can uncrack the eggs or unmake the omelet now. Might as well have breakfast. Speaking of, are you hungry? Because I am starving."

"Can you even eat?"

"No idea. Probably not. But I know what I feel."

"I guess what I'm asking is, how do you even know you're really hungry? Could be like, phantom hunger, or something."

Nate's lips pulled back in a smile Parker didn't like and he let out a wet, joyless chuckle that sounded like something being drowned.

"Was that another joke, Parker? *Phantom* hunger? You're on a roll this morning, bud."

Parker pulled his glasses off his face and buffed them on the bottom of his T-shirt, clearing the grime and steam from the lenses. Beside him, Nate held a hand up to shade his eyes from the sun as he surveyed their surroundings.

"Do you even know where we're going?"

"I have a general idea," said Parker.

"Which means *no*."

"Please shut up."

The two of them came to a break in the trees and found themselves standing at the edge of a small field, grown over with vines and clover and scattered with bare white trees like dead aspens. Did aspen trees grow out here in the Barrens? Parker figured they must, since they were here. But still—there was something about them that he didn't like the look of. He scanned their surroundings while Nate extended a finger toward the farthest edge of the field.

"What the fuck is that?"

Parker saw what he was talking about. The structure rose out of the ground like a rotten tooth from green-and-brown gums, half-buried in the dirt and scorched to charcoal. Looking at it from here, Parker could tell that it had been a house at some point in the past, but now it was just a charred ghost of itself, a dark ruin being lazily devoured by the earth. He'd heard of old houses that had been lost in the Pine Barrens, the homesteads of old Puritans who had wanted to commune with their Lord in the cathedral of nature, but he'd never heard of anything like this. This wasn't decay, or the ravages of time; no, someone had set this house to burn.

Nate's eyes sparkled. "You want to go check it out?"

"I guess, sure."

"Awesome."

"You're weirdly excited about this."

Nate gave him a look. "Why aren't you? I mean, you're the one who wanted us to come out here, man. Don't get pissy now because I happen to be enjoying myself, especially given the circumstances." He made a pistol with his fingers and mimed shooting Parker in the face. "*Pew.*"

Parker bit back everything he really wanted to say to the dead boy.

"Fine," he said. "Come on."

Up close, the house was way more of a disaster than it had looked from a distance. Its walls had fallen, its blackened floor long battered to splinters, its roof collapsed entirely or turned to ash and blown away after the fires had gone out. It would provide no shelter if a storm rolled in, so Parker considered the idea that it didn't even count as a *house* anymore. It was a *thing*, an assemblage of scorched, cracked bones planted in the dirt and nailed haphazardly together.

There was another one of those white trees growing near the center of what Parker thought must have been the living room or the kitchen way back when—not quite a sapling anymore, but not totally mature yet, either. Across from him, near the other side of the ruin, he watched Nate lean in to inspect the burns and the breaks, his beady little rat eyes still glimmering.

"What do you think happened here?"

Parker ran a hand along one of the broken struts. His palm came away black with soot. He held it up and pointed it toward Nate.

"It got burned."

Nate's face curled into a sneer. "Yeah, no shit. I mean, how? Like, do you think this was a forest fire or something?"

"I don't think so," said Park. "Look at the trees around here. See how they're all old? They don't have a mark on them. It wasn't the forest that burned, just the house. I think somebody set this place on fire."

"Like on purpose?"

Parker knelt to lift a fallen pallet of boards. The soil underneath was as black as the house's jagged remains.

"Maybe. Maybe not. Could have been an accident in the kitchen or something. But I suppose it's possible."

"Jesus," Nate said. "How long do you think this place has been out here?"

"Hard to tell. Maybe a long, long time, especially if there wasn't anybody out here to mess with it."

Dropping the boards back down to the ground, Parker stood and dusted his hands off, then he went to the nearest wall to look out at the forest beyond the overgrown clearing. Coming out here as a kid, the endlessness of the Barrens was amazing to him, a wonder to behold. Like it had been plucked whole-cloth out of some storybook. But standing here now, that endlessness filled him with cold dread, laid like a stack of bricks on his chest. He could barely breathe, when he stopped to think about it for too long.

"Dude, are you seeing this?"

He turned to look at Nate. The other boy's eyes were cast down at where one of the skeletal walls met the soil.

"What is it?" Parker asked.

"Just come here for a second. Check this out."

Parker wove through the old wreckage to look where Nate was looking. On one of the remaining walls, there was a row of long, deep gashes, like claw marks hacked into the grain, and a big, dark stain that stood out against the dusty blackness of the wood.

"Does that look like blood to you?" Nate asked.

Parker felt a nervous chill ladder up the back of his neck.

"What the hell could do something like that?"

"My dad always told me there were bobcats out here," Parker said. "Bears too. Might've been one of them."

"Oh, *good*."

"What are you so worried about?" Parker asked, trying to shake off the nerves. "You're incorporeal."

Nate gave him the finger. "Just because I'm not going to get chewed up by some big angry whatever-the-hell doesn't mean I want to stand here and watch it happen to you."

"Aw. That was almost sweet, Nate."

"Great. Can we go now? Place is starting to give me the weirds."

Parker looked around the burned-out old house one more time. They weren't going to find anything in here. It was just a torched-out mess.

"Fine. Sure."

Parker turned to follow Nate out of the wreckage, touching his hand to the pale tree as he passed it by.

Wait.

He stopped and turned on his heel to go back and look.

It couldn't be.

There was something carved in the wood.

Past the edges of the burned house, Nate stopped and turned back to glare at him. "Yo, Parker, what the hell? Are we going or not?"

"Just . . . give me a minute," Parker called back.

"Whatever." Nate razzed his tongue at him, but Parker hardly noticed. He stepped in close to the tree and used one hand to brush some of the ashy pollen from the bare, bone-white trunk.

There were lines scarred deep in the wood, cut by a steady, sure hand. They bled hardened sap, red amber collecting at their jagged corners in a dried-out crust. He couldn't stop himself from touching them, running the pads of his fingers along their deep, deliberate edges, carefully probing at them as if they were razor blades that might butterfly his fingertips wide open if he touched them wrong. Like history could reach out and kill you, if it wanted to badly enough.

DAC.

David Allan Cunningham.
His dad had been here.

7

They packed up as much of the camp as they could carry and headed into the trees, following the same direction they thought they'd seen Parker and Adam go the afternoon before. Josh took the lead, with Nicky close behind him. Chloe trailed the two of them by a car's length, marking their path by chopping a deep, ragged gash in every third tree with the prying side of Parker's camp hammer. Nicky hadn't said anything to her after she'd threatened her cousin's life back at the camp; she'd just silently stood up and gone to pack up all her things. She didn't even speak to Josh while she worked. In fact, for the first time since February, Nicky didn't seem to notice his presence at all.

Breaking down the tent piece by piece, Josh had shot Chloe a furtive look.

What the hell? he mouthed to her.

Chloe shook her head. *No clue.*

Except that was a lie, wasn't it? Another one to add to the list. She didn't doubt that Nicky was mad enough to try and kill Parker if she ever saw him—only her ability to do so. Chloe was starting to understand that maybe she didn't know her cousin half as well as she'd thought she did. He'd already shot two of their friends; no telling what someone could do after they did something like that.

But Nicky hadn't ever been great at listening to reason when she wanted to be right, doubly so when she already knew she was wrong. Hurting Parker wasn't going to do any good, but she was going to try anyway, if she got the chance. She'd probably do it just to prove a point.

Parker had broken something fundamental in all of them the first time he pulled that trigger.

WHACK. Chloe cleaved another scar into another tree, squinting her eyes against the morning sun as she brought the hammer down in a sharp, controlled rhythm. The first few times she'd swung the thing, the impact had rung up into her shoulder, the pain an electric charge arcing through her bones. After that, she'd started figuring out how to ensure maximum impact and coverage without lighting her arm up like that.

WHACK.

The claw tore away another thick stripe of bark and wood, leaving an ugly backslash a foot long in its wake. She was getting better at this. Up ahead of her, Nicky cupped her hands around her mouth to shout again.

"Adam? *ADAM!*"

She'd been shouting herself hoarse ever since they'd left the campsite. Chloe had told her that odds were the gunshot was farther off than they'd thought, but Nicky wasn't hearing it.

"He had all night to crawl, Chloe. All. Night. You don't know how far he might have gotten, okay?"

Chloe had wanted to say *Neither do you*, but that wasn't going to help anything. If Nicky wanted to shout her voice to sandpaper, that was her own business. After all, it wasn't like Chloe had a better idea. Wandering around and screaming like a bunch of assholes was all they had right now. She pushed the thought away and raised the hammer again just as Nicky drew another breath. This time, they did it together:

"Adam! Are you out there?" *WHACK. "Adam!"*

Josh looked back at Chloe as she ripped the hammer free from another trunk.

"Hey, you okay?"

"Yeah," Chloe said. "Yeah. Fine."

"As long as you're sure."

"I'm sure. I just wish we were looking for something specific, instead of waiting for him to shout back."

Nicky spun in place, her face already taut with rage. "Okay, if you don't like what we're doing right now—"

"Guys," said Josh.

"Nicky, I never said that—"

"—then you can piss off back to the campsite—"

"Uh, guys?"

"I just think that if we had a plan of some sort—"

"—because we can do this on our own!"

"Hey!"

Nicky and Chloe both stopped midsentence to look at Josh, who nodded off to the side of the path they'd been walking. "Look."

The two of them turned their eyes to see where Josh was looking. There was a sort of small grove in the middle of a cluster of trees, the growth uneven and battered, like it had recently been torn up. Or trampled over. Josh broke off from the two girls to get a little closer, squinting underneath the bill of his ball cap.

"Stay here, okay? I just . . ." Josh trailed off.

Chloe felt her brow knit itself into deep worry lines. "Just what?"

Josh turned to look at her. "I'm going for a better look."

Before either Chloe or Nicky could protest, he stepped into the brush and the grove, bent low. The two of them watched him hunt around, keeping his eyes trained on the ground.

"Oh, shit," they heard him say after a moment. "Oh, *shit*."

"What is it?" There was an uneasy quaver in Josh's voice that Chloe didn't like the sounds of.

He knelt to pull a plant out of the soil, holding it up for them to see. Its leaves were stained rusty red. "Blood."

Beside her, Nicky gasped. Chloe asked, "How much is there?"

Looking around at the foliage by his feet, Josh's face was grave. "A lot."

The girls followed him into the grove. It was smaller than it had looked from outside, just a small open space in the middle of the endless sea of trees. Nicky crossed over to the far side while Josh knelt back down where the grass had been flattened the most.

"Look, I know I'm not like, some experienced woodland tracker or anything, but this is bad, right?" he asked.

"It's not good," Chloe said, stepping over to stand next to him, trying to not look too closely at the messy red smears scattered across the leaves. The smell of dull copper still hung in the air like a hex.

"There's a trail over here," Nicky called to them. "It goes on for a long ways."

Josh looked at Chloe, anxiety stitched across his face.

"You think it's Adam?"

She nodded her head. "I don't know who else it would be."

"I mean . . . we should follow it, right?" Nicky's voice quavered. Chloe looked back to see that her expression had softened a little bit for the first time all morning. She supposed hope had a way of doing that to people.

"Yeah," Chloe agreed. "Yeah, we should. Nicky, you lead the way. We're right behind you."

"All right," Nicky said. "Babe, you okay to go?"

Josh nodded, tearing his eyes away from the ground. "Yeah, I'm cool. Let's go find him."

Following the thin trail of blood, the three of them filed out of the grove, into the dark of the woods once more. As they passed into the shadows, Chloe brought the hammer down across another tree.

WHACK.

Up ahead, Nicky drew another deep breath and cupped her hands around her lips.

"Adam? ADAM, WE'RE HERE! CAN YOU HEAR US?"

The words danced through the trees like fire, distant but deliberate. Nicky. Parker couldn't tell how close she was exactly, but it couldn't have been that far. She wouldn't be alone, either. Beside him, Nate cracked a wide, cruel grin.

"Well, now, that is definitely a surprise," the ghost said. "Thought you'd left them behind. Looks like it's not so easy to get away from all your problems, is it?"

Parker pushed a low branch out of his way and kept walking. "Shut up."

"They're going to come for you, you know," Nate said. Parker could hear the smile in his voice, that sick little upturn at the edges of each word. "I'm serious, man. They're going to find him, and then after that, they're going to come and kill you."

Parker kept walking, feeling the comfortable pressure of the revolver in the waistband of his pants, the weight of the hatchet in his hand, and thought of his dad hewing his initials into the white tree in the middle of that burned-out house. He was close to him—closer than he'd been in a long time. He wasn't going to stop now.

If his friends wanted to come and hunt him down before he did what he needed to do, they were welcome to try.

He was done hiding.

* * *

It wasn't long before they found the cave: a yawning, jagged hole blown in the side of a house-sized rock that looked like it had been here ever since some elder god had fastballed it into the earth. Josh saw it first, pointing to it through the trees.

"What if he made it all the way in there?" he said in a tone that sounded like he hoped he was wrong, or that the two girls would veto the suggestion.

They didn't.

The three of them had followed the trail of blood all the way out here, and it sure looked like it was leading them to the mouth of cave. They weren't going to stop now.

The area around the cave was rocky and bare, save for the dead white tree that sprouted out of the earth beside it. They closed in on it in single file, their boots rough against the craggy ground. Thin and uneven as it was, the trail of blood was unmistakable, smeared in rusty hooks and scythes across the grass and soil and rocks. The stains led into the cave, but not out again.

He was in there. He had to be in there.

Nicky was the first one to step forward, bending over to call half-heartedly into the dark.

"Adam?"

Nothing.

"Adam, it's . . . it's Nicky. We know what happened with . . . with Parker. We came to help."

More silence. Chloe and Josh exchanged a grave look, but said nothing. Ahead of them, Nicky leaned farther into the cave and cleared her throat.

"Adam, please just say something . . ."

A groan, low and wheezy, shook from deep in the cave. Nicky's eyes bugged out, and before Josh or Chloe could stop her, she dove into the cave in a quick, catlike lunge, her long, lithe body disappearing into the shadows.

Everything went quiet. The moment stretched out until forever. Chloe couldn't breathe, couldn't look away, couldn't do anything but silently pray *Please come back, please come back, please come back* until Nicky emerged again, stooped over and dragging what Chloe thought—at first—was a bag of garbage. It took her a second to realize the ugly truth.

It was Adam, but at the same time, it wasn't. The creature that Nicky had dragged out of the cave had Adam's face, wore Adam's clothes, but it wasn't really him. This boy, this *thing*, was bent and warped, its skin clammy and so pale they could see the web of blue veins running underneath the surface like a madman's atlas. His spine was curved forward like a fishhook, while his head had arched so far back it was nearly pressing between his shoulder blades. One of his legs was soaked in blood, the jeans torn and soaked through with rusty red around the knee. His mouth was ringed with messy purple stains and his eyes fluttered open and shut, bloodshot to bright red; he shielded them from the light with a strained, bony hand Chloe could almost see through. In his other hand he clutched a broken branch, long and sharp and bone white. Chloe was sure he'd torn it from the tree at the mouth of the cave, but she couldn't tell where from. Adam pressed the branch to his sunken chest like a crucifix, his fist so tight that Chloe was sure his bones would break through the skin.

The heat coming off of him was astonishing. He boiled the air around him in thick, cloying waves, the alien radiation revolting against his friends' skin. It was like his fever had caught a fever. He twitched and shuddered in place, muttering to himself, whatever nightmare he was having bubbling to the surface in half-words and syllables sheared from the larger whole, totally incomprehensible.

"*. . . e's he . . . s'tchin . . . Sho . . . l't . . . ve ten th . . . uit . . . let mys . . . d . . . Jus . . . ese . . . jus . . .*"

The three of them stared down at their friend, this broken, monstrous imitation of the boy they used to know, with disgust and horror.

After a moment, Josh whispered, "What happened to him?"

"I . . . I don't know . . ." Nicky's voice was strained and pitched, a violin string tightened to the verge of breaking. "I don't know . . . God, he . . . he didn't look like that yesterday . . ."

No shit, Chloe thought, not unkindly. Still, she knew that they couldn't just stand here and do nothing while he suffered. Josh and Nicky weren't making any moves, so she supposed it was up to her. Again.

She knelt down over Adam, trying to get a better look at his face. His bloodshot eyes rolled back and forth in their sockets without seeing, his hair was glued to his forehead with sweat, and his lips were drawn back in a thin, deathlike rictus, exposing every tooth in his head all the way back to the hinge of his jaw. This wasn't natural. This wasn't okay. There had to be something they could do to help.

Chloe extended a hand to brush the blood-spackled hair away from his brow but paused when Nicky made a choked little animal noise in the pit of her throat.

"No, no, Chloe, don't," Nicky said. "Please."

Chloe turned to look at her. "What? Why?"

"I don't know. Just . . . please don't touch him. Please. I tried to touch him in the cave, and he freaked. The only way I could get him out was by dragging him by the shirt."

"Nicky, it's okay," Chloe told her. "If he freaks, he freaks. He's sick. He's hurt, and he's scared. He needs a doctor."

She set one hand on Adam's clammy gray forehead and immediately knew that it was a mistake. There was something wrong with his skin, something slick and vile, like running her palm across a snake's back. The feel of it turned her stomach in a hard, vomit-inducing flop. She tried to jerk her hand away, but it was already too late.

She didn't see Adam move so much as she *felt* it, the speed and force of him too fast to be witnessed by the naked eye. Underneath her small hand, she felt him lash out and hit her in the stomach with a *whack*, just like she'd been marking the trees along their path. She stumbled back, struggling to take a breath. Operating seemingly of their own accord, Chloe's legs kicked and thrashed out, bicycling her away from her friend, sending her tumbling onto her back with a heavy *thump* where the rocky ground met the forest floor. Eyes toward the sky, Chloe tried to find purchase and get back to her feet, but her body wouldn't obey, her limbs buzzing and gummy. Why wasn't her body working the way it was supposed to?

Nicky screamed, staring at her with wide, horrified eyes, and Chloe followed her eyes down to try and see what was freaking her out so bad.

Oh.

The branch stuck out of her rib cage where Adam had driven it into her, a white dagger punched straight into her midsection. Blood welled out from around the ashy wood, soaking into her shirt in a slow wave that gained speed the longer she lay there and watched it. It was a curious thing, like a growth she'd sprouted abruptly and without warning—part of her, but entirely separate in its newness. Unbidden, her mind vortexed around this new addition for a moment longer, unable to make any sense of it in the framework of what her life and her body had been up until this point.

Then the pain hit, and Chloe started to scream too.

Her entire world contracted into a little shell of bone-wracking agony that set her every nerve on fire. For one awful, fleeting moment, Chloe could feel every inch of herself illuminated by the pain as it traveled through her body, slashing and burning and pinballing back to the epicenter, the new hole in her belly and the jagged trespasser that had opened it. The screams poured from her with the blood, as if they'd been trapped there for years, just looking for a way out. In the fog beyond the pain, Chloe could hear her friends barking madly at each other, their voices draped with panic and confusion. It was a funny noise, totally abstract in its urgency.

"Don't pull it out of her, don't pull it out of her—!"

"Josh, she's bleeding!"

"And she's going to bleed a whole lot more if you pull it out! It's the only thing keeping her insides inside right now!"

"You're not a doctor, Josh! You were only in Boy Scouts for like three years! You don't know shit!"

"My dad's a doctor—"

"I don't care about your doctor dad right now!"

"He taught me some first aid, Nicky! So, yeah, I think that in this case, I know a little bit more than you!"

"Oh, *fuck off*—"

Nicky fell into Chloe's field of vision and smiled at her, the first real smile Chloe had seen on Nicky's face since yesterday afternoon. She was so beautiful when she smiled.

"It's going to be okay," Nicky said. Her voice was like warm honey, or sunshine that had been somehow transmuted into sound. "I promise. I'm going to get this out of you. Just hold on, okay?"

Behind her, Josh barked, "Wait, Nicky, don't—!"

Then Nicky curled her hands around the branch and pulled.

The pain came back like a bomb set off inside Chloe's guts. It was too much; the suffering too enormous to be fully comprehended. Her mind couldn't wrap around the sheer force and scale of it.

Nicky was a liar. She was hurting her on purpose. That was the only explanation.

Nicky pulled on the branch again, jerking it back and forth inside her, and Chloe screamed again, louder, trying to thrash away from Nicky's clumsy cruelties, but it was no good. She couldn't move, pinned to the earth by the pain. Her eyes rolled in nauseous circles inside her head, searching for something, *anything* to distract her from the hurt and the panic and the fear.

In the moments before she finally passed out, Chloe swore she saw Adam, bent and gnarled, rise up from the ground and sprint into the trees. *Parker said he shot him in the leg . . .*

Nicky yanked again. Darkness started to crowd in at the corners of Chloe's vision, and for a moment, she thought *Well, at least if I pass out, it won't hurt as much.* But there was something behind the darkness, something deep and old that wore the emptiness like a mask. Images rose up out of the shadows like memories, clutching at her with cold, stick-like corpse fingers. She didn't know what she was seeing, but it was too late to do anything but sink. The thing in the darkness had her now.

Chloe's eyes sank shut, and she saw.

The young woman ran through the forest, her lungs burning from the cold, but she didn't slow, didn't dare stop. She couldn't afford to. Not now. Not when he was so close behind. She didn't know what he would do to her if he caught up to her. Was it even an if *anymore, or was it simply a matter of* when*? She no longer knew.*

The memories passed through her mind like waves in a river, impossible to catch or hold. Her head felt suddenly full, as if she was no longer alone with her thoughts. She'd been going for too long. She was too tired. She could barely remember her own name anymore. The details had started to bleed away, like she'd been stuck with a blade or something worse, ebbing out of her in tidal pulses that kept time with her heartbeat. She'd been losing pieces of herself ever since she'd fled Mount Holly, she could see that now. She'd had to leave those pieces behind if she wanted any chance of surviving. The woman who escaped this would no longer be herself, but someone—something—else entirely. Until then, she only knew she had to get away, and fast.

She crested a hill and came to a clearing around a great old tree, an ancient, twisted black oak that stood above all the rest. It stood alone in a field of dark soil, its branches thick and curled with age, its roots thicker than a man's legs, knotted and half-buried in the earth. There was a hollow in its heart, an empty, dark space that she might be able to fit into if she squeezed herself just right.

That voice—the Voice of the Lord—has led me here, *she told herself.* The Lord has a plan for me.

The Lord will protect me.

Bracing one foot against the closest root, she clamped both hands around a low-hanging branch and lifted herself up into the hollow. Making herself very small, she nestled inside the trunk, curling back into the soft bark and black, crumbling heartwood, hoping the shadows would be enough to hide her if (when) he came this way. From where she'd tucked herself, she could still see a scrap of sky in the distance, through the other trees, a window leading off into infinity. She could hide here, and with a little luck, he'd pass her by, the skeleton man with his ghosts and his madness, his hatchet and his fires.

She was exactly where she needed to be.

There was a horrible ripping noise from inside her body, and Chloe's eyes snapped open again as she woke to the sound of screaming she only distantly understood as her own.

She was back. Not coffined in some tree. She was here. She was here.

Briefly, Chloe had the feeling of being *unplugged*, as if she was a lamp or a toaster that had been popped from the wall socket, all the power cut in a single yank. Useless. Nicky was still kneeling over her, now cradling the bloody, jagged branch in both hands, her eyes dancing back and forth from it to Chloe and back again.

"See? I told you I'd help," Nicky gasped. "You're going to be okay now."

Chloe tried to speak, but all that escaped her lips was a weak, crushed whine. Then her eyes fell shut again, and everything disintegrated into a great, merciful nothing.

8

Parker couldn't say when it was exactly that he started to hear the waves, only that when he noticed them, it felt like they'd always been there, a soft, lapping undercurrent of sound that had joined the buzzing chorus of trees and wind and wildlife. He thought, just for a second, that maybe he'd walked all the way to the edge of the Barrens, where the trees hooked down and around to meet the ocean. But that was impossible.

Wasn't it?

He looked back at Nate. "I don't suppose you can like, *ghost* your way up above the trees to try and tell me where the hell I'm going, can you?"

Nate spat, but the loogie never hit the ground.

"Fuck are you talking about?"

"I mean, does that teleportation trick of yours work vertically? So maybe we can get a better sense of where we're going?"

"It's not a trick, man. That was me just trying to stick close to you, and to tell you the truth, I don't know how it works beyond that. I focused on keeping up, so I kept up. And, as far as like, *ghost flight* goes? Trust me, that was the first thing I tried. Nothing doing. Turns out being dead is just as bullshit as being alive."

"How lucky for us," said Parker.

"Hey, I don't make the rules. I just live by them. Or, you know, whatever." Nate turned in a circle to look around. "Why are you asking, anyway?"

Park pulled up short and looked at him. "Well, look, I have a general idea of where we're heading, right? The campsite was *here*"—he drew a line in midair with his index finger, punctuating each end with a sharp jab into the empty space with his fingernail—"and the burned house was *here*."

"All right," Nate said. "But so what?"

"I think we need to find the water."

"What water?"

"Can't you hear that?"

"Not really . . ."

"Just listen for a second. Okay?"

"Fine." Nate cocked his head and narrowed his eyes. "Yeah, okay, I hear it now. It's far away, but so what?"

"So I'm thinking maybe we find it and follow it. If my dad heard it, too, he would have done the same."

"Sounds like a lot of guessing to me."

"Trust me, I know what I'm talking about. He's my dad."

"*Was* your dad," Nate corrected.

"Please, *please* stop it with that. Please."

Parker took a long look at their surroundings. The trees around them were massive old things, monsters in their own rights that had been here for centuries before this moment and would likely be here for centuries after they'd all gone. Looking at them like that, an idea sparked in Parker's head, and he dropped his pack to the ground, then the pistol, and the hatchet beside them.

"Do me a favor and stay here," he said.

"What? Why?"

Parker waved a hand in his direction. "Just wait for me, all right? I'll be right back."

"Where are you going?"

Parker pointed. "Up."

"*Up*? What does *up* mean? Parker?"

Parker didn't answer him. He was too busy launching himself up the side of the biggest, oldest tree he could find, climbing the branches like a ladder, lifting himself off the ground rung by rung. Twenty-five feet up, thirty, forty, fifty—the tree bore his great bulk all the way without complaint. Even near the top of the ancient pine, the branches were at least as thick as one of his arms. The tree would hold; Park knew it would. It had lasted this long, weathered innumerable storms and winters. It could carry one climber safely for a few minutes, no matter how small or big they were.

He didn't stop climbing until he could see across all the surrounding treetops. The forest seemed to go on forever. It was a rolling ocean of uneven, paintbrush green that stretched out to the horizon in every direction. The sight of it took his breath away. He knew, on paper at least, how big the Pine Barrens were, but seeing it on a map was nothing compared to standing in the middle of it. Some part of him had honestly thought he'd be able to see a highway or the ocean from here, but there was nothing but trees in every direction, and in the near distance, through a small break in the forest, he could see . . .

Holy shit. *Holy shit.*

"Are you seeing this?" he called down excitedly.

"Obviously I am not," Nate shouted back, annoyed.

Whatever. Park would show him soon enough. He couldn't wait. They were so close too.

Oh my god. This was amazing.

* * *

It took a full quarter of the Everclear as disinfectant and nearly everything Josh had in his first aid kit, but eventually they managed to get Chloe's bleeding to stop. Nicky was impressed; Josh had handled himself well. His time in the Boy Scouts wasn't all for nothing. Sweat still poured off her boyfriend's face in waves, and he wiped at it with the bottom of his own shirt, leaving dark hooks of perspiration in the fabric.

"Let's just hope he didn't puncture anything major," Josh panted, slumping back on the damp grass.

Nicky sat down beside him and pitched both hands onto the ground behind her, leaning back on tired, noodly arms to study Chloe. She looked so small and broken like this. So fragile. As if a strong wind might blow her apart like a pile of leaves.

"How likely do you think that is?" Nicky asked.

"I don't know," Josh admitted. He spoke like his mouth had gone numb, slow and careful. "Not great, probably, and even if we got lucky . . . she bled a lot. And I know I was a Scout for only three years and I should probably shut up about my stupid doctor dad already, but as I understand it, losing a lot of blood's not like, a good thing, generally speaking. If we can get her on her feet by tomorrow, maybe she'll be able to walk out of here. I really don't know."

Nicky let his shitty little swipes pass. Starting a fight with him right now wasn't going to do either of them any good, no matter how angry she was—at Josh, at Adam, at Chloe, Parker, Nate, herself, everyone and everything. The fury churned like a ball of liquid fire inside her heart, rolling and burbling, desperate for release.

That familiar rage, trying to come out in unproductive ways again.

Her therapist had told her that anger was healthy but rage wasn't, and if she insisted on hanging onto the rage like she often did, she needed to learn ways to funnel it into something constructive. Track had been good for that. When she was running, all of her burned because she didn't have any other choice. When she wasn't, sooner or later those fires started to catch inside of her anyway. They always started out so small, too, sparked by a million tiny offenses that built into catastrophic blazes she carried around until she didn't have a choice but to turn them on someone. When she pointed them at herself, it looked like depression, fear, despair. When she pointed them at someone else, the school counselor usually had to call her parents with more bad news.

It was funny—up until the very moment Adam had stabbed Chloe, Nicky had done her best to pretend that Josh was somehow immune to her fury. It had been a silly, stupid little fiction, but it had been hers, secret and true since the first time she kissed him. Pretending that maybe there really was someone she wouldn't get so pissed off at for just being a person, with all the flaws and weaknesses that entailed. That maybe, somehow, he was the one human being out of seven billion who was special.

It sounded so stupid, thinking about it like that now.

And what about Adam? That thing she'd dragged out of the cave had been him, but at the same time, it hadn't. Adam would never have hurt Chloe. Not if he was thinking straight, not if he was himself. The warped boy she'd pulled into the light . . . he was sick, feverish. Warped and scared and delusional. He'd been terrified, or furious, so he'd lashed out.

And then he was gone.

She'd told Chloe not to touch him. She'd practically begged her. And look what had happened.

Thinking about it too much set that fireball alight again, so she turned her attention away from it and scooted a little closer to Josh, trying to smile a little bit for his sake.

"What time is it?"

Checking his watch, Josh sighed through his nose and hung his head, defeated. "I don't know. Apparently this thing stopped running at some point."

"What do you mean, stopped running?"

He unstrapped the old Timex from his wrist and held it up, giving it a shake. "I mean it stopped running, Nicky. As of . . . three fifty-three this morning. It's dead. I didn't even notice. Shit."

"Doesn't it have a battery or something?"

"Of course it does."

"How old was it?"

Josh rubbed at his eyes. "Brand new. I had it changed last week because I knew we were coming out here. Just junk now." He tossed the watch away into the underbrush.

A nervous unraveling popped loose in Nicky's stomach, and she had to cross her arms over her midsection to keep from laughing or screaming or both. She hated this. She hated everything that was happening so goddamn much.

"So what do we do now?" she asked.

"Check your phone or something. I don't know."

"I mean about this. About *her*."

Josh pulled his hands away from his face.

"Well, it's afternoon already," he said slowly. "I don't think she's in any shape to go anywhere. Maybe we just stay here for now. Set up the tents and wait for her to wake up."

Nicky was incredulous. "That's your grand plan? Sit here in the middle of nowhere and wait and see?"

Josh flopped over on his back, wiping his brow dry again.

"Unless you have a better one, yeah. I don't see any hotels around, but you're welcome to go looking if you want."

A long, uneasy silence passed between them. Nicky watched Josh rub the bare spot on his wrist, couldn't help but notice the way that he avoided looking at her.

"You don't have to be such an asshole," Nicky said after another moment.

"I wasn't."

"Yes, you were."

"Chloe could have died, Nicky. She still might. And if that happens, I'm sorry, but it's on you."

"It is *not my fault*—"

"Except it is," Josh cut across her. "It will be. I told you not to pull the branch out of her, and you did it anyway. You didn't even listen to me, you just . . . did it, without a thought as to what could happen," he ranted. "You didn't think about it at all. You never just stop and *think*."

His words slashed at her heart. Briefly, she thought about turning the blaze on him full force, letting him see how it really felt to burn. But she bit it back, and when she spoke again, her voice came out small and shabby.

"We had to do something, Josh. We had to try *something*."

"You should have tried anything other than that."

Nicky watched him for a few more minutes, waiting to see if he had any other mean shit to throw at her, but he seemed to be done, at least for the time being. Dusting her hands off on the knees of her pants, Nicky rolled to her feet and unbuckled her tent from her pack, rolling it out on the smoothest patch of ground she could find.

"What are you doing?" Josh asked.

"Setting up the tents," she said, as neutrally as she could. "If we're camping here for the night, we're going to need shelter, aren't we?"

Josh didn't say anything after that. For a few minutes, Nicky worked in silence, feeling his eyes on her back as she went about assembling the tent. When he eventually got off his ass and started to help, she paid him no mind. She didn't have anything else she wanted to say to him.

9

Parker hit the ground running, grabbing his things without a word to Nate and taking off into the trees.

Nate would catch up. He was a ghost. He could do whatever he wanted—except, apparently, fly. Whatever.

Parker followed the mental line he'd drawn out from the foot of the great oak, ducking and weaving through the lesser trees until he came to a shallow creek. He followed it downstream until the forest broke apart, giving way to the kind of open space Parker hadn't seen since they'd pulled off the highway the day before. It was easy to forget how much forest there actually was in here, especially down among the trees. It was dense, practically claustrophobic, so intimate that it threatened to crush you at every step. It overwhelmed to the point that it was easier to just not think of how big the Pine Barrens really were. But sometimes—sometimes—the trees would give way, and you'd be reminded, its vastness impossible to ignore.

The open space before him was absolutely massive—roughly the size of a warehouse, but round and beautiful, like an oversized crop circle stamped in the trees. In the center of it all stood a crystal-blue lake.

The lake wasn't huge, but what struck him about it was how perfectly circular it seemed, like an impact crater that had been filled in with water. The creek he'd followed fed into one end, and on the far shore, Parker could see the lake draining off into a wide river that disappeared into the trees on a downslope, far past where he could see. But despite the water actively flowing in and out, the surface was completely still, a single pane of blue glass from shore to shore. It reflected the late afternoon sky above like a mirror, absolute and unbroken. Not a single wave disturbed it, not a fish bobbing for food nor bird swooping down to slash at the surface for its lunch. The very idea of disturbing it seemed to Parker like some kind of minor sin, a heresy, an affront against God. Not that he believed in God anymore. Even when things were good, the only gods that his family seemed to hold dear were the New York Jets. After his dad went missing, his mom had added *gin* to the list, and more and more, it seemed like that was taking over the top spot in her book.

Whatever. It was just a lake. It was just water. God, or whatever, could deal.

Parker walked down the rocky shore to where the water met the silt and picked up a flat stone, dancing it in the palm of his big hand. It would do just fine. Curling his index finger around its edge, Park swept his arm out in a tight hook and sent the stone sailing across the surface of the water. He could nearly hear it whistling through the air as it flew, spinning like a Frisbee, tracing its arc with squinted eyes. He'd get at least four skips out of this one, he was sure of it. The rock dipped closer and closer to the lake's surface . . .

And sank.

Park didn't understand what he'd just witnessed. It was like the lake had opened some secret mouth and gobbled up the stone whole. No ripples radiated out from where it had dropped, there was no *plunk* as it struck the surface. It just . . . disappeared into the water. For a moment, Parker even wondered whether he'd imagined throwing it—until he looked down at his empty hand and saw that it was streaked with mud.

What in the hell had just happened?

Standing there, watching the glass lake, Parker felt his head swell and start to swim. His vision blurred and tilted, skewing to one side in a smudgy tunnel while his body swayed the other way to try and normalize. Looking at the lake like this, he felt an enormous isolation creeping up around him, as if he were the very last human left alive on the planet. The forest went quiet, drawing in close to hold its breath, waiting for the right moment to—

"The hell are you doing?"

Parker bit back a scream, his heart hammering inside his ribs, then looked over at Nate, whose smug grin was glued from jowl to heavy jowl. The vertigo instantly dispelled, and Parker felt himself wilt under Nate's eyes, trying to breathe away the spike of nerves that had jolted into his heart.

"Nothing. Skipping stones, I guess."

"And that's what you dragged me down here to do? To show me how good you can throw rocks, or whatever? Because, like, big whoop. I can throw rocks too, man. Or at least I could. *Before*."

"No," said Parker, blushing. "Nothing like that. It was just—"

He looked from Nate to the still lake and back again, feeling incredibly stupid. This was stupid. He was being stupid.

Get it together, Parker.

"Nothing. Forget it." He straightened his shoulders and broke Nate's empty gaze, pointing down the shoreline with a single finger. "Look. There. That's what I saw."

"Holy shit," Nate coughed. "Dude, holy shit."

On the far edge of the lake and maybe a quarter of a mile down, there was a little town. It was gray and stooped and weathered all to hell, the buildings hunched closely together, like they needed the warmth. From the top of the oak, he'd seen that, going farther back, the houses all clustered to surround a sagging, weathered old church. It was obscured by the trees at the moment, but Parker knew it was there.

Perched at the top of the tree, he'd half expected the town to turn out to be a collection of torched-out skeletons, like the one they'd found buried in the forest this morning. But standing here on the lakeshore, he could see that it was so much more than that.

Parker glanced over at Nate with an excited look in his eyes. "Do you want to go check it out?"

Nate didn't look back, just nodded, keeping his eyes on the little gray town.

"Absolutely."

They walked down the shore in silence, watching the town loom larger with every step, becoming more *real* somehow as the little details emerged from the blur: a crooked door here, a collapsed roof there, walls overgrown with lichen and hanging moss, the way the road was scattered with more dead white trees. It was like watching a dream emerge into the real world, something that couldn't possibly exist but somehow *did*, right in front of you.

As they drew closer, Parker kept his stride a tiny bit crooked, his body turned just a little bit sideways, one eye still trained on the lake. Something about it unnerved him. It stuck in his head like a hook, like that feeling you got when you knew you were being watched but couldn't say from where, or by whom. He couldn't put a name to it, but there was something wrong with that lake, and with every step farther from the water's edge, he felt himself unclench more and more.

He thought about telling Nate, even though he knew that he'd only make a joke out of it, or mock Parker about whatever part he found most ridiculous. That was just who he was; things could only be one way with him, a single objective reality that everyone else had to deal with. But what if objective reality had gotten all fucked up when none of them were looking? Wouldn't Nate have to admit that things were no longer what he'd gone through life thinking they were? After all, wasn't Nate the one who'd woken up dead today?

They came to the edge of the town, stepping off the shore to circle around until they found a path that led to a tall, crumbling gateway with no gate attached. Parker stood there, looking up the main road at the collection of little homes and bigger outbuildings, trying to make them all fit in his mental version of the Barrens. He'd heard of homes being lost in the woods before, of course, but never whole towns. Not like this.

"How is this even here?" he wondered aloud.

Nate pursed his lips and whistled. "I'm starting to realize that lots of things can get lost in the woods. Towns, dads, lives. All sorts of shit."

Parker gave him the finger and walked into the town, keeping his head on a swivel, trying to see as much of the little collection of grayed, weathered houses and outbuildings as he possibly could. How long had they been abandoned out here? Two hundred years? More? It seemed to him like the town had been left to harden and petrify in the absence of the people who had built it. He couldn't see any evidence of a fire or an explosion or anything else that would cause people to pick up and leave. They were just . . . gone.

"Hello!" Parker called into the emptiness. "Hello? Is anybody there?"

Only silence greeted him. He called out again, but there was nothing, no one, barely even an echo. The place was completely empty—not that he'd expected anything different of a town slowly being swallowed by the Pine Barrens.

Where they weren't haphazardly boarded over, doors and shutters hung open or had been ripped off their hinges entirely, roofs bowed and cracked with weather and age. There was even an old wooden wagon cart by the side of the main road collecting moss and rot, one wheel split apart, giving it a crooked, lopsided look. That effect wasn't exclusive to the wagon, though; it stretched out across the whole town, much like a jumbled mouth of crooked, broken teeth, all gray and green with decay.

Rotten teeth. Dead teeth.

Park walked quietly along, the crunching of his feet atop the ashy dirt horribly loud in the silent little town. His eyes darted back and forth, looking for anything to identify it—a sign, something, anything—but there was nothing. It was just a nameless little town, lost in the middle of nowhere, like a dead body dumped in an unmarked grave. Even the air was sour out here, sick with stale moisture and the plant life that was overtaking the town, dragging it apart as it grew between the boards and through the foundations, taking the land back as its own.

His dad had been through this place. He felt it all the way down to his bones. If Parker, clumsy and panicked and inexperienced and haunted as he was, had found it, then his dad had to have too. The old man had been camping for decades before Parker was even a glimmer in his eye.

Parker choked back a fist of nerves and squared his shoulders, feigning a kind of courage he didn't truly feel. He wasn't scared, he wasn't starving, he wasn't exhausted—no. He wasn't any of that at all.

Dad had been here. He knew he had. Now all Parker had to do was find the next sign of him.

The two boys—one dead, one alive—headed deeper into the nameless little town.

Muttering to herself, Nicky gathered wood, breaking apart dry branches with her hands and heels while back by the tents, Josh cleared a space to build another fire. They didn't speak, and Nicky's insides silently pinballed back and forth between fury at everyone else and hating herself for being so stupid and broken that she poisoned every good thing in her life.

Her mom's voice echoed in her head again.

I don't know why you insist on dragging everything around you down, Nicoletta. Can't you just let things be nice every once in a while?

Her mom never understood Nicky's mood swings—or at least never acted like she did—even though she had them, too, for as long as Nicky could remember. She should understand better than anyone that knowing about them wasn't enough to stop them from happening.

Another surge of tears welled up inside Nicky's throat, and she had to twist her knuckles into her thighs to push them back down again. She wouldn't let herself boil over. Not here. Not now. She and Josh didn't need to talk, anyway. They could both just work in silence and try and ignore how ugly things could get when they weren't looking. Nicky recognized this kind of mutual rage; it existed in a sort of low-level hum pretty much all the time at her house, constructed and maintained by both of her parents for decades now. And, hell, they'd made it work for them. Maybe this was just how adult relationships were.

For her part, Chloe drifted in and out of consciousness, her lips parting to form half sentences—*What did . . . ? Are we going . . . ? Is this the . . . ?*—before she sank back into sleep. Nicky knelt by her side, checking her temperature, peeking at the wound in her belly under the improvised bandages, occasionally dribbling water between her lips from Josh's Nalgene while stroking her hair softly and imploring her to drink up, please drink up.

Nicky worked where she could see the both of them, never wandering farther than fifteen or twenty feet away, so if she raised her voice even a little, they—or at least Josh—would hear her and be able to help. Not that she needed help. She didn't need anything. Not her boyfriend, not her friends, not even the pills that she'd left at home because they were going to be out here for only one night and it seemed stupid to bring them. Or because she didn't want everybody to see her taking them, because then she'd have to explain them, tell them everything, and it would make all that ugly everything too real. Best thing to do now was try and keep herself distracted from the hot, oily blackness bubbling underneath her skin.

God, but she wanted a cigarette. She'd left her menthols and her little yellow lighter back by the tents and sleeping bags, a small concession to Josh that she was sure he'd missed. He hated when she smoked, even though he never said anything about it. It was impossible to mistake, the way his nose wrinkled every time she lit up, the way he kept their kisses quick and dry after she'd had one. He wasn't nearly as good at hiding things as he thought he was.

If there was ever a time for a cigarette, this was it, but obviously that wasn't happening. So she chewed on the inside of her lower lip until she tasted blood and she gathered firewood, bringing armfuls of dry branches over to Josh, who sat at the mouth of the cave, putting together a small circle of stones for a campfire.

Josh stood up as she approached, rising quickly to walk off into the trees, his back turned toward her.

"Where are you going?" Nicky's voice shook when she asked. Another thing to hate herself for.

"I have to pee."

He didn't even look at her to say it. Like she didn't matter to him at all. Being talked to like that made her want to cry, and it made her want to punch a hole through his face. Trying not to scream, she watched him walk into the forest, half-obscured by the trees, then turned her own back as she heard the faint *zzzip* of his fly.

Nicky brushed her hands off and considered the bare tree by the mouth of the cave. It was so weird, all bone white and hard and dead like that. Inside her head, she called it a *poison tree*, good for absolutely nothing.

Well. Maybe not nothing. It might make decent firewood, at least.

Using her bare hands, Nicky took hold of one of the branches jutting off the central trunk, then pulled down. The branch broke away from the trunk cleanly, leaving behind a dry, crumbly dead spot where it had been attached. Under the bark, the wood was nearly black with rot, dead all the way through; she was sure it would burn. She held the branch up to consider it in the fading sunlight, comparing it to its bloody sister on the ground, the one that Adam had run Chloe through with. Brushing her hand off on the leg of her pants, she took hold of another branch and pulled. It peeled away from the tree as easily as the first. Nicky moved on to the next branch, plucking them off like the legs from a spider until the ground at her feet was stacked with dry, bony boughs.

Behind her, someone coughed. Nicky spun in place—Chloe was awake.

She sat up on the little bed they'd made for her out of their sleeping bags, one arm planted against the ground while she kept the other clamped tightly across her improvised bandage. Her skin was gray, and her hair looked stringy and lifeless . . . but her eyes were on fire, as bright as Nicky had ever seen them.

"Hey." Chloe's voice was weak and scratchy, but there was a smile that pulled at the edges of her words, a smile that was more Chloe than not. Nicky dashed over to her friend, scattering the white branches with one foot, then pulled Chloe into a tight hug.

"Careful," Chloe gasped under Nicky's arms. "Careful."

Nicky let go and leaned back. Behind her, she could hear the soft crunch of Josh's feet in the soil and leaves, walking over to join them.

"Sorry," said Nicky. "I just . . . I didn't expect to see you up and about so soon."

"Well, I'm not exactly up and about just yet."

"At this point I'll settle for just up," Nicky said. "With how badly you were hurt, we thought you'd be out for a lot longer than you were."

"Sorry to disappoint."

"No, Chloe, it's not like that—"

"Hey," Josh said, standing above them with his arms crossed over his chest.

"Hey yourself," said Chloe. "Glad to see you guys are okay. How long was I out for?"

Josh shrugged. "Few hours. Four, maybe? It's hard to tell out here."

"Okay," Chloe said, rubbing at her eyes. "But it's still Saturday?"

"Still Saturday," Josh echoed.

Nicky rested a hand on Chloe's shoulder, gave it a gentle squeeze. "How are you feeling?"

Chloe wiped at her eyes with the back of her hand.

"Honestly, pretty bad. Better than before. But, yeah. Not exactly awesome." She gestured to the bandages lashed to her wounded midsection. "I assume this was you?"

"Yeah," Nicky said. "Both of us."

"Thank you," Chloe told her.

"Seriously though, you're feeling all right? You were really out of it for a while," Nicky said. "It looked like you were having some seriously messed-up dreams. I was worried."

Chloe blinked hard, over and over. "Yeah," she replied. "Definitely some weird ones."

Nicky nodded to the backpack full of food beside them. "Are you hungry at all? Thirsty? We've been giving you water, but . . ."

"No, not really."

Nicky nodded and watched as Chloe closed her eyes for a second. When she opened them again, they'd gone cold and weird, the same way Nicky had seen them get on school mornings before really big tests.

"What happened to Adam?" Chloe asked.

Nicky's mood turned bitter. "What do you mean, what happened?"

"You know, after . . . after he . . ."

"Stabbed you?"

Chloe pursed her chapped lips. "Yeah. That."

"Don't know," Josh said. "Think he ran off into the woods. He wasn't doing too good, though."

"Good enough to run, apparently."

"I suppose," Josh said.

"So we agree we all saw it, right?" Chloe asked. "We saw Adam run."

"I didn't see that," Nicky said quickly.

Josh's face got dark. "Yeah, you did."

"I know what I did and didn't see, Josh."

Josh narrowed his eyes. "I'm not sure that you do, *Nicky*."

"I saw it," Chloe said. "At first I thought it was a dream or something, but now . . ."

"Except that doesn't make any sense," Nicky said. "How could a kid who got shot in the leg . . . ?"

"Run off into the forest like that? I don't know," Chloe admitted. "But I'm starting to think we left *sense* behind back in Randolph. This place . . . I think it plays by its own rules."

Something inside Nicky bristled and recoiled at hearing her say it like that. "No, no, fuck that," Nicky said. "Stop. It's just a forest. That's all it is. Don't make it out to be more than that."

Chloe gave her a look, studying her face.

Nicky wanted to glance away, break eye contact, stop her from doing that spooky-genius thing that always seemed to let her see the insides of people. It was something she'd been doing since they were all little kids.

A second later, Chloe's gaze softened, and she nodded, having come to some kind of decision. "Then how do you want to deal with this, Nicky?" she asked.

Relief cascaded through Nicky's body, like a cool blue wave crashing on the shore. "I think the plan needs to stay the same," she said. "Same as before. We need to get out of here, especially now that you're hurt. But we'll have to stay here for the night. Give you a chance to rest up and heal a little so we can keep moving tomorrow."

Chloe's face fell. "Yeah. Okay. That makes sense."

"Josh is going to build us a fire," said Nicky. "We'll try again tomorrow, find the car, go for help. We have food, and we have water. We're going to be okay."

"As long as you're sure," coughed Chloe.

"As sure as we're gonna be," Josh said, stepping back from the two girls. Using the broken white branches, he laid together a pyramid of wood in the center of the stone circle, stacking the smaller ones first, then the thicker ones around those until he ran out.

Nicky and Chloe watched him work in silence, sitting back on the ground to wait. Nicky could feel Chloe trying to catch her eye, no doubt wanting to know what had happened between her and Josh in the time she'd been out, but what could Nicky even say about it? What would be the point? She just had to let things cool off for now. Things would be better by tomorrow.

Together they watched as Josh sparked Nicky's lighter to life and held the flame to the little thatch of matchstick twigs he'd arranged under the smallest white branches. The twigs caught fire almost immediately, crackling and popping and blackening with heat as the flames swelled up to lick and lash at the white branches. Any second now, they would catch, and the three of them would have a fire to keep them warm through the night.

But the white branches didn't catch, and after a few long seconds, the twigs sputtered and wisped out too.

Josh tried again. With one hand, he held the lighter's little orange tongue to another bundle of twigs, bigger than the first, and when it was good and going, he slid it under the woodpile and waited. And waited. And waited.

The white branches wouldn't burn.

"You kidding me with this . . . ?"

Josh plucked one of the white branches from the pile and then held the lighter to it, waving the little BIC back and forth, but the dry, ashy wood simply would not catch. It didn't even brown under the heat of the flame. It was like trying to set fire to stone. Still, Josh tried again, and again, and again, his face knotting up with rage, his movements increasingly frantic until his temper boiled over and he jumped to his feet, kicking at the campfire, sending the branches flying apart in a lopsided spray.

Nicky recoiled, as did Chloe beside her. "Jesus, Josh!" Nicky said.

He spun around toward the two of them, his eyes wild and wide. "What?"

His voice was calm, but there was a look in his gaze that Nicky didn't trust. She'd never seen this side of him before. He wasn't the type to get frustrated like this. She jabbed a finger toward the place where the campfire used to be.

"What would you even do that for? How does that help?"

"Whatever," he growled, his voice full of poorly masked irritation. "There's other branches, right? There's a million other branches in this stupid fucking forest. I'll just go and get some of those, because the ones you picked out clearly *aren't working.*"

Nicky had had enough of this shit. He could be a moody asshole all he wanted, but she didn't have to sit here and take it. Without another word, Nicky stood and walked away, crossing her arms over her chest to hold herself close, hoping she could get far enough away before she started to cry.

It's just a forest. It's just a forest.

It's just a forest.

10

The boy's bones bowed and bent, then splintered and split inside his arms and his legs. They popped like bottles breaking underwater, the sharpness of the sound muffled by the red meat wrapped so tightly around them. His tongue, dry and cracked, swelled to fill his mouth as his eyes rolled into the back of his head, the purple veins sewn through the sclerae thick as butcher's twine. The boy that used to be Adam screamed without sound and saw without sight as his body contorted into jagged shapes and terrible glyphs, dissecting itself in wave after wave of purest suffering. He lay where he'd fallen, in a patch of pine needles, a thin pink froth leaking from the corners of his drawn, bloodless lips. He clenched his teeth until they cracked and broke; he lashed and scraped at the dirt until his fingers were torn, bloody claws. His back arched and shattered into its thirty-three component parts, each knuckle of tender bone torn loose from the others, trailing shredded tails of nerves and blood vessels and all the stuff of life.

He was dying. This was what dying felt like.

Alone, the boy-thing started to weep. A great yawning fissure opened up inside him, cold and infinite, and he clutched at that emptiness, at that nothing, pleading for it to eat him all up and take his pain away. He would throw himself into the dark if it meant he didn't have to feel this anymore.

He heard the echo before he heard the voice, its sibilant edges creeping up the sides of that frozen inner chasm, slipping out in whispers and tendrils like smoke. The words assembled themselves in strange patterns inside his head, the syllables all out of order, the letters and sounds reversed; but still he heard, and understood.

Hello, Adam.

The boy-thing tried to scream again but found it impossible, his throat locked up against the pain, unable to let any but a small, throttled noise escape. Veins stood out on his forehead. Tendons bulged in his neck like cords. The agony was brilliant, blinding.

The voice reached out to him again, like a beam of white sunlight knifing through an eternal darkness.

Not long now.

The boy-thing ground his teeth to powder, feeling new ones grow into the ragged sockets, pearly white and razor sharp. The sound of cracking bones filled the forest around him, but there was a humming there too—as if he could hear his body knitting itself back together, assembling into something stronger and more terrible than he'd ever imagined.

When it was over, the warped boy-thing could smell blood in the air, rising from the earth with the humidity in great, coppery clouds. In the distance, he could see a dying light surrounded by darkness, frail and red. He was already so, *so* hungry.

His stalk-like legs didn't make a sound as they whisked him into the dark.

The sun sank lower and lower still until it dipped behind the trees and vanished entirely, drowning the little town in soft, inky blackness. Parker had originally wanted to explore, look for signs of his dad, maybe even find another carved set of initials, but it was getting too dark for that. Better to call it for the night and have a look around tomorrow morning. He didn't want to admit it, but the thought of wandering around a place like this in the dark sent a deep chill licking its way up his spine.

Tomorrow. He'd look around tomorrow. For tonight, he'd decided to camp down in the little house connected to the gate, a small, two-room structure with a main room and a dusty, cobweb-draped bedroom beyond that. There was a nameplate bearing the name *HARROW* posted outside, hand carved into a heavy, smooth slat that hung by the door.

Setting up in a corner of the main room, Parker used his foot to swipe away some of the leaves that carpeted the floor, carefully unrolling his sleeping bag on the bare, rough wood. He'd had to pry his way inside, using the blunt side of the hatchet and his bare hands to pull the boards away from where they'd been nailed into the frame. The gatehouse wasn't in great shape—the air inside was musty and ancient, its walls heavy with mold underneath a steadily disintegrating roof—but it would do for the night. He stretched out on top of his sleeping bag, feeling every joint in his big body groan with relief, then dug in his backpack for the little flashlight he'd packed away, clicking it on to flood the room with a white glow that cast corkscrew shadows in every direction.

"Probably not a great idea to build a fire in here, huh?" Nate asked from the far corner of the room, pacing back and forth, craning his head to look around in the light burning out of Parker's pocket Maglite.

"Probably not, no."

"Sucks."

"We have light," Parker said. "And do you even need warmth anymore?"

"Dude, I don't know. It's just . . . campfires are comforting, you know? Something about them just *feels* safe. Fires mean people, warmth, food. I mean, come on. You remember food, don't you?"

Parker's stomach gurgled and growled at the word. Yeah, he remembered food. It had been only yesterday that he'd last eaten, but that was already long enough for him to miss it. He should have brought something for himself, a granola bar or anything. He could have hidden it in the bottom of his pack, secreted away where no one would have even known. He'd learned a thing or two about hiding things in the last year; his mom could probably teach a seminar on that shit by now.

His parents had never really been big drinkers, but Lori had been doing a great impression of one the last few months. It had started out in small ways that nobody would have noticed unless they were really looking—an extra glass of wine at dinner, sometimes two or three. Then Park noticed bottles would go missing from the rack in their little kitchen, only to turn up the next day, bone-dry in the trash cans in the garage, buried under layers of crumpled newspaper. Like she was fooling anybody.

For a while, he thought it was only the wine, but over Christmas break, she'd sent him looking in her purse for her cell. He'd found the phone, but he also found a half-empty pint of Gilbey's gin tucked away in there too. That was the first one, but it was far from the last. After that, Parker seemed to find the little plastic flasks everywhere, secreted away in the rolltop desk or her jacket pockets or hidden among the cans in the kitchen pantry.

He never said anything about it to her. What *could* he say? He didn't have the words to describe what he was feeling, and he wasn't even sure she'd listen if he tried. She'd gotten lost in herself, falling deeper and deeper into the darkness that had opened up inside her since his dad had disappeared. The woman he lived with still looked like his mom, still sounded like her—and on her good days, even acted like her—but she wasn't his mom. Not really. It was there in her eyes, a slurry, runny-egg light that made him sick to look at for too long. It danced on her breath, the plastic juniper stink there to greet him almost every afternoon and evening, and sometimes before he left for school too. He saw it in the way her hands had started to shake in the mornings before she had her coffee, even though he pretended he didn't.

She'd caught him watching her one Saturday a couple of months back, as she uncapped and emptied one of those little airplane bottles into her first mug of the day. She didn't try to call it medicine, no bullshit clichés like that. She didn't call it anything, really. She'd just stood there, bottle in hand, and pretended like she wasn't dosing her coffee, like she wasn't holding anything at all. Parker knew this move; truth was, he'd sort of expected it. Silence had always been her favorite tool, her sword and her shield. So no, she didn't say anything about it. Instead, she just locked eyes with her son as they both tried to figure out how much the other one knew.

When she tried to laugh the incident off a long, agonizing moment later, the sound came out so fake and forced, it made Parker want to scream. But he didn't scream. He nodded and smiled and pretended that everything was okay. Everything was just fine.

He hadn't even said goodbye to her before he left the house yesterday morning. He would have liked to, but she was asleep, curled up in a snarl of sweat-stained sheets in a T-shirt and underwear, the door to her bedroom hanging half open like a broken jaw. Briefly, Park had thought about going in to try and rouse her, tell her that he loved her, but at the last second decided against it. The half-naked woman tangled up in those blankets, with her head buried under the pillows—that wasn't his mom. She was just some stranger wearing her skin.

Somewhere far off, Parker heard a soft whistling, and a moment later, a breeze blew through the shabby old gatehouse, chilling him through his clothes. He rolled onto his side, nestling farther down into the sleeping bag, while across the room, Nate watched him, his eyes darkened by the shadows, unblinking.

"What are you thinking about, Parker?"

The big kid shook his head. "Nothing. Nothing."

"Doesn't look like nothing."

"Yeah. No. Sorry. Did you say something?"

Nate shook his head, making his jowls wobble.

"Nope. You just looked real far away there for a minute."

"I guess I was, yeah."

"Where?"

For a second, Parker thought about lying to him.

"My house. My mom."

"Do you think she misses you?"

Parker shrugged. "I kind of doubt she's even noticed that I'm gone. My problems don't really register with her anymore."

"Double sucks."

"What about you?"

Nate shifted in place. "What about me?"

"Do you think your parents are worried?"

"Doug and Cathy don't really worry about much," he said. "But I don't know, they might've changed their tune in the last thirty-six hours. Stranger things have happened, right?"

"Stranger than your parents worrying about you?"

Nate cracked a grin and blasted him with a finger-gun. "Exactly."

Parker supposed it made sense. He'd met Nate's parents only twice since they'd been friends; perhaps three times. They'd always seemed, well, *fine*. They were fine. Maybe a bit preoccupied, distant . . . he might even go as far as calling them cold. They always just seemed like they wanted to be anywhere but where they were.

"Do you miss them?"

Nate scoffed. "I dunno. Not really. There wasn't a whole lot of *them* to miss, you know? Past few years, the three of us mostly communicated through texts."

"And you were okay with that?"

"It was simpler that way. Easier for everybody to not have to actually talk to each other."

Parker felt a cold twinge dagger his heart. "I miss talking to my mom about things," he admitted. An enormous, awkward silence settled between the two of them.

Nate squatted down and knelt forward, hands laced together between his knees.

"Look, you're tired, man. I get it. Maybe just try and sleep some, huh? You're no good to anyone if you're a zombie. We can start fresh in the morning. We'll go check shit out when it's light out, maybe go and see what that old church back in the trees is all about."

Parker rubbed at his eyes and nose. Despite the sorrow coiling in his chest again, he could feel sleep lurking in the wings, just waiting for its cue to come and swallow him up. He buried himself even deeper into the sleeping bag, reaching down to pull the zipper up and around his broad shoulders, trapping all the warmth he could inside.

"Nate?"

"What?"

"Are you going to be here when I wake up?"

His friend eyed him from across the room, dropping both arms down to rest on his thick, cross-legged knees. He nodded his head.

"I'm not going anywhere."

"Okay. Good."

Nate didn't say anything else, so Parker clicked off the Maglite, drowning the room in darkness so complete, it was almost obscene. He plucked his glasses off the bridge of his nose and folded them up, but didn't, wouldn't, let his eyelids slide shut just yet. He kept them open, gazing into the nothing, listening to the little movements in the air and the woods surrounding the house. He wondered if Nate was still sitting there, in the corner of the room, staring at him with those dead, unblinking eyes that did such a good job of pretending to be alive. He wondered if that's what death really was—just a long, unbroken stretch of consciousness, unable to sleep or eat or touch anything to break up the monotony. Just trapped awake, forever.

If that was death, Parker thought it sounded more than a little bit like hell.

Parker's consciousness had already started to ebb away in little tidal surges, tiny pieces of him lost to the sea of sleep for the night. The waves were warm and comforting, quiet and dark, and he gave himself over to them.

But . . .

The thought floated up from the darkest depths of Parker's mind, a coffin unchained from the sea floor, breaking the surface with a hiss and spray of toxic, moldering air. *I didn't tell him about the church.*

Parker's eyes were open for a long, long time after that.

Josh fed the fire while Nicky lay on her side, pretending to doze inside her sleeping bag. Chloe didn't know exactly what the hell had happened to them in the time that she'd been out, but whatever it was, it must have been bad. Neither of them spoke to each other after they got the fire going; hell, they barely spoke to Chloe, either, but at least they bothered pretending. Nicky had passed out food—another shabby dinner of cold Pop-Tarts and crushed potato chips, but it was better than nothing. Not long after, Chloe had slipped back into sleep with relative ease, but there were nightmares waiting for her underneath the surface.

She'd been working in the Ganderses' home for almost three months when the reverend started coming around. Mary Kane, from all the way up in Ipswich and barely a hair over twenty, had grown up poor, like her parents and their parents before them. Given that, she counted herself lucky to have found any position at all, but that she'd found one with a family as kind and generous as the Ganderses was doubly fortunate. They were good Christian folk. They took care of her at least as much as she took care of them. She really thought it could last forever.

It was a Friday morning the first time the reverend came calling. Dressed in black, he was tall and thin like a scarecrow, with hollowed-out cheeks and a thin, sharp jawline like a viper. He stood outside the front door of the modest little estate house with his back rod-straight, head and shoulders taller than anyone else Mary had seen around the township of Mount Holly, even taller than Anders the blacksmith. He greeted her with a slow, deep bow, this strange, skeleton man, and when he rose again, she could see that his smile was gray and oily to match his eyes. He wasn't old, *he was just . . . withered. As he stood there, the rough, thick fabric of his cloak whipped and danced in the wind, as if it were trying to break free of him.*

"Reverend Simon Phipps, come to share the word of the Lord with the master and the lady of the house," he said, extending a hand Mary did not take. "And who might you be, my dear?"

"Mary Kane," she said, looking anywhere but his awful, viscous eyes. "The Ganderses' maid."

Far across the fields, on the well-trod paths behind him, she could just make out people in the distance, walking along, shielding their eyes from the sun as they made their way toward town. In this moment, more than anything else, she wished she were walking with them, or anywhere else in the world—anything that didn't involve standing in this doorway, trapped under his creeping gaze.

"Lovely to meet you, Miss Kane," he said, moving his tongue around her name as if it were a spoonful of honey. "Would you mind fetching your master for me? I would speak with him."

Without another word, Mary nodded and then turned and fled back deeper into the house to find Mr. Ganders, hoping to keep her distance from the strange, looming reverend.

Later on, as he was about to leave, Mary heard Phipps ask the Ganderses one last question.

"Your maid . . . does she often receive gentleman callers?"

The reverend's visits soon became a regular occurrence, at least once a week, but sometimes more. He came preaching his good word and leering hungrily at Mary from around the corners when he thought she wouldn't notice. He would read from the Bible; he would show the children magic tricks (his funny games, *he called them); he would even help out with the chores, chopping wood and starting fires in the hearth with that damned black hatchet of his, the one he had made special with the flint along the blade edge. He liked them, and the Ganderses him, though every so often she thought she could catch a look of—what, distrust? Unease?—flit across her employers' faces when he spoke. But still, he was the town's reverend. He was owed some measure of respect, no matter their personal feelings. Wasn't he?*

It wasn't long before Simon broached the subject of marriage. He was quite taken with their housemaid, he confessed to them one sunny morning. Through his ashy, uneven smile, he told tale of a life she wanted no part of, a house she didn't want to live in, children she had no wish to bear. He spoke of it as if it was a foregone conclusion—of course *Mary and he would be wed. What other option did she have? What other suitors were there?*

And Mary endured it. She smiled patiently at every sweet-bitter comment. She shied politely away from his long, grasping fingers when he attempted to pray with her. She waited for him to understand his cause was lost, demurring from his every attention.

And for a while, demurring was enough.

Until it wasn't.

When the day came that he cornered her long enough to ask for her hand, Mary did the worst thing imaginable.

She told him no.

She tried to be kind about it, gentle even, but she was unequivocal; she was firm. She didn't tell him "Not now" or "I'm not sure." She did not waver. She told him no. No, there was no changing her mind. No, she did not love him. No, she could never—would never—love him.

She would not marry Reverend Simon Phipps, in this life or any other.

But still he came calling, week after week, under the thin auspices of ministering to the Ganders family. To the family's credit, they stood behind her decision. They pulled her aside one evening and told her as much, though it seemed as if it pained Mrs. Ganders to do so. They made it clear to her: Mary's life, inasmuch as it could be, was her own to live, no matter how Phipps had pleaded or tried to convince them otherwise. They would not force Mary to change her mind.

The last time Reverend Phipps came to preach, she could see that something had broken loose from inside of him, some vicious, slavering thing that had been only barely restrained before. She could see it in the way he watched her with his dead, colorless glare. Before, she had been a curiosity, or worse, an obsession; now, she was food.

There wasn't any reason for it, not that she could see; no root cause to explain it all away. He'd always been this. Maybe the voices in his head had gotten too loud to ignore. Maybe the fires that he so loved starting had finally overtaken his heart. Whatever it was, it was plain to see, scribbled all over him in his expressions, his movements, the things he said and the way he said them. Simon had snapped for good, and there was no coming back from that.

It was pure, stupid luck that she was awake when he came for them. She'd been up half the night already, tossing and turning from nightmares she couldn't remember. Surrendering to insomnia, she dressed quietly and headed to the kitchen to make herself a cup of tea.

She was at the stove boiling water when she heard someone kick in one of the windows. At first, she thought she was hearing things—a holdover from one of her bad dreams bubbling to the surface to rattle her—especially given the absolute silence that followed the sound. How could she have thought anything else?

But then the people upstairs started to die.

Mr. Ganders got it first, judging from the sound of Mrs. Ganders's screams, which were silenced as quickly as they'd began. Next it was the children, dashed to death in their beds one after another as they wept and wailed for the parents who could no longer save them from the hatchet. Cowering there by the cupboards, Mary would have guessed it was Simon no matter what. But then he began to sing as he paced from room to room, and in doing so, banished all doubt.

Hymns. He was singing hymns as he killed them.

But she wasn't dead yet. She could still escape. She could disappear into the night and never be heard from again. The family was already lost—need she be, as well?

Mary's body turned traitor then, freezing when she commanded it to move, to run, to escape. But she was glued to the floor, locked inside her own flesh, unable even to scream. For a moment, she thought that she might fight back, that she could run upstairs with a carving knife from the wooden block and plunge it into Simon's chest, to end this here and now. But she knew that was just a fantasy. She wasn't brave. She'd never been brave. He'd come for her, as he was always going to, and now that the Ganderses were dead, she was going to die, too, just as they had. There was nothing that could change that.

It was the sound of his boots on the stairs that shook her from her horrible trance, the dull and distant click *of hobnails against wood growing ever louder. It was so much worse than the screams, or the sobs, or the wet* thwacks *of metal biting through flesh that Mary had pretended she couldn't hear.*

It was the sound of her death approaching.

That sound charged through her in a wave, her every nerve returning to life in a single rush. Her legs, her entire body returned to her, she didn't dare waste another breath.

Mary ran. She barely touched the floor as she sailed toward the back door, flying like a gale loosed through the house. She could feel her heart pumping blood through her limbs, she could hear the night throbbing all around her; in that moment, she felt alive, so damnably alive.

She was halfway across the far field by the time she started to smell the smoke. Turning back for just a moment, she could see the first glimmers of flame dancing in the windows of the small estate, little more than lamp-light behind the glass. As if the house were still her home, beckoning her back inside with promises of safety and warmth.

But it wasn't her home, not anymore. The glow was another trick, another one of Simon's funny games. She had to keep going. She could lose him if she stayed far enough ahead. There was a forest, a great forest, far south of town. She thought that she could make it by morning, lose him in the trees, but she had to go—now.

She wondered if she'd ever stop running again.

For a moment longer, she watched the house burn slowly. Then the front door swung wide open. She didn't stay to see him emerge from the shadows, carrying that horrible, night-black blade at his side. She knew what wretched fate waited for her on the other side of that.

Spinning on her heels, Mary Kane squared her shoulders and sprinted farther into the dark.

A cold, oily chill shot through Chloe's body as the dream crumbled around her and she came tumbling back out into the real world.

What the fuck was that?

Sprawled on the ground, she blinked, trying to see more than she already could. Nights in the forest were so dark, and from where she lay, only a scattering of stars managed to poke through the canopy of trees that hung overhead. Things were sharper out here after sunset, all the edges like blades. The campfire that Josh had built so carefully in between them had died down to arterial red embers shot through mostly dead logs. No wonder she was so cold. Chloe dragged a hand across her forehead. Despite the fire having gone out, she'd broken out in a terrible sweat, drenching her from top to toes, wicking deep into the fabric of her clothes. Another fever broken, she supposed. Her head felt clearer, her body aches had gone, even the air around her tasted sweet and fresh. She wiped her slick palms on her sleeping bag and gingerly moved to sit up, propping herself at an angle on her elbows and forearms, trying to ease past the bright hooks of pain that yanked at her midsection.

She couldn't see her friends, but she knew they were there, could hear them breathing through the dark. Nicky's mild, droning snore sounded against Josh's wet, open-mouthed snuffles. She was here, and they were here. She wasn't alone . . . as if being together was enough to save anyone in this place.

The names from her—what would she even call it? A dream? A vision?—came back to her in a rush, and she clutched them desperately, trying to keep them from evaporating again.

The Ganders family.

Mary Kane.

Reverend Simon Phipps.

The names, and the bright, brutal images they carried with them, hung in front of her face, as familiar to her as her own reflection, or the woods that she'd seen—*felt*—the Kane girl run through, praying madly to some invisible, whispering god for salvation. The forest had changed in the interim centuries, but not so much as to render it unrecognizable. What she'd seen was true. It had happened. She was as sure of it as she was that there was ground underneath her and a sky above. That psychopath had slaughtered that family . . . and the Kane woman had let him, sacrificing their lives so she could turn tail and run. Chloe's skin still pulsed and buzzed with Mary's fear and shame, a hideous, borrowed sensation she couldn't seem to shake herself free of.

It was that fear that made it hard to condemn her outright. Chloe had never felt a paralyzing fear of her own like that; that kind of fear warped reality around it, bent it to suit its will. Mary Kane could have no sooner ambushed Phipps as take flight by flapping her arms like wings. Chloe knew that. She knew it as well as she knew that Phipps had been a monster, and in the real world, fighting monsters only ever made things worse. She was starting to realize that herself now.

Sleep tugged at the corners of her eyes, but some part of her knew they would need another campfire if the three of them were going to get through the rest of this chilly night without everyone waking up sick. The light and the warmth would do them good. It would see them through until dawn.

Carefully, she rolled onto her side, picking up a small handful of the dry twigs and branches Josh had left beside the rocks. She slid them underneath the scorched, still-glowing logs that had been their campfire until not too long ago. She considered the knot of branches, then added more to it. She didn't know what time it was, but wanted to make sure the fire would last them through the rest of the night.

Nicky's lighter was on the ground beside her, a cheap yellow BIC with a cartoon baseball printed on the side. She really hoped this would work. She'd never built a campfire before. She thumbed the lighter to life with a *skritch* and held the little flame to the fresh kindling, holding as still as she possibly could so the wood would catch. A second later, fresh flames swept through the dead branches with a soft rush, and Chloe pulled her hand back quickly. Flickering yellow light filled the little area around them, and Chloe glanced over at her friends one last time, meaning to let sleep take her again.

For a moment, she didn't understand what she was seeing. It didn't make sense. But even lacking sense, she couldn't stop herself. She screamed.

The figure that stood on the edge of their camp in dirty, destroyed clothes was tall and rangy, totally devoid of all the muscle he'd spent so many years building up at football and baseball practices and gym trips and track meets. He was almost spiderlike now, his limbs drawn long and thin, as if he'd been stretched out by some dread medieval torture machine.

It looked like Adam, but it wasn't Adam. Not anymore. It wore his skin, but it was a bad costume, rendered in tattered cloth and loose loops of fish-pale skin that hung off him in ropes and rags. His eyes—*its* eyes—were dull and milky and shone with a kind of yellow wetness, while his mouth hung agape to reveal rows of broken, splintered teeth, streaked with thin pink mucous that dribbled farther down its chin with every strangled wheeze. Whatever had grown under Adam's skin and warped him into this, it wasn't him. This wasn't her friend at all.

On the far side of the fire, Nicky and Josh tore free from their bags, knocked clean out of sleep by Chloe's shriek. She couldn't see the expressions on their faces; she didn't know what they looked like when they first saw the Adam-thing. She just heard Nicky moan *oh no oh Jesus oh my god* as Josh stepped forward with a hand outstretched, a fake, forced calm in his voice that Chloe thought for a second might actually work.

"Hey, man, it's okay." The way he said it sounded like he was talking to a rabid dog that had gotten too close. "It's going to be okay, Adam, I promise, we're gonna get you help—"

Chloe didn't even see the Adam-thing move. It was too fast, the night too dark, and she was too sleepy. All she knew was that one second, Josh's face was attached to his head, and the next, it wasn't. A heavy wing of blood, almost black in the darkness, floated away from his skull, and he screamed—good god, did he scream, loud enough that it seemed to shake the whole forest. Josh stumbled back, both hands drawn to the place above his neck, the delicate flesh there sheared apart by the gnarled hooks at the end of the Adam-thing's hands. He hit the ground with a heavy, graceless *thump*, and the Adam-thing followed him down, dropping onto his body with a wild screech, ripping and gnashing at him and staining the air with the smell of burning copper.

Nicky didn't even hesitate. She howled and leaped at the Adam-thing as it dug savagely into the soft flesh of Josh's throat, sweeping a burning branch from the fire like a flail, swinging it wildly, her screams filling up the night around them.

"*No no no no NO NO NO, JOSH, NO!*"

The Adam-thing sprung off of Josh, its sharp, hooked hands and razored maw soaked in red, but Nicky didn't stop. She sprinted full tilt at the thing that used to be their best friend, slashing the flames at its face, leaving orange brushstrokes hanging in the air after each swing. The Adam-thing made a wet, choking sound and reared back on its heels, letting Nicky press in closer; Chloe could see exactly what was going to happen next, but she was powerless to stop it.

Nicky took another step closer—*too close,* Chloe thought, *way too close*—and the Adam-thing whipsawed forward, burying one red-stained claw into her chest before savagely raking it back, carving deep, bloody gashes through her shirt and shoulder. The tall, red-headed girl screamed and tried to swing the burning branch again, but it was no good. The Adam-thing ducked out of the way and then handily batted it from Nicky's fist. Yowling, Nicky fell back and hit the ground, and the Adam-thing reared up to fall on her like he'd done to Josh.

So Chloe did the only thing she could think of.

She shouted at the top of her lungs, "Adam, don't!"

And to her surprise, the Adam-thing actually paused, turning its red-smeared head to regard Chloe with those horrible, rheumy eyes. It was like looking into a spider's eyes. There was something primal in the revulsion she felt holding his gaze, but she knew that if she looked away now, Nicky was dead. So she held fast, no matter how much doing so made her want to scream and vomit and then scream some more.

"Don't do this," Chloe begged. "Please."

The Adam-thing watched her, and for a moment, she could see the boy underneath the monster, his handsome, delicate features eroded, but not totally gone yet. She held out a shaking hand to him, wishing she could somehow bridge the distance between them. Wishing he wasn't too far gone.

That's when Nicky struck.

The branch on the ground had nearly gone out, but one end still glowed red with heat, and she jammed it into the Adam-thing's long, distended neck as hard as she could. The tall, pale creature shrieked and recoiled, thrashing its long arms in wild windmills, then twisted free and dashed away into the darkness, crashing through the trees until the sound of it faded completely away.

But it was already far too late. The damage was done. Even in the low glow of the campfire, Chloe could see there was too much blood coming out of Josh. It throbbed from the gaping holes the Adam-thing had left in his body and pooled in a black lake underneath him. Nicky, wounded as she was, crawled over to her boyfriend and crumbled, pawing at him, soaking herself in his blood, the sobs pouring out of her like a freshly loosed waterfall. Wordlessly, Chloe slumped back onto the ground and started to cry, her bleary eyes turned toward the sky, and didn't stop for a long, long time.

SUNDAY

11

Dawn tore through the town in a slow wave, leaving it drowned in dead, gray light. The cold was everywhere now. The night's chill had sunk deep into the nameless little town's slats and corners like stubborn, icy hooks, refusing to be burned away by the little sunlight that managed to filter through the scudding shell of clouds that had overtaken the sky since sundown.

Inside the gatehouse, Parker's eyes slid open as consciousness returned to him in broken pieces. He'd lay awake on the floor for what felt like hours after killing the light, listening to the house around him, straining his ears until they rang trying to hear if Nate was still there or if he'd vanished when Parker wasn't looking. He shifted in place, and his giant's frame cried out in protest. His muscles ached horribly, either from bedding down on the bare wooden floor or from the tension hard-knuckled into his body and bones from the noisy, bloody nightmares that had chased him all night, now receding back into the black drift of sleep.

He rose slowly, fitting his glasses onto his face to look around the small old room for Nate, finding himself alone. Fine by him. He wasn't any good at talking to anyone first thing in the morning, anyway. His brain was too muddled by sleep, the words always coming too sluggishly to make him any kind of decent company. He'd heard coffee helped people with that kind of thing, but he'd never developed the taste for it.

Rolling up his sleeping bag in silence, Park took a look around the little gatehouse, noting how different it looked in the wan morning light. Last night, it had been spooky and ancient, but now it just seemed dilapidated and, honestly, a bit sad. Parker's heart sank at the thought that this had once been someone's home, and that, for whatever reason, they'd just left it behind one day without any explanation.

He packed up the rest of his things—flashlight, hatchet, gun—and slung his pack around his shoulders, fitting his arms underneath the heavy nylon straps. Then he turned and threw open the front door, filling the front room with that peaky gray morning light. The chill in the air licked along his bare skin with the wind, a soft, gentle sensation that made his body feel cold and hard.

Christ, but he ached. Maybe he'd slept even worse than he thought.

Overhead, the sky seemed closer than it had been the day before, the cloud cover drawing the earth nearer to the heavens and the dead oblivion that waited beyond them. Like the gatehouse, the town was a little sadder this morning, a little shabbier, a little more broken. The roofs seemed to sag a bit more than they had the day previous, the walls bowed with deeper curves, and the fences leaned at more extreme angles, where they still stood at all.

Stepping out of the house and onto the rough, dust-blown trail that passed for a main road in whatever this place used to be called before it had died, Parker's neck crawled with the sensation that he wasn't alone—that there were eyes on him from every house and outbuilding. Turning back to close the gatehouse door, or at least wedge it shut in its frame, he nearly jumped his skeleton from his body when he saw Nate standing behind him, hands jammed deep in his pockets, another version of his same old shitty grin pressed between his round cheeks.

Above that, his eyes were beady and black. Rat's eyes. *They hadn't been that black when he'd been alive, had they?* Parker wondered.

"Hey, man," the ghost said. "Sleep okay?"

Parker rolled his shoulders against the spike of nerves Nate's sudden appearance had driven into his spine, tried to play it off like he was adjusting his backpack.

"Yeah. Fine. I guess." He gestured toward the gatehouse. "Were you in there the whole time?"

"I don't know. I guess I was, sure."

"What does that mean?"

"I mean, it kind of feels like I'm a little bit everywhere all the time now. Like I got spread out way, way further than I used to be. It's like I'm stitched into the fabric of this place. I can feel all sorts of strange shit. Little tremors and shakes in the forest floor, the wind through the trees . . . Like, right now, I can tell you that there's a family of deer on the edge of town, drinking from the lake. The mom's heart is running a million miles an hour because she's nervous. I don't know why, but I can feel her pulse racing."

Parker stared at him. "That's fucking spooky, man."

"You're telling me."

"So like, you know everything about the whole forest now? You can see everything?"

Nate shook his head. "No, it's not like I suddenly got connected to the forest Wi-Fi or whatever. It's more like . . . a feeling. I can *feel* the woods around me. Things ring off of each other, like a harp. Strike one string, and the rest of them vibrate back."

"And that seems normal to you?"

"Man, none of this seems normal to me," Nate fired back. "Does any of it seem normal to you? You're the one standing here talking to a dead guy." He stepped out of the gatehouse to slip past while Parker pulled the door shut.

"Point taken," said Parker.

"That's what I thought. Now, let's go have a look around. Place isn't gonna explore itself."

Park turned and followed his dead friend at a short distance, keeping his eyes pinned to the spot between the ghost's shoulder blades, staring knives into him, trying to figure out if Nate could feel it, or if that was all bullshit too.

Hours later, when she opened her eyes again, the first thing Chloe saw was Nicky, still streaked with rusty red, sitting cross-legged on the ground, cradling Josh's torn, crumpled body in both arms. Memories from last night slithered into place inside Chloe's head, fitting together in an ugly patchwork.

The dreams.

The fire.

The blood.

Adam.

Lying there in the dead of night, in the aftermath, Chloe hadn't meant to sleep, but she couldn't stay awake, no matter how much adrenaline her body dumped into her system. The wound in her side, the fever and the exhaustion had all jammed their bony fingers deep into her flesh and dragged her down into a deep, dreamless sleep that had proven impossible to fight off. One second, she was lying there in the glow of the campfire while Nicky wept and screamed herself raw, and then . . . well, then someone had clicked off the lights inside her head, and she was gone.

She was almost embarrassed by the relief she felt. She couldn't have kept staring up at the empty sky like that and stayed sane, running through things again and again and again, trying to see a way through that would have kept Josh from dying so horribly at the hands of the thing that used to be their friend. Sleep was a mercy. Sleep was an escape hatch. No matter how strong you were supposed to be, sometimes it was just nice to not exist for a little while.

Sitting up slowly, Chloe pulled the sleeping bag off her legs and hazarded a few small movements, testing her new limits, stretching her arms out in opposite directions until the hole in her ribs screamed for her to stop. Rolling her shirt up, she peeled the bandage back to take a look at the bloody mess that lay underneath; it was a neat wound, about the size of a half-dollar, the edges already starting to clot over with a dark, crusty scab. She ran her fingertips across the places it had dried, feeling the smooth, bumpy ridges and the thin, flaky parts where it met her undamaged skin. For a second, she had the wild, childlike impulse to dig a fingernail underneath and tear it clean off, just to see how bad it would bleed.

Across the dead firepit, Nicky snuffled and wheezed, and Chloe glanced over at her. She looked as bad as Chloe had ever seen: her eyes big and dark and ringed with bruise-like shadows, her skin filthy and mottled, her shirt in red tatters where Adam had raked her. Those deep, parallel wounds she bore on her shoulder had crusted over in the night, the iron-red lines stark against her ghost-pale skin. Chloe wondered how badly they hurt, or if she'd even noticed that they were there. The hole Adam had punched through her own ribs still throbbed and ached like a motherfucker, even just leaning here like this.

"Nicky," she said quietly, not wanting to startle her friend.

Nicky looked back at Chloe, her eyes crater-wide, but she didn't say anything. She just sat there, curled around her dead boyfriend, totally silent, waiting. In that moment, everything that Chloe thought she had to say to her seemed so stupid, so completely irrelevant. What could she say that would mean anything? All they had was each other now. No Josh, no Adam, no Parker, no Nate. They were all they had left to try and get out of these woods, and Chloe truly didn't know if it would be enough.

"Nicky, listen . . ."

Looking at her friend like that, Chloe wished she didn't have to say it. But she said it anyway.

"Babe, I think we have to bury him."

All the vulnerability drained out of Nicky's face in an instant, leaving a hard, sharp thing behind. She didn't look hurt like Chloe had expected; she looked mad, like Chloe had hauled off and slapped her.

"Why?" The word knifed out of Nicky's mouth in an icy slide.

"You saw what the birds did to Nate yesterday morning. You saw that."

The reality of what she was saying hit her a moment too late. Had that been only yesterday? Only twenty-four hours away from the horror of piling rocks on top of their friend's body, and they were already doing it again? This was so fucked. This was so completely *unfair.*

"You know we have to," Chloe said, trying to keep her voice from shaking. "To protect him until someone can come and get him. His mom and his dad deserve to be able to bury him right."

Nicky made a low moan in the place where her throat and her chest met.

"What are we even going to *tell* them, though?"

Chloe didn't even have to think about it. "The truth. We'll tell them the truth. All of it."

"They won't believe us."

"They will, Nicky. But we have to be honest about all of it. Parker, Nate, Adam, Josh. We'll tell everyone exactly what happened in here. They'll believe us if we tell them the truth. I promise you they will."

"But what if they don't?"

"Then that's on them," said Chloe. "Right now, all we can do is stick together and do our best to stay safe and get out. Fuck Parker, and fuck Adam. They both might as well be dead too, as far as I'm concerned."

"Don't say that," Nicky snarled, her voice quavering on the edge of tears.

"It's the truth. Right here, right now, all I care about is you, and me, and doing the best we can. Right now, I think that means keeping Josh safe, just like we did with Nate, and after that, it means being smart and getting out of here together."

Nicky flinched, casting her eyes down toward the ground.

"This is the only way we can help him now. We can still be good to him, but we have to do it together."

"I really loved him, Chloe."

Chloe's heart winced, hearing her say that. She liked Josh, but she didn't love Josh. She could only imagine what Nicky was going through. Thinking about it too much made her want to cry.

"I know you did, Nicky. I know. Keeping him safe is the best way to show him that."

The redheaded girl rubbed furiously at her eyes. "Can't you just . . . ?"

Chloe sighed and gestured to the lake of blood that had wicked through her entire shirt.

"I wish I could, I really do. But it has to be both of us," Chloe said.

"I can't."

"You have to."

Nicky's eyes filled with tears and spilled over, slashing her dirty cheeks with wet, clean lines that rolled down to her jawline.

"No," she moaned. "I *don't.*"

"Please," Chloe begged. "I need your help. I wish I could do it alone, Nicky, I really do, but I can't. I need you with me on this. *Please.*"

"Okay," Nicky whispered, almost too quiet to be heard. Chloe wasn't even sure if she'd actually spoken, or if Nicky had just moved her lips and let Chloe fill the rest in. Either way.

"Thank you," Chloe said, holding a hand out in Nicky's direction. “Can you help me up? I don’t think I can . . .”

Nicky nodded and delicately laid Josh’s body down on the cold ground, unfolding herself from underneath his dead, bloody weight, then crossed to hold her filthy hands out to Chloe.

Taking them and squeezing them tight, she met Nicky’s harrowed gaze, pretending not to see the way her eyes kept flicking over toward Josh’s crumpled, mangled form.

“Is this going to hurt?” Nicky asked her.

“Yeah,” Chloe said. “Probably a lot. Still, can’t lay around all day, right?”

“I guess.”

“Okay, on three, I’m going to pull, you do the same. Alright?”

Nicky nodded.

“Okay. One. Two—”

“Wait.”

Chloe looked at her. “What?”

“Are we going on three, or is it one-two-three, then pull?”

Chloe thought about it. “Pull on three.”

“Okay.”

“Ready?”

“No.”

“Yeah, me neither. Okay. One. Two. *Three*—!”

Chloe pulled, and felt Nicky do the same. There was a cold, bladed tearing that dragged through the middle of her as they both yanked Chloe up to her feet; she clenched her teeth against it, trying to not scream. Something went *pop* in her wound, and she felt a warm, wet trickle running down her belly to seep into the waistband of her jeans, but still she pulled, feeling her arms catch fire and her shoulders start to burn through with acid. Lurching to her feet, she held on to Nicky for dear life, gasping for air, feeling the pain recede by degrees. Her legs were rubbery and unsure, but they didn’t buckle, and that was as much of a victory as she could hope for right now.

Pressing her hand to the wound in her ribs to try and stanch the bleeding, she scanned the area around them, spotting what she was looking for after only a moment.

"Here, grab that." Chloe pointed to a big, wrist-thick branch that had fallen among the nearby trees. Nicky quickstepped over to scoop it up, passing it to Chloe.

Experimentally, Chloe planted the end of the stick in the ground like a flag or a pick, then, white-knuckled, transferred some of her weight over to it. She felt the wood bow and bend beneath her, but it didn't break. Okay. This would do for now. She nodded at Nicky, who let her go and stood with her arms crossed over her chest.

"Thank you," Chloe panted.

Nicky didn't say anything in response. She just nodded, her eyes a million miles away.

"We should get him into the sleeping bag, Nick. Just to be safe. Okay? That way he'll be protected. Can you help me with that?"

Nicky nodded.

Chloe hobbled over to the place where Josh lay, his skin pale and gray and slack, waxy eyes still hanging open, the shock of his own death frozen there. She watched Nicky gather up his sleeping bag and carry it over, spreading it out across the bare ground, unzipping it all the way.

"I think we can roll him onto it and then zip it up around him," said Nicky.

Chloe watched Nicky's eyes, the way she disappeared down that well of darkness deep inside of her. She'd always wondered what it was that Nicky hid down in that hole, though it was pretty obvious that it wasn't anything good.

"I think you're right," Chloe said, choking back a fresh rush of pain. "Yeah. Let's do this."

Leaning down to take Josh by the sleeve, Chloe braced herself against her new crutch and dug her feet into the soil, while beside her, Nicky bunched one hand in Josh's shirt and the other in one of the pockets of his jeans.

"Same as before, okay? Pull together on three."

"Okay," Chloe said.

"One . . . Two . . . *Three!*"

The two girls heaved at the same time. For a moment, it seemed like Josh wasn't going to move at all, but then he lurched to one side, rolling toward the spread-out bag. Chloe could already feel the fabric of his shirt starting to slip free of her fist.

"Keep pulling," Chloe groaned through her teeth, doubling her grip to try and keep hold. "Almost got him, almost there . . ."

The sleeve snapped out of her fingers, and she threw a hand out to try and grab back on. But instead of his shirtsleeve, her hand closed around the soft, cold skin of Josh's wrist.

The vision hit her like a flash bomb.

She recognized the scene—she'd seen it before. Hell, she'd lived it before, but not like this. Not through Josh's eyes.

The daylight fell away in sheets, giving way to the dark of night as the trees and the forest and the sky above held steady. The campfire, cold and dead only a moment before, rasped to life as the darkness rushed in all around her, the dancing flames painting red-orange afterimages on her eyes. Across the fire, Chloe could see herself, a short, slight little thing sprawled on the ground like a broken doll, her face wide with confusion and shock. Nicky was there, too, hunched shoulders drawn cable-tight as she regarded the creature that stood on the edge of the flickering light—the thin, pale thing that used to be Adam.

Standing there, she felt her arms and legs move, animating on their own, taking a few short, cautious steps in the Adam-thing's direction, stretching one mole-dotted hand out while Nicky and Chloe watched on, barely breathing.

Step. Step. Step.

Her legs moved autonomously, experimentally, carrying her closer to the Adam-thing. In her peripheral vision, she saw Nicky's jaw work and bob like she was saying something, but she couldn't hear what; the words came out muddied and muffled, like they were being filtered through cotton batting. There was a pressure building in the pit of her throat, a strange sensation that she initially didn't recognize as the precursor to speech. Locked inside a body that wasn't hers, she heard herself speak with a voice that wasn't her own.

"Hey, man, it's okay. It's going to be okay, Adam, I promise, we're gonna get you help—"

In the next instant, there was a flash of motion, too fast for her to process. Then something struck the side of her head, and she was falling, chased down by a shrieking, spindly mess of teeth and claws. Chloe tried to scream, tried to thrash away, knowing what was coming next, but she never hit the ground. She just kept falling and falling, past where the forest floor should have been, past the point that she understood it at all. She tumbled through some horrible forever, locked in a body that wasn't hers, wishing she could yell or cry or even breathe on her own. The seconds unraveled into minutes, then hours into years. She never stopped trying to scream her way out.

Then it was gone. Day again. Her own body again.

Chloe unclasped her hand from Josh's wrist, then fell back and sucked in air, on the verge of tears at her ability to move and breathe and blink on her own once more. At her feet, Josh was slumped over onto the fabric of the sleeping bag, while Nicky watched her, pupils dialed to pinpricks.

"Are you okay?"

Chloe forced herself to slow her breathing. *Get it under control, get it together.* She darted her eyes away toward the blur of the forest.

"Yeah," she lied. "Fine. I'm fine. Sorry."

"It's all right," Nicky told her, in the kind of deliberate way that said it really wasn't.

Silently, they bundled and zipped Josh the rest of the way up in his sleeping bag and dragged him into the place where the forest grew thickest. Hobbling on her makeshift crutch, Chloe started to venture into the trees around them.

"I'm going to go look for rocks," she called back over her shoulder. "We'll pile them over the top of him so he'll be safe. I can find them, but I'm going to need your help carrying them when I do, okay?"

Nicky nodded, her eyes glued to the wet, messy sleeping bag at their feet.

"Can you stay here with him until I get back?" Chloe asked. "I don't think it'll take too long."

"I'll be here."

Figuring that was as good as she was going to get from Nicky, Chloe limped off into the forest, her gait uneven and slow, buoyed up by the branch clutched in her fist. Somewhere in the distance, she thought she could hear water.

Once she was far enough away from Nicky, Chloe leaned against one of the great, old trees that surrounded her and tried—and failed—to keep herself from crying again.

When she closed her eyes, she could still feel herself falling.

Parker and Nate followed the main street of the little town, scanning the nameplates on the front of each little house: *CANTON*, *LITTLE*, *GROSS*, *EADWARDS*. Hung outside the biggest house was a nameplate that read *LEEDS*. It must have been an impressive place in its time, just down the street from the church, surrounded by those bare, bone-white trees that stabbed up from underneath the ground. The doors were boarded up, the windows shuttered and nailed tight, the roof and walls crumbling just like the rest of the town. But there was a kind of majesty to it, a faded glory that hung around the house like an aura. There was just something about a house as large and austere as this in a town buried in the Barrens. The Leeds family, whoever they were, had faded into the past, but their house still stood in their wake like a tombstone.

Swallowing his curiosity, Parker followed Nate up the road to where the dirt path curled around and held his breath as the church gradually revealed itself to them. Tall and faded, its white boards had long since curled and gone gray from time and weather, but the simple cross atop its single tower stood firm, nearly black against the drab sky. If the Leeds house was big, the church was massive, to the point where it wouldn't have seemed out of place in Newark, or maybe even one of the smaller neighborhoods across the river in the city proper. Like the rest of the abandoned town, the church was mostly boarded over. But as they approached, Parker could see that a few of the planks blocking off the front doors had been pried away, the ghostly outlines of them still visible in the weather-stained wood.

Someone had been here.

Parker double-timed it up the path, heart throbbing in his throat. His footsteps thundered on the church's front steps, the wood creaking and groaning underneath his bulk. Off to the side lay the discarded bracing boards, pried from the doorframe and tossed away like trash. Nate nodded at them.

"When do you figure that happened?"

"Not sure," Parker said. "But it can't have been that long ago. Look."

He nodded toward the outline the boards had left, their shape weathered into the wood, the grain underneath fresher somehow.

Nate looked back at Parker. "Shit. You think this is him?"

Yes, Parker's mind rasped. "I don't know." *It has to be.* "Maybe, I guess."

"Well, let's not just stand out here playing with our dicks. D'you want to go in or not?"

Park nodded, a little too quickly. "Sure."

He considered the small space left open by the pried-free boards. In the back of his mind, he thought, *Could Dad have actually fit through there?* He honestly wasn't sure, but there was no way in hell Parker was getting through that, even down on his hands and knees.

Fuck it. He had a better way through.

Twirling the hatchet in his hand, Parker brought the blade down hard on the lowest of the old boards, cleaving it in two with a *crack* like a gunshot. Bracing his shoulders, he swung the hatchet again, and again, and again, making short work of the other boards blocking the doors, prying them back from the frame with his free hand and tossing them aside. When they'd all been hacked away, Parker stood back and delivered a sharp kick where the doors met, sending them flying open, revealing little but shadows beyond.

Breathing hard, Parker glanced over at Nate. "We doing this?"

Nate clicked his tongue against his teeth.

"I'm following you, big guy."

Parker nodded, then stepped through into the collapsing old church.

The smell of stale, old air washed over him in a dead heave, pricking his upper sinuses, tickling his brain like a sneeze that just wouldn't come. He snorted against the sensation and spat a fat loogie onto the rough floor, then pulled the collar of his T-shirt up to cover his nose and mouth, observing the place from behind foggy glasses.

The nave of the church must have been impressive once, but now it was faded and decaying to match its outside. Blades of light from long-broken windows poured across blighted pews draped with black dust, while cobwebs collected in every corner of the hall and thistle weeds sprouted up between split floorboards. At the back of the church, above a toppled lectern, a large wooden cross hung on the wall, listing to the side as the building continued to sag and crumble with each passing year.

Even through Parker's T-shirt, the whole place stank of mold and dry rot and bitter chalk; it reminded him of the time his parents had dragged him out to North Plainfield to clean out his grandpa's house after the old man had finally given up the ghost. Clearing out trash up in the attic, he'd found a dead raccoon in the farthest corner, withered with age and shot through with maggots. That same smell was in here. Like something had crawled inside the church to die.

Parker walked a slow circuit of the big open hall, soaking up the details, kicking sweeps of detritus out of his way as he went. High up on the far side of the church, a falling tree had torn through the wall, leaving a scar of light in its wake. Pulped Bibles sat in splintered pew backs, only barely identifiable from the gilt crosses branded in their cracked, rotting covers. Reaching down, Parker tried to pick one up, but it crumbled to dust in his hands.

Around the back of the fallen lectern, underneath the great wooden cross, Parker turned to stand where the priest or pastor or whoever must have stood when this town was still alive, trying to picture what it must have felt like to deliver a sermon here, this deep in the woods. His parents had never really brought him around to the church way of thinking; he could never seem to make the leap of faith required. He got that from his mom. She'd always been solidly interested in the realm of the provable. So when his dad up and vanished one day, all she had to cling to was the fact that he was gone. No wonder she'd spiraled out. Sometimes he'd gotten the sense that his dad used to be, if not exactly *religious*, then at least *spiritual*. He'd never held it against the man, it was just that he thought the idea of life beyond the grave was all bullshit—until he'd woken up to a ghost smiling back at him. Now he didn't know what to think.

He shifted in place, and underneath his feet, the old boards groaned. Glancing down, he saw something there that he hadn't before.

Kneeling, Parker swept away the twigs and needles and dirt with his bare hands until the shape of it was clear—a long, wide rectangle cut in the floor, precisely aligned with the rest of the floorboards so that it was almost perfectly invisible, unless you were looking for it. A pair of rusty brown hinges sat at one end of the rectangle, a tarnished ring handle at the other. Parker ran his hands over all of it, getting a feel before thumping a fist in a quick *one-two-three* in the rectangle's center. Yep, definitely hollow.

"There's a door in the floor," he called out.

At the other end of the church, Nate's head popped up over a pile of pews, beady black eyes burning with curiosity. "There's a what?"

"A door," Parker said again. "Set in the floorboards back here, behind the thing. The lectern."

"What kind of a door?"

"Like for a cellar, or something."

Nate crossed the church, weaving in between the slumped pews, to stand over Parker. "Does it open?"

"Haven't tried yet."

Nate rolled his eyes and made an impatient noise in his throat. "You know, I really cannot believe your lack of curiosity sometimes."

"I was waiting for you," Parker protested.

"Then let's do it," Nate said. "I'll let you do the honors, for obvious reasons."

Parker looked at his friend for a moment longer, then looped a pair of fingers through the brass ring and pulled. The hinges screamed in protest, a grinding screech that bit like pins into Parker's eardrums, but he kept pulling, lifting the long panel door back to reveal a rickety stair-ladder that led into a deep darkness below. He couldn't see down into it; the small amount of ambient light in the church had little chance of penetrating that far. Staring into the dusty dimness, Parker pushed the door away, letting it fall with a *clap* against the floorboards, sending a fresh cloud of dust and dirt curling into the air around it. The impact echoed throughout the big, empty church, but the cellar was tomb-still.

"Now what do you suppose they were keeping down there?" the ghost asked.

Parker set his backpack down and produced the small Maglite from one of the side pockets, clicking it to life. The harsh white beam cut like a lightsaber through the dim light of the church, and he turned it downward, tracing the length of the ladder stair to where it met a hard soil floor. It couldn't have been more than ten feet down, but from where the two boys perched, it seemed easily three times that.

"Let's go find out," Parker said.

Propping the battery end of the flashlight between his teeth, he swung himself around to ease down the steps, submerging himself in the darkness.

Hidden away in some barrow, curled up like a fist, all bones and tendons and wretchedly drawn angles, the bloody boy-thing slept. He dreamed of a voice like ice against his buzzing, blister-hot skin as the sun slid across the sky beyond the trees. It crawled out to soothe him from the tiny, impossible spaces that separated the particles in the air, caressing him with slithering, frost-rimed tendrils that coiled across his sweat-blanched flesh and sent chills through his strange new body, easing back the knives of the fever that had taken up residence throughout.

I am here with you, it whispered to him. *You are not alone. I will keep you safe. I will keep you alive. Just follow me, and stay close.*

The voice and the nightmares and the fever were one and the same—the last, dying scrap of the boy that he'd been knew that. But it was too late to stop it now. He was in its hands. The change almost complete. Nothing to do but sink.

Alone and in agony, Adam let go and disappeared down into the well of himself, and the warped, bony thing that emerged hours later was not him anymore.

I am here with you, Adam.

I love you, Adam.

But the thing did not recognize the name.

12

The rocks were a lot heavier than Chloe remembered them being yesterday. Straining against herself as they four-handed them back to camp, she went slow and steady, trying to avoid tearing the throbbing hole in her side open again. One at a time, she and Nicky lugged the stones from the trees to the place where they'd left Josh.

While Chloe had been out scouting for rocks, Nicky had remained by his side, both her hands curled in his, staring off into the distance. But when Chloe returned from the trees, Nicky was all business. Together, they piled the stones around Josh, wrapped as he was inside his sleeping bag, the stains from his exposed insides still bright red on the green polyester, even in the sallow morning light.

When they'd drawn a full outline around him, Chloe wiped away the lines of sweat from her flushed neck and cheeks. Leaning hard on her improvised crutch, she turned back to Nicky.

"Okay, I think we can start stacking them now," she said. "This should be enough."

Nicky made a pinched face.

"What?"

Nicky shook her head.

Chloe took a step closer to her. "No, seriously, what?"

"I thought about it, and. . ." The redheaded girl let out a choked-back moan and wiped at her teary eyes with dirty hands. Clearing her throat, she said, "Can I do it?"

"What do you mean?"

Nicky nodded toward Josh and the pile of rocks. "Would you just . . . let me handle this part of it? For him?"

Chloe studied her face for a moment, the dirt and the sorrow and the absence tattooed there, never to be banished or scrubbed clean again. She glanced down at the wounds carved through the soft, exposed skin between Nicky's shoulder and her breast, the scabby, parallel lines left there by something they couldn't understand or explain.

"Sure," Chloe said. "I can sit and chill. Probably need to rest, anyway."

"No, I mean—"

"What?"

"Can I . . . Can I be alone? With Josh? Just for like, a little while, so I can . . ."

Right. Of course. "Oh. Sure. If that's what you need, then absolutely. I think I heard a creek down that way, anyway." With her free hand, Chloe pointed off into the trees. "Might head down and see if I can find it. We're running low on water, so probably isn't a bad idea to keep us from dying of thirst."

If we even live that long, her brain snarled at her from the depths. *Two of us gone already, three if you count Adam. Leaving Nicky alone might not be such a good idea—*

She cut the thought off midsentence, clapping her brain shut with a heavy *clack* like a bear trap.

"So, yeah," Chloe said. "I can make myself scarce for a little while. You take your time here." She hobbled over to the packs and unclipped both of their water bottles from the sides, carrying them in one crooked arm. "Just wondering, how long do you think you'll need?"

Nicky shrugged. "I don't know. I never did anything like this before."

"Okay," said Chloe. "I'll shoot for an hour. I won't be too far off, though, okay? So if you need anything, or if you finish early and you want me to come back, just give a shout. I'll come as fast as I can, all right?"

"Okay. Thank you."

Chloe made for the trees.

"Chloe?"

She looked back at her friend, standing over her dead boyfriend in his soft coffin on the forest floor. When Nicky spoke, she did so without looking up.

"I loved him, you know. I really, really loved him."

Chloe nodded at her, tears burning in her own eyes. "I know you did, Nicky. He loved you too."

For a second, Nicky looked like she was going to say something else, but then she shook her head and turned away to start lifting the stones, laying the first one down next to his head. Chloe watched for another moment, then slowly turned and headed into the trees, in the direction she'd thought she'd heard the water coming from.

The cellar was dusty and damp and pitch-black. The beam from Parker's flashlight split the gloom like a blade through a sheet but did little to dispel it. Stepping softly down onto the dirt floor, Parker took the Maglite from his mouth and swept the light around the low, wide room to get a better look.

The cellar was pretty much what he'd been expecting—uneven soil floors, walls bracketed up with thick, old, hand-cut beams, rows and rows of nearly empty shelves. It wasn't small, but its ceilings were low enough that Parker had to stoop to move around. There was a pile of moldering old Bibles to match the ones rotting in the pews stacked neatly on one of the shelves to his right, a few empty glass jars tilted over on the floor on his left.

From up above, Nate called out, "See anything?"

"I don't know," said Parker. "It's dark as hell down here. I've only got the flashlight. Are there any candles or anything up there? Anything you could throw down?"

Park felt like an idiot the second the words left his mouth. Of course Nate couldn't throw anything down to him. All he could do was stand there and talk shit; in some way, this must have been like heaven for his dead friend.

"I don't see anything," Nate said. "But, you know, good luck with the flashlight."

"You're not coming down?"

"Nah, I'm good up here, but thanks."

Parker craned his head up toward the empty hatch and said, "You know, I really cannot believe your lack of curiosity sometimes."

Parker heard a low, throaty chuckle fading as Nate walked away from the door in the floor, leaving him alone again. The sound of it was strange to him; it took a few moments for him to realize that Nate's laugh had changed. It used to be an enormous, bellowing whoop, back when he was alive. That chuckle? That was something else. Never in his life had Parker heard Nate laugh like that.

On the other side of the cellar, the flashlight beam fell on a small whitewashed door set in the wall. Parker could see that he wouldn't be able to fit through it standing normally; maybe Chloe could have, or Nicky, but if he himself wanted to get through, he'd have to crouch and twist himself into angles that he could already tell were going to be painful. Stepping in close, he traced the door's upper edges with his hand, down to where it was held shut by a crude latch made from a heavy chain and a rusty oversized nail.

Looking around the cellar once more to make sure he hadn't missed anything, Parker hefted the chain off the bent nail and dropped it, jumping only a little when it clacked against the doorjamb. He curled his hand around the door's handle and pushed. It wouldn't move. He pushed harder, feeling it give the tiniest bit, but it was stubborn. Leaning back, he scanned the edges of the door to make sure he hadn't missed a second chain, anything like that, but there was nothing. Okay. Fine. Clenching the small flashlight between his teeth again, he braced both hands and a shoulder against the little door and, counting to three, shoved as hard as he could.

The hinges screeched, and after a second, the door started to lurch inward. Kicking his toes into the soil floor, he slowly pushed it all the way back, then dusted his hands off and plucked the flashlight from his mouth like a cigar. Leading with the Maglite beam, Parker stooped and twisted and squeezed his way through the doorway.

When he emerged on the other side, his eyes widened with awe at what he saw there.

Steps.

There was another set of steps heading farther down into the earth, old and wooden, but sturdy looking. Reaching an arm out, Parker shone the beam down the stairway, but the light was too weak; he couldn't see the bottom from here. Twisting to look back over his shoulder, Parker cried out, "Nate? Nate!"

There was a pause, then a distant voice came back: "*Whaaat?*"

"Get down here. I found something!"

"Something like what?"

Parker didn't answer, and a moment later, he heard Nate grumbling close behind him. He turned to look excitedly at his friend who, squinting, pulled a hand up to shield his eyes as he closed the distance between them.

"Sucks down here already. What now?"

"Look."

Parker spun the beam down the little stairway again. Ducking through the white doorway, Nate stepped around him and leaned in for a closer look.

"Okay, that's really weird," Nate said.

"Right?"

"What do you suppose is at the bottom?"

"Don't know yet, but I'm going to go find out," Parker said. "You coming with?"

Nate made a show of thinking about it, then shrugged. "Fuck it," he said. "Why not? Not like shit's going to happen to me down there if things go all sideways. I'm—what did you call it? Oh, right—*incorporeal*."

Parker gave him a strained smile. "You know, that's almost sweet of you."

"Sweet's what I specialize in, bud. Come on, after you."

"Why after me?"

"Because you're the one who discovered it. This is your show, after all. I'm just here to see what happens when it all goes wrong again. Which, make no mistake here, it absolutely will."

"Your confidence in me right now is absolutely staggering," Parker said dryly.

"Now you're stalling. Come on, your future awaits."

Nate ushered him down the stairs, and Parker obeyed, ducking to avoid banging his head on the low ceiling.

"You know, I'm kind of amazed you could fit through that door," Parker said. "Tiny space for such a big boy."

"Man, fuck off with that. Speak for yourself."

Parker smirked in the darkness as he padded down the stairs, following the steady beam from his flashlight.

The stairway went farther down than he would have expected, deep into the earth until the light from the church above was just a distant memory. They were so far from fresh air by now that all

Parker could taste when he breathed was dust. He marched down with Nate close on his heels until the wooden stairway terminated at a hard stone floor that looked worn smooth by age and countless feet. Parker stamped the heel of his boot against it, just to make sure it was solid, then raised the light to look around.

They stood in a small sort of antechamber, with the stairs on one end and another white door fixed in the other. It was the same style as the last one, but this door was larger, the paint brighter, preserved by the remoteness and stillness of the room. There wasn't a chain pinning this door shut, either; instead, it was held in place by a rough iron latch that, like everything else in the church, had been made by hand back in the day, probably by the town blacksmith or something.

"Where is this?" Nate said, his voice soft with wonder.

"Don't know," Parker said. "Deep, though. Really deep. Under the lake, maybe. Or right up next to it."

He stepped forward and pulled back the arm of the latch, keeping his light fixed on it as he lifted it away from the lock plate and pushed the door open. It didn't scream like the one at the top of the stairs, but actually moved quite easily, swinging back to hang open on well-oiled hinges. Nervously, Parker stepped through into the small room beyond, widening the beam of light as much as he could without popping the head off the Maglite.

He wasn't prepared for what lay inside, though, and kept the flashlight trained on what he saw in the center of the room. Behind him, he heard Nate grumbling as he shuffled in.

"What the . . . ?"

"Yeah."

"The fuck is all this?"

"No idea."

The room was small and dark, and from where he stood, light in hand, Parker could just make out the small ceremonial table—altar?—standing in the middle of it, stacked high with odd decorations. He could see feathers and ancient, tied-off bundles of herbs, piles of carved animal skulls and tarnished silver flatware on top of neatly folded scraps of yellowing paper. From the back of the altar sprouted a fan of thin wooden rods, so tall that it nearly scraped the ceiling, adorned with various trinkets suspended by rough lengths of brown, waxy twine. There were iron nails, battered crucifixes, stoppered phials filled with hair and teeth, more and more and more and more. There were dozens of them, all different ages, all crafted and mounted by different hands. Were these . . . offerings?

"Well ain't this some shit," Nate mused beside him. "The hell was going on down here?"

"I have no idea," Parker said, his eyes searching the altar. "I don't . . ."

It took Parker a minute to see it, but once he did, he had to stifle a yelp. Hanging from one of the wooden poles, between a small, rust-spotted knife and a headless doll, was a watch. Not an old pocket watch or whatever they had used back when there were still people in this town, but a silver-and-black Seiko with a rubber strap, *200m* standing out on its face in the flashlight glow.

Parker knew that watch. He'd grown up admiring that watch. More than once he'd asked his dad about it, and more than once, his dad had given him the same answer: *There are some things that, if they're done right, only have to be done once. I bought this watch for myself back when I was in college, and I've never needed another one. No battery, no electronics, nothing. Just springs and gears inside. The thing runs perfectly too. Long as I keep taking care of it, it always will.*

Parker would've known that watch anywhere—the little bends and creases in the strap, the scuff marks and scratches on the metal, the blocky rectangular markers behind the glass. The hands stood still inside the case, the spring inside the old mechanical stopped dead at 6:15:32. Park reached out to touch it, but at the last second, he hesitated. This watch—his dad's watch—shouldn't have been here. There was no reason for it to be hung in this place with all these other offerings. Touching it, holding it—that would make it real. And if it was real, that would unlock so many other questions that he didn't have the answers to.

But he couldn't *not* touch it. He had to. It was his dad's. Closing his hand around it, Park ran the pad of his thumb around the dial, feeling the dull, notched edge, the metal cold from being left underground like this for . . . well, for however long it had been since his dad had strung it up and abandoned it here.

Standing there, inspecting the watch and the altar around it, something else caught Parker's eye. There was a folded note left beside the others, but this one was new, written on a page torn from a spiral notebook, the paper shock-white in the dark, creased down the middle. With shaking fingers, Parker scooped it up and unfolded it, holding the light on the drawings scribbled across the page in hard-pressed black ballpoint.

It was a map. He could make out the town, and the lake beside it, and yeah, there was the church too. But reeling off from the rear of the church was a dotted line, a sort of curling path that led away into the woods, snaking through the little stick-forest to meet up with a crudely drawn car in between a cluster of sharp, wretched white trees. Atop the car, the artist had scratched a thick, panicked X, marking the spot. Across the bottom of the torn page, they'd scratched something else. It was another drawing, an all-too-familiar black hatchet engulfed in the flames of a campfire. Down in the corner, he'd even signed his work: *DAC*.

There was a high-pitched whining inside Parker's head, the pressure building in his veins as the blood raced through his skull. He felt a sort of strange jigsaw sensation in the air around him, as if the pieces of the puzzle were tumbling into place in slow motion, not yet betraying the whole picture. Still, he knew where he had to go next. Hell, his dad had drawn him a map to it. He had expected this; he'd planned everything.

"We have to go," Parker whispered.

"Go?" Confusion muddied Nate's voice. "Why go? We just got here. I mean, look at this shit, this is crazy. You don't want to, like, look? Why would we go? . . . Parker?"

Snapping his father's watch from where it hung above the altar, Parker turned and sprinted out of the little room, barreling past Nate's ghost and up the rickety wooden stairs at top speed.

13

It didn't take Nicky long to pile the rocks they'd gathered all the way over Josh. She started like Chloe had explained it yesterday: a ring of stones around the outside, then building up off of that outline until he was completely covered. She'd expected the act itself to be hard, and it was, but it felt right, her being the one to do it.

It felt good, taking care of him one last time—even if the cold emptiness that moved through her once it was done made her want to die.

After she'd set the final few stones across his torn, battered face—admitting to herself that the body on the ground didn't even really look like Josh anymore—Nicky slumped down next to her backpack and fished in the side pocket for her Newports. Jabbing one between her cracked lips and saying one last silent *Sorry* to Josh, she sparked the yellow lighter to life and dipped the end of the cigarette into the little flame. Breathing in deeply, she let the sweet menthol smoke fill her lungs; after a few more puffs, she felt a plastic kind of calm start to work its way into her brain.

Nicky reached a hand down to the bottom of her jeans and rolled one of the cuffs up, exposing a wide stripe of olive skin. She could feel the little hairs starting to poke through the surface; she would need to shave when they got back to their lives. Cuffing her pant leg up another turn, she fantasized about the shower she was going to take when she got back. It was going to be decadent; she'd make it last hours, scrubbing all the filth and woe from herself, hiding in the steam, alone and safe. The shower had always been a kind of sanctuary for her, warm and soft and clean and peaceful. She'd give almost anything up to get back to that right now. She supposed the next best thing was her and Chloe getting the hell out of this forest as soon as they possibly could.

And, speaking of, where was Chloe, anyway? It wasn't like her to stay away this long, even if Nicky had asked her for space. She clicked her phone on to check the time—she'd been gone more than an hour now, closer to two—then glanced hopelessly at the bar indicator at the top. *No Service*. Still. Of course.

Taking one final drag and blowing out a thin cord of smoke, Nicky clenched her teeth and ground the lit cigarette into the bare patch of skin between her rolled-up pant leg and the top of her shoe, relishing the sting as the ember bit into her flesh. The heat sizzled against her like the fizz inside a can of Coke, a sound she knew she could hear only because of how quiet it had gotten out here.

She held the smoke in place until the glowing cherry guttered out and she felt like she could breathe again. Unbidden, her mom's voice bubbled up inside her head, an echo from the first time the old woman had caught her hurting herself: *You're such a pretty girl, Nicoletta—I don't know why you'd want to ruin that.*

Dropping the dead butt to the ground, Nicky brushed the ash from the blistering red divot above her ankle. Then she drew a deep breath and, gazing up at where the trees started to scrape against the sky, burst into tears.

Parker barreled out the big front doors and around the side of the church, running blindly for the cluster of trees that stood behind it. Somewhere in his wake, he could hear Nate calling out.

"Parker? Parker, what the fuck, man!"

But he wasn't listening to Nate's bullshit right now. He hadn't even stopped to pick up his pack as he'd dashed out of the main hall. All he had with him was his flashlight, the watch, and the hand-drawn map he'd found on the altar. Everything else he'd left where he'd dropped it by the door in the floor, but that was whatever. He could go back for his stuff later, but right now he had to move; he was too close not to. He could feel it all the way down to his bones—that same sensation he'd gotten when he'd found his dad's initials cut into the burned homestead. It was like walking into a house that you could just *feel* wasn't empty.

He wasn't alone in this forest. His dad was out here, somewhere, and Parker was going to find him.

He pushed through the trees until he found the path, a foot-worn dirt trail just as coiled and winding as it had been on the map. Up ahead, there was another cluster of those weird white trees, and as Parker drew close, Nate stepped out from behind them, materializing himself from nothingness again.

"What are you doing, man?" Nate asked.

Parker charged past him at full speed. The ghost could keep up if he wanted, but Parker wasn't going to stop for Nate or anybody else. Not now.

"He's here, Nate. I know he is."

"Who, your dad?"

"Yeah. My dad."

"Do you know that for sure, or are you just hoping it's true? Because, and no offense or anything, but it seems to me a watch and a shitty little treasure map aren't much to go off of."

The words hit Parker like a cold spear driven through his heart in a single, brutal thrust. Tears prickled at the corners of his eyes, and he wiped them away with the back of his hand, no longer caring if Nate saw or not.

The real Nate was gone. Whatever this thing was, whatever remnant piece of the boy he'd known, Parker didn't answer to it. He didn't owe him anything.

"Fuck off," Parker growled at his dead friend. "I know what I know."

Nate smirked. "Yeah, that's what I thought. Fine. After you."

The two of them snaked through the forest, following the path as it curled and cut between the trees, driving endlessly forward, propelled by Parker's blind momentum. A barbed little ember had caught in his chest, so unfamiliar and alien that it took him a moment to recognize it: *hope*. For the first time in days, weeks, *months*, Parker actually felt like all might not be lost. And nobody got to take that away from him.

His dad was an experienced outdoorsman. Park had known that ever since he was old enough to know things about his parents. There were pictures all over the walls in their house from his dad's myriad adventures—fishing in Colorado, hiking the Rocky Mountains and the Appalachian Trail, driving up the Hudson Valley in New York for two weeks of solo camping, biking the trails in the upper Pine Barrens . . . Dave Cunningham knew how to survive out in the wilderness, even through a savage winter like the one they'd had over the holidays. If anyone could do it, he could, and when Parker found his dad, he'd make him explain. Park would finally know why he'd run away like that, without a word or a note.

Maybe he could even convince him to come home.

Up ahead, the path curved away from the track it had been following for what felt like miles, weaving over a small hillock into another copse of those white bone trees. These were younger than the others, though—little more than saplings, really. They looked like they'd bend or maybe even break if Parker bumped too hard against them. He continued along the trail, in between the ashy white trunks. As he passed through them, he saw something that seemed so completely alien out here in the overgrown forest that it made him stop in his tracks.

There was a car lodged in the earth.

It was old, way older than any car Park had ever seen in his life. Broken down, faded, and left here to rot away, it looked like something out of the pages of a history book. The thing was boxy and sleek, its lines clean and sharp. Parker imagined that back in its day, it must have been a hell of a thing, like it had been carved out of solid shadow. These days, though, it wasn't looking too hot. The metal along its black sides was battered and weatherworn, scarred with holes where the rust had eaten through. The windows had been smashed from their frames long ago and braced over from the inside with branches, tightly lashed together. Its wheels and most of its front end had sunken into the earth as the forest had calmly overtaken the old coupe, so only the hood ornament still poked up through the soil: a wheel shot through with a silver arrow, the word *Pierce* just barely legible in the metal.

Parker didn't have to pull out the map to compare. How many cars had been abandoned this far out in the Pine Barrens? Leaning in closer, a cold chill ran through his body when he realized he recognized the way the branches had been tied together. They looked just like the ones his dad had shown him how to make when they'd been camping before, when he had taught Parker how to build a makeshift shelter.

Just like this, his dad had told him the first time, cinching waxy twine into tight knots, binding the wood together in an uneven plank. *It won't keep everything out, but it'll do.*

". . .Dad?"

The word fell out of his mouth like an afterthought; he hadn't meant to say it, but it boomed so loud inside the walls of his skull that it had to escape somehow.

"*Dad!*"

Parker ran for the sunken coupe like he was trying to race the sound of his own voice. Despite the exhaustion, despite the constant shuddering heartbeat against his ribs, despite it all, he ran for the battered car and curled one big hand around the handle on the driver's side door, nearly ripping it from its hinges in his excitement.

He'd found him. He'd actually found him. He'd known he could; he'd known all along. After months of emptiness and confusion, Parker had really and truly found his father, and everything was going to be okay.

He was half-right.

The body that came tumbling out of the car was preserved, almost mummified; it was thin and withered and covered with a fine layer of grime, but it was definitely him. It wore his clothes, his boots, his tattoo—even though his skin had gone dry and gray, Park could still make out the globe, anchor, and eagle emblazoned with *USMC* above the deep gashes in his wrist and forearm. He could see that there was a matching set of slashes hacked into the other arm too. Wispy licks of gray-speckled black hair sprouted from the top of the half-bare skull, rendered feathery and insubstantial, but its color was still familiar to Park.

The smell inside the coupe was hideous; foul and cloyingly sweet, like bad chicken long gone to rot, it rushed out of the car and caught in the back of Parker's throat, refusing to be spat out. He thought that he might smell that wet grave stink for the rest of his life.

Standing there, beside the ancient coupe, Parker didn't look away. He wanted to, more than anything, but found himself held steady by some deep-down, grown-up part inside him that he barely recognized.

It can't be for nothing, it whispered to him. *He deserves to be seen one more time by someone who loved*—loves—*him.*

Pulling the collar of his T-shirt up over his nose, Park knelt down beside his father and leaned in close to check the car and the body—for what, he couldn't exactly say. Maybe just to see if he could figure out why Dave Cunningham had died.

The interior of the coupe was boxy and stuffy, all of its upholstery rotted away and turned to dust decades ago. There was a knife on the rust-stained floor, a folding blade with a red bone handle Park knew as well as the watch. His dad had carried that pocketknife wherever he went—right up until the end, it seemed. There was a sleeping bag spread across the back seat of the car; it seemed like maybe his dad had been hunkered down in here for a while before things went really wrong. His arms and legs were bent and drawn up close to his chest like dried-out chicken wings, the fingers on both hands braided into knotty, uneven points underneath a jaw that hung open far wider than Parker thought a human jaw could spread.

It looked like his dad had died screaming.

Somewhere in the distance, Parker could hear steady, rhythmic impacts, like far-off gunshots. Maybe it was hunters who had wandered blindly into the maw, about to be eaten by the Barrens—just like Parker, just like his friends, the town, his dad. Just like everybody and everything.

"Holy shit," Nate said behind him. "Is that a car?"

"It is," Parker said, without turning around.

"How old is that thing? Like, honestly, it looks a hundred years old or something."

"Might be."

"How d'you think it got out here? Like old-timey bootleggers? Something like that?"

"Nate."

"What?"

Parker shifted to the side, just enough so his dead friend could see the body that lay on the ground before them.

"Oh, shit," Nate gasped. "Parker, is that . . . is that him?"

Parker didn't budge from where he was crouched. "Yeah."

"Jesus, that's fucked up," said the ghost. "What about his stuff? We should check—maybe he left some of his things in there, like a pack or something?"

"There's nothing in there."

"I mean, you don't know for sure, do you?"

"I know."

"Well, did you at least look? I mean, come on—"

"Nate, I *know*," Parker roared, rising to spin on the ghost, eyes wide with fury.

Nate shut his mouth with an audible *click*. The silence between the two of them swelled and contracted, a volatile, living thing that would explode into a storm if provoked.

"Can you please just get the hell away from me for a minute?" Parker whispered. "Please. I just need a few seconds alone right now. With him. Okay?"

Underneath his lips, Nate licked his teeth slow, his black eyes narrowed.

"Fine," he said. "Whatever you need, friend."

And then he was gone.

Dropping down to sit on the dirt beside the body, Parker reached out a hand to run his bare fingers across its withered, papery skin and the smooth parts where the scalp used to be. He was so dry, so brittle . . . like he was made of corn husks. Slumped there, Parker felt all his futures deflate, all the possibilities cut off at the wrists.

He'd found him. But everything was worse now—not better.

Holding his breath against that cloying grave stink, Parker gathered what was left of his father up in his big, thick arms and deposited him back into the coupe, folding the old sleeping bag over the top of him like he was tucking him into bed. Whispering a few quiet words, Parker ran his hand across his father's desiccated brow a final time, then stood back up and shut the door tight again. There wasn't anything more for him in there.

Farther back, Nate's ghost stood in a small clearing, staring at his feet while the white trees swayed and bent in toward Parker like eager eavesdroppers. Parker walked up without looking too long at his dead friend, pausing in place to roll his head around on its pivot, twisting until the joints in his neck popped like overgrown knuckles.

Head cast down like a chastised child, Nate looked at Parker from under the line of his brow.

"What do you think happened?" That bitter edge had crept into the dead boy's voice again, that sick, mean thing that needled at Parker's nerves and had pushed him over the edge to pull the trigger that first time.

"I don't know. Nothing good. Gets cold out here in the winter, you know? Really cold. Maybe he thought he could last it out, weather through the freeze inside the car. He knew how to hunt. He could find food out here if he needed to. He didn't starve."

"Yeah, no, I saw," Nate said with a sneer. "Looked like he was trying to turn his wrists into ground beef with that bone-handled pocketknife of his."

Parker's stomach lurched at the thought. "It just doesn't seem like him at all."

"And what, fucking off into the great green yonder without any warning last year suddenly does?"

Parker glared at the ghost, and when he spoke, his words came out deathly serious and half-whispered. "What's that supposed to mean?"

Nate bugged his eyes out and threw his hands up, the universal gesture for *don't shoot the messenger.* "I'm just saying, given the other weird shit surrounding the situation *in toto*, isn't it possible that you're not the authority on what he was and wasn't capable of?"

"Shut. Your. Mouth," Parker said, his voice like something rising out of the grave.

"Or what?" Nate taunted. "You gonna hit me? Shoot me again?

Do it, pussy. See what happens. See who looks fucking stupid then. Face it, asshole—you're stuck with me."

Parker didn't move, feeling the tension coil and vibrate in his shoulders, an overwound spring on the verge of exploding.

"You can never go back," Nate said. "You have to know that by now, don't you? You've gone too far, you've done too much bad shit for them to ever forgive you for it. Even if you manage to skip away from shooting me in the fucking face, what are you going to tell your mom? That you found dear old dad withered up like that? Or are you going to lie and say you never found him at all? You really think that you can lie about something like that for the rest of your life, big guy? Or the rest of hers?"

"Fuck you," Parker said, holding his ground. "You don't talk about them. You don't know shit about them, or me."

Nate's eyes flashed to the side, just over Parker's shoulder, and his lips pulled into a bitter smile.

"Yeah, yeah, yeah, fuck me. Got it. But you know what? Me and your dad are both dead, but only one of us came back for you. So maybe—just maybe—I might know a bit more than you think. Make do with what you've got, prick. I'm just trying to help you out. Keep you moving forward, onward and upward, you know, all that inspiring-type bullshit."

Hearing him say it like that, something caught in Parker's head, like a thread yanked from a knit sweater. He could already feel it all unraveling.

"You're not, though. You're not trying to help at all," said Parker.

"The fuck are you talking about? Of course I am."

"No, you're not," said Parker. "You're just trying to wind me up. This whole time, all you've been doing is driving me crazy, making things harder than they needed to be. I was fine out here before you showed up," the big kid said. "I was doing okay. And then I open my eyes yesterday morning, and you're there with some song and dance about how you're like, tied to me or something? What even is that? How would that even work?"

"You think I know?" Nate jeered. "I'm just trying to deal with it, man. I don't know why you're not."

And just like that, Parker felt the thread pull completely loose, the knit falling apart around him. The question was so obvious, he truly couldn't believe he hadn't asked it before now.

"You're not Nate, are you?"

Skitch.

WHACK.

Skitch.

WHACK.

Skitch.

The tip of Chloe's improvised crutch bit into the ground as she stalked away through the trees, until the stiff clacking sound of Nicky piling rocks on top of rocks faded into the background noise of the forest. She marked the trees on her path with the hammer to guide her way back, leaving deep divots in the trunks as fast as she could swing her arm. She wasn't complaining about having some time to herself. With the breeze, it was actually almost nice out here. As if anything in this stupid fucking forest could be called *nice.*

She tried not to think about Josh. She tried not to think about Adam. That . . . *thing*, whatever it was . . . it wasn't their friend anymore. Adam wouldn't—couldn't—have done the things that creature did. Chloe imagined it out there, long and pale and spindly, watching from the shadows, waiting for the right time to strike. She'd wandered too far already; it was too late for her now. Nicky wouldn't even hear her screams when she died.

No, stop it. Stop that shit right now. You can't think like that. Might as well lie down and die right here if you let those thoughts take over, so stop already.

She was falling down that same black well that had taken Nicky so completely, she could see that. What her own mother called *doom spiraling*. And she knew that if she gave into that kind of thinking now, none of them were ever going to escape. She had to keep it together, just for a little longer. Just until they got out.

Squinting her eyes against the light, Chloe turned her head up to see how far the sun had traveled across the sky since she'd been walking—not very far at all. She'd been gone for twenty or thirty minutes at the most, hiking away from camp, scoring the trees as she limped, trying to clear her mind. An hour away from each other would doubtless do she and Nicky both some good.

WHACK. Chloe hacked out another little gap in another big tree and pressed on. The hole in her ribs ached something terrible, but it was at the very least a little familiar. She could rely on it, sort of like her new crutch. The branch under her armpit wasn't even that uncomfortable anymore. It was a hundred times better than no crutch, anyway. She checked the sun again. Yeah, she could go a little farther before she'd have to turn back.

Through the trees, Chloe limped along, listening to the hush and warble of the forest around her, the blood ringing in her head. It was so quiet out here. Stopping for a second, she leaned backward, carefully stretching her spine, feeling the wind blow across her small, skinny frame, and heard the wind trill like it hadn't before. She turned her ear to the wind, listening closer. It took her another minute, but yeah, she was able to pick up on it again. There, in the distance, a murmuring through the trees, the sound of something rising and falling, punctuated with furtive silences.

Were those . . . voices?

She stood there, listening to the round, muffled sounds of people speaking in the distance, too far away to make out individual words, but close enough to hear the music in it—the rising and falling, the pauses, the abrupt interjections, the stutters and false starts. There were at least two people out there, she could tell that much. She was definitely hearing a conversation.

Without warning, her mind flashed to images of police officers, firemen, some team of well-prepared emergency workers dispatched to find them and bring them out of this endless green wasteland. Her heart leaped at the notion. *We're going to get out. We're going to go home.*

Home. Even the word sounded beautiful inside her head. Marking the trees as she hobbled along, Chloe followed the sound, listening to the voices as they grew clearer. There were two of them, one softer, the other louder.

"What do you think happened?"

"I don't know. Nothing good. Gets cold out here in the winter, you know? Really cold. Maybe he thought he could last it out, weather through the freeze inside the car. He knew how to hunt. He could find food out here if he needed to. He didn't starve."

"Yeah, no, I saw. Looked like he was trying to turn his wrists into ground beef with that bone-handled pocketknife of his."

"It just doesn't seem like him at all."

"And what, fucking off into the great green yonder without any warning last year suddenly does?"

Cutting in between the low-hanging conifer branches, Chloe drew closer and closer to the argument. The voices themselves were familiar, somehow. Not firemen, not emergency workers. Something else. Keeping low and quiet, she crested the little hill that stood between her and the voices and peered through an open space in the branches.

Down ahead of her, there was a collection of those evil-looking white trees, the same kind as the one Adam had run her through with. She'd seen them scattered all over the forest, but their placement had never been so dense and deliberate as this. Bare and scabby, the white trunks all stood at attention, like watchful guards. *Sentinel trees*, she thought idly to herself. It almost would have been funny, if the thought of it didn't creep her out so much.

Beyond the sentinel trees, she could see an old-timey car sort of buried in the ground, like it had been driven halfway into a pit and been abandoned. She'd never seen a car like that before. Standing not too far away from it were a pair of young men arguing in tense, raised voices. One of them, she recognized right away—she'd know her cousin's enormous frame from a mile off—but her brain had to work to process the sight of the other one. He was familiar, but in a way that made her brain shiver a bit, like a frozen breeze had blown across its surface. It took her a second to realize, but when she did, her breath caught tight in her chest like an icy hook.

No.

There was no fucking way.

Nate?

In the middle of the clearing, Parker was talking to their dead friend, his broad back knotted tight with tension, his voice drawn and thin. Across from him, Nate stood with his arms crossed, a mean smirk stitched from cheek to cheek. Stooped there, Chloe had to admit that for someone who used to be dead, Nate looked pretty all right. The hole Parker had blown through his head had even healed over. Good for him.

"What's that supposed to mean?"

"I'm just saying, given the other weird shit surrounding the situation in toto, isn't it possible that you're not the authority on what he was and wasn't capable of?"

"Shut. Your. Mouth."

"Or what? You gonna hit me? Shoot me again? Do it, pussy. See what happens. See who looks fucking stupid then. Face it, asshole—you're stuck with me."

Chloe listened to the argument, shifting to try and see both of their faces, but she couldn't get a good view of Parker's. Nate's, on the other hand, she could see just fine. He was grinning at Parker in that same superior way, his lips drawn thin and tight, the smile not even close to his beady black eyes. It was a crocodile smile, the kind you saw just before you got chomped and dragged under the waves.

Chloe knelt there in the trees, totally transfixed by the sight . . . and then Nate turned that smile on her.

It wasn't an accident, a muscle twitch or an errant flicker of the eyes; it was too deliberate for that. No, he meant to do it, to turn his cinder block head and look her right in the eyes. It happened fast—so fast that she was almost sure that Parker missed it. But to Chloe, pinned there by fear and confusion, it was clear as day.

Nate saw her, and he fucking grinned.

Chloe flinched away from that horrible, dead-eyed smile and shrank back into the foliage, desperately trying to hide herself again, crouching down as low as she could against her crutch. Balancing herself precariously on the rough branch, Chloe tucked herself away and watched her cousin argue with a dead boy, praying that neither of them would turn and look her way again.

The ghost's face twisted up like a pretzel, all its features turning in nauseating knots before bouncing back to its original configuration.

"I'm sorry, what?"

"You're not him," Parker said to the apparition. "You never were."

As he said it, Parker reared up, making himself as large as possible. He wanted to be angry; he wanted to explode with a blast of that same volcanic fury he'd felt back at the camp. But that rage had long burned off and buried itself in the ground, gone somewhere so deep that he couldn't lay claim to it anymore. In its place, he'd found a kind of stony resignation, a chilly stubbornness that spread through his body like his veins were freezing. That adult voice, ringing in his head again.

"You look like him, and you're mean like him, but you're not him. You're just wearing his face. So I'm done listening to you."

The ghost scoffed. "What are you talking about, man?"

"The church. The knife. The way you keep knowing things before you should've been able to. Like you've been here before. Like you've seen all this before."

"The knife? You gotta be fucking *kidding me*," Nate raged. "Parker, you saw what I saw. Guy slashed his wrists all to shit. What d'you think he did it with, a rock or a leaf or something?"

"You said *bone-handled*," Park said, his voice drawn like a garrote. "Why would you have said that if you didn't already know?"

"Parker, you don't know what you're talking about. This is crazy. You realize that, right? You sound like a crazy person." Nate—or the pretending thing that had assumed his form—didn't say anything further, the smug grin on its expression melting away to a cold, dead neutral.

"No," Parker said. "Crazy was believing that you could really be him. But Nate's dead, and wherever he is, I don't think he's coming back. You're just a shitty imitation."

Underneath its stolen face, the ghost licked its teeth again and flashed a wide grin at Parker. The silence between them was enormous and obscene, and it lasted a lifetime.

"I tried to do this nice," it said. "I really did."

"What are you?" Parker asked.

"I'm a shitty imitation," the ghost oozed, smiling. "I'm every awful thing you've ever done. I'm nothing. I'm whatever you want me to be."

The dead thing's face began to bubble and droop, a wax mask left to bake in the sun. It stepped back from Parker, looking less human by the second, a sly smile playing at the corners of its dribbling lips. "None of you have any idea what's waiting for you out here. There are horrible things buried in this forest, and you children think you can dance atop the graves and walk away clean. But you'll learn."

Park shivered at the thing's words, at the thought of all the awful dead things hiding in the trees around him. Left to the imagination, this place was filled with horrors. The ghost was proof enough of that. Shame and fear overwhelmed him. Parker had led his friends into a starving, open mouth, and then he'd been fool enough to fall for its tricks. No longer. The spell was broken, the glamour was falling off. The ghost bled like a watercolor. Its features smeared and melted into the air around it, slipping away drop by drop, leaving behind only the vaguest outline of a person, with two burning black eyes set deep in the smudge that used to be its head. It didn't even bother using Nate's voice now; the sound that issued forth from it was a malignant, guttural thing.

"None of you are going to last out here," it said. "This forest eats people. It doesn't matter how careful you are, it doesn't matter how hard you fight—you'll die begging, and broken, and alone. Just like he did." The ghost pointed one runny arm toward the car half-buried in the hard forest floor.

Then—legless, armless—it drifted toward the pale trees, blown along by a breeze that wasn't truly there.

"You deserve what you get," the ghost muttered as it seeped between the white trunks. "All of you."

Then the ghost was gone, like he—*it*—had never been there at all.

Parker felt numb, like his whole body had been struck cold and dead. Standing there, hands bunched into bloodless club fists, he realized he couldn't feel much of anything. His ears rang with the ghost's threats, his mind reeling at the image of the hateful spirit melting away into nothing. *This forest eats people.* Parker was starting to understand how true that was.

There was a rustling close by. He turned and looked toward its source—a cluster of low trees at the top of the little hillock by the path. Suddenly, without the hatchet or the gun, he felt very exposed, almost naked. Nothing to do about it now, he supposed. Strapping his father's watch tight around his wrist, Parker squared his shoulders, ready to throw himself at whatever it was that came through those bushes—ghost, monster, whatever.

Of all the things he was expecting to burst out of the forest, the small brunette girl with the sad smile carrying herself on an improvised crutch didn't even make the list. At first, he didn't even really believe it was her.

"Chloe?"

His cousin raised a hand toward him, a limp, half-hearted wave. "Hey, Parker."

He rushed over to the bottom of the hillock to meet her, holding his arms out to catch her if her legs gave out, but she made it to the bottom despite her unsteady gait and waved him off, keeping her distance.

"What are you doing here?"

"I, uh . . . it's complicated," said Chloe.

"Is it . . . are you actually *you*?"

"Of course I'm me," she said. "Who else would I be?"

He reached a hand out to touch her, but she flinched away, opening up a wound deep in his heart. Still he persisted, bridging the distance, feeling his fingertips sparkle with nerves. *Please be real*, he thought over and over, like a mantra, like a summoning. As if he could make it true if he wanted it hard enough. *Please be real. Please be her. Not another trick. Anything but that.*

When his hand made contact with the fabric of her shirt, the familiar weight of her thin shoulder, a great rush broke free from the core of him, a tidal wave of relief. Automatically, he pulled her into a great bear hug, enfolding her in his thick, long arms, squeezing her tight.

"Jesus, I'm so glad it's really you," he said, fighting back a sob. "I missed you, Chloe. I'm sorry, I'm so, so fucking sorry . . ."

When he let her go, Parker noticed her wincing, one hand pressed to a bloody spot on her shirt that he hadn't noticed before.

"Shit. What happened?"

"Long story," she said. "I'm fine, just . . . just leave it alone, okay? Back up."

Parker quickly drew away from her, like he'd been burned. Or like he'd burned her.

"Where's everyone else?"

Chloe's expression darkened. "Nicky's back at the camp," she said.

"The camp . . . ?"

"Not that one," she said shortly. "Somewhere else. It's not far, straight back that way." She gestured over her shoulder with the camp hammer. "We've been doing our best to keep moving. Trying to get out. It's a lot harder than we thought it was going to be."

This forest eats people.

"Million square acres," Parker said, adjusting his glasses so she wouldn't see the tears collecting in his eyes.

"So helpful," Chloe said. Her tone jabbed at Parker like a dagger. "Really what I need right now, so thank you."

"Chloe, I—"

"Don't," she snapped, her expression suddenly full of fire. "Whatever it is you're about to say, just save it. Okay, Parker? I really don't want to hear any more apologies right now, and especially not from you."

Park swallowed against the lump in his throat.

"What about Josh?" He asked. "And . . . Adam?"

Chloe shook her head, looking away from him. "Josh is gone. Same with Adam, but that . . . that's different."

"Wait, what do you mean *gone*?"

She looked at him like he was stupid; instantly, he understood her meaning.

"Are you kidding?"

She shook her head.

"What the fuck happened?"

Chloe turned evasive. "Something got him."

"Something . . . ?"

Her intense green eyes darted away from his. "Long story." She made a show of shaking off whatever it was she was thinking. "What about you? What have you been doing since . . . yeah. Everything."

"Camping. Looking for my dad." Parker spoke deliberately, carefully, feeling his way around the words like his mouth was filled with razor blades.

"Jesus," Chloe sighed. "Is that why you brought us all the way out here? All the blood and the awfulness, this whole nightmare—it was because you wanted to find him?"

Park couldn't bring himself to say the words, so he just nodded, wincing away when she met his gaze.

"You should have told us," she seethed. "You should have said something, *anything*. We would have understood. We're your friends, you *fucking asshole*. You didn't have to—"

"I know, I know—I'm sorry," Park said, desperate to change the topic.

"Sorry. Doesn't. Fix. Anything, Parker."

"I know."

"So stop saying it."

"I know, I know . . . I just . . ." His voice was shaking something awful now. Parker puffed out his cheeks and blew air through pursed lips, blinking real fast to keep himself from crying. *Not here, not now.* "I'd take it back if I could."

His cousin's eyes were cold and furious.

"So would I."

She turned away from him and hobbled a few steps back toward the little hillock, her shoulders rising and falling in a slow, metronomic wave.

"How'd you get all the way out here?" he asked, watching her go.

Chloe stopped, then glanced down and gave her branch-crutch a little shake. "Limped. Nicky wanted some space so she could bury him. Josh," she clarified.

"*Bury* him? How . . . ?"

"Same as we did with Nate. Collected up some stones and cairned him down. Nicky wanted to do Josh alone, so I took a walk. Ended up out here, saw you talking to . . . yeah."

Something like cold, shivery relief hummed inside of Parker, like crystal struck with the side of a fork.

"You saw him too?"

Chloe nodded. "Was it really him?"

Parker shook his head, clearing the noise away. "No," he said, with grim finality. "It wasn't."

"Then what the fuck was it, because it sure looked—"

"I don't know," Park said, cutting across her sentence. "Something else. Something angry. Something from the forest."

Chloe glared at him, and after another moment, nodded toward the broken-down old car. "So what's in there?"

Parker felt another pointed sob knock at the pit of his throat, and he had to struggle to speak around it.

"Dead body."

Chloe's brow wrinkled. "Whose dead body?"

Parker watched her study his face. Watched her wonder whether he'd killed someone else out here. He hated that he'd given her a reason to consider that.

"Dad," he said.

Her face contorted and fell, the rage there all but evaporated.

"Oh. Oh, Jesus. God, Parker, I am so, so sorry. How did . . . ?"

"I think he did it to himself," Parker said. "Pretty sure, at least. He had marks on both of his . . ." He gestured to his wrists, unable to finish the sentence. "He's been out here for a while."

"Shit. What do you think . . . I mean, why was he all the way out here?"

"Honestly, I don't know," Parker admitted. "Maybe he was just looking for a quiet place to die. He definitely spent some time in that town—"

Chloe held a hand up, stopping him midsentence.

"Wait, wait, wait," she said. "What town?"

14

Walking along the little corkscrew path, he told her all about what had happened to him since Friday, every crazy detail. The ghost, the burned-out house, the town, the church, the altar—he told her everything.

When he finished his side of the story, Chloe didn't hesitate to catch him up on hers: Nicky's rage after she'd overheard Chloe and Parker on the radios, finding Adam in the cave and how he'd gored her with the branch, the vision (or nightmare, or whatever) that had been waiting for her when she'd passed out, the flashes of twisted, alien consciousness while Nicky and Josh had patched her up. How Adam had come back to them, all twisted and broken, how he'd torn into Josh like a rabid wolf.

She even told him about what she'd seen this morning when her skin had touched Josh's. Parker absorbed it all.

Eventually, the path led them to the town Parker had told her about: a hunched collection of homes and buildings backed up against a looming white church. She followed Parker along the footpath until they stood in the middle of the dusty main road, then he jerked his head toward the big church doors.

"I left my stuff in here."

"And underneath the cellar, that's where you found the altar, and the . . . ?" She nodded at the watch on his wrist.

"Yeah. We don't have to go down there if you don't want to."

"Yeah, I wasn't going to ask for a tour. Thanks, though."

"Do you want to at least come inside?"

Chloe turned in place, scanning her eyes around the little town, letting her gaze wander down the main road, all the way out to the crystal-blue lake beyond the town's edge and the wall of white trees that stood on its far shore. It looked like they went on forever over there. Like someone had come along and painted that one section of the Barrens bone white.

There was something about the idea of standing here alone that she didn't like; it filled her with that same kind of prey-type vulnerability she'd felt when the ghost had looked at her back by the car. It made her skin crawl—like she was sticking her arm into the jaws of some ravenous, slavering beast, hoping it wouldn't bite down.

"Sure," she said, trying to sound calmer than she felt. "Might as well."

She followed him up the front steps, standing back while he placed both hands on the heavy double doors and pushed. They swung open with a groan, the rusted metal hinges grinding against themselves.

Inside the church, the light was already fading, what mottled old glass there was left in the windows blocking more sun than it let through. Over by the toppled lectern, Parker's backpack lay on the floor in a jumble, next to a rectangular hatch cut into the floor. Parker knelt to lift his things back onto his shoulders, but all Chloe could look at was the impenetrable darkness beneath them, a perfect void ready to spread and cover the planet the second it broke free of its prison. She clenched her shoulders tightly together and felt the church go silent as she stared at that hole in the floor. The darkness, the silence—it was crushing, an impossible, hideous pressure that would drag you under if you dared dip even a single toe in.

How had Parker descended into a hellish darkness like that only to climb out again like it was nothing? How could anyone do that?

"Ready to go?"

Her cousin's voice loosed Chloe from the cellar's hypnotic pull, but it was what he held in his hand that gave her pause: long and spindly and black, with a silvery line of flint along the blade edge. Warmth rushed into her cheeks as her panic rose anew.

"Parker, where the hell did you get that?"

He raised an eyebrow. "Didn't I tell you about this? I think it might have been my dad's. Found it in a campfire—I think he tried to burn it or something. Here."

He held the black hatchet out to her, but she didn't take it. Memories that weren't hers played across the back of her eyes—screaming children, a woman hiding in a hollow tree, a house engulfed by fire. Just looking at it set every nerve in her body alight with anxiety.

Chloe shuddered. "No," she said. "No, I'd really rather not."

"What? Why?"

"Because I've seen that thing before," she said slowly. "Remember I told you about the reverend, the one who started the fires? In the nightmare?"

Parker nodded. "I remember."

Chloe raised a finger toward the hatchet in his hand. "Yeah, well, I'm pretty sure that that's what he used to do it. There's flint in the blade. You can see it there, if you hold it up to the light."

Parker hefted the hatchet and considered the line of silver along the outermost edge. "But how would something like that even be possible?"

Chloe started to tally off her fingers: "The ghost. The dreams. Adam. Hell, even this town. How is any of this possible? Listen to what I'm telling you. Wherever that thing came from, it has some really seriously bad mojo attached to it."

Park drew the hatchet back to press it against his chest, almost like he was protecting it. "You don't know that for sure. I mean, come on, it's just a hatchet, and it's been helpful, having it. It's seen me through a lot in the past couple days. I can't just . . . get rid of it."

"I know what I saw," Chloe told him. "Whatever that thing is, wherever it came from, it's not just a hatchet."

"Are you positive?"

She didn't even bother saying it again. She just met his eyes and nodded, slow and definite.

Parker dropped his arm, going quiet and letting the hatchet hang down by his side, his eyes dancing from the floor to Chloe to the hatchet and back again.

"I'm still going to keep it," he said, with grim finality.

A surge of fury raced up Chloe's spine at his stupidity, his stubbornness. She thought about barking at him, raging at him, but what good would any of that do?

"Fine," she said with a sigh of resignation. "Just . . . please be careful with it, okay?"

"I will."

"But like, really careful, Parker. *Really* careful."

Parker made an annoyed sound in his throat. Without another word, he turned and walked away, beelining for the church doors. Chloe stood there for another moment, feeling herself drawn again toward the gaping darkness that boiled up from the floor. Setting her shoulders against its gravity, she kicked the hatch door shut with a *BOOM* and then turned and followed her cousin out into the wilderness once again.

The walk back to the camp wasn't as arduous as the trek out here had been, or maybe it just didn't feel like it. Maybe the weight that had lain on Chloe's heart since she saw Parker standing out in front of that old car, arguing with a ghost, had finally started to slip away, bit by bit. The farther they walked together, the more things felt . . .

well, *normal*, for lack of a better word. Like they were just *them* again, two against the world. For a little while, it didn't matter that Chloe was limping because she'd been fucking stabbed or that Parker had shot their friend and stranded them all here. The gun and the black hatchet didn't matter. The nightmares or the ghost. None of it. All the details just fell away, and it was like they were six again, going walking in the creek by their grandpa's house—*going adventuring*, they'd called it. They'd stay out for hours, soaking their jeans and sneakers, digging in the dirt, hurling rock after rock into the water, trying to decipher what the graffiti left by the older kids on the cement pylons meant, both of them playing at their own imaginary versions of Indiana Jones.

Chloe hadn't felt anything like this in years, and she was glad to have it returned to her, if only just for a little while. Back at the camp, she knew reality would be waiting for them there, with all of its stubborn, ugly horrors. But reality could wait. For now, for a little while at least, they could just walk together and be okay.

Guided by the orange afternoon light, the cousins followed the deep green gashes hacked into the trees to where a small campfire popped and crackled in a clearing. Nicky slumped beside it, her eyes a million miles away.

Chloe emerged from the trees first, and Nicky smiled with relief when she saw her. But when Parker trailed Chloe out of the woods, Nicky's smile vanished, like a magic trick. She was on her feet in an instant, rushing over to the cousins in long, furious strides, her hands knotted into hard, bony fists.

"You *motherfucker*," she seethed.

Behind her, Chloe heard her cousin come up short and say, "Nicky, wait—"

"You *fucking asshole*," Nicky spat at him. "You total fucking *cunt*."

Chloe took a step forward, trying to put herself between the two of them, but on the crutch, she could only maneuver so much. The fact of the matter was that Nicky was still way more agile than Chloe had ever been, even at her healthiest. Now, hurt and riddled with infection, Nicky wove around her like she barely existed at all.

Leaning on her crutch, Chloe twisted around just in time to see Nicky lash an open hand across Parker's face, the sharp impact of it *crack*ing between the trees. Parker recoiled, his head snapping back on a hinge, but he didn't try to stop her. Incensed, Nicky reared back and hit him again, harder than the first time. Chloe could already see a pair of glowing handprints rising on Parker's cheek, one on top of the other. She hit him, and she hit him, and she hit him some more, each successive impact ringing out louder than the last.

"Fuck you, Parker," she snarled. "Fuck you! They're dead because of you! Because of you and your *bullshit*!"

"Nicky—" Parker began, but she slashed at him again, drilling another full-force blow across his chops. A bit of blood had started to collect at the corner of his lips, and he licked it away, his eyes big and sorrowful.

Chloe could see Nicky running out of steam. Carefully, she took her by the elbow and pulled her away, marveling internally at the tension in Nicky's body; she was practically vibrating with rage. Holding her, Chloe watched as the hate tattooed into Nicky's face mutated again, melting like candle wax into anguish and desperation. Unbidden, tears spilled from the bottoms of her eyes, leaving shiny silver tracks down her freckled, sunburned cheeks.

"It's his fault," Nicky gasped into Chloe's shoulder. "All of it. He should have died out there. He should have fucking died out there, Chloe."

"I know it is," Chloe said, her voice a tender hush. "I know. But we need to stick together if we're going to get out of here. Right?"

Nicky sobbed and shuddered, but a second later, she nodded.

"I know," she choked out.

"I'm sorry," Chloe whispered to her. "I wish it didn't have to—"

"I understand," Nicky said, cutting her off. "But fuck. *Fuck.*"

Behind them, Parker cleared his throat. "Nicky . . ."

Suddenly, Nicky turned free of Chloe's grasp again, thrashing like a fury, stabbing a long, sharp finger out at Parker, who just stood there and took it, like a cow on a factory belt.

"No, no, no, no," she screeched in his face as she drummed him with tiny fists. "You! Don't! This is your fucking fault, Parker! You did this to us! We wouldn't have ever come out here if it wasn't for you. We wouldn't be stuck, Nate and Josh wouldn't be dead, *none of it!*"

"I'm sorry," Parker whispered. "Nicky, I'm so sorry."

"Oh, you're *sorry*?" she fumed. "He's sorry. Chloe, did you hear that? Parker's *sorry*. Except sorry doesn't fix a goddamn thing, and it sure as hell doesn't bring anyone back from the dead."

For a second, she looked like she was going to hit him again. Chloe stepped forward to rest her free hand on her shoulder, as if that might calm Nicky somehow.

"You're *sorry*," Nicky spat. "Sure you are, you miserable piece of shit."

Park's expression fell, and he held his hands out to his sides, utterly defeated. "Nicky, I never meant for any of it to happen like this. You have to believe me. I didn't mean for any of this—"

Underneath her hand, Chloe felt Nicky bristle in the half moment before she dashed forward, crashing into Parker and bunching both of her hands into the fabric of his shirt as she reared up to scream in his face.

"No, no, no! No! Shut up, shut the fuck up!" Nicky howled at the top of her lungs. "You don't—you *don't*—get to do that. Not now, not ever, you fucking, fucking *murderer*."

Chloe watched that word—*murderer*—land against Parker like Nicky had hit him with a sledgehammer. In an instant, he recoiled and wilted, all the life knocked clean out of him. But Nicky wasn't done. Not quite yet. Stumbling back from him, her face twisted into a mask of hate, black fire in her bloodshot eyes.

"You should be dead already," she said, her voice terribly calm. "I wish you'd had the balls to do what was right and killed yourself after what you did."

Nicky jerked her shoulders, like she was going to leap at Parker again, maybe rake his eyes out this time, but Chloe stepped forward and crossed an arm over her breastbone, holding her back. Let Nicky tear through her first, if she wanted to get to him that bad. She knew she couldn't actually stop her if Nicky decided to do it, but Chloe was done letting her friends kill her friends. There weren't that many of them left now.

So she dug her feet into the loose dirt, roadblocking Nicky as best she could. "Nicky, don't—"

"No," said Nicky, shifting her bloodshot gaze down toward Chloe once more. "I can't. I won't. I'm done."

She wrenched herself free of Chloe's tenuous grasp and stalked away, past the fire and the sleeping bags, into the trees where the shadows were heaviest. Chloe stared at the ground until she was sure Nicky was gone.

"She's okay," she said after a moment.

Parker shook his head. "No, she's not."

"She will be. Eventually. She just needs time. She's been though a lot, man. We all have."

"I know," said Parker. "Chloe, really, I'm—"

But Chloe waved him off. "Do me a favor. Stop apologizing, okay? It's just making things worse."

Parker opened his mouth as if to respond, but then closed his lips again and just nodded at her. Chloe nodded back, then limped over to her sleeping bag and eased down to lay flat on her back with her eyes closed, hoping for sleep. Maybe in dreams, things would be better.

Eventually, Nicky came back from wherever she'd stormed off to, but when she did, she did so wordlessly and without even a side-glance at Parker. She was still fuming, but at least she was doing it quietly.

Chloe was thankful for that. She'd half expected Nicky to come back having built up another head of steam to take out on Parker, and the hell of it was that he would have let her. No doubt about it. Fortunately, it didn't come to that. Nicky simply materialized out of the shadows and paced over to her place by the fire, then sat down and fixed her hollow gaze on the flames. Chloe knew better than to ask if she was okay. She knew she wasn't. None of them were okay anymore.

Parker made up his own part of the camp in the golden light of the coming sunset, setting up his sleeping bag next to theirs, working silently while Chloe started checking over their provisions. They had food, sleeping bags, their backpacks, Nate's bag of fireworks, Josh's med kit, and little else. The food was already running low too; she and Nicky and Josh had worked through more than she'd thought the past two days, and today hadn't been much different, even without Josh there to help. Still, Chloe couldn't help feeling like there was more missing than there should have been. Maybe that was just hunger distorting her perception.

From the bottom of the bag, she fished out a can of sardines in hot sauce and tossed it to her cousin, along with a skeevy off-brand granola bar. Then she passed a packet of Pop-Tarts and a sheet of gas station jerky to Nicky, setting aside a Twix and a small tube of honey roasted peanuts for herself. Splitting their last warm can of beer between the three of them, they ate in silence and fed the fire as the light streaming through the trees dimmed and died.

When she'd polished off her dinner, Nicky crawled into her sleeping bag and rolled over, pointedly showing her back to her friends. For a minute, Chloe thought she was faking, but after a minute, they could both hear that familiar, tiny handsaw drone floating out of

Nicky's mouth. She'd never fake a snore like that—not to sell a lie. It would be too silly, and while Nicky was a lot of things, even on her best day, silly didn't rank.

Still, Chloe waited a few minutes longer before she twisted in place to look at her cousin, and asked, "Can we talk?"

Parker wiped crumbs and oil on his jeans. "About what?"

"Nate."

"Thought we already did," said Parker. "He's dead. Murdered," he corrected himself grimly. "What else is there?"

"Not him. The other one."

Across the fire, Parker clenched his eyes shut and rubbed at them with his thumbs, the expression on his face creasing his forehead into a series of deep canyons.

"Oh, right," Parker said. "That."

"Listen, we don't have to if you don't want to—"

"No, it's fine." It was most definitely not fine. "What do you want to know?"

Chloe shot a glance over toward Nicky's sleeping form, eyeing the slight rise and fall of her chest underneath the soggy nylon.

"Maybe we should . . . ?" She nodded toward the trees, then back at Nicky. "Even with what she's seen, what she's been through . . . hearing it might be too much for her, asleep or not."

"Yeah," her cousin said. "Sure."

Parker rose quietly and stepped over to offer her a hand up. Chloe popped the last little handful of sugar-crusted nuts into her mouth, then stitched her fingers through his and let him lift her off the ground like she weighed next to nothing. She always forgot just how gigantic he was, how powerful he'd gotten in the last few years. To Chloe, he was still the same size as her. She thought he might always be, at least in her head.

Together, they walked off into the encroaching darkness and folded themselves in between the trees, the dancing light from the campfire still close enough to cast shadows across both of their faces. Taking her crutch in both fists, Chloe pitched her back against a bare tree trunk while Parker stood with his hands stuffed deep in the pockets of his jeans, shoulders hunched up around his neck.

"So what do you want to know?"

It didn't take a genius to see that Parker really, really didn't want to talk about this, but Chloe needed to.

"So, you said he—it—showed up yesterday morning, right?"

"Soon as I opened my eyes, yeah. He was just *there*, waiting for me to wake up," he said.

"And it was always him? It always looked like Nate?"

"Yeah. I mean, no. I'm not sure."

"How do you mean?"

"He was . . . blurry," Parker said. "Like he was out of focus. All his edges were sort of soft. At first I thought it was me, you know? Bleary from sleep or something. Wasn't wearing my glasses. But you saw what happened."

Chloe remembered. She'd watched as the ghost's form had bled away, leaving behind an indistinct, person-shaped smudge in its place, a hateful thing with void-black eyes and a long, Cheshire cat mouth filled with crooked teeth.

"Yeah," she said, shuddering. "I saw. I know."

"No, you don't," Parker said. "You don't know. It didn't just look like him, it talked like him—fuck, it even walked like him. Like a nearly perfect copy, Chloe."

"But you figured it out. You saw past it."

"Yeah, after two days," he said. "Hooray for me."

"What was it that did it?"

Parker shook his head and turned his sad, intense gaze out toward the darkness of the woods.

"It was the small things," he said. "Lots of little stuff that just . . . built up."

Chloe leaned in, meeting his eyes. "There had to be something. Something that started tipping the scales."

Park shook his head. "Honestly? It was the way he laughed. That . . . thing, it laughed differently than Nate. I didn't notice it at the beginning—or at least, I told myself I didn't notice it. But it wasn't Nate's laugh. There wasn't any joy in it—it was just this ugly, hollow noise. Nate only ever laughed when he meant it," he said. "You remember."

"Yeah," Chloe said. She knew what he was talking about. His laugh was one of the things that had drawn them to Nate in the first place—the way he would crane his head back and let these big belly laughs fly when something was really, really funny. It could fill up a room, Nate's laughter. "He had a really great one, didn't he?"

Park opened his mouth to speak, but no words came out. Chloe understood.

"That thing . . . the way it laughed was this wet, dead noise. Like it was choking on its own blood," he said after another moment. "Everything about it was like a fun house mirror version of Nate, all the mean parts and none of the good. Like being shitty and cruel enough would keep me from noticing what was missing."

Chloe looked down at their shoes. "I don't know, Parker. He'd been doing a pretty good job of that back before you shot him, too."

It was true—in the past year or two, something fundamental had changed inside of Nate, and while he still laughed sometimes, it had grown rare, reserved only for the times when he absolutely couldn't hold it back. There had been something hard and bitter growing inside him; they'd all noticed it. His tongue had sharpened to a razor point, while his sense of humor had started to verge closer and closer to vicious. Maybe it was kids at school, or his grades, or his parents; none of them could have said for sure. Even at the best of times, Nate didn't talk about his life much, and nobody ever felt like they could ask. Maybe that was the point. So instead they'd just kept on pretending, letting him get away with it, acting like there was nothing wrong with him shooting his mouth off—until it had finally gotten him in the kind of trouble none of them could take back.

"What do you think it was?" Chloe asked. "The ghost, the, the . . . whatever. If it wasn't him, what was it?"

Park turned away from her. "Something else. Something that eats the things that die out here, maybe. Whatever it was, I think it was wearing his face to get me to do what it wanted . . . but we never got to what that actually was."

"You're welcome," Chloe said with a half-smirk.

"I'm serious, Chloe. It was trying to keep me away from you," he said. "Whatever else it was planning, it wanted me alone."

"Then why give you what you want? Why let you find your dad?"

Parker's face wrinkled up. "Because if I found him dead, there was one less giant reason for me to ever go back."

"But why keep you here?" Chloe asked. "What good does it do, keeping you around? What does the ghost, whatever it really was, get out of it?"

Parker blew air through his nose. "Why turn Adam into some horrible, bloodthirsty thing? Why do any of it? It's just being cruel for cruelty's sake. We're ants under a magnifying glass. It wants something to torture."

"I really don't think that's it," said Chloe. "Listen, imagine it's not about keeping you as a blood doll or whatever. It's not about punishing you, nothing like that. Just think. Why would anything—anybody—not want you to leave here?"

Park's eyes searched hers, his brows sloping off to the sides.

"Maybe it doesn't want to be alone."

Chloe shrugged. "It's possible, at least."

"But that still doesn't answer the question of *why*, though. Why torture us, why warp Adam and kill Josh? Why take away everything good I have, every quiet thought, every moment of peace? Why make life so fucking awful for me, for all of us?"

Chloe shook her head. "Because if there's nothing left in the world for you, then nothing outside of the Pine Barrens matters. You could just stay here forever."

"What, like my dad did?" His eyes were suddenly full with tears, and he wiped them away with the back of his hand before they had a chance to spill over.

"He came out here for a reason. Maybe he was seeing ghosts too," Chloe said.

"What, like it tried to get in his head? You really think that's possible?"

"You guys have been coming out here for years, Park. Him even longer than you. No one could blame him if it got inside his head after all that time. Especially if it was wearing another mask. I mean, come on, it had you fooled, and you're the smartest person I know," Chloe said.

"I'm not that smart," he told her. "I still fell for it."

"That's the point. Anyone would have. I did, and I only saw him for like thirty seconds," she said. She reached a hand out and took her cousin's oversized one, giving it a firm squeeze. "Let yourself off the hook for that, at least."

"You know, the fucked up thing is that I wanted it to be real," he whispered. "I wanted more than anything for it to really be Nate. I thought that if it was, maybe I could get a second chance with him, do things different, or at least try and make it right."

Parker slumped back, letting his shoulders fall. He looked like he was going to start crying again.

"When he first showed up, I thought he was a hallucination. Like, I really thought I'd lost my mind." Parker sighed, pulling his hand away. "Like he was something I'd dreamed up, an imaginary friend to keep me company or something. After he stuck around, I don't know. I thought, why not? Why can't it be him? Looks like him, sounds like him, so . . ." He jerked his head out toward the trees and the growing dark. "It was just nice to not be alone for once. Even if it was Nate."

"Parker, you're not alone. You haven't ever been alone." She tried to take his hand again, but he jerked it back.

"Yeah," Parker said, "I have been. For months now. Ever since my dad left."

"That's not true—"

"It is," Parker cut her off. "You know it is. My mom's barely functional and getting worse. She holds it together just enough to not get fired from her job and to buy another pint of gin. But she's not my mom anymore, Chloe. She's just this sad, bled-out shell that I live with. Another ghost to add to the list. Don't act like you don't know what I'm talking about, because I know you do."

Chloe shook her head and looked away from her cousin, hoping he couldn't see her cheeks and neck burning apple red in the soft darkness. Yeah, she'd had some idea of what Uncle Dave's disappearance had done to Aunt Lori. She'd seen the red-thread veins breaking out across her nose and cheeks, the glassy glaze that filmed her eyes. Hell, even as far back as Christmas, with the splotches and stains on her clothes, the juniper fumes on her breath, Chloe had known something was really wrong. Everybody knew. It was way worse than normal family-holiday drunk.

Parker had barely spoken to anyone that day. He'd just sat in the corner on his phone, his face knotted with rage. After they'd finally left, the rest of the grown-ups, her parents included, all stood around the kitchen, gossiping and bemoaning the sad, tragic state of the Cunninghams. Except none of them had bothered asking if Park or Lori needed help. Nobody had said anything. They were content to sit there and smile and open their presents and ignore everything that had gone so terribly wrong. It was easier for everyone if they just pretended.

On the way home, her mom and dad had actually asked her if she'd had a nice time. Like nothing had happened at all. Like they'd forgotten.

"Okay, but you've had us," said Chloe. "Me, and Adam and Nicky and—"

Park shook his head. "No, I didn't."

"What? Of course you did—"

"No," he said, "I didn't. Ever since Dad disappeared, you guys have pulled back from me. All of you. You know you have."

"Parker, come on, that's not fair—"

All of a sudden his hands were on her shoulders, holding her at attention. His eyes were still wide and watery, but there was a seriousness there that she hadn't seen before. A Parker she'd never met, filtering through to the surface.

"No, listen to me. I don't blame you—I get it. It's a lot to deal with. *I've* been a lot to deal with. You've done what you could, but you can only do so much. You have your own problems to deal with, your own shit that doesn't have anything to do with me. You have your own lives. I'm not mad." He let her go and leaned back again, wiping at his eyes. "Shit's just been hard, you know? It sucks, dealing with something like this on your own."

He wasn't wrong—she *had* pulled away from him. They all had. It wasn't like they'd all gotten together one day and decided *Fuck Parker*; it wasn't even a conscious choice. He just hadn't been the easiest person to be around since his dad had vanished, so it was easier to not be around him. They still ate lunches together, they still hung out, but yeah, they did it a little less than they used to. Or they'd just not invited him as much. Chloe had hoped he wouldn't notice, but of course he had. He wasn't stupid.

"I'm sorry, Parker," Chloe said, her voice quavering. "You deserve better than that."

"Almost everybody deserves better," said Parker. "It doesn't mean we necessarily get it."

She looked up at him again, and in the shadows and low light, she caught another glimpse of the man he'd grow up to be someday. Quiet and thoughtful, and more than a little weary. She could see where the wrinkles would dart in at the corners of his eyes, the lines of his cheekbones that would thin out and grow blade-sharp with age, the way his hair would get shaggy and go salt-and-pepper long before it seemed like it should. Just like his dad's.

"So what do we do now?" Chloe asked.

"I think we do what you guys have been trying to do since we first showed up."

"We pack up and get the fuck out of here."

"Yep."

Chloe took a deep breath and blew all the air out of her lungs in a tight, thin stream. "Okay. How do we do that? You're the camper here."

"Forest has got to end at some point," said Parker. "We just keep walking the way we've been walking. Eventually we've got to hit something. This is New Jersey, for god's sake, not the wilds of Montana or whatever. There'll be an expressway or another campground or something eventually."

"Except for the fact that the forest doesn't want us to leave," she said.

"Yeah, except for th—"

A distant scream split the night around them, the sound of it ragged and horrible and far too clear to be anything but human. Chloe nearly jumped off the tree, twisting her whole body to look back toward the glow of the campfire, her eyes painfully wide. She couldn't see much from where they stood, just the fire and three empty sleeping bags.

Wait.

A blast of cold exploded in her stomach.

"Oh, Christ, *Nicky*," she gasped.

15

The voice, high and lilting, cut through Nicky's dreams like a hot razor, starting at the very outermost edges, slicing deeper and deeper inward until the sound of it was all she could hear.

"*Nicky . . . Help . . . Help . . .*"

Curled up in her sleeping bag on the bottom of the ocean, she rolled over and fought to stay underneath the heavy black waves. Sleep was good. Sleep was safe. When she was asleep, she didn't have to think about or feel anything that she didn't want to. At night, in dreams, she could be anywhere she wanted, be anyone she needed to be. Yet the voice pierced every last layer, a bright, bladed beacon sent to raise her from the half-death of sleep, back to the land of the living.

"*Nicky, I'm . . . hurt . . . Nicky, please . . .*"

She felt herself surfacing from the depths, crashing through vertical miles until she found herself laying on the forest floor again, bundled in nylon and still as scared and angry as she'd been when she'd closed her eyes. Gradually, she let her eyes hinge open, adjusting to the darkness that had fallen around her, watching the campfire shadows that danced and played across the trees in the distance. She lay there and gazed at the flickering shapes as they jumped and skittered, warped in on themselves and became something new, then changed again.

After a time, she blinked the fog of sleep away and craned her neck farther out of the bag, straining to hear that voice wending through the night again. A moment later, it came to her once again, floating on wings wrought from the breeze itself. So light, so delicate, but there. Undeniably there.

"*Babe, I'm here . . . I need . . . help . . .*"

Josh.

He was out there. He was still alive. Jesus Christ, she'd buried him alive.

Screaming out in horror, Nicky was out of her sleeping bag in a heartbeat, her pulse a machine-gun death beat in her temples. Her whole body throbbed along with the rhythm, the veins in her neck and in her legs nearly singing with pressure. She took off into the dark without hesitation, fleeing the light, not even pausing to pull on her shoes. She could go barefoot. Her soles could take the drubbing; it was a small price to pay to get him back.

"*Just like that, love,*" his voice urged her on, louder now, clearer. "*Come on, I'm so close. All you have to do is reach out, and I'll be there . . .*"

Nicky scrambled into the woods, madly flailing her hands out in front of her face, slapping away low-hanging branches and patches of scrub that dared stand in her way. Thorns and broken sticks and brambles slashed at her bare skin, leaving red-hot welts in their wake, but she didn't notice or care if she did. Getting to him was more important.

"I'm coming," she whispered to herself.

"*I know you are. I'm so excited to see you. I love you so much . . .*"

"I love you too," gasped Nicky. All around her, the forest hunched up its shoulders and enfolded her inside itself while she outraced the campfire light, sprinting madly into the dark. She'd always been fast on her feet, ever since she was a little kid, but only now did it feel like there was a purpose to it, a reason. Josh was out there, and she would find him, wherever he was. She could be there in an instant if she wanted to. Her legs would carry her.

He was somewhere out there, and when she found him, everything was going to be worth it. All the blood and pain and loneliness would have paid for something, and she was never going to let him go again.

She was so close now. She could almost feel the warmth of his skin in the trees ahead of her, barely out of her grasp. But not for much longer.

Nicky kept running.

They followed the sound of her crashing through the trees as fast as they could, limping through the darkness in pursuit of their friend. The hole in Chloe's ribs screamed with pain as she juddered along, so much worse than it had been before, but she swallowed back the agony and kept pace, nearly dragging herself forward by the stick nocked tightly under her armpit. The ground was rough and uneven, hard to navigate in the shadows, but she managed it, though going slower than she would have liked.

Pausing for a moment, Chloe drew a deep breath and raised her head to the night sky.

"Nicky!" she howled. "Nicky, wait!"

Overhead, the moon slipped free of the clouds, a cold, white scythe shearing the darkness apart, casting scattered light across the forest floor. Chloe squinted through the scant glow, trying to see any sign of her friend, but finding nothing.

"What would she run for?" chuffed Parker, a few strides ahead. "Why would she even do that?"

"I don't know," Chloe panted back. "I have no idea."

Somewhere in the distance before them, the scream came again—closer now, but no less horrible. Chloe drew up short and pulled in another lung-bursting breath.

"Nicky, we're coming! Just tell us where you are!"

Only silence greeted her. Up ahead, Parker stopped and turned back to face her. "We can't keep going like this," he said. "We're going to get lost."

"Just a little farther," said Chloe. She could still see the campfire behind them, though judging by how small it was, they'd already gone deeper into the trees than she'd thought. "We can go a little farther and be okay, right?"

Parker's face looked unsure. "I don't know," he said. "Maybe. Probably."

"Good enough for me." Chloe threw herself forward again, ignoring a fresh howl of agony from her wound.

They were going to find Nicky. She couldn't lose anyone else.

The two cousins dashed into the night until the fire back at their camp was just a far-off pinprick of light in the distance. That's when the wave hit her. At first it had been faint; another tidal rush of the low-level dread she'd been nursing ever since Parker had pulled the gun on Friday, exhaustion and nerves fucking with her again. But when the wave really hit, her body lit up with a searing black light that rose from the earth and soil, from inside her, and dragged her completely under.

Instantly, the dread was all she could feel. It eclipsed the burning in her lungs, the pain blowing through her ribs, the rubber in her legs. It all washed away, little more than thin silt to that churning black crash. Stumbling underneath its weight, Chloe stabbed her crutch out into the soil to keep from toppling over, then pitched forward anyway and retched.

Beside her, Parker recoiled, then lunged forward to catch her, as if she were falling. She might have been falling. She might have never stopped. She couldn't tell anymore.

"Jesus, Chloe—"

"We shouldn't be here," she gasped, dribbles of green vomit from her lips staining his forearms. "We shouldn't . . . something's wrong.

Something's really wrong here. It's in the earth, and the trees . . . Jesus, Parker, *what the fuck is happening*?"

"What is it?" Parker asked, bracing her in place, holding her upright, his big slab arms surprisingly tender. He'd always been gentle with her, even when they were kids.

"Just . . . oh, *god* . . ." she gasped, trying and failing to suppress a dry heave. In the distance, another scream rang out, pinballing madly off the trees, but she only barely heard it over the din roaring beneath her skin.

"We can stop," said Parker. "We can stop here for a minute."

"No, we can't! Parker, she's out there—she's out there, and she's going to die," Chloe stuttered, straining uselessly against him. It was like trying to shove past a brick wall. "We're the only ones who can help. We have to, we have to help—"

"I know. I know, Chloe. Here, just breathe for a second," he said. "Okay? We'll catch up with her, I promise. Just try and catch your breath."

Eyes still shut, she let him lead her, one arm locked around her shoulders.

"Here," he said, guiding her to a place where dead leaves crunched underfoot. "Just lean here for a minute, all right? There's a tree right in front of you, okay? All you have to do is reach out and lean against it. Do you think you can hold yourself up?"

Eyes shut tightly, she sucked cold air into her lungs and held it there, trying to get her body back under her own control. Breathing out in a thin stream, she nodded in what she thought was his direction.

"Okay," Parker said. "Okay. Just . . . here. Just keep your hands out. It's literally right in front of you. Just like that, okay, easy now . . ."

He guided her slowly until she was moving under her own power again. For half a second, everything was quiet. Everything was calm. She was going to be okay.

Then she opened her eyes and saw it at the last moment—a flash of dead, ash-white bark, the exact texture of a scab.

"*Oh fuck, Parker, no*—!"

But it was too late. Chloe pitched forward, and her body, the traitor, reflexively stuck both hands out to catch itself against the sentinel tree, despite the voice in her head screaming *Don't touch it don't touch it, please don't fucking touch it*—

Her bare palms slapped the ugly white wood as one, and for a second, she didn't feel anything.

Then, she felt everything.

Reality fell away from her in mangy clumps. She felt it collapse out from under the soles of her shoes, leaving her floating in an empty void, her heart and guts stuck in that motionless, held-breath moment before the roller coaster plunge. She tried to draw breath, but there was no air for her to breathe. She tried to move, but there was nowhere for her to go. She was trapped in the nothing and nowhere, locked in her own body for a single, horrible moment that lasted lifetimes, until a new reality began to assemble itself around her. Piece by piece, it materialized, and she found her footing, coming to rest on a tiny patch of dirt while the forest fell into place.

It was daylight again. Or still. She had no idea how long she'd been standing here, bathing in the cold white glow like this. She craned her neck toward the bleached-out sky. The sun hung overhead, perfectly still and punishingly close, yet she felt no heat. She watched as the trees swayed and danced in the breeze, but felt no wind against her skin. The forest around her seemed somehow thin, *as if it were made from papier-mâché. Like all it would take was working her bare hands into the fragile cracks to tear it apart in sheets.*

This was the forest, but it wasn't her version of the forest. She hadn't seen this place yet.

She surveyed her surroundings as they drifted into place. Close by, she could hear footsteps, quick and light, getting closer. Chloe turned to look and saw a young woman come running out of the trees. She wasn't much older than Chloe herself—perhaps twenty—and she was wearing a long black dress, her battered leather shoes moving briskly underneath its hem. Her face was blister-red around spaced-out eyes, puffy cheeks smeared with earthy black stains, slashed through with tear tracks. Standing there, watching her approach, Chloe raised a hand and waved, but the girl took no notice of her. She didn't seem to see her standing there at all.

Chloe knew who she was. She'd seen her before, in the middle of the night, standing in a field as an estate house burned behind her.

Mary Kane. Her name was Mary Kane.

The girl whipped past her without a glance, and as if dragged along by some invisible cord, Chloe followed. Automatically, she winced and braced herself against a fresh shock of pain from the hole in her ribs, but the pain never came. Padding after the strange young woman, Chloe found she could move effortlessly, like she'd never been gored at all. Idly, one of her hands went to the spot in her side where the wound had been punched into her, but there was nothing there. No blood, no sodden hole driven through her flesh, no explosion of hurt.

She looked down and felt a sickening vertigo lurch when she realized she couldn't see her feet. She couldn't see them, because her feet weren't there. They weren't anywhere. They were just . . . gone. It was the same with her legs, her midsection, her arms, her chest, all of her. Oh. She was in another memory, vision, nightmare, whatever. Good to know.

Letting herself be pulled along through the trees, Chloe took a mental inventory of the things she'd seen before. There had been the scarecrow man, the maid, the dead family, and the burning house. The escape into the forest. The strange, hypnotic voice whispering to Mary from inside her own head. The massive old oak. She could feel the way Mary had felt, escaping the tall man's clutches again, the elation of escape and bottomless shame at what she'd let him do to the Ganders family. They hadn't deserved that. They'd been patient and kind and good, and Simon had slaughtered them like they were cattle, while Mary ran.

Every so often, Chloe would glance at their surroundings, pausing to get as best a read as she could on where they were, where they'd been, where they were going. She knew that Mary didn't have any sort of plan, but still the older girl ran on with blind determination, Chloe dogging her every step. Every so often, a sound would slip free of the trees behind them, an odd note here or there, too musical to be a mistake. It happened a few times before Chloe understood.

Someone back there was singing.

The two girls sprinted past a winding creek and over another hill to a place where the trees suddenly just . . . stopped, making way for a wide clearing that looked like a scar riven into the earth, a stretch of empty ground surrounding an ancient, gnarled tree. Chloe had seen this before too.

It must have stood a hundred feet high, maybe two hundred, with heavy, knuckled branches grasping out from its massive, knotted trunk, and leg-thick roots stitched into the earth around it in a rough circle. There was a hole torn in its side that she liked the look of—a man-sized hollow filled with shadow, sheltered from the midday sun.

Black soil crunched under Mary's feet as they approached the enormous old oak tree. Chloe looked to Mary, her face scrunched up in thought, and felt what the girl was feeling: her lungs burning, her legs nearly dead, her head pounding, her hands starting to go numb. A body wasn't meant to go this far for this long. She didn't have much left in her now. All she wanted to do was rest.

Mary didn't hesitate. Chloe watched as she braced herself against the half-buried roots and then heaved herself up and into the hollow part of the trunk, nestling her body down to hide in the shadows. Everything went quiet after that. Even Chloe, invisible as she was, held her breath.

He burst from the tree line only moments later, tall and deathly lean, with a joyless grin held so perfectly still on his face that it might as well have been carved into the flesh. In one hand, he held the black hatchet, spinning it around and around like the counterweight of a clock.

When had he closed the distance between them? How had he moved so fast?

He walked like a cartoon skeleton or a broken marionette, his movements jerky and awkward; it was as if at any moment, he might burst apart into all the individual pieces that made up his hideous whole. Crossing the clearing to stand beside him, Chloe inspected his face up close. He wasn't good-looking to begin with, but the gauntness of his body and the way his skin looked like wet paper draped lazily around a cheap Halloween decoration made him look positively ghastly. He carried himself with the bearing of a once-bigger man who had grown terribly thin. His mottled, liver-spotted skin hung in loops and folds around the edges of him, the loose flaps of his jaws and neck drawn tight by his god-awful, gray-toothed smile. There was something wrong with his eyes too—the irises were too pale, the pupils too wide.

Instinctively, Chloe conjured up his name from another stolen memory.

Phipps. Reverend Simon Phipps.

Chloe followed him over the black dirt of the clearing, careful to keep her distance, even ghostly as she was. Humming to himself, Phipps danced across the clearing, the hatchet turning lazy flips in his knobby fingers, cutting a straight line toward the great oak—after all, where else could she have possibly gone?

Chloe wanted to scream out to the girl in the tree, tell her to run, hide, go anywhere but here, *but Mary wouldn't—couldn't—hear her. Because this wasn't really happening. Chloe understood that now. She hadn't fallen into an alternate dimension, a different world, nothing like that; she'd crashed through into a memory that wasn't hers, and memories didn't change just because you wished hard enough.*

Slowly, almost delicately, Phipps stepped in close to the ancient tree, running one skeletal hand across its ashy old wood, getting a feel for its texture. He didn't even look at the girl curled inside the hollow as he stroked his fingertips across the trunk.

"Hello, my dear."

For a moment, Chloe was unsure if he'd actually spoken or if someone else had snuck up on them while she wasn't looking. Where Phipps's singing voice had been a sonorous, almost beautiful baritone, when he spoke, the words came out parched and reedy, like a broken rattle. Inside the tree, Mary shrank back into the little corner of shadow that she had left, crossing her arms over her chest, like that would protect her from anything. Chloe could feel the way her nerves chattered under her skin as he drew near, worsening when he spoke to her. Mary didn't say a word, too paralyzed with fear to even move her lips.

Standing there, Chloe watched as the reverend's smile split wide open, revealing rows of crooked yellow-gray teeth, all mismatched, like they'd been pulled from a dozen different heads and assembled haphazardly inside Phipps's lopsided mouth. He rolled his shoulders, then his neck, twisting until the joints all popped. With a flash of his arm, he buried the hatchet blade in the wood just above Mary's head, cleaving a line down the grain, then reared back and did it again, horizontally this time, leaving a crude cross hacked into the wood. Mary cried out with each impact, flinching away from each swing, but Phipps didn't seem to hear her; he just went on, driving gash after gash into the dry trunk, stopping only when he'd covered the big old tree with crosses. When he was finished, he juddered his bones around to stand before the hollow once more, holding his arms straight out to his sides, grinning face turned up toward the sky, like a man reveling in his own crucifixion.

Inside the tree, Mary began to quietly weep.

"Simon . . . Simon, please . . ."

His smile didn't falter. He didn't speak, didn't move. A disgusting, wet clicking noise ground out from the pit of his throat, a sound that Chloe only recognized too late as laughter. From where she floated, Chloe could see fresh tears falling down Mary's cheeks as she braced herself against the dry wood. The reverend twirled the hatchet like a little girl with a dolly.

"Simon, don't," Mary gasped.

"Goodbye, Miss Kane," Phipps said.

Then he swung the hatchet.

A streak of white sparks exploded from the blade as it slashed across the rocky soil, a brilliant fan that sprayed the dry bark of the great old oak and immediately burst into flames. Inside the tree, Mary screamed, and Chloe gritted her teeth and screamed with her, feeling the heat race across her own skin too. Beside her, Phipps stood back and fanned his arms upward, urging the flames higher as they consumed the tree and the girl trapped inside it. That dry grinding shook free from his mouth again, that horrible laughter, but it was only seconds before it was drowned out by the roar of the fire. Chloe could see Mary inside the tree thrashing and flailing madly, trying and failing again and again to claw her way out of that awful, blazing coffin as her skin blackened and curled, her burning hair dancing like a living halo around her head.

Chloe didn't know how long she stood there with Phipps, horrible scarecrow that he was, watching the tree burn, feeling the hateful flames dance across her own arms and neck and back as they consumed the girl trapped in the hollow trunk.

Eventually, Mary stopped making noise. Her movements slowed, then stopped. As Mary died, Chloe could feel her own consciousness crumbling away and sinking into the earth, pulled ever downward by some unseen force. In her rapidly tunneling vision, just before the soil dragged the fragmented pieces of the thing that used to be Mary Kane completely under, Chloe could just barely make out the shape of Simon Phipps standing there, arms raised to praise the growing fire as it lashed at the sky from the outermost tips of the tree's heavy, bent branches.

At last, everything was still. The silence of the forest floor was cold and absolute. It reached on and on into infinity, and Chloe could feel herself settling into the mercy of oblivion. She'd been so foolish to fear something like this. Death wasn't painful, nor was it scary. Death was a release from pain and fear, a final, gracious rest, and she let it take her over.

But she wasn't alone. They *weren't alone. True, she could still feel the burned girl's lingering presence in the earth beside her, but that wasn't all now. There was something else here, buried in the clay beside them. If she could hear anymore, she would say that she was hearing small whispers from the depths of the earth, but it was more than that. It was physical somehow, these little wisps of sound, distant but intense, carrying themselves through the dirt to shake what was left of Chloe and Mary to their shared core. Chloe tried to reach out to them, to trace them to their source. Thinking of the flames, and how she'd felt them skip across her own skin, Chloe thought that Mary must have felt it too. How could she not? Even in this soft, silent grave, it was impossible to not notice something like that.*

She reached out for Mary beside her, trying to feel where the older girl had gone to. She couldn't have been far, they'd sunk together . . .

The second she made contact, it was like an explosion had gone off in Chloe's head—the raw power of her, the sheer scale, was almost too much to bear. She could feel that distant whisper drumming against her own head, yes, but it was boring into Mary, feeding into her, amplifying her beyond the scared girl she'd been moments

hours

days

months

years

before. The explosion carried out in an incredible shock wave, and it was all that Chloe could do to hang on to the rolling wave of energy that used to be Mary Kane, praying she wouldn't be noticed. Chloe felt herself growing and spreading out under the soil with Mary, her consciousness fracturing and dividing into a dozen tendrils, a hundred, a thousand, more. Blades of Mary's consciousness, and Chloe's with it, branched off through the forest, driving up through the topsoil in hard, bone-white spears while the rest of her/them spread underneath the ground. She could see the trees, and the vines, and the wind stirring the dirt in loose, lazy cyclones. She saw time out of order: a village being built, a rickety man in a long black coat dying alone, delirious and desperate in the woods. All through the forest, the seasons passed and the earth grew larger and yet smaller, somehow—and together, they watched it happen. They listened to it. They saw people, funny little monkeys, changing and growing to fit their new environments as the two of them spread farther and did the same.

Together, fueled by the whispers from the deep, they became the forest, snaking along through the stone and veins of clay, the soft earth and roots and rivers, and as the earth surrounding them grew colder, damper, Chloe had the feeling that they were heading toward deeper water.

Together, they hammered through the soil into the freezing cold and found themselves floating in the center of a great, round lake filled with crystal-blue water, nearly black at its darkest corners. The water was still as it held them, but even in that stillness, it was so loud *in here. What Chloe had once taken for whispering was like drowned thunder in this lake, the sound huge and churning and impossible to escape.*

Looking around, she could see that there was something at the bottom of the lake, something that shone bright and cruel at the center of the basin, like a distant star twinkling through the blue-black darkness. It had been here forever, and would be here long after the planet was a smoldering cinder hurtling through the vast emptiness of space. They were already connected to it, the two of them—they had been ever since they'd left their bodies behind—and yet, its true nature evaded them.

Formless, Chloe swam for it, desperate to see what it was that shone so brightly in the dark, that whispered to them so loudly. Down and down she paddled, sinking farther into the water, but the spot of light never seemed to get any closer. Ignoring the pressure from the water and the warped shiver of reality around her, Chloe dove deeper and deeper, determined to see the source of all that light and noise and power. She was going to see what it was. Even if it killed her, she would see it.

She dove and swam and fought her way down until she came to the bottom, and that blazing light that shimmered all the way through to the surface.

Here, at the frayed edges of everything, she could finally see: the light wasn't light at all, at least not as she knew it. It was a hole on the lake floor that seeped energy, heat, noise. It only seemed like light because that's all her mind could interpret it as, but it was so much more than that. Unmoored and so far afield from her flimsy human form, she could now see it for what it truly was. It was a tear in the fabric of reality, a puncture, a wound left over from some great, grand violence committed here before humanity was even a glimmer of a glimmer in God's eye. Whatever had left a mark like this was incomprehensible in its power and its enormity; whatever it had been, the wound had never stopped bleeding.

As she watched, oily, bladed ghostlight poured from the messy split. She felt herself falling into the refracting glow, tumbling formless through the hole she'd found hiding at the bottom of the world. It unfolded around her, endlessly shimmering and refracting at the seams, pulling itself apart until she could see beyond.

Underneath the light, the energy, whatever it was, she could see shapes, lines, hard angles, all assembled into a brutal architecture that stretched from horizon to horizon. A city. Gray and cold and long, long dead, it stretched wide across the entirety of whatever strange earth it had been built upon. Its towers stabbed into the pallid sky, disappearing among the distant clouds. She'd never seen anything like it, as if the city had grown here of its own accord or else been carved from a single, continuous block of ashen stone. Floating down farther, the details carved into the towers and streets and rock walls made themselves apparent to her. Intricate and coiling, they made her head throb, made her feel like her eyes were going to bleed and burst.

The emptiness of the city—that was what she kept coming back to. It was overwhelming, crushing in its indifferent totality. There had been life here once. Something had etched these nauseating arabesques into the stone. Something had walked the streets and climbed to the obscured tops of those corkscrew towers.

Far off, near where the sprawling city met the blanched, dead horizon, she could see a mountain sprouting from the ground, its soil black and diseased and piled up just so. Her brain wrinkled a bit, seeing it there. Strange place for a mountain.

No, *her brain whispered to her.* Not a mountain. You've seen mountains before. You know hills like that—you've built hills like that. You know what lies beneath them.

Her mind reeled at the notion, at the sheer size and scale, but no mat-

ter how she tried to deny it, she understood the truth now. She had since she first laid eyes on it.

No, it wasn't a mountain.

It was a burial mound.

This city was a grave.

Far below, the landscape began to shake and rumble, and she could see the great cairn shedding curtains of soil as the ground below it shuddered. Thunder broke across the sky, enormous and brutal, and she recognized it too late as the voice she'd heard before, that whispering that had lilted through the trees and seemed so soft in the forest far above. So fragile. This was anything but. This was the voice of something ancient and infinite and cruel. She understood then that just because this was a memory didn't mean she was safe. Just because something was buried didn't mean it was dead.

Somewhere deep inside her skull, Chloe felt a pair of jaundiced eyes peel open, yellow with age and neglect, shot through with crimson threads, the pupils black as crude oil. The voice that blasted through her then wasn't the buried, wet thunder that shook the city below; it was sharper, smaller. Infinitely more human.

INVADER

TRESPASSER

THIEF

INVADER

TRESPASSER

THIEF

A moment or a lifetime later, an icy claw plunged through the blue water, through the light, through this dead heaven to close tightly around Chloe's brain. It was like nothing she'd ever felt, like panic given form. As the pain and fear mauled at her, she felt herself dragged upward, out of the memory of this cold city beneath the lake.

And then, once more, she was screaming soundlessly, falling forever.

It was like an electric shock. She felt it all the way down to her bones, like someone had stitched a copper wire through her and then hooked it up to a raw power line. She screamed, or at least thought that she did, and tumbled back onto the ground, curling up in the dirt, sucking air through clenched teeth, waiting for the pain to recede. Instantly, Parker was kneeling over her, cupping her face in one of his big hands, the night an explosion of stars far behind him. He was saying something, but the words didn't make sense to her brain. His voice lilted and swung low at the wrong times, like it was being played backward at her. Shaking off the

vision

memory

nightmare, she gagged on a hot mouthful of bile and tried again to focus on what he was saying, on the way his lips moved. After a few seconds, the sounds coming from his mouth seemed to right themselves, and she was back to reality once again.

"Chloe, hey! Chloe! Hey, say something, okay? Just say anything so I know you're alright. Please. Please, Chloe."

She coughed and spluttered and retched, pitching forward and feeling the wound in her side erupt in red agony. Her back and neck curled at the memory of those horrible yellow eyes opening inside her head, and she felt her spine curling in opposite directions as she dry heaved against her own body. Both of her hands went out to grasp at the fabric of his shirt, pulling him closer, or trying to drag herself off the ground. The pain was everywhere. The pain was everything.

"Parker, I . . . I . . ."

Her cousin's eyes went plate-wide with relief, and he worked his jaw without saying anything. A few seconds later, he seemed to find the words.

"Chloe, what the fuck was that?"

"I . . . oh, Jesus. I saw . . ." she gasped. "Parker, I saw everything."

The wind died down, and Nicky slowed to a trot, crossing her arms over her chest, trying to keep warm. The light from the moon was chilly and hard, and standing still in it for too long felt like it might freeze her in place, like that guy at the end of that hotel movie. She had to keep going—but where? Spinning around and around, she strained her ears to listen for the voice floating through the trees. *His* voice. It felt like it had been hours since she'd last heard it. But there was nothing out here. Just the soft undercurrent buzzing of the Pine Barrens.

"Where are you?" she whispered to herself. "Where did you go?"

There was a rustling behind her, and she whirled around to meet it. Was it possible? Could he be so close and she'd not even known it?

"Josh?" she called out into the windblown trees. "Josh, is that you? Josh, it's okay, it's me, it's Nicky. You can come out now. You're safe. I'm not going to hurt you . . ."

She peered deeper into the darkness, feeling her heart *thud* against her ribs. This time, when the voice came, it came from just over her shoulder, like he was whispering right into her ear.

"*Nicky*?"

Spinning around again, her heart swelled, a beautiful lightness spreading across her back and shoulders as the whisper slithered through the trees. She imagined she could fly away if she liked, no longer subject to the rules of this stupid, hateful world, because he had come back for her. There, in the distance, in the trees, she could see him now. Just a shadow, little more than an outline, but him, him, wonderful him! She could imagine the relief that would be on his face, the joy at having been returned, the relief she would feel being in his arms again. He was running for her, she could see that now, sprinting through the trees, ducking low, as agile and quick as he'd ever been.

"I'm here!" she called out to him.

She held her arms out to catch his flickering silhouette, only recognizing the bent, stretched shape scrambling madly toward her with its torn-up hands and broken teeth too late.

Then she screamed.

MONDAY

16

After a few restless hours, Chloe rose from the shallow sleep she'd managed to scrape together in the uneven quiet before the dawn. She'd have liked to keep sleeping, but the sun had grown too high, too bright. Impossible to hide from now. In the winnowing, reddish darkness behind her eyelids, she could still hear the whispers from under the lake, Mary Kane's furious screeching, the sound of the claw augering through her skull to clamp around her brain.

Chloe had seen Mary—the real Mary, and the endless thing that had claimed her for itself—last night, and she'd paid the price for skulking around in places she wasn't supposed to be.

The wound in her ribs was worse this morning. That was the first thing she noticed when she opened her eyes and tried to roll over. Laying there, the constant buzz-saw ache was the same, but the pain became unbearable when she touched it or tried to move. Parker would have to help her change the bandage in a little while. Unzipping her sleeping bag from the inside, Chloe sat up, sucking cold forest air against the agony drilling through her ribs.

The morning around them was quiet and bright, almost peaceful. The wind rustled through tree branches, while puffy white clouds drifted overhead. Almost by reflex, she reached in her backpack for her phone, holding down the power button until the cracked screen skipped to life, displaying a time that didn't mean anything to her anymore. The battery was in pitiful shape too—a paltry 13 percent even after keeping it off for three days. She quickly dialed the screen brightness down to try and conserve the power she had left. Up at the top, the banner read *No Service.* Big surprise. Turning it over, she seriously considered just throwing it into the trees, sending it all the way to hell. It wasn't doing her any good in the Barrens anyway, and even if they ever actually got out—

The phone buzzed.

Chloe froze, staring down at the little brick of plastic and glass in her hands, not wanting to look at the screen and see that she'd imagined it. Losing her mind, inventing things like that and living comfortably in her delusion—that was one thing. But being aware enough to know just how far gone she really was . . .

That would be so much worse.

Then it vibrated again, and again, and again: *Bzzt-bzzt. Bzzt-bzzt. Bzzt-bzzt.* Over and over her phone shook with alerts. She wasn't imagining this. This was real. It had to be. Turning the phone around to look, she watched as a single service bar flickered and guttered while the screen filled up with notifications. Text from Mom. Text from Mom. Text from Dad. Text from Mom. Voice mail from Mom. Voice mail from Dad. Voice mail from a number she didn't recognize, then another from a second number. Voice mail from Aunt Lori. Text from Mom. Text from Dad. Text from Aunt Lori. Voice mail from Dad. Text from Mom. Text from Mom. Text from Mom.

Oh, fuck.

Nimbly, her fingers leaped into motion, dismissing all the notifications in a single sweep and bringing up the keypad function. At the top of the screen, the little service bar fluttered back and forth. Chloe tried to hold her hands as still as possible, not wanting to lose the little reception she still had. Three numbers, that was all she needed. Three little numbers. Her thumb traced the pattern: *9-1-1.* Heart racing, Chloe hit *Call* and held the phone still, waiting for the soft digital *click* of connection. And she waited. And she waited.

And then the line went dead.

No, no, no, no, no—

A notification popped up in the center of the screen.

No Service.

Up at the top, the service bar had vanished, replaced by an X icon. Hands trembling, Chloe resisted the urge to scream. Of course. Of course it had happened like that. Why would anything start being fair now?

Still. It had been enough to download her messages. That wasn't nothing, she supposed. Chloe brought up her texts and thumbed at the most recent one, from her mom.

Chloe, please just come home. We're all so worried about you. We love you more than anything and we just want you to be safe. Please come home.
4:02AM, 5/28

Sorting through the rest, she found they were all variations on that same theme, steadily decreasing in panic as Chloe wound the clock back, scrolling through four days of Mom-texts, all the way back to the one she'd fired off Friday evening.

Have fun with your friends, sweetheart! You earned it. Senior year, here you come! I'm so, SO proud of you. Love, Mom.
9:30PM, 5/25

She'd even followed it up with a string of emojis, because of course she had. Nobody used emojis when anything was seriously wrong. Stifling a surge of tears, Chloe stared at her mom's text messages for a long time before thumbing over to the voice mails, picking one stamped yesterday morning, from her dad. Selecting it and hitting *Play*, she held the phone to her ear.

"*Hey, Scooter, not sure if you're getting this or not, but I just thought you should know I love you. We love you. Your mom loves you. Whatever's going on, wherever you are right now, I hope you're okay. I miss you, and we'll be waiting for you to get home. Just come home soon, okay? Please come home. As quick as you can. Please. I love you.*"

She went through all of them, one by one. Aunt Lori's messages—both voice and text—were garbled, but Chloe got the gist. It wasn't a surprise that she was drunk, especially now, but at least she was trying. That was something. The numbers she hadn't recognized were from the Randolph Police Department, then from someone at the New Jersey State Police. Both basically the same. Totally useless.

The phone buzzed in her hand again, and she pulled it back from her face to look. It read *5% Low Battery!* for a moment, then the screen went black and stayed that way.

"No, no, no!" she wailed, clicking madly at the power button. But it was no good. The battery had finally given out. She was alone again. Wiping a fresh spill of tears from her face, Chloe jammed the dead phone back into her backpack, almost more by routine than anything else. She didn't know what good it would do her, but throwing it away still felt *wrong* somehow.

Reaching for her branch, she pitched herself up to her feet and started looking around for her cousin. Beside her, his sleeping bag lay empty, his backpack unopened next to the other orphaned bags they'd been carrying with them—Nate's, Adam's, Josh's, and now Nicky's too.

After they'd returned to the fire last night, Parker had helped her climb into her sleeping bag and said that he was going to stay up for a while, to keep watch, *just in case*. But he wouldn't say *in case* of what.

Chloe supposed he didn't really need to. They both knew what was hiding out there, waiting for them.

Through the trees, she could see him sitting on a weathered log just beyond the edge of their camp, facing the way they'd ran after Nicky last night. She wondered if he'd slept at all or if he'd just sat there, staring off into the trees, wishing things were different than they'd turned out. Leaning heavy on the branch, she limped toward him, leaving the camp in disarray as she closed the distance between her and her cousin.

"Hey," she called out to him when she got close.

"Hey yourself," he said back, without turning to look.

"You okay?"

He shook his head. "No. You?"

"No."

"Okay," said Parker. "Glad we got that sorted out."

Chloe circled around to ease herself down next to him, gazing into the shadowy green void they'd gone crashing madly through only hours before. Nothing moved, not even the boughs against the wind. It was still and dead. Just like everything else in this forest.

"I don't think she's coming back, Parker."

"I know she's not."

Chloe lifted one slender hand and set it down over the top of his giant paw, curling her fingers in between his and giving them a good squeeze.

"Were you out here all night?" she asked. "You're cold."

"I don't know," he said. "I guess."

"Well, why don't you come on back and we can get a fire going, maybe warm you up a little bit."

"This is all my fault, Chloe."

He wasn't wrong, but it didn't feel right to agree with him. Instead, she said nothing and squeezed his hand a little bit tighter.

"I brought the gun," he said, unbidden. "I pulled the trigger. I made my choices, but we all have to deal with them now. I'm sorry, Chloe. I'm so, so fucking sorry. None of you deserved any of this."

She leaned over and rested her head against the curve of his big, broad shoulder. "No, none of us did. Including you," she added. "But the best thing we can do now is get out of here while we're still standing."

Parker nodded.

"Are you still hearing her? That woman, Mary?"

"It's not really her," Chloe said, shaking her head. "No more than it was really Nate. She got trapped here, just like we did, and when she died, this place made her part of itself. Another mask in its collection. Just like everything else that dies here."

"But it's still there?"

Chloe let her eyes sink shut again and listened to the silence that filled up the forest around them. She'd been hearing it in the distance ever since they'd hobbled back to camp last night—the voice of the thing under the lake. At first she'd thought it was an echo, some lingering remnant of her last vision, but the longer she listened, the louder it got. Not a remnant. Not an echo. She'd been stealing the signal before, tapping into something she'd hardly understood. Now she was hardwired into it.

Craning her head, Chloe strained her ears, listening. After a moment, she heard it—a sharp susurrus, folded underneath the sounds of the woods, threaded through them, so well-hidden that it was barely there at all. Tuning into that noise—*the voice*—Chloe found that she couldn't make out the words anymore, but maybe that didn't matter. Maybe the things it took had thought in individual words, but what ran through the head of the thing buried in that dead city was far more feral and baroque: emotions, images, urges, acts. That was what Chloe could hear now, woven into the fabric of this place—hate, pure and true.

She opened her eyes again.

"Yeah. It's still there." Chloe felt him wilt, hearing that. "How about you? Anything weird happen while I was out?"

He shook his head. "No."

She could tell it was a lie. "No more ghosts?" she asked.

"Not that I've seen."

She looked away from him. "Well, that's a good thing, right?"

"I guess. You sleep okay?"

There were a million different ways she could answer that question, but none of them seemed to fit. "I don't know. No. It was sleep. You sure you don't want to try and get some?"

"I'm fine."

"Are you?"

He turned to look her in the face, his brown eyes glassy behind his dirty spectacles.

"I will be," he said. "Eventually. Once we get out of here."

"And how are we planning on doing that?"

With two fingers, Parker pointed out at the trees to their right. "Well, the sun came up over there this morning, so that must be east, right?"

"I guess."

"I'm thinking that we walk that way until we hit a highway or the ocean. Whatever comes first. New Jersey doesn't go on forever, and neither does this haunted house of a forest. It's got to end at some point."

"All right," she said. "Great. Good plan. I like this plan. Let's get going."

He held up a finger. "Except."

"Except what?"

Nodding to the right again, he said, "Thing is, if we go that way, I think we're going back the way we came yesterday. Through the town. Past the lake. Into the trees."

Her heart pinched, then fell. "Shit."

"Right," said Parker.

"So we find another way," she said, spinning her wheels. "There's got to be another way. It's New Jersey. There are highways everywhere."

"We've been saying that for four days now," Parker reminded her. "Look where it's gotten us. Shortest path back has gotta be the way we came. We keep on that line, and we'll probably hit something sooner or later. But we need to keep to the line."

"Except there's no guarantee it'll work, right?" Chloe asked. "There's every chance the forest keeps fucking with us, turning us around to keep us trapped inside. What happens then?"

Parker sighed heavily. "I don't know. We fight it, keep pushing, hurt it bad enough to make it let us go."

"Any ideas on how we might go about doing that?"

"No," he said. "Nothing. What about you? Any brilliant ideas?"

Chloe turned halfway around to look at the backpacks piled by their sleeping bags, wincing at the way the motion pulled against her wound.

"Actually, yeah. Now that you mention it, I think I might."

17

Weighed down with backpacks that were and weren't theirs, Chloe and Parker set out along the path they'd walked the day before, through the trees and scrub, back toward the buried car and the empty town and the dead white forest beyond the lake. Because he'd asked her to, she talked Parker through every part of the vision again—all the things she'd seen, felt, everything. Together, they examined every detail, every little moment that she'd experienced, just to make sure they hadn't missed anything. It wasn't exactly an easy task; it was already fading from Chloe's mind, like a dream that she couldn't cling to, no matter how hard she tried. Every time they went through it, she could feel herself leaving out details she'd included before, but found herself unable to recall what they were or why they were so important. They'd simply thinned out and disappeared, like morning mist under dawn's burning eye.

She let her cousin lead them through the woods, following as fast as the crutch would carry her, wincing against the pain that burned through her midsection pretty much constantly now. She wasn't sure when the acid throb had started. Maybe when she'd woken up this morning, maybe while she'd been sleeping, maybe even before—last night, perhaps, when they were dashing through the woods to try and catch up to Nicky. Maybe she'd torn it wide open while they were out there in the dark and hadn't noticed because of the adrenaline pumping through her bloodstream. It could have happened any time, but she supposed the *when* didn't really matter that much. All she knew was that it hurt more now than it had since she'd first been gored.

Stopping on the path, she rolled her shirt up and peeled the makeshift bandage back to look. The wound was already worse than it had been early this morning, purple-red around the edges and black across the middle, slithering out under the surface of her pale skin with bright-red tendrils she didn't like the look of. A few steps ahead, Parker rolled to a halt and turned back to see.

"Shit. That's not looking so good, Chloe."

"Gee, thanks, Dr. Cunningham. I hadn't noticed."

"Does it hurt?"

She nodded. "Yup."

"Bad?"

"Really bad."

He took a step closer to her. "Yeah," he said, stepping in closer. "That's seriously infected."

From under her furrowed brow, she shot him a death glare. "I do have eyes, Parker."

"What do you want to do about it?"

She drew a deep, slow breath through her nostrils as she probed with bare fingers at the edge of the black scab. Right by the tip of her finger, the scab had torn away from her skin slightly. Pinching the edge between her thumb and forefinger, Chloe pulled it farther back, sending a thin trickle of yellow-and-red fluid down her skin. Little waves of pain jumped through her body as she tugged. *Stop it, stop it, stop it.*

Rolling the bandage back in place, she pulled her shirt down and looked at her cousin, a weary look on her face.

"Your guess is as good as mine," she said.

"What about like, antibiotics?"

"That's a great idea," Chloe snipped. "Did you bring any?"

Parker's cheeks flushed red, and he turned away. "Stupid question," he said. "Sorry."

Chewing the inside of her cheek, she felt shame needle at her insides. "No, *I'm* sorry. I'm not trying to make you feel bad. You're just trying to help."

Parker nodded. "Yeah. Okay."

"But it was a pretty stupid question."

She cracked a grin in his direction, and she was relieved when he smiled back, even if it was sad and tinged with worry. It was better than nothing.

"Well, try to hang on, okay?" Parker said. "We're getting the fuck out of here."

"Hooray." She pulled the backpack higher on her shoulders and tried to ignore the pain chewing relentlessly at her ribs. Parker walked on, and Chloe followed him.

After a while, she started to recognize the terrain. She figured that at some point behind them, they'd passed the little footpath that led back to the ancient car that had become her uncle's grave. She felt a little pang of guilt for not having seen it as they passed by, or for asking Parker if he wanted to stop and pay his respects. But maybe he'd seen and hadn't wanted to stop. She wouldn't have blamed him for it. If it was her dad's bones out there, she wouldn't want to see them again if she could help it. Especially if they were surrounded by all those sentinel trees.

They lined the path as they walked, those trees. They were everywhere, if you looked for them. The forest was sick with them, bony spears of *it* stabbing up through the cursed earth, its own private network, Mary Kane's body and soul twisted and brutalized into this horrible new form until it was impossible to tell where the forest stopped and she began. Chloe watched the trees, and she was sure that they were watching them back.

Eventually, the path wound through a thicket of pines and down a hill, then the trees verged off to either side as the town came into view. They rounded the church on the left and came to stand in the middle of the wide, dusty main road that led through the town proper. From where she stood, Chloe could already see the lake. Being this close to it made her want to jump out of her skin.

"*Eeaugh.* I hate it here."

"Yeah," he said. "There used to be people who lived here. Families . . . Whole lives. Now it's just . . . empty. Gone."

"Sad, when you put it that way."

He gave her a look. "Was this the . . . the thing? Do you think it did this?"

A cold wire of unease snaked through her. "Maybe. Probably. Not like we can do anything about it now. Can't resurrect a dead town."

"Guess it's just us and the ghosts, then," said Parker.

"I guess."

He led her down the path and through the hunched little settlement, cut from gray wood and broken shingles, stepping carefully to minimize the crunch of their shoes against the dirt, which echoed so goddamn loudly in the empty town. As they made their way down the hill, Chloe gave in to the familiar, curious tug at the back of her head; she wanted to know what happened here, wanted to break into every house and outbuilding that still stood to try and figure out where they'd all gone. It was just like Parker had said: there were people here, once, with lives and secrets all their own, and that stubborn part of the old Chloe ached to unearth everything they'd hidden away, just to know *why.*

She tried to look at it like a puzzle to keep her mind off the lake. There had to be a reason. Nothing ever happened for no reason. That wasn't how things worked. Cause and effect were universal truths, and more often than not, the cause was hiding in the little things, details you wouldn't normally notice or even think to look at. Like the fact that they'd walked past that church three times now and she hadn't seen a graveyard anywhere. Like the fact that most of the houses around them were all still standing, despite time and weather and the natural creep of decay. Like the fact that her uncle Dave hadn't been the only one to leave an offering on that altar below the church; he'd just been the latest. It was a riddle, and she knew she could solve it, given enough time.

They were about halfway down the hill when Parker turned around to look at her, taking the incline backward.

"You ready for this?"

"Absolutely not," she said. "What about you?"

"I don't know. I guess. If I have to be."

"You have a real way of inspiring confidence," Chloe said.

"We just need to get around it," he said. "We're not swimming across it, we're doing our best not to touch it."

"We're not touching it at all," she said, her voice stony. "At all. Understood?"

Slowly, he nodded. "Understood."

She let her eyes sink halfway shut as she followed him, conjuring up the vision of the light at the bottom of the water again until she felt those yellow eyes start to hinge open inside her head, old and heavy and cruel.

Walking ahead, Parker led her around a corner that signaled the end of the little clapboard town. "Here we go," he said.

Chloe rounded the corner after him and resisted the urge to scream. The lake was enormous, crystal blue, and perfectly circular, as if some cruel god had jabbed a finger into the surface of the earth, leaving a perfect divot in its wake. Standing here, looking at it like this was like watching a nightmare come to life, building itself out of whatever body and blood it could steal from the air around her.

Inside her head, she felt memories start to crystallize and sharpen again as she gazed out across the water, so vivid and knife-like that she feared they might actually slice her open.

Except it wasn't just memories. Standing there, she could *feel* the grave at the bottom of the lake, the way the weird, poison light still shone in her, radiating out from those hideous, jaundiced eyes all the way down to her bones, as sure as she'd felt it shine in what was left of Mary Kane. Being this close to it made her spine curl. Instinctively, she took a step back, clasping a hand around Parker's wrist.

"Okay, maybe this was a bad idea," she said to him. "Parker, we shouldn't have gone this way. There are other ways out of here. We just need to keep looking."

"There's no other way," Parker told her, even though she could tell by his voice that he didn't entirely believe that. "We have to get out of here. That hole in your side isn't getting any better. How much longer do you think you can keep walking like that?"

She studied his face, wanting to tell him he was wrong, she felt fine, but that wasn't the case, and both of them knew it.

"We have to do this, and that's our path." He pointed out across the lake, where the far shore was filled with giant white sentinel trees like dead, withered arms digging their way up through the soil. "You can do this, okay? You can do this."

Unclasping her fingers from his wrist, she looked up at him. "Okay," she said, swallowing against the stone in her throat.

"We're just going to be extra careful, alright?"

"Yeah," she said. "Sure."

Wordlessly, careful to not touch the small, chopping waves, they started to circle around the lake, making for the creek on the far shore.

As they passed into the low shade of the sentinel trees, Parker felt it again, that same little itch that had come needling at the back of his neck ever since they'd returned to the abandoned town. Like they weren't alone, being watched from nearby. It wasn't the trees, either—this was something animal, something immediate. He hadn't said anything to Chloe about it, because what good would that do? She couldn't run, couldn't fight, couldn't do anything if things went sideways. They just had to keep on walking and wait it out. Something would happen or it wouldn't, and either way, they'd deal with that when the time came. Not before.

"Uh, Parker?"

He looked back at his cousin. Her face had gone bone white. She was pointing at the trees out ahead of them. He looked, and for a minute, he didn't understand what it was that he was seeing.

There was a body hanging from the trees.

She was mounted high in a cruel parody of the crucifixion, her arms strung out wide to either side, wrists spiked clean through with sharp, broken branches. Her clothes hung off her body in rags, revealing drying wounds and gashes; her arms and legs and midriff were exposed, scourged to bloody tatters. Her red hair spilled down around her head in limp, lifeless sheets. At some point, she'd lost a shoe.

Without saying a word, Chloe started forward, and Parker reached out to lay a hand on her shoulder, holding her back.

"Hey, what are you doing?"

She gave him a deadly serious look. "I have to see, Parker."

"Wait, what!" A bright white shock coursed through Parker's whole body. He knew what happened when Chloe touched things anymore. "No, Chloe. No, you don't."

"Yes," she insisted. "I do."

She shrugged his arm off of her and moved closer, the slow *pick-thrush*, *pick-thrush* of her uneven gait slashing loudly through the silence that had descended around them.

"Chloe, please don't do this," he called after her.

Standing there, underneath Nicky's bloody, torn body, his cousin looked so small, but the look on her face was anything but fragile. She was determined. She'd already made her mind up about this, and Parker wasn't going to be able to change it.

"It's okay," she said without looking back. "Really, I'll be okay. Just stay here and keep watch, all right? Try and catch me if I fall."

Face dark with worry, Park uncrossed his arms from over his chest and moved to stand behind her, but he didn't say anything more. He tried to shut the thoughts of Mary Kane, of the sentinel trees, of the horrible thing at the bottom of the lake, clean out of his mind. Chloe knew what she was doing.

Standing there, he winced as she reached out to cup the pale, cold skin of their dead friend's bare calf. Instantly, her shoulders knotted up tight as she braced herself against the mental surge that came boiling up out of the ether to drag her under.

She was ready for it this time. She told herself she was ready for it this time. But as her hand touched Nicky's dead skin, she realized too late how wrong she was.

"I'm here!" they called out in tandem to the silhouette between the trees.

Slitting her eyes, Chloe felt Nicky spread her arms wide to embrace the shape in the distance, realizing too late that the bent, stretched thing scrambling madly toward them was not—had never been—Josh.

They screamed together, the sheer force of it straining their lungs. The sound was enormous, shattering the night around them, but it wasn't enough to startle the creature from its purpose. With a wet snarl, the creature that used to be their friend fell on top of them, scrabbling and tearing at them like a rabid dog, ripping through their shirt like it was wet toilet paper. It was too late to fight back now. Everything had already gone so wrong.

The creature—handsome features still recognizable underneath the warped animal—leaned back and raised one of its red-streaked claws high, then hissed and buried it deep into their throat. Nicky/Chloe gurgled and thrashed as the Adam-thing curled that claw into a fist and hauled it back out again with a hard snap, *like a rubber band breaking. Chloe expected it to hurt, but it didn't. There was just a sickening cold that spread out from the place where their throat used to be. She could already feel Nicky slipping away, and quickly. Above them, the Adam-thing's fist came away filled with a mess of torn red chunks; it brought it to its mouth and started eating noisily.*

Chloe felt her back arch and leave the ground, then she was floating and falling, alone again in that infinite void, with nothing to do but close her eyes and wait for it to be over.

Nausea crashed through her as she came back, stumbling away from Nicky's body and driving the walking stick deep into the soil, trying and failing to keep herself upright. She went sprawling to the ground, barking her ass on the hardpacked soil, the impact lighting the hole in her ribs up like a firework, flaring bright, brilliant red. She groaned and sucked air through clenched teeth and clapped a hand to her side, pressing down on the wound despite the bitter throb.

A second later, Parker squatted down over her, holding a hand out. She didn't take it.

"You okay?" he asked.

She didn't know how to answer that question. Every part of her hurt. The wound in her side throbbed in time with her pulse. Her limbs were shaky and numb with exhaustion, and a beacon of bright white pain had opened up behind her right eye, like someone was twisting a fork around in her brain, trying to spool it up like spaghetti. That was new.

"Yeah," she said. "No. I don't know. I guess. I told you to catch me."

"Chloe . . ."

She waved him off, instead using the crutch to drag herself up off the ground. "I'll be alright."

"What did you see?"

Chloe turned her head and spat, then used the bottom of her shirt to wipe the remnants from her lips. She didn't know what to tell him.

"Was it him? Was it Adam?"

She nodded. His eyes narrowed and went dark.

"Was it . . . bad?"

The images played across the backs of her eyes again, scarred permanently into her memory.

"Yeah," she finally said. "It was bad."

"Fuck. Did you see him . . . ?" He nodded to Nicky's body, the way it had been hung.

"Shrike her to the tree? No."

Parker's shoulders fell. "Probably for the best."

"Yeah," she said, taking a deep breath, trying to dispel a fresh surge of sickness at the back of her tongue. "Probably."

She watched as Parker owled his head around at all the old sentinel trees that surrounded them. "You think he's close?"

"Maybe," said Chloe. "It's possible he's been following us since we passed through the town, maybe even before. Hard to tell."

"What's he waiting for?"

"I don't know. Maybe for us to slow down, wear out. Easier to kill us if we're both fucked up instead of just one of us."

"Look," he said. "Maybe it doesn't have to go down like all that. Really. I guess I just wonder if we could try to talk to him—"

She didn't mean to laugh, she really didn't. It just happened, exploding out of her in a bitter, cruel rush. Even the sound of it seemed wrong, now; foreign, almost. Like laughter was an alien concept to this place.

"You want to try and talk to him. Really?"

"Yeah, Chloe. I do. I just think—"

She held up a hand, cutting him off. "No. Parker, listen. He's not him anymore. I don't think you understand how bad it really is."

Parker shook his head. "There has to be some part of him that's still him. No matter how bad it's gotten. I mean, come on, it's *Adam*."

"Parker, I know you want to believe that that's true, but you haven't seen the things I have. You didn't see what this place turned him into. That's what it does. It happened with Mary Kane. It happened with Nate. It happened with Adam. Whatever you're imagining, however bad you think it is, I promise you that it's worse."

Parker's face flushed, and his eyes fell.

"Do you want to try and get her down?"

She sighed. "I wish I could tell you yes. But we're burning daylight. I don't think we can spare the time. Or the energy. We have to keep going."

"Okay," he said, then nodded toward where the creek weaved through a wide place between the trees. "Come on. I think that's our way through."

Chloe heard it first.

Crunch. Crunch. Crunch.

The sound was faint and far off, so distant that she barely noticed it at first. Just another nothing-sound of the forest as they followed the water. But she'd long since learned not to trust the impulse to disregard or take anything for granted. That impulse had a body count now. So she listened, and the harder she did, the louder it got.

Crunch. Crunch.

Crash.

It was getting closer.

She reached out and slapped at her cousin's shoulder, stopping him in place. "Parker?"

"What?"

"Did you hear that?"

Parker cocked his head to the sky, listening to the breezy roll of the forest. Chloe listened, too, straining her ears as the creek went silent and still and the wind died down, hoping she'd just imagined it, that there wasn't any—

Crash. Crash. CRASH.

Parker's back bolted up rail-straight and he dropped the packs, pivoting his head around like a panicked animal.

CRASH. CRASH.

The sound came again, and again, louder every time. Then, just as the sound seemed like it was going to come smashing down on their heads, everything went quiet. Ahead of them, just along the water, the underbrush parted, separating from itself to allow the vile thing to emerge from the shadows.

"Oh god," Parker coughed. "Oh my fucking god."

He was still painted with Nicky's blood, long dried to sick, flaking rust. From where Chloe stood, she could make out crisscrossing highways of venous blue and arterial red throbbing steadily under spongy, spoiled-milk flesh. His clothes were in tatters around the grotesque shape of his body—torn and stretched and perverted into configurations unintended, as if he'd gotten trapped in a taffy puller, like the ones down the shore. His legs were bowed and banded, terminating in raw, bloody feet. His ropy arms hung down below his knees, nearly scraping the ground with hard, red claw-hands that looked like the flesh had been shaved from them, leaving only jagged bones behind. His face only barely read as human—his lips thin and fish-belly pale, drawn back nearly to his ears, exposing a gruesome, toothy smile; his nose a withered, crumpled remnant of its former self; his eyes stone black and set so far back in his skull that Chloe was surprised he could see anything at all. A few stray wisps of hair still clung desperately to his mottled scalp, sprouting out in stray clumps.

Neither of them moved. They barely even breathed. Chloe thought she'd already seen how bad Adam had gotten, but the thing that hunted them from the shadows was nothing compared to the grotesque horror that stood before them now, grazing its bloody fingers through the dirt. Beside her, Parker stepped forward and drew the black hatchet from his belt. With his free hand, he passed the gun over to her. She wondered what he expected her to do with it. She'd never shot a gun in her life.

"Just keep back, okay?" he instructed her quietly. "If this goes wrong, you shoot him until the gun clicks empty. Should be four shots left in there. Okay?"

"Uh, what are you going to do . . . ?"

Out of the corner of her eye, she saw Adam move first, a smear against the white trees, and it was all she could do to shove herself out of the way as Parker howled and leaped forward to meet him.

They'd done this before.

The two boys crashed into each other with a hard *smack* that Parker felt all the way down into the marrow of his bones, the impact knocking him dizzy while the Adam-thing scrabbled at the dirt to stay upright, hissing and snapping its jaws. It kicked one bone-thin leg out at him, a cheap shot, but he was too far back for it to connect. A second later, it rushed him again, faster than before, but Parker was ready for it this time. Sidestepping the lunge, he ducked and drove one big fist into the spindly thing's breadbasket with a hard, meaty *thunk*. The Adam-thing keened as it fell, and Parker backed up, keeping its attention on him and not Chloe, trading the black hatchet from hand to hand, keeping it out in front of him like a talisman or a ward.

"Please don't do this," he said. "Adam, *please.*"

A glimmer of recognition danced across the Adam-thing's eyes, but then it was back on its feet again, sprinting forward, slashing its gnarled, bloody hands out in tight, knife-like swings. Taking another step back, Parker braced himself, tightening his stance to sidestep it again, but when he tried, the Adam-thing pivoted midstep, leaping to latch onto Parker's bulk. With a satisfied snarl, it reared back and buried a claw into his midsection, shearing through the fabric of his shirt until it found purchase in the soft flesh of his belly, digging in with psychotic intensity.

The pain was immediate and immense, dwarfed only by the revulsion at having those hideous bone-fingers digging into the meat under his skin. Parker's mind screamed at him—*Getitoffgetitoffgetitoffpleasefuckingjustgetitoff!*—and through the hurt and the noise, he could feel hot rivers rolling down his stomach to pool in the waistband of his jeans. Somewhere far removed from himself, he felt the hatchet fall out of his hand, its usefulness lost in the frenzy, his brain defaulting instead to a primal, apelike urge to batter the thing off of him. Over and over he drilled his elbow down between the Adam-thing's shoulder blades, hammering its spine as hard as he could until it shrieked and unlatched, dropping to the ground with a wail.

Parker didn't waste a second. Throwing himself forward like a linebacker, he shoulder-speared the thing with the full weight of his body, lifting it off the ground, feeling it slash at his shoulders and back with its sharp fingers before they both crashed into the earth with a skull-juddering *crunch.* The two of them went rolling, swinging and swiping at one another with bloody hands.

When they broke apart again, Parker crawled quickly to where he'd dropped the hatchet, feeling some small measure of rationality return to him. He didn't hear the Adam-thing race over to loom above him; he only realized what had happened when the thing jammed its claws square into his back, driving in so deep that he could feel the tips wriggling inside his body like hungry worms. Parker screamed and tried to roll away, sweeping the hatchet off the ground with panic-numb fingers. He brought the blade end around in a wild twist and felt it *clang* off of something solid. There was a wet shriek, and a second later, the claws slid free from his flesh. Hatchet clutched tightly in his fist, Parker rose on rubbery legs. A few feet away, the Adam-thing was prodding at the deep red stripe that Parker had opened up in the flesh between its arm and shoulder. Dark purple blood pattered to the ground at Parker's feet, falling freely from the blade.

Emboldened by the adrenaline dumping through his system, Parker advanced on the wounded creature that used to be his friend. The Adam-thing swiped at him, and Park ducked back, then dashed forward again, swinging the black hatchet over his head in a wide arc, screaming like a barbarian. He felt the wicked blade sink deep into something soft half a second later, but he couldn't keep his balance. The two of them crashed into the icy creek. Cold water bit into Parker's flesh like knives and held him down as he struggled to get back to his feet, the black hatchet still clutched in one fist, streaked from head to haft with thinning red.

The Adam-thing dropped down onto Parker's chest with a vicious retching noise, pinning his bulk to the creek bed. With one claw it batted the hatchet from Parker's numb fingers, and then it reared back the other to finish the kill.

Thunder boomed in the distance, and the Adam-thing's body jerked to the side—once, twice, three times. Not willing to miss his shot, Parker gathered what strength he had left and punched the thing in the ribs, as hard as he could. His knuckles came away bloody.

Adam's body shuddered and rolled off of Parker, crumbling to the bank of the creek in a twitching, fetal mess. Dragging himself away from the fallen thing, Parker saw Chloe standing over them, the gun smoking in her tiny fist.

"Chloe . . ." he gasped.

She raised the gun toward the crumpled Adam-thing and pulled the trigger one last time, blasting a messy red hole through its throat. The creature went still and stayed that way.

Chloe held the revolver out to Parker. "Are there any more bullets for this?"

Park shook his head in the negative, trying to catch his breath, in awe of the frost in her voice.

"Did you want to keep it?"

He thought about it for a second and then sighed, "No."

"Fine by me," she said and dropped it to the ground beside their friend with a dull thud. "Now, can we get the fuck out of here, please?"

Parker nodded and started to pick himself up off the ground again. "Yeah, of course. Sure."

"Great," she said. "Lead the way."

18

They followed the creek east, or at least what Parker thought was east, tracking its path as it widened and grew through the white trees. They moved haltingly, constantly detouring around trees or over fallen logs, but nonetheless, Parker couldn't help feeling like they were making progress. Walking a few steps ahead, he prodded at the wounds Adam had gouged in his back, then peeled back the wet rags of his shirt to examine the throbbing gashes sliced into his belly. An uneven red crosshatching decorated the soft, pale skin there. Not exactly shallow, either. There'd be some nasty scarring after they healed over. Tearing a length of fabric from his shirt, he blotted at the cuts, trying to stanch the bleeding.

"You okay?"

Parker wiped away a fresh rivulet of blood, leaving a thin red smear behind that spackled the hairs on his belly down to the skin. He thought it looked like maybe the bleeding was slowing a little.

"Yeah," he said. "I'll be fine. You?"

She laughed at that. "I mean, sure? I don't know. I don't think I'm going to fall over and die this second, so I guess I got that going for me."

Eventually, the water led them to a little cliff, where the creek tumbled over the edge in a chuckling waterfall, spilling down nine or ten feet to a rocky patch below. At the bottom, the water pooled and widened and then rushed away along its track, the current stronger than it was above. In the distance, they could see where it started to grow into something more akin to a river. The white ghost trees branched off to follow the line of the cliff, heading deeper into the woods—heading, Parker had no doubt, toward *her*. They were a part of her, after all. As much as she was part of the forest and the thing that slept beneath it. The whole of the Pine Barrens was an ecosystem of fear and horror. But they were going to get out. A small amount of relief prickled his skin as he stood there. Surely they were close now. Closer than they'd been in days.

Chloe limped over to stand at the edge of the cliff while Parker turned his face skyward to gauge the angle of the sun, and the time they had left until night fell.

"Now what?" Chloe called out to him, raising her voice above the waterfall. "Do we go sideways, or down?"

"I mean, down seems right," Parker said. "I'm thinking that if we can get down there, we can probably just follow the creek all the way through. Should lead us straight out, so long as it doesn't turn around on itself and lead us deeper in."

Next to the cliff, Chloe turned on her crutch to look at him. "Do creeks usually do that? Turn around on themselves?"

"I mean, not usually, but in this place?" He gave her a look.

"Yeah, no, I get you."

"So, like I said, as long as the creek follows the sun, and we follow the creek, we'll make it out, I think."

"You're sure about that?"

He shrugged.

"About as sure as I can be of anything in this—"

His hand suddenly seared with agony, throbbing like an overfilled water balloon, the skin swelling with pins and hot blood. Automatically, his fingers clamped shut around the handle of the hatchet, so tight that he could feel the grooves in the wood grain scarring into his palms. The pain was electric, coursing up his arm past his shoulder and into his neck, his jaw, his brain.

Kill the listener, Nate whispered, his voice quick and sharp like a scorpion sting, burying itself so deep into the meat of Parker's brain that for a fleeting moment, Parker truly believed that the thought was his own. A knotted fist of nausea blew through Parker's whole body, a hard twist of sickness that fired like a mortar shell on the Fourth of July, exploding in a green wave behind his eyes.

A groan slipped loose from his lips as the world went sideways. He could feel himself listing, his feet bicycling underneath to try and compensate for the sudden inversion of gravity.

Do it, Nate hissed. *Do it, do it, put the blade in her head put the hatchet in her fucking head do it NOW DO IT NOW—*

Parker felt like he was going to throw up. He thought he'd gotten rid of the ghost, whatever it was, banished it from his head. But of course he hadn't. It was too stubborn and mean, too powerful to just give up like that. It'd keep its hooks in him for as long as it could. Even if they managed to get out of here, it would probably never really let him go. He'd be stuck hearing his voice—*its* voice—for the rest of his life.

It was so loud too. So impossible to ignore. Parker's face pinched tightly into a knot as he took a measured step closer to his cousin at the edge of the cliff, then another. She was so small. It would be so easy. He could still hear his dead friend—*not him*, he reminded himself, *not him, not him, not him*—hissing in the back of his head. He wanted to fight against it, to deny the truth of the matter, but in that moment, he knew that he didn't have any choice. He had to do it.

The boy-thing was lost deep inside itself, beating a panicked retreat from its own bloody wounds, all the damage that the two little creatures had hammered into its broken, bent body. Deeper and deeper it ran into the dark, looking for a place to hide among the hard stone tunnels of itself, finding no comfort; the voice wouldn't allow it that, no. The boy-thing didn't want to return to itself, to the terrible world, with its pains and bloody horrors. It didn't want to go back, but no matter how deep inside its horrible, distorted, wounded form it traveled, there wasn't anywhere to hide from the light and die in peace. There was nowhere it could be alone, not anymore.

Nowhere to go but back.

Bleeding into the dirt, the boy-thing opened its eyes. It could already smell where they'd gone.

Parker closed the distance between the two of them and rested a hand on Chloe's slender shoulder, giving it a squeeze he hoped was reassuring as he watched their shadows gliding across the ground: hers slight and painfully thin, propped up by her crutch; his broad and hulking, the hatchet clutched tightly at the end of one tree-trunk arm. Slowly, she turned around to look at him with a soft little smile, a look of actual hope that he hadn't seen on her face in what felt like a very long time. She nodded down toward where the water collected itself after the fall, and the forest beyond, sunlight dancing through the trees and across the churning surface of the river. It was beautiful out there. Another one of the forest's pretty lies.

"How far do you think we have left?"

"I don't know," he said. "Few miles, maybe. Could be more. You know, give or take."

She pricked an eyebrow up at him, that same bright, questioning look she'd been giving people ever since they were little kids.

"Hey, you okay?"

It ached his heart to hear her ask that, knowing what had to come next. But there wasn't any way around it. Not that he could see.

The hatchet was so heavy in his hand, the voice so loud in his head. He leaned in and gave his cousin a big, gentle bear hug, trying to show her all the love he had for her in a single, perfect gesture. He hoped it would be enough.

"What was that for?" Chloe asked, pulling away from him.

"I . . . I just . . ." he stuttered. "I'm so sorry about this."

"What?"

Then he pushed her.

She fell.

Entirely unmoored from the constraints of gravity, Chloe went tumbling off the edge of the cliff, windmilling her arms as her feet left the ground, her stomach lodging itself in her throat. It had happened too quickly for her to understand what had transpired at first. One second they were standing side by side, and the next she was spinning over the edge. She didn't even have the time to scream or shout before she was plummeting toward the ground.

But the falling was familiar. By now, falling was an old friend, that feeling of being suspended in midair, turning in languid circles before the inevitable impact. Hanging there like Wile E. Coyote, she thought to herself, *Shit, this is probably going to hurt, huh?*

And then it did. It hurt a fucking lot. Chloe slammed into the ground in a graceless heap, limbs splaying out in an awkward tangle. The wound in her side screamed against the impact, and the rest of her followed suit. It was like someone had set a bomb off inside her body, the detonation ripping through her at the speed of sound. Her eyes blurred with red and black, and for a moment, she thought she might pass out from the agony. When her vision cleared a moment later, she pawed at her tender midsection, the fresh charge of dark-brown blood pouring out of her impossible to ignore.

Crying out again and biting back a flood of tears, she struggled to roll over and look up at her cousin, who stood on the cliff's edge with a sad, shameful look on his face. He'd pushed her. That was the only explanation.

"Parker, what the *fuck?*" She wept as she tried unsuccessfully to rise to her feet. The pain was like a boulder that had been laid across her, pressing her into the earth, keeping her immobilized. "What did you do that for?"

Above her, Parker worked his jaw open and shut, open and shut, like he was trying to think of the right thing to say.

"Sorry," he said, after a second. "I . . . I had to."

"You had to *throw me off a cliff*?"

He nodded. "Yeah."

"What the fuck for?"

He made a tired face, the tiniest of smiles creeping into his round, dirty cheeks. "The ghosts . . . the thing under the lake . . . they're still in my head. I can hear them now, too, talking to me. Whispering. They don't like you. They wanted me to . . ."

He broke her gaze and twirled the hatchet around in his hand. It didn't take her long to understand his meaning.

"So you pushed me down here instead?"

" Are you . . ." he muttered. "Are you okay?"

She shook her head at him and forced herself to stand up, groaning as she did. It felt like she was going to rip her whole body clean in half.

"I have no idea. Probably not. I mean, goddammit already," she said to him. Moving closer to the cliffside, she held her arms out. "Would you just get down here or help me back up? We're don't have time for this."

He didn't move.

"Parker, come on. Enough of this bullshit, let's go. Stick to the plan, c'mon."

He shook his head at her.

"Sorry, Chloe. I don't think I can. They're . . . they're too loud. I wouldn't be able to . . ."

A tiny fire of rage sparked inside her chest, fueled by the pain that had so completely gripped her body.

"Parker, come *on*. We have to go *now*."

"I know." He nodded off behind her, to the river that flowed away from the cliff and along the path of the sun. "You go that way, okay? Stick to the plan."

He tossed one of the backpacks down the cliff to land at her feet, and then, after a long moment of deliberation, he tossed the black hatchet down after. It thumped against the dirt and stayed where it fell. Chloe gave him a confused look.

"What do you think you're doing?"

"You need it more than me."

Unbidden, her mind flashed to all the horrible things she'd seen done with that hatchet. All the ugly, evil shit she'd downloaded over the last few days.

"I don't want it."

"Neither do I. It's yours now."

"No, it's not!" she insisted. "It's not mine, and I'm not touching it, because everybody who does fucking dies."

"I'm still here," Park said, with a weird smile. "Come on, you don't know what this place is going to throw at you between here and wherever it is we end up. You need something to protect yourself with."

"What about you?"

He smiled at her and, with one big hand, produced the camp hammer she'd used to mark the trees from his backpack. She didn't know when he'd lifted it from her, but it was a neat trick.

"I'll be fine," he said. "I'll catch up. I've just got something I need to take care of first. You just stick to the plan. I'll see you at home, okay? Promise. I love you."

She didn't believe him at all, but she couldn't get back up there to stop him, either. Her shoulders slumped, and wrapping her hand in the remnants of an old T-shirt, she limped over to pick up the hatchet. Maybe not touching it directly would dull some of the bad mojo radiating off of it. Even so, the second she curled her swaddled hand around that black haft, she felt it. Like whispers in the dark. Blood in the water. The T-shirt didn't help much, but it was still better than mainlining any more of this place's twisted magic. It would have to do. She'd had enough doors of perception kicked open without her permission already.

The hatchet was heavier than it looked, more like a cast iron pan than something lightweight and stainless steel you'd buy at the hardware store. It felt substantial in her hand, old and bitter. She gave it a few practice swings, testing out its balance. Wounded as she was, Chloe didn't know if she could even defend herself at all, but she'd rather have it and not need it than need it and not have it.

"Fine," she said at last, raising her head toward the rocky edge above her. "If it'll make you happy, I suppose that I can make this w— . . . Parker?"

But the cliff was empty. He was already gone.

19

Step by hitching step, Chloe tracked the river downstream, walking along the soft earthen bank, following what she thought was the path of the sun. All around her, the forest seemed to breathe in and out, drawing in closer and then farther away as she passed through it. Her nerves had gotten worse since she and Parker had split up, drawing themselves tight like piano wire. Beside her, the water had begun to darken and pick up speed. But it wasn't the river that was bothering her; it was that no matter how far she seemed to go, the forest was still riddled with sentinel trees. Every few feet, she'd spy another one, standing in her path or just peeking out from the distance. She'd thought that getting farther out would mean she'd be able to leave them behind. Guess not.

Up ahead of her, the river bent to one side and then straightened out. As Chloe *pick-thrush*ed around its bank, she saw what the water was leading her toward. It was a row of white trees, clustered so tightly across the bank that it might as well have been a wall. Big enough that she couldn't walk around it, tight enough that she didn't dare go through them; she wasn't going to risk accidentally jacking into the fear-Matrix again.

Walking up a little farther, she stood in front of the wall of trees and looked them up and down, the knots in the bark like dead, unblinking eyes. Somewhere along the line, she'd started thinking of the trees like individual nerve endings, all interconnected, forming a web throughout the whole of the Pine Barrens. The thing under the lake was stitched through all of it, Chloe understood that better than anybody.

The only way it lets us go is if we make it, she'd said, sitting on the log, staring out into the wilderness with Parker. *And I think the only way we can do that is by giving it bigger problems than us.*

Bigger problems like what? he'd asked.

She'd spat then, and hoped he couldn't see the tears collecting at the corners of her eyes.

Like us burning this forest to the fucking ground.

It made sense on paper, but there was something else to it, something stubborn and cruel that she desperately hoped he wouldn't notice. The Pine Barrens had bled her, violated her, turned her inside out. This forest and the awful, craven things that lived inside it had hurt her, and she wanted to hurt them back.

The plan wasn't complicated, really: they'd follow the river as far as they could, and if (really *when*) things got dicey, they'd use the rest of Adam's Everclear to start a fire the Barrens couldn't ignore. The river would be their way out. They'd swim, if they had to. Even if they didn't know where it led, anywhere was better than here.

Unslinging the backpack from her shoulder, Chloe used her crutch to steady herself while she knelt down to unzip the bag. She knew the white trees wouldn't burn on their own; she'd seen as much when Josh had tried to light their branches for a campfire two days before. That was okay. She had all the propellant she needed right here. Drawing the bottle of clear liquor from the side of Adam's pack, a Molotov cocktail waiting to happen, she uncapped it and brought it to her lips, taking a deep slug off the top. It tasted like a dozen different shitty, stupid nights, dragging napalm down her throat as she fired it back, resting in a ball in her belly. Ugh. She'd always hated this shit. Things always got too messy when they drank it. It was like jet fuel for bad decisions.

Unfortunately, bad decisions were all she had left at this point. In front of her, the sentinel trees swayed in a breeze she didn't feel, back and forth, like they were waving to her. She upended the rest of the bottle onto them, shaking it until she'd dumped every last drop onto the trunks and ashy roots. Tossing the bottle into the river, she watched it float away, then fished Nicky's little yellow lighter from her jeans pocket. *Skritch*ing it to life, she held the flickering little flame away from her face and touched it to the nearest trunk.

Nothing happened.

Goddammit, come on. The only thing more flammable than 190 proof liquor was like, pure gasoline. This should have worked. She waved the little flame back and forth across the booze-drenched bark, over and over, trying to force the issue, but the trees refused to take. It was like trying to set fire to stone; the Everclear didn't catch, the bark didn't blacken. She held the fire to the tree until the cheap little flint wheel grew hot and sizzled against her skin, forcing her to douse the flame.

Of course. Of fucking course it wasn't going to be that simple. They were insects scrabbling at the ankles of ancient, cruel powers that could no doubt crush them at any time.

A great, black desolation settled into the pit of her chest. If the Everclear hadn't worked, then what would? There wasn't anything else.

Actually, wait a second.

She did have something that might do the trick—and if not?

Well, she'd think about *if not* when it happened.

Stepping back, Chloe unlooped the black hatchet from her belt and held it up high so the silver line of flint in the blade's edge glinted in the sun. She could do this. Of course she could. She'd seen that Phipps asshole do it enough times, and he was a psychopathic primitive. All she had to do was snap it down into the rocks like this—

Sparks exploded at the foot of the closest tree as she raked the blade over the stones, blooming into tongues of gasping blue flame that spread quicker than Chloe had expected—the Everclear, finally doing its job. In an instant, the fire grew and raced up the length of the white trees, turning from blue to orange-black as it jumped eagerly from branch to branch, a forest fire in fast-forward.

A mad, desperate wail split the inside of her head, like it was sawing the two hemispheres of her brain apart. Chloe screamed through clenched teeth and doubled over, raking at her eyes with numb fingers, her crutch dropping out from under her arm, useless. The sound was enormous and catastrophic, and when it finally subsided, the silence that settled in between her ears in its wake was deafening. She barely had a chance to catch her breath before the sound ripped through her again, even louder this time, angrier, and she felt a terrific heat scorching her hand, so terrible that she thought that she'd caught fire alongside the trees.

Looking down, she saw the black hatchet pulsing and throbbing in time with the heartbeat of the fire, forming stress cracks along the wood and metal that radiated a kind of sour red light. The forest's own bad magic, working against itself. Chloe could have laughed.

Then the hatchet shattered, detonating in a spray of fire and shrapnel that bit into her face and arms and neck and chest. Chloe reeled backward, trying to escape what had already happened, her body bright with new pain, falling, falling, falling until she hit the ground.

It didn't take Parker long to realize he wasn't alone. There wasn't any one thing that tipped him off to it—no nearby footsteps or heavy breathing. It was more like a feeling he got every few seconds, as if sharp, reptilian claws were plucking at the sweaty spot between his shoulder blades.

Stopping for a moment, he stared back into the trees and the shadows that had surrounded him when he wasn't looking. The darkness was nearly absolute; it was like the night never quite left this place, instead hanging on like grim death in the places where it could hide itself, underneath branches and brambles, in between the white trunks and buried under knotted roots. He thought about calling out to whatever it was that was traveling along in his wake but knew it couldn't or wouldn't respond. Not in any recognizable human way, at least. Not anymore.

Hiking Nate's overstuffed bag higher on his shoulders, Parker kept on the path, listening to the crunch of his shoes against the ground, the wheeze in his lungs, his heartbeat thudding inside his temples. The trees were growing closer together the farther in he went. Parker had seen pictures of trees that had grown together like this in Earth Science class. Mrs. Sandoval had said that trees growing into one another like that usually meant a forest fire was inevitable, to clear the ground and make way for new life. Fires were good, she'd told them. Fires were change incarnate. Nothing in this world walked away from fire unscathed.

Parker smiled at the thought. He was getting close now.

Some part of Chloe knew that she was bleeding, that there were dozens of new wounds blown into the soft, dirty skin of her face, like she'd been blasted with a shotgun or a pipe bomb. But somehow, that didn't matter much right now. Inside her head, the scream had turned itself into a physical thing, a black, razor-toothed tendril that had curled around her brain to bore through the middle, like a finger trying to wriggle through a raw steak.

"No, no, no, no, no," Chloe whimpered on the ground, clutching at her head, curling up as small as she could. "Get out, please, just stop, get out, let me go . . ."

The tentacle burrowed deeper, excavating memories she hadn't thought of in years: her seventh birthday party when her dad got too drunk; the first time she'd ever kissed anyone (Stacy Cale, at a sleepover in eighth grade, on a dare); her childhood teddy bear, a battered yellow Pooh, sitting on the windowsill of her bedroom, draped in sunlight.

Distantly, Chloe understood what was happening here. She was being probed, explored, cored like an apple. The forest—and the thing underneath, for they were one and the same, she saw that now—had had its fun. Now it meant to take her too; just like the others. Mary Kane, Uncle Dave, Nate, Josh, Nicky, Adam—they were all long dead, thrown into the gaping maw of the Pine Barrens as sacrifices, or worse, food.

Chloe didn't plan on joining them.

Marshaling her strength, Chloe gave a mental *shove* against the black tendril and felt it withdraw—not much, just the tiniest bit, but that might have been enough. Forcing her eyes open, she saw that the fire was spreading too quickly, racing along the ground where she'd previously spilled a trail of the grain alcohol, crackling and thrashing. It had already jumped from the sentinel trees to the regular pines and oaks now, too, blooming out in a wave of destruction—heat and smoke and light all working in concert to cause as much damage as possible, painting her face and skin with a brutal, dry heat that stole her breath. She could tell that this was only the beginning; things were about to get a whole lot worse for the Pine Barrens.

Inside her head, the forest thrashed and screamed, consumed by the flames. Then it withdrew, leaving a kind of impression where its presence had dug in, another scar in Chloe's collection. The thing had taken the bait; now it had bigger concerns than one broken, bleeding little girl. The fire was spreading, and left unchecked, it would grow to consume everything. She could imagine it happening already—the entire southern half of New Jersey ravaged by fire and smoke and cinders. She'd started something she couldn't control, and the only thing to do about it now was let it run its course.

Smoke, thick and billowing, rankled at her throat and her lungs, dancing through her insides, leaving pinpricks of bright, itching pain in its wake. Chloe grasped at the skin underneath her neck as she forced out cough after cough, trying to catch a breath of clean air. No such luck.

Moving on her hands and knees, she clambered over to the river's edge, feeling the foamy, rushing waves slap coldly against her palms and wrists. The water was deep here, so deep that she could only barely make out the silt and rocks at the bottom. Her skull throbbed terribly where the forest had attempted to wrench its way through, but for now, she was alone inside her own head again. Not that it would last. Once the thing realized that there was nothing it could do to stop the burning, it'd be back to finish the job. Better for Chloe to not be close by when that happened.

Wincing from the pain that pulsed through her entire body, Chloe drew deep breath after deep breath, then dumped herself into the rushing waves below.

Cold, stone-hard and absolute, dragged her down, snatching the air from her lungs and the sight from her eyes in a single shock. But already she could feel herself moving through the freeze, hurtling away from the banks, propelled by the river. She could feel herself spinning in the icy waves, glancing off rocks and dirt and sunken logs, but the impacts barely registered.

She would have laughed if she had been able. She'd done it. She'd actually gotten away. All she had to do now was ride the river all the way to wherever it took her.

She bobbed upward without meaning to, breaking the surface of the water in a heaving, bubbling mass, drawing air into her lungs so hard that it pained her. The river rushed her away, growing wider and deeper and faster by the second, churning with whitecaps as it carried her along through straits and perilous turns. Holding her hands out, Chloe tried to brace herself from colliding with more flotsam, but she could only do so much; she needed her hands to stay afloat, and couldn't do both at the same time.

Underneath her, she could feel debris whipping past her legs, roots and rocks and the like, but she didn't truly realize just how fast she was being dragged until the waves dipped, then spun her in place and caromed her off of something hard and sharp. She heard a soft, meaty *crunch* inside one of her legs—and for a moment, she went numb from the thigh down, a curious sensation replaced a moment later by pure agony.

Another scream came clamoring out of her, and she thrashed at the water, trying to right herself, trying in her pain and panic to somehow gauge the extent of the damage done to her leg. Something was wrong, she knew that much. Something was very fucking wrong here. Spitting out a murky, bitter mouthful of river water, she tried to push away from another tangled cluster of branches, but her hands had already gone numb from the icy water, and she only sent herself spinning around again, careening sidelong toward a rock that jabbed out of the surface of the water like a broken tooth.

She caught the edge face-first, the impact rocking her whole body with a sharp, hollow *crack* that she felt all the way down to her toes. A blade of white light tore through her skull, clouding her left eye with a curtain of muddy red that ebbed away and replaced itself every time her face dipped under the waves. She tried to scream again, tried to cry out, tried to wipe the blood away, but it was too much. She was all bad angles and numb digits now. Nothing worked the way she told it to. As she was swept downriver, Chloe could already feel herself spreading out and fading away, a single drop of blood diluted in too much water. In the last glimmers of consciousness, she hoped that Parker was right, that this river would lead her out of this fucking forest and not into some deeper part of the nightmare they'd been trapped in all this time. All she wanted was to get out, and to see him again.

Then she passed out and didn't feel a thing anymore.

20

Lightly, Parker stone-hopped across another bent hairpin creek. He could smell it in the air now—a sort of cinnamon sweetness buoyed along atop a hot, billowing musk. It smelled like campfires and fireplaces and his dad's cigars, all at once. He couldn't *see* the smoke yet, but yeah, it was definitely there.

As he walked, Parker smiled faintly to himself. She'd really done it.

He walked on and on, and time grew loose around him, warping like he was trying to scoop up melting butter with his bare hands. He didn't know if he'd been walking for minutes or for hours, only that the farther he went, the more the white trees grew taller and thicker, crowding in together so tight that he felt like he needed to hold his breath and turn sideways just to squeeze between them.

Up ahead, just past another copse, he could see the ground rising up into a steep little hillock, blanketed in trees so tightly packed it looked like a head of hair. He had no idea how he was going to get through something like that, but he'd have to figure out a way. No sense in coming this far and not seeing it through to the end.

Chloe had told him about this place. Back at the camp, she'd searched her memory and told him that if they came to a hill like this, they'd gone too far off the path and they needed to turn back. Beyond this was the place where Mary Kane had died.

They were supposed to give the tree a wide berth; that was the plan the whole time. Same as the lake. The whole forest was cursed, but there were some parts that were worse than others, and according to Chloe, the tree was about as bad as it got. But plans changed. And Parker still had some things that needed doing before he could be done with this place.

A chill wind blew in from behind him and swiped at his sweat-dappled neck, raising the hair there to stiff attention. Whatever inhuman thing that had been dogging his path, it was close now. Maybe close enough for him to reach out and touch.

As if on cue, a shape emerged from behind one of the largest trees on the hill—short and round, his face snarled up with bitter contempt, his T-shirt drawn too tight across his broad, soft chest.

Nate.

Except it wasn't. The forest made it so easy to make that mistake again, to take what Parker was seeing as truth. But the longer he stood there and looked at the thing wearing his dead friend like a mask, the more he saw the places where the glamour was imperfect. He'd seen it before, the way the ghost's face seemed to melt and churn when he looked at it for too long. At first, he'd written it off as trick of the light, a side effect of Nate being somehow-dead-yet-here; now he knew better.

Parker slowed to a halt, feeling his heart wilt and fall into his guts. His body ached, his head hurt, his feet were little more than swollen bags filled with blood and bone. He pulled his glasses off his face and buffed the lenses on the bottom of his T-shirt before slipping the frames back over his nose and ears and fixing the impostor with a hard, exhausted look.

"Don't you have anything better to do?"

Nate—not-Nate—shrugged and cracked a smile.

"What can I say?" it said. "I like you, Parker."

"Just like you liked my dad?"

"That was different," the apparition told him. "That was complicated."

"And this isn't?"

"Your dad was looking for something that he wasn't ever going to find out here," it said. "Wasn't a good fit for anybody. But you know him. Soldier to the core. He kept pushing, kept trying to force the issue. Tried that all the way up until he put the knife to his wrists."

"Stop."

"I mean, does that sound familiar at all to you? You knew him pretty well, so—"

"Just fucking *stop*," Parker moaned.

The ghost held its stolen hands up—*I'm just saying*—another perfect pantomime of Parker's dead friend. "Listen. You're anything but weak. You came out here looking for answers, and you found them. Not everybody could do the same. You can hold steady, stay strong. You can really make a difference here."

"What are you saying?" Parker asked warily.

"I'm saying this doesn't need to be the end. For anybody. I know why you did what you did—I know why you left her behind and came looking for me, for this place. It's the same reason you came out to the forest looking for the truth. All you need to do is change your endgame a little bit. We can both get out of here. There's still time."

Parker spat. "I'm not your Renfield."

He started walking again. The ghost kept pace with him.

"Why are you still wearing his face, anyway?" Parker asked. "I—*we*—know what you really are underneath it all."

The ghost sneered. "I'm sure you think you do."

"Chloe told me all about what she saw. The city under the lake. Mary and the reverend. Philips, or something."

"Phipps," the ghost corrected. "Simon Phipps."

"That's the one. Phipps. Whatever happened to that guy?"

"He died."

"That's all? Sounds like he deserved worse than he got."

The ghost shook its head. "You have no idea."

"And you still haven't answered the question."

"Maybe I like wearing him," the apparition mused. "Maybe I like the way he fits, the way he looks. Why, not a fan?"

Parker didn't say anything.

"Oh, what, did I strike a nerve? Not a fan of having your fuck-ups thrown in your face? I mean, I get it. There are so many of them. There was Nate, obviously. Adam, Josh, Nicky, now Chloe and you too. Not to mention your poor mother and all their parents too. Brothers and sisters. Teachers, friends. Everybody who hears about what happened here. People notice when kids die, Parker. Especially when they die ugly. Really, there's no counting the number of people you've hurt in four short days. All with one little bullet."

"Not Chloe," said Parker. "Not her. She got out."

Not-Nate leaned in, grinning. "You sure about that? Because last I saw, she'd split her skull open on a rock while she was trying not to drown. What are the odds she'll be able to swim for her life, unconscious and bleeding from a head wound? I'm not sure, friend. I don't like her chances much at all."

Parker looked at the ghost, grinding his molars, trying to tell how much of it was a lie. He bristled at the thought of Chloe hurt, but he had to believe she was going to be okay. He reminded himself that he could already smell the forest fire on the wind. She'd done it. She was going to get out. She was going to be okay.

"Hey, let me ask you something," Parker said casually, straightening his expression. "Did it hurt? When Chloe set the trees on fire, did that hurt? Did you feel it?"

Not-Nate laughed at the question, not a damp, throaty chuckle now but a full belly laugh, a perfect replica of the one Parker was so used to hearing from the boy he'd killed just days ago.

"Physical pain is a small concept for small things," not-Nate scoffed. "You children have no idea what true pain really is."

"That's a *yes*," Parker said, snapping a finger-gun at the thing's melting face. "Good." He drew another deep breath, the heat and cinders and burnt sugar of crackling sap syrupy in the back of his throat.

Not-Nate laughed again, but it was harder this time. Colder, older, and meaner.

"Fine," it said. "Have it your way. But when he's ripping your guts out, I want you to remember I gave you a chance."

The ghost's face drooped into one final hateful glower, and then not-Nate dissolved in midair as quickly as he'd appeared. Through his fading frame, Parker could just make out another silhouette crouched at the foot of the little hill. Its body and limbs were warped and distended, its pallid skin draped in wounds and blood, pockmarked with holes it shouldn't have been able to survive.

Adam.

From its crouched position, the twisted thing watched him approach with glassy, inhuman eyes, wide and unblinking. Parker wanted to say something to his former friend, anything, but the words wouldn't come. He wasn't sure if there was any Adam left inside the broken shell that would hear a word he said, anyway.

The Adam-thing waggled its pale tongue between broken little razor teeth as it rose up to its full height and began advancing on him. Parker briefly wished he'd hung on to the black hatchet. Rolling his shoulders until the top part of his spine crackled, Parker braced himself. He could still feel every cut and bruise from the last time they'd done this.

The Adam-thing leaped at him, claws out, and Parker lunged forward to catch it in midair, hammering its ribs with tight, heavy fists as fast as he could piston them. It slashed at his shoulders, opening fresh, deep cuts around the straps of the backpack, but Parker tried to ignore the pain, locking his hands on the creature's midsection to throw it away from him with a mighty heave. The warped thing bounced off a cluster of trees with a bone-crunching *thunk* but was back on its feet as soon as it hit the ground.

This time, it was Parker's turn to rush in. He barreled toward the creature, but the Adam-thing quickstepped forward and struck Parker in the shoulder with one sharp claw, opening up long red streaks through his flesh. Parker cried out and winced back, then riposted, slamming one safe-sized fist into the side of the creature's head. Shrugging off the blow, the creature clacked its teeth at him and swung again, then Parker did the same, backing up the hill as he swung, desperate to keep the higher ground.

Punch, swipe, punch, swipe. They traded shots as they climbed the hill together, and when they reached the crest, the Adam-thing ducked down and dodged around his side to strike low. But Parker was ready, firing an uppercut home into the soft meat of its distended neck, the ragged wound blown into the flesh when Chloe pulled the trigger the last time. The creature trilled and recoiled, and Parker tackled it as hard as he could, sending both of them careening over the hill and down the other side.

Rolling in a knotted clump, they fell, bouncing off trunks and over fallen logs, exchanging wild body blows until they crashed past the trees into a wide-open clearing covered in black soil and dry branches. In the center grew a massive, warped old tree, burned black as oil and cut all over with coarse crosses.

It towered above him; it towered above everything, really. Two hundred and fifty feet tall if it was a foot, it stood ancient and heavy with bent, knobbled branches that sprouted like disfigured arms from its blackened, horrible trunk. From where he'd fallen, he could see the hollow hacked roughly into the side of the tree—an upright doublewide coffin.

Flattened on the ground, Parker lay in awe of the tree. He'd never seen anything like it in his life. He'd never even *dreamed* of something like it. It looked like it had been ripped from another time, some brutal, prehistoric era, and then abandoned here to take root and spread. He could perfectly imagine this great, malignant thing growing and hammering its way out of the earth, cruel and hard, out of time and space. Another horror that had sprouted here and never stopped—a dead thing still growing, fueled by the curse that had been poisoning this forest since time immemorial.

A growl came from beside him. He tried to roll away, but he was too late. Pain erupted across the side of his head. The right side of his vision went red and then black immediately after, and stayed that way. Parker screamed and recoiled, scrabbling his feet in the dirt, fingertips searching his bloody face until they sunk into a hot, wet split in the flesh that lit up with panicked, desperate agony as he touched it. Every instinct in his body told him not to touch it, just put pressure on it, stop the bleeding, but he kept his hand where it was, exploring. He had to know.

The gash ran from the backside of his skull all the way to the bridge of his nose, bisecting his eye, slashing the skin deep and bloody. He could feel that his ear had been mangled, sheared in half as the Adam-thing had raked his skull. The lower half hung loosely by a few strings of skin and sinew, useless. He blinked, or at least tried to—he could only see out of one of his eyes, now. Pain, still far off but razor sharp, radiated across half his head, and when he tried to breathe, his lips sputtered against each other, warm and wet. The taste of copper filled his mouth, and he spat as his other hand went pawing for the glasses that had been stripped off his face when the creature had struck him. Somewhere in the back of his mind, he knew that the Adam-thing had slashed out his eye, but it hardly seemed to matter now. It was just an eye, just an ear. He had spares.

When his fingers alighted on the molded plastic of his specs, Parker fit them over his face once more, shuttering his surroundings into what little focus he could lay claim to. He wasn't dead yet. He could still do this.

Out of his left eye, Parker saw the Adam-thing rise and start to advance, stalking toward him with a rictus grin pulled across its mottled, papery skull. Parker scrambled back, spiking his arms and legs beneath his massive frame to try and get purchase, catch his balance, something, anything. Then the bleeding, snarling, claws-and-teeth thing that used to be his friend was on top of him once again, digging at him with those horrible, ragged barebone hands, opening up fresh rivers of blood in his chest, shoulders, forearms. Biting back a howl of rage and pain, Parker clamped one hand around the creature's throat, gagging inwardly at the soft, gelatinous feel of its skin, and pounded at its skull with a fist knotted tight as steel cable. After a few brutal punches, he felt the Adam-thing's grip loosen, and Parker kicked him off, sending him flopping to the ground in a graceless heap.

They were both slow to get back to their feet, but when they did, Parker was just a little faster on the draw. Rearing back as he rose, he threw his full weight into the swing.

The Adam-thing never saw it coming.

Parker hit him like a car crash. He felt bones breaking under the crush of his knuckles; heard the sick splitting sound the second his fist made contact with the creature's skull; saw the way his warped, bleeding friend dropped to the ground like a cut-string marionette. Except that wasn't enough. It was never going to be enough. He was going to get up again, and again, and again. How many times had he come back already? How much more damage could he be allowed to cause?

No, this was Parker's chance. He could stop it for good, right here, right now. Fear and panic, paranoia and rage boiled in his head like a writhing fist of black tentacles. Before he knew that he was really doing it, he'd fallen on top of Adam's crumpled, grotesque form and started hammering him with both fists, drumming his head with a monstrous fury that seemed to grow with each successive blow.

He hit him until his hands, numb from the beating, came away soaked in red, like he'd dipped them in a bucket of blood. Underneath him, the Adam-thing lay deathly still, head caved in like a rotten jack-o'-lantern, the uneven flicker of his lungs filling and purging the only sign that he—*it*—was still alive.

Just one more, a voice that wasn't his own whispered to him. *That's all it'll take to spill that head of his all over the forest floor. One good hit. Better make it count.*

He almost did it, too. Parker reared up like a blood-crazed bear, lacing his cracked, split fists together and raising them high to swing like a sledgehammer before the fire that had caught inside his head and his heart sputtered, then went out and stayed out.

"Do it."

Park turned his head to look for the source of that new voice, with all its cold cruelty. From around the great tree emerged a girl, not much older than he was, with dark hair and big, expressive eyes. She was tall—not as tall as Parker, but not far off, either. Her skin was pale, but not clammy or dead. It made him think of marble, like she had spent her entire life hiding from the sun. She wore a plain white dress, the fabric soft and thin, so thin that he could nearly see through to what hid underneath. He blushed when he realized he was staring.

The girl took a few steps closer to him and held her hands out.

"He's going to come back," she said. "You know he is."

Parker's arms fell to his sides and hung there, useless—dead things that had been nailed to his shoulders. He couldn't hit Adam again even if he wanted to.

"Because you keep bringing him back," he snarled.

Inside his chest, Parker's heart knocked and hammered against his ribs at a madman pace that didn't seem to be slowing. Forcing himself to draw steady, even breaths, he let his head hang down until his chin settled on his collarbone.

He didn't hear her move. Same as always. She didn't make any noise, but then suddenly, she was right beside him, kneeling down, watching him watch Adam, all of reality drawn into a perfect little bubble that held the three of them together. A quiet, awful little universe all their own.

"Not this time," the ghost said. "Not anymore. I'm done dragging him along. If he gets up again—*when* he gets up again—that's all him."

"But he's not him," Parker said. "Just like you're not you. You never were."

"Of course I'm me," the ghost said. "I've been me this whole time. I don't know what your cousin told you, but she doesn't know what she's talking about. Now *finish it*."

Parker's shoulders fell.

Underneath him, Adam's breathing had quickened, but it was shallow. He'd seen breathing like this before, back when he was a kid and his dog Baxter had gotten bit by a snake. Bax had lain in the garage breathing exactly this same way for hours before he finally died. *Nothing to do now but wait*, his dad had told him, tears in his eyes. *Be with him. Remind him that he's not alone. Nothing in this world should have to die alone, Parker.*

"He's already gone," he said. "And I'm not gonna be your new monster."

The giant boy rolled off his fallen, dying friend and rose, his movements achingly slow. Parker turned away from the ghostly girl's cold, dead gaze, turning in a slow rotation to take in the whole of the clearing. Smoke was rising up beyond the trees on the other side of the hill. They didn't have much longer. He glanced over his shoulder to catch another glimpse of the pale ghost that had stood beside him just moments before. Of course she was gone.

With one hand, he wiped a fresh curtain of blood from his jaw and smeared it on his T-shirt, leaving a messy red handprint on the torn fabric. He could hear it now—the roar and crackle of the flames as they grew and devoured in the distance. Except the fire wasn't so distant anymore. He could already feel the heat spreading through the air like a terrible fever. Limping, he stepped away from the body on the stick-strewn ground, moving toward the great black tree.

"Parker . . ."

For a moment, Parker imagined he could actually feel her fingers grazing his bare skin. Her touch was cool and delicate, but firm. More parlor tricks. More bullshit.

"What do you think you're doing here? You gonna try and break the curse, set her free? Is that it? One last good deed before the curtain falls?" the ghost's disembodied voice called to him. "That's not how it works. You can't help her, and you can't stop me. Hell, it's too late for you to get away now too. Most you can hope for now is a quick death. After that . . . *poof.* Dust. Barely a memory."

"Better dust than an eternity here. And whatever you are, you'll die, too, someday. Don't think that you won't. Everything dies. Everything."

The ghost scoffed. "You can't kill something like me, Parker. You can't stop the eternal."

"But we hurt you," Parker said. "We made you feel it. Didn't we?"

Pulling Nate's pack up onto his shoulders one last time, Parker closed the distance between himself and the tree. He felt like he was dragging himself through a swamp, his legs wobbling and threatening to give out at any moment. His body was worn and exhausted, beaten bloody and drained of energy. He was done. He had to be done now. Even though the branch-carpeted ground was dry and firm, he felt himself sinking down to the knees, forcing him to pull his legs from sucking mud with every step.

With one foot braced against the roots of the great black tree, Parker curled both hands around the rough edge of the old hollow and pulled. He didn't even have to put any muscle into it—with a soft *crunch*, the wood and bark came away from the trunk, crumbling in his hands and between his oversized fingers like dry clay. He pulled it off in dusty fistfuls until the hole was wide enough that he could see inside.

The bones in the tree were a blackened wreck, scorched and caked with filth and age, yet still they hung together in a nearly complete skeleton. Its arms were folded over its gritty, cracked rib cage like a stubby pair of frontal wings, the spine bent and crimped like a broken Slinky. The skull was a ruined, crater-marked planet that leered out at him with a drawn, joyless smile. Looking into its grime-packed eyes filled Parker with a curious, vertiginous sensation. Like he was staring into the past and the future simultaneously, the directions of time laid over one another in a double image.

"This won't redeem you. You've gone too far, done too much. It's not going to go the way you think," the ghost said from behind him. "You small things have no idea of the kind of suffering that waits for you at the end of this dream you call *life*. When you see it, you'll beg me to keep you here. Just like they did."

Parker didn't turn to look. He curled his hands into the brittle wood and pulled again, stripping away a dry slab as big as a side of beef, tearing the hole wide enough that he could step through. Tossing the plank aside, Parker shucked the duffel off his broad shoulders and unzipped the top, spreading it wide. Inside, it was the same as it had been when Chloe had passed it over to him this morning, the same as it had been when Nate had first shown it off on Friday afternoon: packed full of fireworks and firecrackers, Black Cats, bundles of sparklers and Roman candles, and—because Nate had been a psycho long before Parker had shot him—ziplock bags bulging with black powder, filched from his dad's gun safe. There was enough in here to level an entire apartment building.

Or one giant old tree.

A shuddering, cracking noise split the stillness of the great clearing from far behind him. He turned to look and, with his one good eye, saw that above the forest, gray-black smoke was already rising from the wild flames that were consuming everything nearby, cutting off all routes out. The blaze was everywhere now. From where he stood, Park could see columns of black and red and orange and yellow thrashing in between the trees on the hill, growing brighter and brighter.

Chloe's fire was finally breaking through.

Carefully, he fixed Nate's bag in between the skeleton's folded arms, tucking it tight so she could hold it for both of them. Then he stepped inside the tree with her, burrowing down to sit against the dry, crumbling bark.

Across the clearing, the fire spilled through the trees in a burning tidal bore, dripping flame that splashed to the earth and spread, catching the tinder-scattered ground alight within seconds. Parker crossed his arms over his chest and looked up at the skeleton long-grown into the wood, and the duffel cradled tightly in her arms. He wondered who she'd really been, all those centuries ago. He wondered if she'd been a happy person, before the Barrens had gotten its hooks into her, before everything had gone wrong. It felt like it had been years since he'd been happy.

He missed his friends. He missed his dad. He missed his mom. He hoped that whatever happened after this, she'd be okay. Maybe more than anything else, he hoped Chloe got out of the woods all right. There was so much he wished he could change. There were so many things he'd done that he would give anything to undo. But it was too late. Nothing to do now but wait.

He breathed deep, letting the smoke work its magic, summoning up little flashbulb pops of light in front of his eye and a numb, drowsy feeling in his head. Like he could just sit here and go to sleep and everything would be just fine. He blinked, and when he looked again, the fire had gotten so much closer—when did that happen? Another blink, and the flames were nearly on top of him, so thick and bright that he couldn't see beyond the edges of the tree anymore. The fire had swallowed it—them—up whole, thrashing at the space inside.

From his pants pocket, Parker drew a battered silver Zippo, the letters *DAC* engraved on the side. He popped the lid open and struck it to life, the flickering little light almost laughably small in the face of the blaze that surrounded him. With one shaking hand, Park held the little flame out to one of the fuses sticking out of the duffel. It caught quickly, the spark curling around closer and closer to the bag. Parker snapped the lighter shut again and clutched it tight in his hands and started to cry.

Broken, half-blind, and self-entombed inside the tree, Parker didn't feel when it happened, and yet, he felt so much more than that. For a single, impossibly small moment in between the waiting and the nothing, he felt everything—the whole of the forest around him, alive with fire, twisted and ancient. He could feel it all, writhing in pain and rage, dragging him bodily into itself. He could feel the wind grazing across the dirt, he could feel the flames chewing into tree after tree, the creeks and rivers rushing across his body like beads of sweat racing down his back. For a single, perfect moment, he was finally connected to everything, and it felt—

Boom.

APRIL

The smell. That was what hit her first. Not the humidity or the gray sunlight drifting through the low cloud cover. It was the smell. Dry and rich and earthy and sweet like pipe tobacco, rising up from the earth alongside the freeway. It was just like she remembered, waking up nearly dead—riddled with infection, one leg broken and her head split half open—on a silty riverbank underneath a smoke-clotted sky early on a Tuesday morning last May. She'd dragged herself along in that smell for an hour or more until she found a stretch of blacktop and a friendly stranger in a pickup truck willing to take her to the closest hospital. She'd breathed in that smell in great lungfuls, not committing it to memory so much as tattooing it deep into her soul.

Some days, she still woke up with it in her nostrils. She knew she'd probably carry the smell of the burning forest with her for the rest of her life.

The soil was black here, still scorched to match the grasping, burned bones that jabbed out of the cindered earth. It was going to be a long time before the forest healed from what they—what *she*—had done to it, and even then it would still bear the scars for decades to come. She could sympathize. Chloe understood scars better than anyone she knew.

Up along the shoulder of the freeway, she heard the car's engine cut out. Turning to look, she saw the little Hyundai's emergency blinkers switch on, metronomic in their steadiness. She'd had to recruit someone to drive her here; she hadn't driven anywhere since she'd gotten out of the hospital. She wasn't allowed, legally speaking. Too many injuries still healing. Too much of a liability. She wasn't about to ask her parents to cart her down here, either. They would have shit themselves if she'd even mentioned it, probably would have locked her in her bedroom for good measure.

She wouldn't have blamed them. She would've thought she was crazy too.

But knowing that wasn't enough to stop her from making the trip. She'd just needed to find alternative transport out of Randolph. She waved to the little sedan—*I'm fine, thanks, be right back*—then hobbled over to the steel embankment and swung her legs around and over the top. She didn't plan on staying long.

Pick-thrush. Pick-thrush. Pick-thrush. The girl swept her hardened aluminum cane through the black dirt at a steady pace as she trekked between the dark trees to a place where she could only barely hear the hiss of cars whipping by on the Garden State Parkway. The smell was stronger the farther in she went, to the point that she was almost gagging on it, back here among the remnants of the blaze. She'd watched the fires churn and swell on the television in her hospital room in Saint Clare's for weeks until the firefighters and FEMA and the forestry service got them under control. When it was all over, the sprawling forest that made up the lower third of the state was left blackened and crumbling.

Eventually, the doctors had been able to stem the infection that had been chewing its way through the trunk of Chloe's body. When she was finally discharged from the hospital, she left behind a kidney and three feet of small intestine, sporting, among others, a scar like a lightning tree from her ribs to her navel, thick and ridged like wood grain. Her leg had never healed right, either, but she was never going to go out for the track team, anyway.

Carefully, she climbed over another fallen tree and wended her way through a tangle of broken, ashy branches, feeling the thorns catch in the fabric of her jeans, drawing tiny beads of blood from her shaky legs. Bracing herself, she used her cane to clear the path before her, limping along until she came to the clearing. It looked exactly like it did the first time she'd seen it: bright, verdant green despite the ash and destruction that surrounded it, filled with broken tree stumps, and almost perfectly circular. *Like the lake*, a bitter little voice hissed inside her head. *Like the grave.*

Swallowing the tongue of bile that had crept into her mouth, Chloe stepped into the clearing. The memories, however bad they were, were just that. Memories. Besides, it wasn't the clearing itself she'd come here to see. Not exactly, anyway.

She'd first had the dream a few months after her release from Saint Clare's, with all its beeping machines and procedures and tired-looking grown-ups in stained mint scrubs. Initially she'd thought it was like the others, another haunted vision left inside her head from her time spent lost in the Barrens. But this one was different. While the others were cold and gray and dead all the way through, this one positively brimmed with life, with color, overflowing to the point that when she woke from the dream, she could feel it pulsing and crackling like a live wire woven through her skin. There was a clearing near the edge of a forest, still green and alive despite being surrounded on all sides by ash and death. In its center, a sapling grew—young and slender to the point of seeming fragile, but it was already tall, well over six feet, its underdeveloped branches heavy with green leaves. Swollen with life, despite its blackened surroundings.

The image of that tree had stayed with her all the way into waking life, growing in the center of her brain as stubbornly as she'd seen it sprouting through the soil of the clearing. It was only a matter of days before it had started to slither into the rest of her life, peeking quietly around the corners and edges, barely there at all . . . until it became impossible to miss. She saw it in her other dreams, and again when she woke up, as if its outline had been tattooed onto the insides of her eyelids. When she wasn't paying attention, she'd find it hiding in the streetlight shadows splashed across her bedroom walls at night; scarred into the tile of the girls' room at school in cracked, stained grout; once, she'd even found it curled atop her mom's windshield, drawn in the shallow January frost.

It was another three months before she decided to go and find it, that tree—*her* tree. Erin, a girl from Trig class, had offered to drive the second she mentioned the idea. She liked Erin, as much as she liked anyone these days. Friendships were harder since she'd come back. But Erin was nice, and unlike basically everybody else, she didn't ask too many questions. Plus, with her shock-purple hair and nose ring and bright, friendly demeanor, she kept people from looking too closely at Chloe.

She felt it as soon as they were on the road, pulling out of the school parking lot on a beeline for the freeway—a pressure building behind her right eyeball, like a tumor blossoming high in the socket, sudden and unwelcome. It didn't hurt; it was just a pressure, much like a sinus headache, but strong enough to distract her from the fact that at the same time her head started pulsing, the gnarled scar hidden away underneath her shirt had started to throb too. That was fine. She could deal with a little more pain. She ground her teeth against it until it got to be too much, and then she told Erin to pull over. They were here. The pressure, the ache, the drumming—they all vanished the instant she stepped out of the car, and the first thing that hit her was the smell.

The tree stood in the middle of the clearing, exactly like she remembered it. Or dreamed it. Both. Neither. Leaning most of her weight on her cane, the girl limped over to the lone sapling, watching its branches and envy-green leaves sway in the spring breeze. Standing there, looking at it, as real as anything else in this world, Chloe's heart flinched in her chest. She didn't want to be standing here like this, because if she was really here and the tree was really real, then everything was nearly over.

But she wasn't going to turn around and walk away from him. Not now. Not again.

Easing herself down onto the closest stump, she ran the fingers of her free hand over the sapling's soft, cool leaves, feeling the gentle pulse of connection.

"Hi, Parker."

She sat there for an hour or more, just venting to him, unloading every feeling and thought everyone else in her life—parents, friends, teachers, court-mandated psychotherapist—had been trying for months to get out of her. They said it was *healthy to externalize.* So she externalized. She told him everything, unburdening herself of all the secrets she'd kept since she'd crawled out of this place. She told him about the hospital—the smell of it, the way the lights gave her terrible headaches, the elderly internist who wouldn't (or couldn't) stop farting. She told him about school, and how there seemed to be a hundred different versions of what had happened to them in the Pine Barrens, and how everyone who told it swore up and down that theirs was the no-shit, hundred-percent capital-T Truth.

She told him how everyone in every grade seemed to know her name and face now, and even though they all played nice, she still caught them whispering behind their hands when they thought she wasn't looking. She told him about the worried expressions that never seemed to leave her parents' faces, and the nervous, careful way they treated her. Without even really meaning to, she even did the thing she'd promised herself she wouldn't do, and told him as much as she could remember about the funerals—all five of them. She wanted him to know. He deserved to know. If he'd kept his promise, he would have been there with her.

It all just came pouring out of her like a waterfall. There was no stopping it once she got started. The only thing that she did manage to hold back was the horrible thing that Aunt Lori had done, at the end of everything. He didn't need to know that. No one did.

Chloe talked, and Parker listened. It was just like when they were kids, except without the radio, and now, one of them was dead. Or maybe not dead, just . . . different. Further away, yet far more immediate than he'd ever been. She could feel him humming in the bark of the tree, the heartwood, the leaves and roots and the ground beneath her feet. It was him, he was here, and yet . . . it wasn't. He wasn't.

Because they weren't alone, the two of them. Beyond the tree and the burned soil and all the destruction that lay between, she could feel it. The lake. The water. And the ancient, dead, dreaming thing far underneath. Still there, still waiting, still listening. Patient, cruel, and eternal. She'd brushed up against it twice before; she wasn't eager to make it three times. Not if she could help it.

In her jacket pocket, her phone suddenly trilled with a text message. She checked the screen. Underneath the weak, flickering service display read the name: Mom.

When are you going to be home, Scoot? I'm making meatball casserole for dinner!
5:43PM, 4/15

And just like that, the spell was broken. She'd stayed too long. At this point, she'd be lucky if Erin hadn't abandoned her out here.

"I gotta go," she said to the tree, planting her cane in the ground to rise to her feet again. "Sorry. Say hi to everyone else, if you see them, or whatever. Tell them I'm sorry."

She could already hear the thrum-and-hiss of passing cars on the highway. Bringing up the keyboard, she tapped out a short response to her mother:

Home in a couple hours—might bring a friend if that's okay?
Love you!
5:44PM, 4/15

She waited for the phone to get a strong enough signal to send, then pocketed the thing again. She looked back at the sapling. It already seemed less colorful, less lush. Its leaves were just leaves again, drifting in the muddy sunlight. Was it shorter now too?

Chloe's eyes played across the black trees that stood around the clearing like tombstones. Wherever he'd gone to, whatever he was now, she couldn't blame him for not hanging around. She wasn't planning to, either. Fact was, she didn't have that many months left in Jersey before she moved away and stayed away, going as far as she could without giving her parents a stress-stroke. These days, she was thinking California. UCLA wasn't offering her a full ride, but she was smart. She was going to be fine. Eventually.

Slowly, she made her way back through the trees and ash, clearing another path with practiced swipes of her cane. Emerging from the underbrush, she climbed back over the embankment and onto the pavement, then limped up to climb into the battered little four-door. Behind the wheel, Erin was drumming on the steering wheel with slender fingers and mouthing the words to some song Chloe didn't know.

Chloe pulled the door shut while Erin killed the music and turned to look at her.

"So?"

Chloe didn't turn to look back her way. "So."

"You find what you were looking for out there?"

"I don't know. I guess."

"Cool. Where to now?"

"Home," said Chloe. "I just want to go home." She thought about it. "You want to come over for dinner tonight?"

"That'd be great," Erin said. "What're we having?"

"I think my mom's making meatball casserole."

"That'd be cool, thanks. Are you sure you're ready to go?"

Chloe stole another look out at the burned forest. She couldn't even see the clearing anymore.

"Yeah," she said. "Yeah, I'm sure."

Without another word, Erin switched the hazard blinkers off, kicked the engine to life, and then merged back onto the highway. They melted into the traffic as if they'd never stopped and could just pass the wreckage on by. Like it wasn't there at all.

Without thinking, Chloe reached over and turned the music back on, back to whatever Erin was listening to before. It didn't matter what the song was, as long as it could drown out the silence.

THE END.

ACKNOWLEDGMENTS

This book would not have happened at all without the guidance and support of some really fantastic people that I am profoundly fortunate to have in my life.

Thanks first go to my amazing agent, Nicole Resciniti, at The Seymour Agency. Nic, you're one of the most insightful, driven, encouraging people I've ever known; thank you for your loyalty and wisdom, and for telling me to keep writing even when the writing wasn't easy. A big thank you also to Lynette Novak and the rest of the Seymour crew for reading an early draft of the book, providing crucial feedback and not getting too grossed out to keep going.

All the credit in the world goes to everyone at Turner Publishing who worked so damn hard to make this book the best it could possibly be: Stephanie Beard, Heather Howell, Kathleen Timberlake, Lauren Smulski and Kathy Haake, thank you for believing in the story and taking a chance on it. Working with all of you has been a joy since day one.

Massive thanks are due to my oldest friend in the world, Emma Price, who generously read the very first draft of this novel, saw something worth pursuing and pushed me to make it better and better and better.

A big thank you goes to Liz Claps, for loaning me her hometown, and for teaching me how to speak the mysterious language of New Jersey's myriad highways.

It should come as no surprise that my family has been instrumental in the creation of this book (and everything else I've ever written). To my Mom and my sister Lucy: you two have been my fan club from day one and have always encouraged me to follow the writing, wherever it took me, and there is no way for me to express how much that means. You've propped me up and you've cheered the hardest, and I love you two so, so much. To the rest of my family: Steve and Anne and Aaron, Dave and Kris, you guys are nothing short of amazing. Thank you for believing in me. Serious credit is also due to my very patient parents-in-law, Rick & Val Emmelhainz: thank you for understanding every time I said *"I'm sorry, I can't; I have to finish writing this goddamn book"* during vacation.

All my love and thanks go to Pat Marshall for reading my stuff, even the bad stuff (hell, *especially* the bad stuff), way back before I had a chance in hell of publishing a word of it. Thank you for your patience and your encouragement, and for always pushing me to try something new, even when it scared the absolute hell out of me. Sorry I said *fuck* so much.

I owe an enormous debt of gratitude to Rusty Barnes, Editor in Chief of *Tough Crime.* It's not an exaggeration to say that literally none of this would have happened without you first believing in my work enough to send it off to seek out bigger and better things. Thank you, Rusty. Next time I'm in your neck of the woods, coffee's on me.

Kevin and Amy Sims, you two have been a constant source of encouragement ever since I first told you *"So, I've got this idea for a book about these kids that get lost in the woods..."* over drinks. Having the love and support of two such phenomenally talented artists has made all the difference in my life. Thank you, thank you, thank you. I'm humbled by the both of you, and am incredibly lucky to count you as my family. I love you both so much.

My love and appreciation go out to the numerous other folks whose enthusiasm, kindness and patience saw me through the process of getting this book into the world: Ashley Marudas, Rebecca Agatstein, Dragan Radovanovic, Kim & Scott Collins, Cindy Socci, Jennifer Russell, Lauren Bochat, Rachel Brody, Rebecca Gorman, Elizabeth Copps, Marni Salmon and anyone else I might've missed. You're all amazing and I don't deserve any of you, but thank you for sticking around all the same.

Finally and most importantly, *The Night Will Find Us* would not exist in any form without my wife, Chelsey Emmelhainz. This book is dedicated to her, and if it's worth a damn at all, it's because of her. She is the best, scariest, most insightful reader I'll ever have and there's nothing I've written that she hasn't helped make better in some way. Thank you for the unending love and support, the sage insights and the brutally hard questions. Thank you for choosing me.

Thank you, for everything, forever.

I love you with my whole heart, Chelsey.

CPSIA information can be obtained
at www.ICGtesting.com
Printed in the USA
LVHW041631311020
670365LV00004B/20

9 781684 425426